W9-CDC-766

Talker 25 Series

TALKER 25

INVISIBLE MONSTERS

JOSHUA McCUNE

GREENWILLOW BOOKS

An Imprint of HarperCollinsPublishers

Talker 25: Invisible Monsters

Copyright © 2015 by Joshua McCune

All rights reserved. No part of this book may be used or reproduced in any manner whatsoever without written permission except in the case of brief quotations embodied in critical articles and reviews. Printed in the United States of America. For information address HarperCollins Children's Books, a division of HarperCollins Publishers, 195 Broadway, New York, NY 10007.

www.epicreads.com

The text of this book is set in 12-point Fournier MT.

Book design by Paul Zakris

Library of Congress Cataloging-in-Publication Data is available

ISBN 978-0-06-212194-3 (hardback)

15 16 17 18 19 LP/RRDH 10 9 8 7 6 5 4 3 2 1

First Edition

 GREENWILLOW BOOKS

For Ehlorea Rayn,
Welcome to the world.
Make it beautiful.
Make it yours.

PART I

THE OTHER SIDE

1

When I asked Colin to teach me how to shoot a gun, I should have considered the consequences. Now he's right behind me, waiting for me to fire, and despite my thermals, snow pants, heavy jacket, and wool cap, I can't stop shivering.

Ever since Colin and his dragon arrived on our remote Alaskan island four weeks back, I couldn't shake the feeling that I'd seen him before. I didn't know why until a few hours ago, wish he'd never told me his reason for deserting the army and joining the insurgency.

Trying to ignore his presence, I focus on squeezing the trigger, an action I've repeated a thousand times over these last several days. The empty supply crate at the cave entrance, cast in Randon's red glow and papered with bull's-eyes, is crumbling from all the holes I've put into it. Kill shots, Colin calls them. Always go for the kill shot.

Until today, firing the Beretta gave me comfort, didn't bother me in the least. Didn't remind me of all the people I killed or helped kill during my time in Georgetown. Of Claire.

Colin's sister.

He comes closer and places his hand on mine. I've faked nerves for that touch, for the tickle of his breath on my ear, but my heart stalls a beat for a different reason this time, and my shivers intensify.

"Another flashback?" he asks.

"I'm fine."

"Why don't we do this later, Melissa?"

No, I need to be strong. For Allie, for Baby. I speak a silent prayer, begging any god that might exist for forgiveness, for strength, then pull the trigger.

Again and again. Nine times in fast succession. No breaths, no blinks. Even trembling, flinching at the thunderous echo of gunfire rattling through the cave, I nail the center of three targets, come close on three others.

"Good job. Fifty feet. You were born for this." He's told me that before. It no longer makes me happy.

"Natural born killer," I murmur. I turn and force myself to look at him.

A sandy crew cut that's grown fuzzy frames a hard

military face that once reminded me of Dad, the pre-paralyzed version. Round it out, add a heavy dose of madness to his big brown eyes, lengthen his hair . . . how could I have missed the resemblance to his sister?

Unlike the others Keith has sent to monitor us, Colin doesn't normally treat me like damaged goods. Tonight, however, there's deep concern in his eyes.

"I'm gonna go on my rounds." I pull out my earplugs, stick the gun into the holster beneath my jacket, and head for the ladder that leads from the cave into the modified shipping container where we sleep and eat and try to live a semblance of a normal life.

He falls in stride a step behind me, putting a hand on my elbow. Like he's worried I'll fall.

"By myself," I say, more harshly than intended.

He doesn't respond, but my footsteps echo alone now. I reach the ladder, climb the rungs fast, my vision blurring with tears I can't afford if I'm supposed to protect those I love.

Kill emotion, human, Grackel says. The old Red's adopted the role of my dragon-talking mentor. Whether I like it or not.

Originally, I wasn't pleased about the idea of other people or dragons on the island, but Keith insisted. Sentries, he calls them. Grackel's a permanent tenant, a dragon with a sharp tongue who knows how to keep a low profile when she hunts for food and doesn't hesitate to singe Baby whenever she deems fit. We're becoming friends of a sort.

But I'm in no mood for friends right now. Too many of my friends of late have ended up dead. I open the hatch that separates the cave from the shipping container. "Leave me alone."

Your thoughts are transparent.

"I'm working on it. Leave me alone."

Allie looks up from the book of poems she's reading on her cot and jabs her yellow highlighter at me. "Speak in your head. How many times do I have to tell you? It makes you look crazy, yes, yes."

"Sorry." I grab the binoculars and flashlight from atop a supply crate and head for the door at the other end of the container. "I'll be back in a couple hours."

"Not taking Sarge with you?" she says. "Go shoot some more shit?"

"Watch your language. Colin's a friend."

"A good friend? How many dragons has he killed, how many?"

"How many have you?" I snap. She flinches, and tears well in her eyes. "I'm sorry, Allie, that's—"

"Go away! I hate you! I hate him! Go away, go away!" She rocks back and forth, alternating between screaming at me and shouting apologies to dead dragons, her left hand closing and opening around the silver dragon pin I gave her the day I arrived in Georgetown.

I start for her, but she ducks beneath the covers and screams louder at me.

Leave her be, Grackel says. *Kill emotion.*

"Leave me be." I slip on a pair of gloves, replace the cap with a balaclava, loop the binoculars over my neck, and escape into the cold, blustery night. I flip on the light that hangs from the end of the shipping container, then run toward the cliff, a quarter mile away.

Kill emotion, human.

"Leave me alone, dragon."

Your thoughts are transparent.

"I heard you the first time," I say between breaths, and run faster. Adrenaline doesn't kill emotion, but it does overwhelm it.

You cannot run forever.

"Help Allie."

She is too tangled to endanger us.

Tangled. Dragon for crazy. Allie can communicate with a hundred dragons at once if she wants, but regardless of her emotional state or willingness to share, not a one can make sense of her thoughts.

I stop and clutch at my knees, wishing I were tangled right now. "That's not what I meant. She needs somebody to talk to. Someone to tell her it's not her fault."

Arabelle and Randon have her. Who do you have?

I scan the sky in a quick, useless sweep, shivering despite all the layers. Until Keith dropped Allie, Baby, and me here, I'd never heard of Saint Matthew Island, a barren strip of land in the Bering Sea a hundred miles from anything. With the stiff wind and the near-constant night of winter, it's often colder here than it was in Georgetown. According to the thermostat, at least.

I scan again, more slowly, trying to actually spot enemies this time, trying not to think about the maelstrom that is my life. *In nae.* Persevere. *Baekjul boolgool.* Indomitable spirit. I must be strong.

"I don't need anybody."

Maybe, Grackel says in her insufferably calm way. *But Allie needs you. Arabelle needs you.*

"Don't you think I know that? Don't lecture me, dragon."

It is not your fault. We do not blame you for Georgetown. Colin would not blame you for his sister.

"I don't want to talk about it. Where are you?"

Northwest.

I turn in a half circle and spot two pinpricks of light near the horizon. One a faint red, the other a silver beacon that cuts through the darkness. Arabelle . . . Baby. "How is she doing?"

Well enough. She still cannot pace herself. She gets too excited. And she is stubborn. It seems a common trait around here.

I ignore the jibe. "Don't get too far."

She needs to spread her wings, gain her lungs, learn to hunt and fight.

"No, Grackel. Not yet. And tell her to damp her glow. She's not listening to me."

You cannot protect her forever, human. A storm is coming, she says, not for the first time. I lower the binoculars, waiting for the lecture to continue, but when I focus inward, shutting out the world the best I can, listening for her mental signature, Grackel is gone.

I find a boulder near the cliff edge and sit. I close my eyes, remind myself that Claire's death was an accident. The wind cries a mournful wail around me, the ocean crashes against the rocks far below, the first flakes of snow fall.

A dragon roar startles me. I push away from the boulder and drop to my knees. I scour the dark heavens, but there's nothing. Machine-gun fire and screams echo behind me. I look over my shoulder. Nothing . . .

Wait. A flash of something. I whirl around—spot a Green, fire forming in its mouth. Another dragon pops up on my left, an insurgent with a rocket launcher raised to his shoulder atop it. A man's face melts under flame in front of me. A woman and her baby die to my right in a swarm of bullets.

Not real.

I plant a hand on the rock, fighting the urge to crawl as my lungs seize up. I throw my face into the snow. The shock of cold rips through me, and the roaring and screaming dwindle to muted agony. When I lift my head, the hallucinations are gone.

I reach into my pocket for the envelope I keep stashed there. It contains my security blanket. Something to pull me back from the horrors of my Georgetown reconditioning.

Allie has her silver dragon pin to help fix her to reality. I have Dad's letter, now heavily wrinkled. My hands are shaking so much that it takes three tries to remove it from the envelope. Not Dad's handwriting, but I can hear him saying everything transcribed, and by the end, I no longer see him in that wheelchair when they rolled him in for my *Kissing Dragons* interview; I see him like he was in the picture he kept on the living-room mantle. With Mom, young and vibrant, smiling down at their baby girl.

Knowing someone out there loves me like that makes everything go away for a bit. I fold the letter into the envelope and return it to my pocket, then stand and head south along the cliff line.

The snow intensifies, but the wind settles. I tuck the

binoculars into my jacket. Not much point scouting given the limited visibility, but I enjoy how the white breath of winter makes the world seem innocent and pure.

I think of Mom and Dad and Sam as I walk aimless patterns in the snow. And inevitably, despite my best efforts, I think of James.

The last time I saw him was in an Ecuadorian cave, a few days after Loki's Grunts rescued us from Georgetown. Keith decided to reassign him to the recon squadron to scout our next hideout while we stayed behind and waited for the all-clear.

"It'll keep him busy," Keith had told me. "He needs time to recover. It's for the best."

Yes, but not because of recovery. Some scars run too deep. *In nae*. Survive, find a purpose to keep you going. Bury the memories in the darkest corners and hold them down however you can.

I was in the reconditioning chamber four days, but fabricated memories still haunt my dreams and confuse my senses. James was in the reconditioning chamber for almost four weeks. He survived somewhat intact. Broken, but not destroyed. He wasn't Twenty-Six, but he wasn't James either. His love of dragons had been tainted by dark rage. I understand his torment far more than I'd like, but wrath and vengeance won't protect Twenty-One or Baby.

That was more than three months ago. I didn't even say good-bye. I didn't know how.

We "talked" after that, here and there, sending messages via Baby. *How's the weather? How's Keith? How's Allie?* Short conversations, long silences. Our answers were all variations of "Fine" until they just became *Fine.*

A month ago, we had our final conversation. Started off the normal way. *How are you doing?*

"Fine," I said. "You?"

Good.

Which was not what I expected. Normally there'd be a long pause, or maybe that would be the end of the conversation altogether, but his next words came quickly.

It'll get better, Melissa. One day, this will be a bad memory. You'll be able to go home.

Baby was holding back.

"All of it," I ordered.

She cowered and her glow dimmed, but she eventually spat it out. *He said you won't have to worry about things like Georgetown, stupid TV shows . . . or insurgents. He doesn't mean it.*

But we both knew he did.

My legs begin to weaken, so I find another rock and lean against it. I roll back the balaclava and welcome the snow that falls onto my lips, feel the coolness melt to warmth, and let myself imagine that I'm being kissed. Then I make two angels in a snowdrift, side by side. I watch until they fill and disappear, praying that the hurt will fade soon. I've already got too many problems.

I continue south, switching between walking and sprinting, the fatigue and sharp spikes of coldness in my lungs distracting me from thought. I'm not sure where I'm going, just that I need to get more tired before I return home. Exhaustion helps the nightmares, sleeping and waking.

The snow lightens to flurries, and the first stars peek through the shadowy haze above. I find little comfort in them anymore. With the thick winter clouds, our island is invisible to military satellites and enemy dragons, but on clear nights, we are naked and exposed.

I turn back toward home as the clouds continue to part. I'm within shouting distance of the shipping container when the sudden feeling of being watched envelops me. Goose bumps prickle my arms.

I crouch low behind a boulder and tug out my binoculars. The light from the shipping container illuminates a small patch of snow-dusted bleakness, but nothing else. Behind me, darkness stretches into forever.

I scan the sky several times. Not a soul in sight.

I scoop up a handful of snow and press the frozen wetness

to my face. Biting into my lip, I slow my breaths and wait for the feeling to go away.

Instead, it intensifies.

Eight months ago, at Blue Rez Five, I felt a similar watching sensation. Minutes before I discovered I could talk to dragons, and my life spun into hell.

Those invisible eyes at the rez were withdrawn and cautious.

These are . . . eager.

No, not eager.

Ravenous.

I hear something at the edge of perception. I desperately want it to be a trick of the wind, but when I cover my ears and concentrate, it's still there. A whispered voice. No, multiple voices. Aggressive and guttural. All repeating the same phrase.

Where is the child?

2

Kill *emotion, human,* Grackel reminds me as I stumble through the snow toward our makeshift home.

Guilt, fear, anger—negative emotions, the telepathic lightning rods that allow invasion of thought. Unfortunately for us, I've got 'em in spades.

When I arrive at the shipping container, I lean against its corrugated wall, shut my eyes, focus on deep breaths, and recite my tae kwon do mantras. *In nae, baekjul boolgool.* A part of me always knew this day would come, but I never thought Oren and his sociopathic army of Green dragon riders that call themselves the Diocletians would start the hunt for Baby this soon.

"She can't be of breeding age yet," I insist, terrified.

It is only a matter of time.

Grackel doesn't know why dragon reproduction requires cross-pollination, why a Red and a Blue spawn a Silver, a creature that breathes ice and has no blindness to the color black. What she does know is that Oren and the Greens, the erstwhile alphas in the dragon hierarchy, will be drawn to Baby's superior genes. If Red and Blue make Silver, what will Green and Silver make? What horrible influence will a Green's wrathful temperament have on its progeny?

We should notify Keith, human.

"No!"

We'd have to contact him via dragon, which means we'd have to go through James. Or Evelyn. God help me. "Please, Grackel. Colin and Randon are leaving in a few days. I'll just add it to my shopping list." *Socks, underwear, a couple of textbooks, dozens of candy bars, another book of poems for Allie. P.S. The Greens are on the prowl. Kisses.*

Silly human. She sighs. *If you cannot control your emotions, imagine you are somewhere else.*

Mars. No annoying or hungry dragons there.

I flip off the light and head into the shipping container. Colin rises from a chair and offers me a coffee mug filled with brandy. Need to update the list I send to Preston, too. Brandy. Scotch. Vodka. Double the quantities. At least.

I accept the cup, lift the balaclava, and take a long drink.

Bottoms up, Grackel. Nothing quite kills emotion like a good drunken stupor.

"You shouldn't have waited up," I say. He always waits up, though this is the first time he's acknowledged my drinking habit.

"Anything?" he asks.

I swallow. "All clear."

"Can we talk?" he says. Claire? Did he figure it out? Or maybe Allie told him to spite me. I glance toward her cot, but she's not there.

I follow him to the folding table positioned between a supply crate and the backup generator. "Allie's in the cave?"

"Yeah. Away from me," he says with a brief, toothless smile.

"She just needs to get used to you."

"She won't have to worry about me much longer. Though she's gonna miss Randon."

I can't help but smile. "Only because he lets her fly him upside down."

"And races with them."

I roll my eyes. "Laps and laps around the island. Not listening to anybody."

"Twelve going on sixteen."

I snort. "Twelve going on eight."

He laughs, and for a moment, it's like it was a few days ago.

The moment passes. "So, when does Howard come?" I ask.

"You eager to get rid of me now, too?" he says. This laugh seems too lighthearted.

"That's not what I meant." Not exactly. "This isn't what you signed up for. Babysitting a pair of broken girls in the middle of nowhere."

He doesn't say anything, gives me that stoic look of his. It was the first thing I noticed when I met him. He resembles an army poster child, with his close-cropped hair, square jaw, broad shoulders . . . but it was those brown eyes that had most distressed me. They hid so much. I immediately distrusted him, immediately hated him.

And then he had smiled, and it all slipped away. His eyes came to life, and I saw kindness in them. I wanted to believe he wouldn't hurt me.

Now I know what lies behind that guarded look, and I wish I could make him smile again, but smiles seem very not real at the moment. He grabs a half-filled mug from the table, tops it off, and takes a long swig.

He sits, gesturing for me to join him.

I fake a yawn. "Can this wait until tomorrow?"

"It won't take long. Promise." Pause. "I'm not very good at this. Guess it's best to just come out and say it."

"Wait, Colin—"

"No. No interrupting." He takes a drink. "Look, I'm sorry. I'm sorry about this afternoon. I didn't mean to upset you."

"Nothing to be sorry for," I say, glad my voice comes out steady. "You haven't done anything wrong."

"That's kind of you." He swirls his brandy with a finger in slow back-and-forth arcs. "I shouldn't have brought up Georgetown or Claire or any of it. I've tried not to think about her, about everything, but . . . I don't know how to let go."

Looking at him right now, I realize something terrible and wonderful. He's as lost as I am. I know I can't give him answers, tell him what's right or wrong, because I don't know myself. I'm not sure I can give him anything except more bad memories, but he deserves the truth.

That'll require another half bottle at least, so I slump into the chair opposite him and refill my cup. "I never knew what Claire was really like. She was already reconditioned when I got to Georgetown—"

"You don't have to do this, Melissa." He rises. "It's late. You need sleep."

"Sleep doesn't do me much good. Tell me about her. Please."

He leans against a supply crate, looks toward the ceiling. "Claire wanted to be an ice-skater, a ballerina. 'Someone pretty.' She never told me that. I read it in her journal after she disappeared. Didn't even know she kept one."

"She had such soulful eyes," I say, sneaking a glance at him. Such soulful eyes.

"She knew she was built like a truck. Our parents reminded her often enough. What is it like to have impossible dreams people would laugh at if they knew about them?" His features harden. "I wanted to be an All-Black for as long as I can remember. I enlisted the moment I turned sixteen, passed the tests in a breeze. Claire was so proud."

"I would be too. It's not easy."

He snorts. "It is, as far as dreams go. Nothing like hers. She was so beautiful. . . . I never told her that. I never told her how damn proud of her I was."

Colin sits, stares into his mug, seems surprised to find it empty. I offer him the bottle, but he waves me off. "Claire was fourteen when she told me she was hearing voices. She came to me, not my parents. She was worried what they might do to her. You know what I did?"

I shake my head, drink some more.

"I told my parents about my crazy little sister. They institutionalized her. Two weeks later, insurgents broke her out. I figured it was crazy joining crazy. I never saw her again after that. . . ." The stoic look falters. "Not until Preston's videos."

Three more long sips. Before leaving Georgetown smoldering behind us, Keith made sure to collect all the evidence he could, including file footage that showed soldiers and scientists abusing talkers, torturing dragons, using both to attack human enemies domestically and abroad.

Preston's uploaded several clips to the net, earning himself quite a following and a place with me in the Bureau of Dragon Affairs card deck. He understands the benefits of exposure, but he's failed to realize how much pain those vids might cause the surviving prisoners and their families.

That pain's etched deep into Colin's face right now. Preston's Claire webisode started with footage from the reconditioning chamber, then segued into surveillance video of her sitting catatonic on the bathroom floor, mesmerized by the *Kissing Dragons* episodes they played on constant repeat in our barracks. It ended with scenes from the battle room, Claire almost ravenous as she snarled orders at dragons to kill innocent civilians.

After several deep breaths, I slip a hand from my glove, reach across the distance, and thread my fingers through his. He's shaking even more than I am. He squeezes my hand, gives me an empty smile, then lets go and pushes himself away from the table.

"I'm sorry. This was . . . pointless." He grabs his jacket, reaches for the binoculars, knocking the flashlight to the floor in the process. He scoops it up, muttering to himself, and hurries toward the exit.

"Colin, wait. It's not your fault."

He looks over his shoulder, and I see something very Claire-like in his eyes. He smiles, a wicked thing. "If I ever find the sonofabitches who did that to my sister, I'm gonna feed them to a dragon, piece by piece."

He leaves, slamming the door behind him, and I decide I won't drink another sip of alcohol until he's off the island.

After updating my lists, I write a letter to my brother Sam—telling him how proud I am of him—and add it to the outbound pile. I curl up in my cot and eventually fade into the nightmares.

3

I spend Saturday morning downstairs with Allie, trying to get her to focus on basic algebra. She wants to discuss Greens. I remind her she can't talk to anybody she doesn't know. She throws a tantrum, screaming all sorts of colorful curses at me before hopping onto Baby and flying out of the cave. I yell at them to come back. They ignore me.

I make my rounds with Colin, letting him scout while I bitch about Allie and Baby. He tells me they're young and will grow out of it. They better damn well hurry up. He laughs at me when I say that, and I tell him Tuesday can't come soon enough.

We don't talk after that.

Which leaves me stuck with Grackel and her three favorite words. *Kill emotion, human.* She asks me why I'm angry. I don't know. Could be because I've got an army of psycho killers striving to bore into my brain. Could be because I've got a pair of insolent children running around without a care in the world. Or maybe it's the fact that the first boy I've liked in ages is lost in a darkness that is not mine, and the second one, well, I just happened to kill his sister.

She goes into lecture mode, pretty much telling me to quit sulking, then disconnects.

After a dinner of beans and a Kit Kat, I return to the cave and chide Allie and Baby until they fly off again. I blast some holes in the crate, and for a few minutes, at least, I don't have to worry about pretending I'm exploring Mars, lounging on a tropical beach, or walking the streets of a city protected by a kick-ass dragon defense system.

Sunday, I get my emotions halfway under control. I ignore Allie and Baby and apologize to Colin. We scout the island in silence. Not comfortable, but not too awkward. Not until I catch him staring at me. Like he's trying to decide something.

I tell him I need to pee and sprint home. I unlock the cabinet where I keep my gun and pull out the hand mirror I swore I'd never touch again. After wiping off the dust and suppressing the hope of normalcy, I check my reflection.

On the list of hideous, I'm not sure which I prefer most. Sunken cheeks set in a face a dark shade of sallow, the monkish patch of black hair, or the faded CENSIR scar that still peeks through the tufts. All worthy of consideration, but I'll go with the eyes. Brimming with wetness, like they know they used to belong to someone who didn't resemble a loony-bin escapee.

I snatch the gun from the cabinet and descend into the cave. Ignoring Randon's cocked head and Grackel's toothy grin, I hurry to the entrance. Five hundred feet down, through an abyss of blackness, ocean waves play a faint tune against the cliff wall. I hurl the mirror into the void and chase it with bullets.

Monday, I have no mirror, and Colin's too busy packing to join me on my rounds. The watching sensation dissipates. When I concentrate hard enough, I can still hear the Greens; otherwise, not a peep.

Howard, Colin's babysitter replacement, doesn't show on Tuesday.

Or Wednesday.

Thursday, Colin unpacks Randon's saddlebags while I call on almost every dragon I know. No response.

They are asleep, Grackel says when I ask for her help. In the dragon telepathy world, asleep might as well be dead.

"All of them? Keith wouldn't do that."

Grackel doesn't answer, which is answer enough.

Thursday night, I resume drinking and pretending I live elsewhere.

Friday, I break another vow and call Maren. When James's Red doesn't answer, I swallow what remains of my pride and attempt to contact Evelyn's dragon.

Nothing.

Maybe the military found Loki's Grunts and wiped them off the planet. Or worse, sent them to another prison camp.

"What's protocol?" I ask Colin.

"We have two weeks of fuel for the generators. After that, we can bundle into the cave. A month of food, maybe two if we go extra skinny. When that runs out, we live off the land. Not ideal, but doable."

I dilute my cup of brandy with a few splashes of bottled water. Conservation mode. "We should leave."

He smiles. "Don't like the idea of eating lichen every day?"

"I'm serious."

"We wouldn't know where to go."

"There's a map of hideouts in the escape crate," I say.

"It's probably outdated."

"What about the emergency cell phone?"

Colin shakes his head. "Need to hit the mainland before it'll get a signal."

"Sounds like we should leave."

"We're safer here."

I inform him about the Green voices that have been serenading Allie and me for the past week. "According to Grackel, they're in full broadcast mode. She compared it to a worldwide loudspeaker."

"Sounds like they don't know where we are."

"They're looking for us. And my emotions will make it easier for them to find us."

He rolls his eyes. "Maybe you should leave, then."

I chew at my lip. "Maybe I should."

"I was kidding, Melissa."

"It's a good idea. Grackel and I can vanish somewhere. Plant false trails or something."

"No. I'm not letting you out of my sight."

"I wasn't asking permission, *Sarge*."

He flinches. "That's not how I meant it. We should all stick together. Lord knows I wouldn't be able to handle Allie and Baby by myself."

I allow myself a brief smile. "They were ready to throw a good-bye parade on Tuesday." And have been moping ever since.

"So you'll stay?"

"For now."

A scream awakens me from an unpleasant sleep. Followed by three gunshots in fast succession and a pair of dragon roars. I cling to the sheets, waiting for the rest. But no images come, and the scream fades. No more gunshots either, but the dragons continue to growl, deep and throaty, volcanoes readying to erupt.

Real. Coming from the cave. I bolt from the bed, calling for Colin, but he's not in his cot. Two steps from the hatch, Grackel's raspy voice sounds in my head. *You probably should hurry up.*

I lift the metal cover and am nearly blinded by the bright red-silver light coming from below. "What's going on?"

A misunderstanding among children. They are ruining my meal.

I slide down the ladder to find Randon and Baby circling each other, wings spread, heads arched, teeth bared, and glows at full shine. The ground rumbles beneath their prowling steps. Ice daggers drip from Baby's nostrils. A thick layer of Randon's smoke clouds the ceiling.

"A little help, Grackel," I say. The old Red lies against the back wall, her attention focused on the half-eaten walrus carcass pinned beneath her forepaw.

If they are going to disturb my meal, I might as well be entertained.

"Randon, what are you doing? Stand down."

The dragon shifts his glare to me. *Do not tell me what to do, human. I will not be disrespected by children.* He drops a wing and puffs smoke through two small holes near where it attaches to his body. *Look what that tangled human did to me.*

"I wasn't aiming at you," Allie shouts from somewhere out of sight. "I apologized, yes, yes."

Dammit. Colin had warned me giving Allie her own gun was a bad idea. I duck beneath Randon's wing and realize just how bad. Colin's standing astride a puddle of blood near the cave center, one hand raised in surrender as he clutches at a wound in his side. Allie's beside my target-practice crate, her pistol trained on his head.

I sprint forward and put myself between them. "What are you doing, Allison?"

Colin tries to step in front of me, but I push him back.

"She's not safe," he says.

"She won't hurt me. What's going on, Allie? Why did you shoot Randon and Colin?"

"I didn't mean to hurt Randon. Colin dodged my first shots."

"Put the gun down, Allie." She ignores my plea. "Why were you shooting at Colin?"

"He tried to hurt Baby, yes, yes." Her face squeezes up. "With a needle."

"I wasn't—" Colin begins.

"Shut up!"

I hold up a hand. "Colin's a friend, Allie. It was a bad dream. A flashback, probably," I say. "I know sometimes it's hard to—"

"No! You never believe me. James would. He always did before you made him leave."

Made him leave? "Allie, he was never here—"

"His dragon no longer talks to me, no, no," she says, tapping her head with the gun barrel. "Your fault." She spins around and dashes two steps to the cave precipice. "You don't love me anymore."

I run for her, dodging the gun she hurls at me, but I know I won't make it.

"We were supposed to be on the island together," she says. "You, me, and Baby. Not him. He's not one of us."

She jumps.

"Allie!"

Baby pulls her wings tight, straightens her tail, and dives after her in a silver flash. I skid to a halt at the edge. Colin wraps an arm around my waist, securing me as I search the vast emptiness below. I can't see Allie. Just Baby's light growing smaller . . .

. . . a fading star . . .

. . . almost invisible . . .

Gone.

Seconds stretch into minutes. I spot a pinprick of light flickering at the edge of perception, a silver firefly floating in and out of the darkness. Baby must be searching the icy waters for Allie's body.

I stare into the abyss, wondering why I can't seem to wake from this nightmare. Allie had been upset with me since Colin arrived, but I never thought she'd go beyond tantrums and sulking. Maybe shoot Colin, but nothing suicidal. All those months she survived Georgetown.

Why now?

"Tell me it's not my fault," I whisper.

Colin puts his arms around me and pulls me back from the edge. "You know it isn't."

"I'm sorry she shot you." I push away, focusing my attention on the gash in his shirt, the bleeding hole in his skin. I fumble for the utility knife I keep tucked in my belt.

He grabs my trembling hands with his bloodied ones. "Melissa . . ."

"Let go. You're injured." I cut a jagged swath from the hem of his shirt but can't figure out how to wrap his wound. "I've been shot before. You're handling it better than I did."

"It's a flesh wound. I'm fine." He takes the strip of fabric and presses it to the bullet hole. A gesture of kindness, because it's useless.

"We need to get you upstairs."

He doesn't argue, which means he's in worse shape than he's letting on. We're walking toward the ladder, Colin supporting me as much as I am him, when I spot the hypodermic needle near the blankets Allie sleeps—slept—on when she spent the night down here with Baby.

"How could you?"

"I was trying to help, Melissa."

"Help! I trusted—"

"It's a tracker, Melissa. I wanted—"

"Without telling any of us?"

"It's safer that way."

"Don't give me that bullshit. You know what they did to Baby in Georgetown. You know what they did to us. And now . . . and now Allie's . . ." Two choices. Cry, or . . .

I hit him in the chest with both fists. Over and over, until he's pressed to the wall. He covers his wound but doesn't try to block me.

I hear laughter behind me. Wild and full of impishness. Real? I push away from Colin and turn around.

Baby hovers in the cave entrance, Allie straddling her neck. Both grinning like lovely fools. There is something in Allie's eyes that tells me she's made that jump before.

The tears come. Allie's smile vanishes. She leaps from Baby, lands in a graceful somersault, and races into my arms, where she cries apologies into my shoulder.

Sorry to interrupt your strange ritual of fake death, Grackel says, *but you should probably ask yourself why your boyfriend felt the need to inject Arabelle with a tracker tonight.*

He's not my boyfriend. I wheel on Colin. "What were you thinking?"

Allie tries to wriggle free, but I hold her tight, afraid she might go hunting for her gun. She settles on sticking her tongue out at him.

"Was just trying to keep her safe," he says between labored

breaths. Blood seeps through the fingers covering the hole in his side. He gives me a wan smile. "Sorry. Should have . . ."

He crumples to the floor. I release Allie and kneel beside him. I press my hands over the wound, feel the blood pump against my palm. "Get me the first-aid kit."

Allie doesn't move.

"Come on, Allison. You know he wasn't trying to hurt Baby."

"Fine, but he has to leave the island when he's better, yes, yes."

I nod. She skips off, humming to herself.

The blood's leaking more slowly now. Not sure if that's because I'm doing something right, or because he's already lost too much. "You better not die on me. Why tonight, Grackel?"

Listen, she says. *Feel.*

"I don't have time for riddles."

You are angry, scared, worried.

"Yeah, kill emotion, I know. Go to hell."

Listen, feel.

"You just enjoy watching us suffer, don't—" Watching. The watching sensation is gone. I listen for the distant, garbled voices of Greens but hear nothing.

Two things occur to me, both frightening, though for far different reasons.

Colin's a dragon talker.

"They've found us."

4

Colin's breaths come short and fast, and sometimes with blood. The blankets beneath him are spattered crimson, and the bandages taped over his ribs are soaked through, but at least that bleeding's stopped.

"We need to go, Grackel." He's pale and won't stop shivering, even with Grackel lying beside him to provide extra heat.

Too dangerous. She doesn't sound concerned. Never does. *It could be a ruse, human.*

"Oren and his Diocletians are coming, Grackel. Help me move Colin to the crate."

The old Red doesn't budge. *They want you to panic, human, and you are doing a good job of it.*

"Please."

Will you sacrifice Arabelle for him? What if the Greens do not know our location? I protest, but she interrupts me. *This is what they want. They are sly, the Greens. Perhaps they are looking for someone else altogether.*

"Perhaps pigs can fly," I snap.

How can you be certain it is Arabelle they are after? They never mentioned her by name.

"Who else could it be?"

If it is Arabelle, you must ask yourself why they went silent.

"I don't know, but I can't let him die, Grackel."

Because of his sister. A statement, not a question.

Because of that, because the short list of people I care about in this world might already be significantly shorter. Keith, Preston . . . James . . . "Stop reading my thoughts, dragon."

The truth is on your face, human. You know my opinion, but I will follow your lead.

"I can't let him die."

You and your emotions, she says without malice. With surprising deftness, she scoops up Colin in a claw and carries him across the cave to the escape crate, a modified military drop box that Preston and his dragon brought to the island two months ago. She kneels and sets him on the bed bolted into the side wall.

I prop him up with pillows. "You got the go bags?" I ask

Allie, who's sitting in one of the jump seats on the opposite side of the crate.

"Yes." She doesn't look up from her book of poems. "Under the bed."

"What's your name?"

"Kim Cosgrove."

"And I am?"

"Sarah Cosgrove." She smiles over her book. "My sister. Always."

I ruffle her ever-unkempt hair. "Yes. Sisters forever. I'll be back in a second."

When I'm out of the crate, I retrieve the hypodermic needle. My hand drifts to the scar on my arm where my best friend, Trish, once injected me with a tracer. It's the only reason we escaped Georgetown. The only reason Baby's alive right now.

Oren and his legion of cold-blooded insurgents and colder-blooded Greens won't kill her, not in the bullets-and-chainsaws, Georgetown sort of way. But they will in a deeper way, in a way Georgetown killed part of me.

I can't allow that. I refuse to allow them, or anybody, to hurt her or Allie ever again.

No, Melissa, Baby says, blue eyes focused on the needle clutched in my hand. She skitters away, shooting a narrow stream of ice at the space in front of me.

"I can't lose you." I step around the frozen puddle. "If we become separated, we need to know where you are."

I know you're mad at me. I'll behave better.

"I'm not mad."

She darts past me to the back of the cave, sheltering behind an uninterested Grackel. *You can't make me.*

"We don't have time for this, Arabelle," Allie says. She stomps from the crate, shoots me a glare, then marches over to Baby and waggles a finger under her nose. "What if you get lost? We won't know how to find you."

Baby snorts thin slivers of ice over her. Allie brushes the shards from her hair and kicks the Silver in the shin. It couldn't possibly hurt, but Baby yowls.

Based on their changing expressions and the occasional physical exchange, they must be continuing their conversation in private. Baby's no longer focused on me. I tiptoe my way into her blind spot and thrust the needle into her flank. It takes all my strength to break through her scales, but she doesn't seem to notice.

"Fine. Be lost," Allie says. She folds her arms across her chest but can't suppress a grin as she stalks, with comic exaggeration, into the crate.

Baby shifts her attention to me. *We decided. No needles.*

"Nope." I show her my empty hands. "I'll make you a deal. You promise to listen to Grackel out there, everything she says, and I won't ever bring up a needle again."

She leans down until her snout's an inch from my face. *Kiss on it.*

I gladly do, then wipe the frost from my lips and return to the crate.

I close the wall door, press my palm to the adjacent hand-print scanner, and enter the numeric passcode Preston made me memorize. The magnetic lock engages; a strip of LED lights powers up along the rim of the ceiling, and an electronic map flickers to life along the back wall.

"You did a good job with Baby," I tell Allie as I secure Colin to the bed with buckled straps.

"You should have told me what you were going to do. Sisters don't have secrets. Don't be like him."

"You're right, but you can't shoot people just because they upset you."

"It was like the Georgetown vultures who came in at night sometimes while we were sleeping," Allie says. "Sneaking up on Baby. I thought he was going to hurt us, yes, yes."

Her words make me think of Lorena and Whiskey Jim and how we did whatever was necessary to survive. And how some of us didn't.

"That's over," I say, as much for myself as her. I retrieve her book of poems from the floor. "Find one you think I'd like."

Allie takes it and buckles into a jump seat.

I grab the overhead hand railing. "Ready when you are, Randon."

The screech of talons on metal ripples through the crate. We rock back and forth slightly, lift up a bit, and move forward. Slow at first, jerking along, then faster, and I imagine myself back in Arlington, where I grew up, shooting out of a Metro station, the constant thrum of wind cocooning us. We reach our cruising speed, and I no longer need to brace against falling.

I'm tempted to turn on the LCD that connects to cameras on the outside of the crate, but there's nothing to see but darkness, and Preston encouraged us to save power whenever possible. After making sure Colin's secure, I reacquaint myself with the rest of the escape crate.

Besides the bed and jump seats that double as flotation devices, there's an altimeter, an oh-shit lever in case we need to manually deploy the parachute, a thermostat—currently set at a balmy fifty degrees Fahrenheit—and an electronic map of North America decorated with colored circles and a red arrow in the Bering Sea with the words *You Are Here* written beneath it.

The legend at the bottom of the map identifies the multitude of black circles as *Avoid at All Cost* locations, the few reds scattered through the evacuated territories in the middle of the map as *Allies*, and the remaining beiges, most outside the U.S., as *Neutrals*.

I press the beige pin nearest our arrow. Aerial photographs, demographics information, and a street map of Dillingham, Alaska, appear beside it. A coastal town near a mountain range. Perfect for dragon anonymity. I search the street map until I find the hospital, a building not much larger than the minor-care clinic in Mason-Kline. Not perfect for gunshot victims, but Dillingham's an hour closer than any of the other pins, so it'll have to do. I send an image of the map to Grackel.

"That's where we're going?" Allie asks.

"Yes."

"Then what?"

"After Colin's all fixed up, we'll get in touch with Keith and figure out what to do from there." I force a smile. "Piece of pie."

She grins. "Easy as cake. Ooh, you think we can eat at a restaurant, and I can have some? I haven't had cake . . ."

She goes quiet, but I know she's thinking of her parents, dragon-talking insurgents who were assassinated days before her capture and transfer to Georgetown. "You bet. You can have all the cake you want if you promise me you won't try to hurt Colin again."

"Cross my heart, yes, yes."

As she returns to her poems, I sit on the floor next to the bed and retrieve the backpacks lodged beneath. I listen to Colin's raspy breathing for a while, occasionally wiping the blood that dribbles from his lips, then investigate the contents of our go bags. Fake IDs, national registration numbers, backstories written on flash cards. A change of clothes, a bathroom kit, some cash, MREs, and one emergency cell phone.

The phone won't have a signal until we reach the mainland, so I attempt to contact the dragons again. Tell them where we're headed. Plead for information and help.

Nothing.

Between the silences, I read over my flash cards until I know my new identity by rote. I check our location on the map, give course corrections to Grackel and Randon, talk to Baby, reexamine Colin. After memorizing his backstory, wondering if he chose the particulars or if it's Preston's unfunny idea of a joke, I quiz Allie on her character until she's too tired to continue.

I slide the book of poems from her small hands, roll up the sweatshirt from my go bag, and place it behind her head. Once I'm sure she's asleep, I return to my spot on the floor and read the page she'd bookmarked with her finger.

"The Fatal Sisters" by Thomas Gray. Long and dreary. My breath catches in my throat as I scan the final passage she's highlighted.

Horror covers all the heath,
Clouds of carnage blot the sun.
Sisters, weave the web of death;
Sisters, cease, the work is done.

I tear out the pages in a neat line so you wouldn't realize they were missing unless you checked the numbers. Allie doesn't notice that sort of thing. I search for other poems about death and war—a few here and there, but the ones most highlighted—and rip them free, too.

The remaining pieces that she's dog-eared revolve around sorrow and love. I used to seek those out myself, but now I skip them for ones I don't quite understand, ones I'm happy not understanding.

I must drift, because when I next look at the map, we've reached the mainland. I check on Colin, positioning my cheek inches from his lips. His breaths are uneven and shallow. I press two fingers to his neck. It takes a few more seconds than last time to find his pulse. Fast—as if he just finished a sprint—but weak.

No signs of trouble, Grackel informs me. *Drop will occur soon.*

"At the edge of town. Out of sight, right?"

All will go well, human.

It must. We'll land safe as the dragons take cover in the mountains. I'll call 911. On our way to the hospital, as the EMT informs me that Colin's in no danger whatsoever, I'll phone Preston, but James will be the one who answers. He'll hang up fast, because he doesn't want to waste another second . . . he'll already be on his way to rescue us.

I laugh because the alternative hurts too much. I climb into my jump seat, buckle up, and wait for reality to set in.

5

Reality sucks even worse than I thought.

My ears pop, my chest tingles. The altimeter spins up. Allie clutches my hand until our knuckles turn white. We settle at fifteen thousand feet. High enough that the locals might mistake dragons for stars or comets, but now in radar visibility, according to Grackel.

Which means the dragons need to zip in fast, drop the payload—us—and bolt. As Randon accelerates, I think about how eight months ago, my worst days involved suffering through Lieutenant Spencer's boring lectures on projectile motion.

Never imagined I'd actually *be* a physics problem.

If a crate's dropped from fifteen thousand feet, traveling at a horizontal velocity of two hundred miles per hour, how far will it go before it lands? A long damn way. What if the crate has a parachute attached to it? When should that be opened? And then there's the real stuff like drag and wind shear that we never learned about because those weren't ideal conditions. No kidding.

You worry too much, human, Grackel says. *Trust me. It is not much different than a rock thrown from a cliff.*

Even if Grackel's an Einstein in the dragon world, there's no way she can account for weather, parachute open time, Randon's exact speed at release. . . .

Too many variables.

We're gonna end up landing in the woods a mile out. Or maybe the tributary. We'll plunge through the icy film and sink into the murky depths. The crate's probably airtight, so we'll sit at the bottom of a frozen river, waiting to run out of oxygen or turn into Popsic—

Drop will occur in ten seconds.

Allie tightens her grip, her face gone paler than Colin's. I remind myself that there's only room enough in here for one scared girl, and smile at her. "Kind of neat. Think about the stories you can tell all your dragon friends. How you flew a crate into Alaska."

She gives the slightest nod and squeezes harder.

Five seconds.

I reach over my shoulder and flip the switch that activates

the LCD. Four squares appear onscreen. Grackel and Baby occupy most of the upper left-hand view. Two are tinged red by Randon's glow but are otherwise dark. The final square, from the camera embedded in the crate bottom, shows a smattering of yellow lights, distant cat eyes peeking out at us through the abyss.

Two. Good luck, humans. One.

Grackel says something else, but I don't hear, because my stomach's suddenly lurching into my brain. I bite my lip hard to keep my shriek from joining Allie's.

Deploy the parachute, Grackel says.

"Now?" I break a nail fumbling with the buckle. Why the hell is the oh-shit lever out of arm's reach? "I thought it was supposed to open on its own?"

You will overshoot if you wait.

I finally work the clasp free, spring up, and tug the lever. The parachute unravels with a loud *whoosh*. I stare at the ceiling. There is no backup. Preston said we wouldn't need one. Of course, he also said we wouldn't need to manually deploy—

The whip-snap of fabric expanding and catching wind sounds a glorious melody. Then the crate jerks up, and I slam to the floor. Pain blasts my kneecaps, fades as the feed from the bottom camera settles enough to show a concentrated cluster of cat eyes staring back at me.

We're right over the town.

But drifting.

East.

Toward wilderness and water and death.

I spring up and hurl myself at the opposite wall. The lights of Dillingham continue to disappear off the screen. I try a dozen more times. My efforts only succeed in igniting a fiery ache in my shoulders.

"Cover your ears," I tell Allie, drawing my gun. I load the chamber and fire. The explosive noise of gunshot rattles through my head, and there's now a small hole in our crate. Useless. The lights continue to wink out. Almost gone.

Hold on, Grackel says. I spot a flash of red on the LCD and reach for the handrail as she smashes into the crate feet first. We hurtle sideways. I lose my grip, stumble backward, and collide with the edge of the jump seat.

My ribs crack; I scream. A million tiny sparks ignite behind my eyes. The squeal of talons on metal shrieks through the crate. We lurch to a steady descent, and I tumble to the floor, gasping for breath.

After my vision clears and air slips back into my lungs, I check the LCD. The bottom right screen shows streetlights and empty roads and quiet buildings awaiting our late-night arrival. Grackel's a hazy red glow on the adjacent screen. She flaps toward the shadowed teeth of mountains in the distance.

I examine Colin, grimace a smile. He somehow managed to make it through our joyride none the worse for wear. Grackel was right. Battered, terrified, but we're alive, on course. Should land shortly.

As I gain my feet, Allie breaks into a hysterical wail. I try to ask her what's wrong, but my words come out a groan. I'm staggering toward her jump seat to comfort her when I hear the rumbling purr. Barely audible behind the ringing in my head, the hiss of wind, and Allie's cries, but distinct and terrible. It is a sound I hear often in my nightmares.

Real?

I look at the LCD. Several pairs of fiery orbs dart across it. Headed in the same direction as Grackel.

Grackel, dragon jets are after you.

Painted black, invisible to dragons. Designed for speed, stealth, and execution. A couple can take down a bright Red in under a minute. Grackel's old, not very fast to begin with, and she must be exhausted from the night's flight.

Do not worry about this one, human. Arabelle is safe. Contact Randon when you are ready, she says, ever calm. *Until then, you are on your own. Be brave.*

"Thank you," I whisper to the LCD, then shut it off.

"Grackel's stopped talking to me. It's my fault, my fault," Allie says between hiccupped sobs as she worries at the silver dragon pin clutched between her hands.

"It's not your fault." I press my forehead to hers. "Nothing is your fault. She's just conserving her energy. She'll find shelter in the mountains. The jets can't fly there."

"But the helicopters can, yes, yes."

I shake my head, remembering the dragon-hunting gunships and ax-wielding soldiers who decapitate old Reds far too well. "Grackel's a smart one. I bet you all the money in my go bag that she outlives us all."

Allie sniffles. "That's a silly bet. How am I going to collect if you're wrong?"

"Good call. I bet you a big piece of cake we hear from her before we finish breakfast."

"Deal." She squeezes her eyes shut. "She won't go Georgetown on us, will she?"

Captured and sent to a hidden research facility to be tortured and executed. "No, of course not." They'll probably just kill her outright. As the altimeter ticks toward zero, I hope for that.

I check my Beretta to make sure it wasn't damaged when I fell, load a full magazine, then ready the chamber. I won't be a prisoner again. Death is preferable. Anything but capture.

6

In between inserting an IV, administering an oxygen mask, and checking Colin's vitals, the EMT keeps looking at me. And not in the "I don't believe your ridiculous gunshot story" sort of way. More like he's trying to figure out where he's seen me before.

I'd hoped the scruffy hair, gaunt face, and lack of makeup would hide me from the scrutiny Preston warned me would occur. Had hoped to fade from public memory, maybe visit Dad and Sam in a few months—but on his last visit to the island, Preston informed me that I'd need to lay "Yoda low, Dagobah style" until the war ended.

Then he pulled out his tablet and loaded the final scene from the *Kissing Dragons* midseason finale. Heavily edited with CGI effects, it showed me executing Baby, who'd been digitally transformed from a Silver into a Red because dragon children aren't supposed to exist. And of course they took out the part where I stabbed James.

According to Preston, a week after they released the video, the president's press secretary announced our defection back to the other side and offered a reward for information leading to our capture.

Half a million dollars. Each. A lot more than any EMT makes.

"So where did you say you were from again?" he asks.

"I didn't."

"You a cheechako?"

"I don't know what that is."

"Yep, she's a cheechako. A foreigner. A Southerner," Driver says, affecting a horrible accent. Something between Georgia and Canada. He laughs to himself. "Everything's south of Dillingham. How'd you get up here?"

"We flew, yes, yes," Allie murmurs. Her head's resting on my lap.

I stroke her hair, glance up to find Driver examining us in the rearview mirror. "Look, we're tired. Don't want to be rude, but could we quit it with the questions?"

"I really should take a look at your ribs," EMT says.

Which means me taking off the jacket, him seeing the gun. Me using it. "I'm fine. Worry about him."

I force myself to sit up straight, hide my grimace behind my hand, and return my attention to the window. We speed past old wooden homes and shops, most fishing related. A town, a real town. Feels strange. Maybe because nothing in Dillingham is painted black. Maybe because I've lived in a prison camp or a shipping container the past several months.

"You see anything funny while you were waiting for us?" Driver says.

I shake my head and slide my other hand over Allie's mouth, but she seems to have fallen back asleep.

"Heard them jets, though, right? Sheriff says they were DJs. Dragons in Dillingham? That'll be front page for a week. Everyone'll be sending in photos of junk they didn't see, calling 'em dragons or UFOs. At least it'll be a changeup from sasquatches."

I can see EMT's expression in the window reflection. The mention of dragons has his gears turning. I reach under my jacket for my gun.

"Thought there weren't any dragons in Alaska?" I say.

EMT shrugs. "The Mengeles say it's too cold for them, but you never know."

Cold has little to do with it. Not enough food supply to sustain numbers, according to Grackel. Nothing palatable, at least. A part of me expects her to pop up into my head at any moment and decry the polluted taste of caribou. But she doesn't. Randon and Baby have gone to sleep, safe in the mountains, and I tell myself Grackel's sleeping, too.

"What about that research base of yours they found in Antarctica?" Driver says.

"Twisted, bro. Straight twisted what they did."

Driver snorts. "You gonna believe some YouTube fool who calls himself RedJediGrunt? It's all CGI."

"Bro, that stuff is real."

"I've got a holy glove I want to sell you." Driver wiggles his gloved fingers at us. "Worn by Jesus himself."

"It's real, bro. It was on the news."

"You believe in dragon exposure, too?" Driver scoffs, rolls his eyes. "Get too close to a dragon, you'll go crazy?"

"It's happened. Just watch *The Other Side* and you'll know it's true."

Driver hooks a thumb over his shoulder at EMT. "Dragon boy's got a real thing for those dragon shows, don't you know? Spinoff after spinoff. Infects the neurons."

EMT's face lights up. "That's it. I couldn't figure out who you looked like. That Melissa Callahan girl. Shame about what happened."

"I don't know what you're talking about."

"*Kissing Dragons?*"

I shut my eyes, give a slight shake of my head.

"Don't mind him," Driver says. "He had a poster of that girl in his bedroom." They made posters? Of course they did. I was world famous three months ago. "Don't worry, Sarah, you're much prettier than she is."

I can't help but laugh at that. "How's he doing?"

"Bro's a fighter. Something about him, too. I'd swear I've seen him before. The front lines, maybe."

"Him?" I say, opening my eyes to find EMT squinting at Colin. Is this guy an ex-A-B who platooned with Colin? A Bureau of Dragon Affairs agent? Sam once told me they have sleepers everywhere.

Driver chuckles. "He thinks everybody looks like somebody, don't you know? Add some sideburns, and he says I could be Elvis's son." He puffs out his chest and glides a hand down his profile. "What say you, Melissa Callahan? Am I a Presley?"

"Sure." If Elvis had adopted. Deep breaths, Melissa. These are just people. Not BoDA agents in disguise. Not ex-military. Just ordinary people. I have to tell myself that a few more times before I release my hold on the gun.

When we arrive at Kanakanak Hospital, a single-story strip of a building that seems more like an extended barn than a medical facility, a team of scrub-dressed men and women unload Colin and roll him away. I grab our bags, loop them in triplicate over my shoulders, and carry Allie into the lobby. A lanky man bundled in a fur-lined sheriff's coat strides toward me.

"You Sarah Cosgrove?" he asks.

I set Allie on a chair, put the bags beside her. "Yes, sir."

"You injured?"

I exaggerate a wince. "Ribs."

The faintest smile touches his lips as he powers up his tablet. "From the car accident?"

I nod, unable to meet his gaze. It was a ridiculous story, but I panicked when EMT asked me why we were on the side of the road in the middle of the night, me with fractured ribs, Colin with an hours-old gunshot wound, and Allie without a bruise.

"You got ID, Ms. Cosgrove?"

I retrieve my wallet from my go bag and show him my Washington State driver's license.

He types info into his tablet. "What you doing up here in Dillingham?"

"Heard it's dragon free. Good boarding," I say.

His smile broadens into a full smirk, and I consider going for my gun. One of the first things Colin taught me was how to quick draw and fire. Not as accurate, but the sheriff's at close range. It'll be the end of the road for all of us, but I won't be a prisoner—

The tablet beeps. He appears mildly surprised. "Where

you staying, Ms. Cosgrove?"

"With our uncle."

"What's his name?"

My heart flutters. I spit out the first thing I can think of. "Preston Keith."

"Don't know him."

"He just moved here. From Michigan. Tired of dragons and everything."

"Hmmm. Now tell me what happened again?"

"We were out late . . . partying," I say.

He glances toward Allie. "Partying, huh? And after you left this party, that's when you were shot at?"

"I don't know if it was someone aiming for us, or just . . . like a hunter."

Sheriff's looking at me hard, like he knows my thoughts, but he's still holding his tablet, his own gun holstered at his side. Can I kill him without warning?

"A hunter? Mistook you for a bear? What kind of car were you driving?"

Do I have a choice? "Prius."

He fixes me with a stare I saw many a time when Dad was about to lecture me or Sam for screwing up. "My deputy has yet to find this mysterious car of yours. This magic Prius that looks like a bear and can drive through Alaskan snow. My deputy did, however, find this near the end of C Street.

Very close to where you got picked up."

He shows me the tablet screen, and I slide my right hand beneath my jacket. There's our crate, wide open. "What is that thing?"

"I would reconsider," he says. I'm not sure whether he means my story or if he knows I'm carrying, but I hesitate. "Found blood inside. Now, if I wanted to, I could throw you in holding while I run some of that blood against some of your friend's."

"That's not necessary, sir."

He purses his lips. "I don't know what strangeness you're up to, but we don't want any of it here. You got twenty-four hours to clear out. We understood?"

"Yes, sir," I say, redirecting my hand into my pocket.

"Smartest choice you ever made. Now give me the piece. Slowly."

I don't delay.

"This ain't bear insurance," he says, examining the Beretta. "Don't ever come back here, Ms. Cosgrove." He calls over a nurse whose mouth seems set in a permanent frown. "Get these two cleaned up. And this one's got some busted ribs that need tending."

"What about the GSW?" she says.

"After he's fixed up, discharge him. Off rec." He gives me that stare again as he walks past. When I turn to track him,

I see a second cop holstering his gun. He grins, tips his hat, and leaves with the sheriff.

Nurse Frown uses her ID badge to get us through an automated door that opens into an antiquated section of the hospital. Track fluorescent lighting, half of it flickering or burned out, illuminates peppered tile that was probably last in fashion fifty years ago.

Puckered scowl never faltering, the nurse leads us past an office and an emergency stairwell, then through a swinging door into a room with a half-dozen lockers and a single shower. She provides us towels, orders us to meet her back in the lobby in twenty minutes, and hurries off.

While Allie heads into the shower, I return to the hallway, make sure it's empty, then power up the phone. I dial the number Preston made me memorize. I don't expect anybody to answer, but when someone picks up on the third ring, I'm so happy I almost forget the ridiculous code phrase I'm supposed to provide. "Obi-Wan Kenobi, you're our only hope."

"Sarah?" Preston says, sounding worried. Preston never sounds worried.

"Yes. Pres—" I begin before remembering that's not his identity anymore. "Michael, we're in trouble. We used the crate. We're in—"

"No locations. Can you make it to the white mountains?"

"Huh?"

"You have the SIM card?"

"Yes." I pulled it from the map in the crate.

"Put it in the phone. That'll tell you what you need to know."

"What's going on? I couldn't contact—"

"Bad stuff, Cosgrove."

"What about Papa?" I ask, which is Keith's code name.

"Fine. No time to talk. Get here if you can. Sorry we can't help. Good-bye."

"Wait! Is Jame —" I catch myself. "Is Jay okay? We haven't heard anything from him in a month."

"You don't know?" he says. There's something else in his voice now. Also something I've never heard. Melancholy? Despair? "I'm sorry."

"Sorry?" I mumble. "Is he okay? Tell me."

"I don't know, Callahan. I just don't know," he whispers. The fact that he slipped and used my real name terrifies me almost as much as his words. "Everything's hosed. I'm sorry."

"What do you mean?" I ask, but the phone's gone silent. I look at the screen. *Call ended.*

When I tap out the number again, a message appears— *Locked*—and I'm asked for a passcode. After my third failed attempt, the screen goes blank.

Preston must have programmed the phone to deactivate after I called him. Worried that I might try to contact someone else. Like my father or brother. How could he do that to me? What if we needed an ambulance again? And what about James?

Deep breath. *In nae.* I fetch my pack, retrieve the SIM card, and slide it into the phone's back. The screen lights up, and that digital map from the crate appears in miniature. I jab at the red pushpins that dot the evacuated territories. Touching one pulls up the name of a city, mountain, or national park and assigns it a code phrase. No other information. No photos. No detailed maps. Nothing.

Worse, "the white mountains" are Denver. That's at the edge of the drone zone. The city's a pile of rubble, abandoned to nature and the ghosts of the dead these past ten years. Maybe a place for humans to hide, but not dragons.

I scan through the remaining hideouts, committing them to memory, for all the good it'll do. When I remove the SIM card, I test the phone again, but it might as well be a drink coaster. I hurl it at the wall, then stomp on it.

I stare unblinking at the broken remnants and feel a familiar sting behind my eyes.

"No!"

No more tears. I did not cry for Grackel; I will not cry for James.

7

After showering and changing into our spare clothes, Allie and I return to the nurse's station. Nurse Frown's not frowning anymore. She wraps my ribs extra tight, gives Allie a lollipop that's instantly gobbled, and tells us Colin's looking good and should be out of surgery in an hour.

I thank her and ask if I can use her cell phone to call a cab so Allie and I can get breakfast. Nurse Frown starts frowning again, then lectures me about cell phones causing cancer, extra so because of Dillingham's poor reception. Once she's exhausted her fund of knowledge, she escorts me to the hospital's old-school push-button phone and looms over me until I hang up.

Ernie's Cab drops us off at the Twin Dragons restaurant, which the driver informs me used to serve Chinese before being converted to a diner when some "cheechakos bullied their way in." Two fire-breathing, interconnected neon dragons adorn the front window. Long, snakelike, wingless. Nothing at all like real Reds or Greens, other than the bright glow.

The first thing I notice when we enter is the unhealthily delightful smell of grease and bacon. A waitress greets us with a perfunctory hello and shows us to a booth. The few other patrons in the diner at the early hour don't pay us any attention.

For the first time in more than half a year, I almost feel normal. Just two sisters out for an early breakfast.

"There's no cake," Allie says, pouting at the menu.

"Cheesecake."

"That's not real cake."

"They have pie."

"I want cake."

The waitress, Estelle, drops off a Pepsi for me and a Mountain Dew and a Dr Pepper for Allie. "What can I get you?"

"The lumberjack trio." Hash browns, three pieces of bacon, three buttermilk pancakes, three scrambled eggs, and three sausages smothered in gravy. More food than I could eat in a day, but I don't care, I'm gonna eat it all.

Estelle nods to Allie, who's full-on glaring at the menu.

"What about you, little lady?"

"Do you have any cake?" I ask.

"We have cheesecake. Frozen."

Allie thrusts the menu at our waitress. "That's not real cake."

Estelle shrugs. "We got pie. Fresh as of last night."

"That's not cake either, no, no." She stands and pulls on her coat. "Where's there cake?"

People are definitely paying attention to us now. Most in that embarrassed covert glancing sort of way, but four teenage boys on the other side of the diner are staring at us in that same intent manner as EMT.

"Allison, sit down," I hiss. She flops into the booth and sulks. "Is there anywhere else that serves cake?"

"There's a bakery on the other side of town. Won't be open for a few hours, though," Estelle says.

"She'll have the cheesecake," I say. Estelle shrugs again, collects my menu, and walks away. "Allison—"

"It's Kim, remember? I wanted cake."

"I know, but we can't cause problems. We have to keep a low profile." I glance toward the boys' table. One of them has a tablet out. Another waves at me. I scowl, pull my ski cap lower, and grab the wallet from my pack. I put money on the table to cover our order. "Come on, Allie, let's get outta here."

"Maybe cheesecake is all right."

"We can get cake later," I say. The guys have clustered around the computer tablet.

"But we have to have it now, yes, yes," Allie says. "You said . . ." She chokes up.

I join her on the other side of the booth, keeping one eye on the boys' table, wishing for my gun. "What's wrong?"

"I have to eat my cake before you finish breakfast." She sniffles. "That way you can't collect on our bet. Cheesecake can count, right?"

I kiss her on the head. "Of course it does." I call over Estelle and hand her the money. "Could you box that cheese-cake, please? Don't worry about the rest."

"She has to be all right," Allie says. "It's my fault, my fault. Always my fault."

"It's not your fault, Allie. You know that." I zip up her jacket. "Grackel made her decision. You didn't do anything wrong."

"Yes I did. I didn't want to tell you, but . . ."

"What is it?"

She shakes her head. "You're going to be mad at me, yes, yes."

"Out with it. I won't be mad."

"I blabbed to the Greens," she blurts, then erupts in tears.

I hug her tight, half to comfort her, half to muffle her.

"It's okay." I try to sound calm, but my voice comes out a hushed whisper. "When . . . when was this?"

"Last week," she mumbles into my jacket. "I'm sorry. I know I wasn't supposed to, but you had Colin, and Arabelle was spending all that time flying with Grackel, and—"

"Shhh." How damn long does it take someone to pack up a piece of frozen cheesecake?

"Why didn't you talk to Maren or Syren or any of the other Reds?"

"I did, at first. But then they all went to sleep."

"You didn't tell the Greens where we were?"

"No, no. Never. They wanted to come visit, but I told them we were full."

"Good girl. You didn't do anything wrong," I say.

"But we had to leave the island. And Grackel . . ."

"We would have had to leave one day anyway," I say.

The waitress sets a brown bag on our table. I stuff it into my pack, grab Allie's hand, and head for the exit. The group of boys moves to intercept. I keep my eyes fixed on the linoleum floor and quicken my pace.

A semicircle of eight legs and boots forms a blockade in front of me.

"You're that girl from the net, aren't you?"

"You're confused. Excuse us." I shoulder between two of them, pulling Allie along after me.

"Hey, man, we just want to help. That's wicked backward how they treated her."

Her? I look over my shoulder to find three of the guys scrutinizing Allie. The fourth, who I almost bowled over in my effort to escape, glowers at me, but doesn't show a hint of recognition.

"What are you talking about?" I ask, afraid I already know the answer.

"RedJediGrunt's new vid, man. It's straight trending."

I make a mental note to castrate Preston the next time I see him. "Let me see." I step in front of Allie, placing a firm hand on her shoulder as she tries to get a peek. Tablet guy loads a clip, and yellow words make a slow crawl down a black background, set to "The Imperial March."

"Turn the sound off."

"But . . ."

"Turn it off. I don't want her to hear this. These things give her nightmares." Me, too.

"The United States of America, once home to freedom and democracy, continues to claim that Georgetown and other facilities of its kind are fabrications of the growing, global Dragon Awareness Movement. Despite international pressure, including threats of sanctions and war, the U.S. government refuses to allow U.N. investigators into the country.

"Since the government continues to hide behind a military wall and the cloak of propaganda, it has fallen on the Jedi of the world to expose the truth. Many terrible things occurred in Georgetown. Unspeakable atrocities against dragons, unprovoked attacks on foreign countries, assassinations of sympathizers, abuse of prisoners. These pale in comparison to what you are about to witness.

"Some think that, to keep the world safe, the ends justify the means, no matter how great the cost to our humanity. This final video in our series is for those of you who still believe this."

The words and background dissolve to a high-def infrared video shot from the ceiling corner of an octagonal room. My legs almost give out. My lungs, too.

The reconditioning chamber. The bastards were observing us the entire time. Watching us go crazy.

Not just watching. Making.

Allie crawls into view, her eyes saner than I've ever seen them, and filled with the terror of a newly caged animal. She nears a wall, hands extended, searching for a boundary to the dark prison, and I flinch, knowing what comes next. The CENSIR encircling her head delivers a series of sharp electrical jolts until she changes course.

For a moment, the walls—giant thinscreens or something—light up with images of dragons breathing fire, insurgents with machine guns, corpses everywhere.

The vid shifts to the short period between terror cycles when everything was quiet and dark, and in some ways worse, because now you could agonize over the awful images and sounds you'd witnessed. Real or not real? Allie's rocking on the floor in the middle of the room, knees pulled to her heaving chest, head tucked between them. Every few seconds, she twitches.

On to a later cycle, Allie slipping toward the wild-eyed, crazy girl I met when I arrived in Georgetown. A girl I still see in some way every day. A girl currently obsessed with eating cake because she doesn't want to add another dead dragon to the long list of blame she carries in that invisible space between heart and soul.

I take several breaths until I'm sure my voice'll come out indifferent. "I see what you mean, but it's not her. Excuse us."

Ignoring their rapid-fire questions, I spin around, grab Allie, and rush out of the Twin Dragons into the cold Alaskan morning. Dark, flurries swirling, it doesn't take long before the neon glow of the restaurant fades from view.

When I'm sure nobody's following us, I stop walking, unzip my pack, and retrieve the doggie bag. Allie leans against a plowed snowbank, wiggling her butt back and forth until she's fashioned herself a makeshift chair.

"Cake time?"

"Cake time." I plop onto the mound next to her and squeal at the trickle of slush that squirts into my pants. I sigh theatrically. "Whatever happened to our tropical island?"

Allie laughs. "We'd melt, yes, yes."

"I don't think I'd mind melting," I say, unboxing the cheesecake.

Allie's laughter ends as she looks from the dessert in my hands to the clouded sky. "Grackel didn't like the cold either. You think she's in heaven, Melissa? You think God allows dragons up there?"

She's asked me that before. I resort to an answer that's worked in the past. "He's a fool if he doesn't."

She nods, but doesn't appear soothed. "What about me? Will I?"

This is a new one. "Of course."

"I don't think I will, no, no." Her matter-of-fact tone pierces me deeper than her words. "I don't remember being normal."

I set the cheesecake on the sidewalk, remove my gloves, then take her face between my hands. "Look at me, Allie. I don't know if heaven or hell exists, but I do know that if there's some special place where special people go, you're first in line. You and Baby and Grackel."

"But I killed all those dragons. And Major Alderson. And I shot Sarge. And I don't remember feeling bad about a lot of it. I know I should, but I don't. Because I'm not normal."

"Normal's far overrated. All the normal people I knew growing up were boring. You and me, we get to talk to dragons and live on our own islands—"

"You don't like that."

"Yeah, I wish it was warmer. I wish I wasn't a reality TV star. And honestly, I'm not a big fan of parachuting in a crate or living in a shipping container, but it's a lot better than the alternative."

"Georgetown?" she whispers.

"No, silly." I run a finger from her forehead to her chin. "My mom used to do that to make Sam and me feel better when we were scared or upset. She's not here anymore, but every time I look at you, Allison Tanner, I realize that's okay, because I've got somebody just as wonderful at my side. So you can take your normal and shove it."

She beams. "You're crying."

"It's the snow. You gonna have your cheesecake now, or what? It's probably already frozen again."

She laughs and hugs me. "I love you, Melissa."

"I love you more."

"I love you most, yes, yes." She picks up the cheesecake

and takes a large bite. "Ooh, that's good. Your turn."

"Nope. I'm not a fan."

"Liar." She jams it into my face until I take a nibble. "You have to eat. You're getting pretty scrawny."

It's my turn to laugh. I tickle her. Way too skinny. "Pot or kettle?"

"Pot." She shoves a handful of snow down my shirt.

I thrust a handful down her pants.

Then we're both laughing and squealing. Quite loudly. Quite abnormally. And it feels wonderful.

8

As we walk hand-in-hand back to the hospital, Allie rattles off names and stories of her new Green buddies. I interrupt with repeated reminders to avoid future discussion. She gives her assent each time, then jumps right back into telling me how great and friendly they are.

I don't know if her unwavering love of dragons is some reverse side effect of her reconditioning, or if she's too young to remember life before the blackout policy. The Reign of Flame, as the media named it, ended almost a decade ago, when a task force led by my father discovered dragons couldn't see black. Tipped the scales. Five years later, the war was over, the monsters were defeated, the humans were safe.

There was a point in my life when I clung to those lies,

particularly after Mom died. Then I discovered my dragon-talking abilities and got shipped to Georgetown, where I learned that not all monsters come with glowing scales attached. And not all dragons are monsters.

Unfortunately, most of it's a gray, globby mess. When the wingless Blues stampeded north, ravaging rain forests and villages on the way to North America, they did so because they were supposedly fleeing the invisible monsters that chased them. In one of our more heated discussions, Grackel informed me, in so many words, that the Reds obliterated our cities in retaliation for the incessant military onslaught, hoping to dissuade further aggression.

Most everyone can agree on one thing: Greens are the most dangerous dragons, ragers who seem to thrive on war and death. They don't much like anything, including one another. Which is probably the only reason they don't currently rule the world.

I was six when a quintet torched half of New York City. Took them less than thirty minutes. Required ten squadrons of jets to bring them down. Worldwide panic ensued because nobody had ever seen Greens strike in unison before.

Luckily, it was an aberration.

Until Oren arrived on the insurgent scene with a unification plan. If he gets his hands on Baby and breeds her . . .

Allie doesn't know that on the monster scale, Oren and

those Greens rank right up there with our Georgetown captors. And I don't want her to know. Right and wrong make sense to her in some crazy way I both envy and dread.

"You can't talk to them anymore, Allie," I say as she continues to prattle on about a dragon named Bornak who claims he can roast a deer from five miles away. "Not until I meet them and they get my seal of approval."

"Okay, but you can't be tough. Bornak would make a great camping buddy. He likes to hunt and he makes good fires."

When we reach the hospital, Nurse Frown informs us that Colin's in the recovery room, waking from the anesthesia. "Once he's stable, you guys are on your own." With a stern warning not to excite him, she leads us to the patient wing.

"Mr. Janson, your girlfriend's here to see you."

"Melissa," Colin says. Slurred. Groggy. But my name.

Heat rises in my cheeks, and I'm glad for the dim lighting. "His ex," I say. "No, Frank, it's me, Sarah."

"I knew a Frank," he says, followed by an extended yawn. "Frank and Kevin and Mac—"

"From TV," I interrupt.

"The fab four. Kissing dragons everywhere they go. Until J.R. got too close. Poor Junior." His chuckle fades into a quiet snore.

"Don't worry, this is normal. The anesthesia should wear off soon," Nurse Frown says, and leaves.

I send Allie to the vending machine with a few dollars and instructions to wait in the lobby, then pull up a chair beside Colin. The color's returned to his cheeks, and his breath comes easily.

A part of me wants to get into bed beside him, wrap his arm around me, and lay my head on his chest. Stupid. Even if there were time for something, anything, what would he want with someone four years his junior with almost as many physical scars as emotional ones? And even if he could somehow look past all that, there's the small issue of his dead sister.

But I like the dream—don't have many good ones anymore. I lower my head onto him ever so gently, slow my breathing until it matches the rise and fall of his chest.

I must doze, because the next thing I know, his hand's on my neck. He seems to be asleep. Maybe it was an accident, maybe he didn't know I was here.

Maybe he did.

When I grasp his fingers to disentangle myself, he murmurs, "You're fine where you are. Quite fine."

I sit up and exaggerate a stretch. "Sorry about that. Got tired. Glad you're okay."

A dopey smile crosses his face. "You're my girlfriend, huh?"

I look away. "That's our cover. Your idea?"

"Should have been," he says, then launches into another ramble about *Kissing Dragons*, ending with "It didn't get good again until you were on there. Absolutely stunning."

"It was all fake," I say, standing. "That girl never existed."

I'm almost to the door when he says, "You're wrong. I see her every day."

I make the mistake of glancing back. He's looking at me. Such soulful eyes.

No! I spin around and break into a run, but I'm too slow.

"So beautiful she doesn't even know it. Like my sister."

I flee. Through the lobby, outside, down the empty road toward the morning moon that hangs low over the darkness of the river. My lungs knot up, my legs turn to dry ice, and my heartbeat thunders in my ears. But it is not enough to drown the memory of that look and those words.

I'm almost to the river when my feet slip from under me and I fall hard onto my injured ribs. Mewling, I roll onto my stomach. Behind the blood pounding in my ears and my own pathetic moans, I hear dragons.

Then the jets come, with their percussive gunfire and shrieking missiles. I push myself to my knees and glance toward the eastern horizon. The clouds are ablaze with abstract blue streaks, a chaotic collage of tracer dots, and fuzzy green balls of light. An aurora borealis of war.

Not real.

I dip my hands into the snow and press them to my face. The cold stings, but the cacophony remains. When I split my fingers and peek skyward, the air battle looms, ever bright.

Two Greens emerge from the clouds in fast pursuit of a jet that's lost one of its thrusters. They pinch in around him, blasting fire in turns. Not orange like normal dragonfire, but azure. Beautiful.

A stream of flame envelops the wing. The plane wobbles, twirls into a flat spin. The pilot ejects, his black parachute cast in a vivid green glow. There's a brief roaring match between the dragons. The smaller one darts under the larger one and inhales the chute.

I look away. "Not real. Not real. Not real."

Can't be. Sirens would be blaring. People would be scrambling for dragon shelters. Standard operating procedure for—

For cities painted black, for cities where dragons aren't confused with UFOs.

I spring to my feet, calling for Randon and Baby, but neither answers. Still asleep? I look toward their hiding spot in the outlying mountains. Far from the battle. Safe for now.

But Allie and Colin aren't. At any moment, a jet could spin out of control and crash into Dillingham, or dragons might break loose from the battle and decide to have an impromptu shish kebab of locals and cheechakos.

I search the surrounding cars, find a beat-up black Jeep the owner didn't bother to lock. No keys inside, so I sprint to the adjoining house. I start to knock, but then test the knob. It gives. I sneak in. It's dark inside. I fumble around, locate a pair of switches, turn on the porch and foyer lights. I snatch a set of keys from a bowl on an end table and race back to the Jeep.

I grind the gears twice before the clutch engages, then floor the accelerator. A rooster tail of snow explodes behind me, and the car hurls forward in chaotic swerves. Thankfully, the road's wide and nobody's on it. I ease off the gas pedal, gain control, and speed toward the hospital.

I'm a couple of blocks away when a trio of Greens swoops out of the clouds, the figures atop them little more than snowy specks. They break from the battle and dive toward Dillingham.

I lay on the horn to wake the residents. The dragons grow larger in the rearview mirror, their reflections rippling across the river. The shoreline buildings are well within range, but they don't open fire.

What are they waiting for?

The hospital sign comes into view faster than expected. I slam on the brakes and turn the wheel a sharp right. I leap out, leaving the engine puttering in neutral. A police siren whines in the distance.

The sheriff's calling out orders over a bullhorn from somewhere that sounds a few blocks away. "Keep clear of outer walls and windows. Seek cover beneath tables or in bathtubs or closets."

Useless. The residents of Dillingham might survive a tornado, but not a dragon attack.

The hospital lobby's empty. I hurry through the heavy doors at the rear, toward Colin's room. But he and his medical equipment are gone. I yell for him, Allie, and Nurse Frown as I scour the other rooms in the patient wing. Nothing.

The residents of Kanakanak Hospital have vanished.

I return to the lobby. Through the windows, I see that the town's now bathed in an eerie Christmas-light glow.

What are they doing?

Though I can't see them, I can feel their eyes on me. Searching. Ravenous. I bite hard into my lip until the pain overwhelms the fear. As the watching sensation lessens to something manageable, I focus inward and listen.

Where are you?

It requires all my nerve to ignore the dragons' words and skulk to the window. I get a clear view of the sky. At least three dozen Greens trace slow figure eights above the town, in alternate streams.

Melissa. I almost scream at the sound of Randon's voice inside my head.

"You need to get Baby to safety," I say aloud. Too loud. Everything feels too loud.

We are already flying, human. There is no indication of pursuit.

I drop into silent communication. *Do you know where Colin and Allie are?*

The shelter from dragons, he says a few seconds later.

I look over my shoulder at the access door that leads to the offices and the changing room where Allie and I showered. I'd forgotten about the emergency stairwell. It didn't occur to me before, because I was worried about contacting Preston, but why would a one-story building need a stairwell?

I breathe a little easier. "What to Do During a Dragon Attack." One of our annual school seminars. They gave us ebooklets full of rules. "If outdoors: seek safety at a library, school, or hospital." Not because dragons understand the critical importance of education and health, as some teachers joked, but because of a federal mandate that required every public building to construct a subterranean bunker.

Please tell them I'm okay and that I'll be there—

A gunshot rings through the air. A dragon overhead unleashes a torrent of flame that engulfs a home catty-corner from the hospital. A woman with a toddler cradled in each arm bursts onto the road. A couple seconds later, a burning man tumbles out and immerses himself in a snowbank.

The Green lands in front of the family, and his white-cloaked rider dismounts via a rope ladder. The dragon collapses onto its haunches, licks its lips. The kids wail. Mom's crying too as she gets on her knees. Dad, steam rising from his body, raises his arms high.

The rider shoots him in the head, then motions to the dragon. I turn away and cover my ears, but the crunch of corpse and shrieks of children play loud in my head anyway. Not real, and real, all at once.

"What do you want?" Sheriff asks via the bullhorn. Sounds terrified. Another Green—the brightest dragon I've ever seen except Baby—dives toward the source.

"We mean you no harm." The austere voice that booms from the bullhorn a minute later fires a shiver through me. Though I've only heard it a couple times before, I'd recognize it anywhere. Oren White, the Diocletian leader. "However, if you attempt to harm us, we will be forced to retaliate. We're looking for a pair of girls."

He doesn't know Baby's in the area, I realize, turning back toward the hospital. But somehow he knows about Allie and me. Will undoubtedly torture us for information.

"They landed in Dillingham within the past day," Oren

continues. "One of them is seventeen. Five-ten. Short brown hair. Brown eyes. Probably skinny. Name's Melissa, though she's likely using an alias. The other—"

He stops talking. Sheriff must be in his ear.

It'll be seconds before Oren relays the information to his dragons and they pounce on the hospital. I stare at the Jeep, still idling in the emergency lane. I have to lead them away, hope I can occupy their attention long enough to give Colin and Allie a chance to escape.

I relay my thoughts to Randon. *Tell Colin.*

He says that you must not do this. That it is foolish. I agree, human.

There's no other choice, I say, and break cover at a full sprint.

I climb in, thrust the Jeep into first, and take off. The Green on the ground whirls around, blocking the road that leads out of town. Another pair of dragons slams down behind me, sending up plumes of snow. I accelerate toward the riderless one.

The dragon spreads its mouth wide so I can see the mass of fire gathering in the back of its throat. I jerk the car toward the sidewalk and plow through a low snowbank. I emerge on the other side, fishtail, almost run over that woman and her two children.

The rider opens fire with his machine gun. My rear tire

blows out, and the Jeep pitches left, toward the Green. I tap the brakes, veer right. The Green dances sideways, will squash me between its elephantine leg and the house ahead if I don't stop. My only chance is to try to split the gap between its legs. Clear sailing on the other side.

I point the Jeep at the dragon's enormous foot and smash the gas pedal to the floor. My heartbeat echoes the frantic *bump-bump-bump* of the blown tread. Blood rushes my ears.

"Baekjul boolgool!" I bellow, and jerk the wheel a hard left.

The Jeep careens across the dragon's talons. The front end lifts up. The Jeep goes airborne, sails through the emptiness between its legs. As the dragon roars its pain, a triumphant euphoria fills me.

Then the Jeep crashes back to earth, and I crash through its front window.

9

I wake to the pungent odor of ammonia and a colossal head-ache that dwarfs the dull throb in my midsection. The whir of an alarm siren fades in and out. Large hands appear at the haloed edge of my vision. I catch the glint of silver between the fingers.

Something is put on my head.

Cool and metallic and familiar, but I'm too disoriented to place it. I reach up to investigate, but my hands are cuffed to something. My ears warm, the pressure inside my skull intensifies, and the circlet cinches into place.

A CENSIR.

"No." I groan.

"A precaution."

Another whiff of ammonia, and the world comes into

view. I'm in the hospital, handcuffed to the bed railings. Oren straddles the chair at my bedside, long arms folded across the upholstered back, a tablet dangling from his hand.

He checks the tablet, which can show him my general mood—I focus on wrath—then regards me with a curious smile. "That was quite a stunt you pulled out there. Much like your mother, aren't you?"

"Don't talk about my mother."

"You should learn to take compliments better."

"You should learn not to kill people."

He drags a finger from his left ear to his chin, tracing the knotted edges of a scar that stands out pale and angry against his dark skin. "Considering what happened to you in Georgetown and considering your brother, I'd think—"

"Sam? What's happened to Sam?"

"Keith was always good at keeping secrets," Oren says, but doesn't elaborate.

Sam is safe with my aunt and uncle in Michigan. He must be. So what if he never responded to any of the letters I sent via Preston? He's probably still pissed at me about everything. If something had happened to him, Dad would have mentioned it in his letters to me, wouldn't he? Unless Keith filtered them. I can't put it past him; he hid his and Mom's involvement in Loki's Grunts because he wanted to protect me from the truth that my mother was an insurgent. Oren's right. Keith was always good at keeping secrets.

No, Keith wouldn't do that to me. This is nothing more than a cruel lie from a cruel man. I can be cruel, too. "Do you know how much Lorena—"

Oren's hand flashes to my throat. "Be careful what you say about my daughter."

"Handcuffs and CENSIR not enough for you?" I say between gasps. "I see why Lorena despised you."

I expect him to crush my windpipe—a part of me hopes for it. But instead he releases me and leans back. "You even look like Olivia."

His words, spoken with sad fondness, hurt more than his hand ever could. "Did you come all this way so we could reminisce about the dead?" I glance at the CENSIR tablet and bite my lip. I will be strong. "You wasted your time. I don't know where she is."

"We already have what we want, Melissa. You just put on your big-girl face, act like everything's okay, and say good-bye. Then we'll be out of your hair." He gives me an apologetic look. "Don't worry, she'll be safe with us."

"She's not even of breeding age. Please—"

"The Silver?" He squints. "Figured Keith was smarter than that."

He opens the door and speaks to someone in the hallway. "Make her presentable." Then he looks back at me.

"She thinks you're coming with us, but I told her you'd have to wait until you're healed. She insists on saying good-bye. A favor for you, Melissa, for the friendship you gave my daughter."

She? My chest tightens. They were never after Baby. "Allie? Why?"

"Multichannel telepathy," he says, as if that should mean something to me. "Cumbersome, isn't it? I prefer what the dragons call it. 'Tangled.' Not quite right, but it has a certain simplistic elegance."

"Please, she's just a kid."

"You should have seen her face when she saw all those dragons outside." He beams as he rises. "Reminded me of the first time I showed my Lorie. Allie wants to come, Melissa. She wants to help us save her dragon friends."

"She doesn't know what that entails. Please."

"We are not the enemy," he says, and leaves.

Evelyn struts in. Even with the bulky body armor, white cloak, and goggles resting on her dragon-print headscarf, she manages an annoying beauty and grace. Worse, she reeks of roses. "Hello, Twenty-Five."

I gape. "Real?"

She pinches my arm, smirks when I grimace. "Guess so."

I don't get it. In Georgetown, Evelyn was Talker One, the perky sycophant who did everything the All-Blacks wanted her to do and shunned everybody who didn't. I hated her and thought she was evil, but only in that high-school popular-girl sort of way. The only time I ever saw anything authentic from her was when rescue came, when she was in the ER, huddled with James . . . I bite hard into my lip.

"Where is he?" I say, quivering. I want to cry. I want to strangle him.

She lifts my backpack from the floor and drops it on my bedside. "You look awful. "Don't know if I'll be able to pretty you up. Shame how this—"

"Where is he, Evelyn?"

"Where is who?" she asks. She unzips the pack. "You have nobody to blame but yourself, you know? Don't suppose you have makeup in here? Never were much concerned with keeping up appearances."

While she investigates my pack, throwing barbs whenever she can, I focus on making sense of her words in an effort to stave off the looming darkness. "Nobody to blame but yourself?" James and Evelyn knew about our hideout on Saint Matthew Island, so why did Oren and his Diocletians wait to pounce? After we left, there was no guarantee he would find us again. Nobody knew our location—

Until I panicked in the escape crate and attempted to contact every dragon I knew. Told them where we were headed.

But why the subterfuge? Why flush us out? Why not capture Allie on the island beforehand?

"Those mental cogs of yours still clunking along, Sarah?" Evelyn asks, checking my fake driver's license. She flings it to the ground. "You'll thank me later. Preston got your worst side."

She wets a pair of towels at the sink, returns to the bedside, and vigorously scrubs dried blood off my face. She drapes the towels over my handcuffs, then pulls a ski cap from somewhere inside her cloak and tugs it down over my CENSIR.

"Well, you're presentable. I guess. Be on your best behavior. Twenty-One's enough of a pain in the ass when she's in a good mood."

She's at the door when I cave. "Why, Evelyn?"

"If you can't figure that out, you're even dumber than you look."

Before I can make any sense of her parting shot, Allie bounds into the room, all hops and skips and squeals. She jumps onto the bed and nuzzles into my chest. I groan, and she pulls back.

"Mr. O said not to touch you because you're hurt and I already screwed up." Her smile returns with a delighted laugh. "I'm so glad you're okay, Melissa. Did you hear about the dragons? Mr. O says that when you get better, you can join us at HQ—that's what Mr. O calls it. We can all be together like we're supposed to. And we don't have to be afraid of anything again. We'll be safe. We need to convince Arabelle. She's being stubborn and won't talk to me."

She is so full of joy. It makes my own smile that much harder. "Don't worry. I'll set her straight. Now come on, give me a hug. A real one this time."

She wraps her arms around my neck and presses her cheek to mine. I relax to the pain in my ribs, allowing her slight weight to sink into me. When I can feel her heart beating above mine, I close my eyes. Behind the lilac of the shampoo, there's the faint smell of iron that will grow stronger in the company of Greens, and the hint of woodsmoke and winter that I always associate with Baby.

This is how I will remember her. At peace. Content.

"Time to go, dear," Oren says from the doorway.

Allie kisses my cheek. "See you soon."

"Yep. Be good. I love you."

She waves once, and then she is gone.

"Please don't do this. I'll do anything you want. Just leave her out of this. Please."

Oren gives me a rueful smile. "Move on with your life, Melissa."

After he leaves, I let myself cry.

10

"Do you understand your rights as they have been read to you?"

The sheriff repeats himself as a shift in light pulls my attention to the shadowed figure in the doorway. Claire? Her ghost here to take vengeance on me? A waking nightmare? I hope for the former. She skulks toward us and presses a finger to her lips. No worries, I will not make a peep. She reaches Sheriff and snaps his neck in one quick motion.

Sheriff falls, and through the wetness that clings to my eyes, I see that the shadow is Colin. He removes the towel over my left hand and inserts a broken hairclip into the handcuff keyhole. After unclasping the second one, he rolls up my cap.

He retrieves defibrillator paddles from the wall and places

them against the CENSIR. The machine emits a gradient whine, then beeps. He brushes his lips to my forehead. "Stay with me, okay? This will hurt."

A jolt of hell blasts through me. When awareness returns, I'm in Colin's arms and the CENSIR's off. He presses me close and carries me through the hospital, past a deputy sprawled on the floor with his head turned the wrong way, Nurse Frown weeping in a chair, several people huddled in a group, and a couple of shrieking kids whose father got devoured by a dragon.

Outside, the sun's sitting on the horizon, and I'm not sure whether it's rising or falling. He loads me into an ambulance, buckles me in, and says something about getting us to safety. We drive off, the sky darkens. I stare out the window at a world that seems tranquil. Rebuild the burned-down house across the way, fix the wrecked Jeep we just drove past, clean the random spatters of blood and mounds of dragon crap, and Dillingham's good as new.

If only humans could be repaired so readily.

"You okay?" Colin asks.

When I don't reply, he proceeds to tell me his strategy for our escape and rendezvous with Loki's Grunts. I hear maybe half the words, provide him my limited information.

Somewhere in all of his talking, he's put his hand on my thigh, and he keeps glancing at me. I think he's worried I might open the door and jump. No, Mom taught me better than that. If you're gonna go out, do it in a blaze of martyrdom for the entire world to see.

But the world's seen enough of me already, and I've seen more of it than I ever planned. I'm done with all this. When we get to Denver or wherever, I'll leave Baby in the hands of the competent, and I'll go visit Dad and hopefully Sam. I'll stay with them as long as I can. And I'll make sure to have a gun with me at all times in case—

Kill emotion, human. Her voice is strained and distant.

"Grackel!"

"She's alive?" Colin says.

I nod. *Are you okay? Where are you?*

Do not worry about this one. You cannot even take care of yourself. Her growl echoes through my head. *I wake and find myself buried in the darkness of rubble because of the invisible monsters. My tail is shattered, my back foot is missing, and my fire fails me. This is manageable, but then I hear you acting as if the world is over.*

They took Allie.

Cry some more, then. What good will that do her?

I'm glad you're alive, Grackel, but I don't need your lectures right now.

Block me, she says, knowing full well I can't in my current mood.

Leave me alone.

She does, for about a minute. *Your boyfriend tried to talk to me. Is that what you need, human? A knight to protect you?*

For a moment, I think she means James, but then I remember Colin's a dragon talker, too.

I know what you're doing. It won't work. I lost her, Grackel. I promised I'd protect her, and I failed.

You behave as if she is dead already. And what of Arabelle? Will you abandon her to your sullen reverie?

What can I do? I don't have an army. I can't protect Baby. I can't even protect myself.

Give up then. Call it over and go home. Oh, wait, you have no home. You are stranded with yourself. I do feel bad for you now. I shall let you wallow, for I should conserve my energy for something useful. I cannot believe I sacrificed my beautiful tail for the likes of a coward such as yourself.

"I hate you," I say aloud, but she's already gone.

Colin steers the ambulance onto a gravel road. The shadows of evergreens loom like silent executioners on either side. A mile or so in, he stops and turns off the headlights.

"Randon and Arabelle will be here in a little bit. We'll have to fly them out. Grackel can take care of herself. Everything will be okay."

"Yeah."

He cranks the heater to full and flips on the cabin light. "You wanna talk?"

I remove his hand from my leg and lean against the window. "No."

"I'm always here for you, okay?"

"I need some time to myself."

"I want to help," he says.

"I know. I just . . . I'm fine. Please."

After a long stretch of silence, he says, "Don't shut me out, Melissa. I know what you're going through, I know how—"

"You have no clue!" I say. "Everybody I care about . . ." Lost. Taken. Gone.

He reaches for me, and I slap his hand away. There's hurt in his eyes, but also that stubborn persistence that tells me he won't back down. He'll always want to help me, rescue me.

I know of but one way to convince him that I'm not worth the trouble.

"I killed your sister, Colin. I killed Claire."

I wanted to come off neutral, I'd have settled for cruel, but his bewildered expression starts another bout of tears. I throw open the door, desperate to escape, but Colin catches my arm and jerks me to him. "No you don't. You don't get off that easy."

"Easy? Fuck you! Let me go. Please, let me go."

But he doesn't. I struggle to break free, but I am weak and he is not. He waits for me to play myself out, then he kisses me. I'm so stunned I respond by impulse alone. My tears come faster, but I don't stop kissing him.

He pulls back, leaving a hand on my cheek. "I'm sorry. I didn't know what else to do."

I cannot bear the way he's looking at me, the way that kiss shattered the darkness for a few seconds. No, I cannot bear losing that, too.

I flee.

Fast as I can. Into the woods. Across a frozen creek. Up a hill. My legs fail me and I land knee-deep in the snow. I push myself up before thought and memory can return, but my arms give, and I get a face full of winter.

I roll onto my back, hyperventilating, and look past the canopy of shadowed branches into the sky. Even with my vision blurred and my thoughts numb, it doesn't take long to identify the constellations shining back at me.

I never showed Draco or Cygnus, or even easy ones like Orion, to Allie. Because I was terrified of what she might see. Evil dragons or evil jets, or maybe nothing at all. So I spent time teaching her math and English and history because I wanted her to feel normal, so on that day when our names and faces became forgotten footnotes, we could merge back into dragon-fearing society without difficulty.

I should have taught her the stars. I should have taught her something important.

There is still time, human.

"I thought you were done with me, Grackel."

Your thoughts bleed into mine. Your emotions are a virus.

I sniffle and wipe at my nose. "If you're trying to cheer me up, you suck at it."

You remind me of her.

"Her?"

Your mother.

"You knew Mom?"

Why do you think I came to your island, human?

"Because you were told to," I say, and croak a laugh. Nobody tells Grackel what to do.

She was the one person I ever permitted on my back. A most resilient human, but her heart often interfered with her brain.

"Yeah, I've got the emotion part nailed."

You have her strength, too. You need to find it.

"I don't know how, Grackel."

You must stop running away from life.

I make a snowball and toss it into the darkness. "This isn't life. I'm not equipped for this."

Nobody is. But you have no other option. Be brave or die, human.

She's right. Two choices. Lie here and cry forever,

waiting for someone to rescue me from reality, or . . .

I climb out of the snow, glancing skyward. I will find Allie. I will teach her the stars. "Please contact Allie. Tell her you're okay. Tell her I'll see her soon."

I already did, human.

I smile. "Thank you, Grackel. Also, have her send us images of where she's headed."

Your boyfriend and Randon are deciphering that.

"He's not my boyfriend."

Perhaps you should reconsider.

"Don't you have some rubble you need to dig yourself out of?"

That is the easy task for the day.

"And I assume you've already finished the hard one?"

She doesn't answer, but I'd swear I hear her grin.

11

Flying a dragon without a saddle is about as fun as riding a roller coaster without a harness. A little bit exhilarating, and a whole lot terrifying. It doesn't help that Baby's pissed at me and makes random dips or climbs, brightening at my shouts.

In the moments when I'm not focused on clinging to her neck, I find myself watching Colin. Bent over Randon like a jockey aboard a racehorse, he guides us between frosted mountains, above snow-gilded treetops, across frozen lakes. It often looks like he's smiling, though maybe it's my imagination. But what if he's thinking about that kiss, too?

Baby plunges. Wind stings my face, blisters my lips. My hands slip from her neck. As I reach out, shouting for her to settle, she swoops up at a steep angle and coils into a helix, laughing as I struggle to keep my stomach from inverting.

I tighten my grip. "Knock it off."

She arcs into a glide, spins her head around, and fires a cone of ice over my shoulder.

"Finished?"

I get another blast of ice.

After we follow Colin and Randon past more mountains and emerge over an expansive lake, Baby's wing-flaps ease to their natural beat. I take the chance to rest my eyes, my thoughts drifting back to the kiss. Did that count as my first real one? James kissed me in Georgetown, but that was for the cameras. No, this didn't count either. It was just a way to calm me down. Stupid, but why else would he do that after I'd confessed about Claire—

Baby dives hard, then lurches to a near standstill. I smash into her. Pain explodes in my nose, and a warm geyser of blood pours down my lips. My scream gets swallowed by the wind. With a smirky little laugh, Baby levels out and resumes her rhythm.

I pinch my nose. "I don't know what's gotten into you, but you have to stop it."

Why don't you complain to your boyfriend?

"Is that what this is about? Do I have to block my thoughts from you?"

Baby darkens, losing the small amount of heat radiated by her glow. *He's a scale chaser!*

"Not anymore. He's here to help us. He saved my life."

She bucks again, almost throwing me off. I smack her as hard as I can. A vibrating sting runs up my arm, and she yowls loud enough to draw Randon's and Colin's attention. They circle back and pull up alongside us.

"Everything okay?" Colin shouts over the wind.

"We're fine. Baby just forgot how to fly for a few seconds."

"We'll land shortly."

As the first rays of dawn stretch across the darkness, we take shelter in a low mountain cave. Instead of bending down to let me dismount, Baby dips her head forward and bucks her rump, pitching me off. I land hard on my flank. The wind rushes from my lungs. Slivers of ice drip from her nostrils as she stalks to the back of the cave and curls into a ball next to Randon.

Colin rushes over, but I wave him off. "I'm fine."

"The Diocletians made camp about an hour ago." He shoulders out of his pack and unzips it. "They're in some destroyed city I didn't recognize. Canada, maybe. I think it's a stopover. Allie's in a good mood, and she told Randon to tell you hi."

"Randon's kept me in the loop," I say.

He rummages through his pack and pulls out a pair of MREs. He sits on an outcropping of rock, removes a tow-elette from one, and hands it to me.

I wipe crusted blood from beneath my nose. "Thanks."

He holds up the MREs. "Meals Rejected by Everyone. We have beef ravioli and cheese tortellini. Pick your poison."

"Tortellini."

"Excellent choice." After opening the MRE, he removes the tortellini bag and the flameless ration heater. He tears the top off the FRH and pours some water into it. He seals the FRH, wraps it around the tortellini, and sticks it in a container sleeve.

After repeating the process with the ravioli, he tosses me a pouch of crackers. "Seriously, might be the most edible thing in the cave."

We eat crackers and move on to cobbler while we wait for the main courses to heat up. In between mouthfuls, Colin jokes about the various MRE acronyms (Meals Rejected by the Enemy, Meals Rarely Enjoyed, Meals Refusing to Exit), wonders if cavemen lived here long ago, admires the sunrise and panorama of snow-covered mountains. I've never heard him talk so much. Not once does he look at me.

Mumbling about "three lies for the price of one," he sets my tortellini in front of me and offers me a plastic fork. "Guess it beats canned beans."

I grab his wrist and wait until he lifts his eyes from the fork. "I'm sorry I sprang Claire on you like that."

He shakes his head and shrugs. "It doesn't matter. Eat up

now. We got to get some chow in us and some shut-eye—"

"I'm sorry, Colin. I should have told you earlier."

He rubs at the fork tines and stares out the cave opening. "You know, at first, I thought you were making it up so I'd leave you alone. Then I realized you weren't." He looks at me. "I know you blame yourself for a lot of things. Don't blame yourself for Claire."

"You don't even know what happened," I whisper.

"In A-B boot camp, they load you up with this hundred-pound pack and run you up hills and through sand and swamp. You want to up and die with every step. After dinner, it was an effort to get outta your seat and crawl into bed. Hit the pillow and the next thing you know, reveille's ringing in your head and it's hump time again."

He traces a line down my cheek, following the path of a wayward tear. "The first time you see one of your friends die, you learn the difference between a hard day and a bad day. You can't look back on bad days, because you can't get over that question. What could I have done? 'Cause there's gotta be something. And while you're thinking about how you should have saved him, your next friend goes down."

He thumbs away another tear. "You have to learn to look forward."

"You don't even know what happened."

He cups my face and kisses my eyes. "Claire was already

dead in spirit. Whatever happened doesn't matter."

But it does to me. So I tell him. First about Claire, but once I start, more pours out. He's seen some of Preston's videos, so he knows what they did to us in Georgetown, but I need him to know how it felt.

The hopelessness inspired by CENSIRs and an endless world of frozen tundra interspersed with scientists and soldiers who'd shock you as soon as look at you. The terror of not knowing your day's assignment, whether or not you'd have to participate in dragon torture or battle-room operations that killed innocent people, knowing if you failed to comply, they might hurt your family.

The oppressive guilt. No matter what you did, somebody got hurt.

He holds my hand as I recount slaying half-dead dragons for TV and an audience of soldiers. How their catcalls and jeers faded into the background because James was there, a victim of reconditioning.

Colin slips his fingers from mine. "I didn't know you two were . . . involved. He never mentioned you."

His words sting, and I hate that they do. "We weren't. But there was a time when we were friends, I guess. Then we both were reconditioned. Rescue came before they were finished with me. I got lucky. I'm only half crazy."

"I wasn't with the group long enough to know James.

He always struck me as distant, but his heart seemed in the right place."

I snort. "You're defending him?"

"I don't want to step on any toes."

Heat rises in my cheeks. "What are you talking about? He's a Diocletian now. I don't even know who he is anymore." Did I ever know?

Colin stands. "After I . . . in the ambulance . . . I saw something in your eyes." He stares at the ceiling for a good minute. "Why did you run?"

I burst to my feet, livid. "Not because of him."

"When you talk about him, I hear something in your voice. . . ." He shrugs. "I don't know what I'm saying. I'm tired. We need to sleep."

Colin tries to step past me, but I don't let him. I take his face between my hands, stand on my tiptoes, and kiss him. His lips linger on mine for a moment before he retreats. "It's okay, Melissa, you don't have to convince—"

I kiss him harder. And this time he kisses me back.

12

Perhaps it's the fact I slept without nightmares, but when Colin wakes me, I feel light of body and mind.

"I've never seen you smile in your sleep before," Colin says as I sit up and stretch.

I ignore the kicking urgency in my bladder and lean back onto my elbows. "I didn't know you watched me sleep. That's a bit creepy."

He laughs. "You should smile more. You're beautiful."

"When was the last time you saw an optometrist?"

"Got a physical every six months."

"Drop your socks and grab your . . ." I arch my eyebrows.

"Your dad teach you that?"

"Among other things. Like not trusting All-Blacks. Especially when they tell you you're beautiful."

"Fine then, you're hideous. So hideous I can't stop looking at you."

Smiling through a yawn, I push myself to my feet. "Be right back, Romeo."

After relieving myself in a dark corner of the cave, I decide to confront Baby. She's coiled against the side wall, facing away from me. Her glow goes dim at my approach. The last time I saw her so dark, she was on the Georgetown slaughter slab, awaiting execution.

"I know you're upset." I glide my hand along the scales of her rump. She used to brighten at my touch. I take in her faint smell and think of Allie. "We'll get her back."

No response.

"If you need to yell at me, that's fine. Don't hold it in."

No response.

"We'll get her back. I promise. I know you don't like Colin, but—"

She leaps to her feet and whirls on me, baring her teeth, her glow going supernova. Squinting, I see a ball of frost pulsating at the back of her throat, in rhythm with her breaths.

He's a scale chaser!

I step forward, inches from her lower lip. Ice crystals sprinkle my sweatshirt and face. Footsteps sound behind me, and I raise my hand as Baby's eyes narrow to black slits and the ball pulses bigger, colder.

"Make us breakfast," I say without looking back.

Always sneaking around, Baby says as Colin retreats. *He tried to needle me.*

"He should have asked you. It was a mistake, but he wanted to make sure you were safe. He's not a bad person, Baby."

He's the same as the rest of them. And you are blind to it. The joy leaks from you when you are near him. He is a scale chaser!

The ball of ice slips from her throat into her mouth. I don't know if she's losing control or threatening me, but I don't budge.

"He didn't join the army to kill dragons. He did it to protect his family. He knows he made a mistake."

She gives a frantic shake of her head. *I saved your life first.*

"What are you talking about?"

In the mountains with the metal monsters where men like him killed that Red.

"I know you did, but I don't understand what that has to do—"

Everything! The ball rolls to the spot behind her teeth. If she opens a few inches wider, it will tumble out and crush me.

"Whatever I did to upset you, it wasn't intentional. I could never hurt you, Baby. You know that, don't you?"

She turns aside, spits out her anger, then slumps down,

her brilliance fading to nothing. She ducks her head into her tail. Soon, I hear an odd sound, something between a snort and wheeze. She's crying.

I clamber atop her and wiggle my way headlong into the tight gap between her tail and body until I reach her snout. If not for her tears, bright and warm, my head would be locked inside a dark freezer.

"You know what got me through Georgetown?" I pause to compose myself. "You. Knowing that you still glowed kept me going. The day I discovered I was supposed to kill you, that was the worst day of my life. When rescue came, and I learned you were alive . . . that was the best. Hands down."

She opens an eye, as large as my head. The tears stop, and her glow intensifies enough that I don't crystallize. *You never remember me. You're always thinking of the scale chaser.*

"Look into my heart, listen to my thoughts, do whatever you must, but know that you are my family. I would give my life for you."

And him?

"Him? Maybe a finger. He is a distraction that keeps my thoughts off Allie."

She brightens. *He kisses well?*

I laugh. "Not as well as you, but a good deal warmer."

I want you to be warm, Melissa.

"Not too warm." I wriggle forward and kiss her frosty muzzle.

She goes blinding again, but in a good way. *Sisters?*

"You, me, and Allie. Forever."

We fly east over the ruins of a city Colin tells me is Calgary, then turn south into Montana as the sun sets. To avoid radar and the automated anti-dragon artillery hidden across the countryside, we change altitude every half hour.

Besides the fierce accelerations when she dives to near ground level or climbs toward the clouds, Baby maintains a steady gait. Randon refuses to relay any "noncritical" messages to Colin, and Baby's following strict no-talk orders to conserve energy, which leaves me with nothing to do but mull over the train wreck of my life.

My thoughts keep circling back to my conversation with Evelyn. She would have betrayed me in an instant. But she didn't. Connecting those dots is easy. James must have convinced her not to divulge our location, must have played dumb for Oren.

So what? He could have warned me about Oren's plans. If he still cared in any way, he would have. Unless he didn't know. He wasn't in Dillingham. Of course he knew. He must have. Then why was Evelyn so angry?

We encounter our first drone as the moon is cresting.

Following Colin's instructions, Baby loops in and ices it from above. Colin and Randon dive after the falling drone.

By the time Baby and I land, Colin's on his knees, digging through fragments of black metal cast in a crimson glow. Broken clumps of trees and puddles of water surround him. Randon carries a frozen part of drone in his mouth, sets it down, and blows out short bursts of fire to melt the ice casement.

Stepping around branches and a pair of iced missiles, I work my way to a mound of discards: twisted fragments of plane, a shattered camera, the tip of a propeller.

"What exactly are you doing?" I ask. "DJs could be here any second."

"No, this is one of their perimeter drones. They're not equipped with zenith cams. No way it saw us."

"I still don't see why we're here."

"Every drone is equipped with instrumentation," Colin says, not looking up. "Blade tachometers, thermocouples, transceivers, that sort of thing."

"Oh, sure. You know I have no idea what you're talking about, right?"

"This." He wrenches loose an apple-sized black box from the wreckage. "Soon enough, the military will realize the drone is down. They'll see the temperature readings and discover why it went down. And they'll come looking for it."

"So why are we here?" I say.

"The wonderful thing about today's unmanned aerial vehicles is that they're all operated through the DoD mainframe." He taps a jagged piece of metal with his foot. "In a couple minutes, the mother system will relay this bad boy's zero-output parameters to DOCOM, and a task force will be sent to investigate."

"You have to speak human for a little bit, Colin. Pretend you're talking to someone who wasn't in military intelligence."

"We're going to play a little trick." He explains his idea on the way back to the dragons. "Drones sometimes relay faulty information due to weather, dropped signals, minor malfunctions. You can't deploy a response unit every time there's a blip on the radar, so there's a built-in delay to ensure it's not a false signal. Why are you smiling at me like that?"

"You don't look like a nerd on the outside." I laugh at his pained expression and kiss him on his scruffy cheek.

"Thanks," he grumbles.

"You were saying. Delays and false signals and all that fun stuff."

"The critical parameter the mother system relies on is drone speed." He interlocks his hands. I step onto them, and he boosts me onto Baby. "The other sensors are secondary. As long as we're flying, we're in good shape."

"So we're going to pretend to be a drone," I say. "Why is this a good idea?"

He grins. "Best part. The mother system knows where all the children are. She tells them where to fly. Due to recent resource redirects, the herd's been thinned in the evac territories, so there's only one drone per sector. We'll be free and clear. . . ." He notices my amusement. "Hey, I'm not a complete nerd."

"You're cute like this. Now you're blushing. Very cute."

"Could you shut up now? We need to fly."

Baby stomps in agreement.

"Won't this mother system know there's something wrong when we don't follow its orders?" I ask as I shimmy into position around Baby's neck.

"Eventually. It'll recall the drone for a maintenance check, but we'll have ditched our cover by then. By the time they realize anything's wrong, we'll be safe and secure in Denver."

"And if it doesn't work?"

"Perhaps I should get another kiss. Just in case."

Baby nudges him to the ground with her tail and lifts off.

"I'll kiss you, too!" he shouts after us. Baby blasts a bolt of ice that explodes between his legs.

I laugh. "Good shot."

I missed.

We skim across an abyss of darkness broken only by Randon and Baby's reflections over rivers and lakes. I keep my head on a swivel, certain every new star on the horizon is a searchlight from a drone or dragon jet that's discovered our ploy. Every couple minutes, I remind Baby to remain vigilant and annoy Randon with update requests about Allie.

He always gives the same answer. *She still sleeps.*

Which means she's been asleep for more than twelve hours now.

Near dawn—no signs of enemies, no word from Allie—we reach the outskirts of Denver. The white mountain-shaped roofs of the airport stand out in sharp contrast against the backdrop of charred fields. The scorched and splintered husks of skyscrapers protrude like spears from the horizon.

I remember the exact date Denver went from city to graveyard. I remember every day Mom was called away to war.

I begged her not to go; she smiled and kissed me and said everything would be okay. Told me to be strong for Sam and Dad. Hiccupping back tears, I stood on the curb outside Groveton Elementary with Principal Markinson and watched her drive away. That night, it was all over the news.

I'd never seen so many dragons, so much fire.

To save Mom, I made promises to God. I don't recall them all—they changed each time—but I'm sure I've broken most of them. When Mom returned home, I cried and urged her to quit the army. The next day she signed me up for tae kwon do. Said it was because I skipped school and needed to learn discipline. But a few months before her death, I think she revealed her real reason, written on the back of a picture she'd sent from her final salvage mission.

Congratulations on the black belt, Mel, Mel. I'm prouder than you'll ever know. In a world filled with darkness, you have found your inner light. Hold on to it, no matter what. I love you. Always. Mom.

With her customary heart and smiley face.

I can't help but think she was also saying good-bye.

She couldn't have realized my inner light would die with her.

It's rekindled in fits and spurts, but never for long. Dad broken. Sam, who knows? Allie lost. James . . .

As we glide toward the airport, I look away from the sorrow of past ruin and banish the dread of future heartache. *Baekjul boolgool.*

I am my mother's daughter. I am strong.

13

Baby follows Randon through a jagged opening in the airport roof, toward the far side of the terminal, illuminated
faint red by Grackel's prone form. Fractured tiles, shattered glass, and unidentifiable debris litter the area. The old
dragon opens one green eye when we land, mumbles, *It is
about time,* then resumes her throaty snores.

Keith emerges from the shadows, a large-caliber rifle
looped over his shoulder. He looks as if he's aged ten years
since he dropped me off on Saint Matthew Island three
months ago. A beard, scraggly and streaked gray, sprouts
from a face wrought by fatigue.

He embraces me. "You're looking good."

"You too," I say, and we share forced smiles. "Oren
took Allie, Keith. We haven't been able to contact her in

almost fifteen hours—"

"We can discuss this later. You must be tired."

"We didn't fly all this way to sleep."

"What happened? Where is everybody?" Colin asks.

"Just me and Preston for now. Come on, let's get out of the cold."

Keith takes us to an access room that resembles a cross between an anarchist's bunker and a hacker's paradise. Gun racks and ammo cabinets occupy the left wall. Touchboards and thinscreens cover the rest. Several are set to the twenty-four-hour news stations, currently focused on mounting tension between U.S. forces and their European counterparts; a few seem to track military operations, and one large screen on the right displays a map of the U.S. similar to the one I saw in the escape crate, with a couple of key differences.

Fewer *Avoid at All Cost* locations—black pushpins—than before. The drone zone's been pushed east into Kansas, which explains the lack of drones in the area. The ruins of Denver are now part of the evacuated territories. I wish I could feel relief, but my gaze keeps coming back to the red pins that represent insurgency hideouts.

Only two remain.

"You'd be surprised how much can change in a few weeks," Preston says from the doorway. He sets a tray with four coffee cups on a nearby table. He joins me at the map and offers me one. "Sorry, Cosgrove, no special sauce."

Shoulders slumped, dark blotches beneath his eyes, black hair rumpled, Preston appears even more defeated than he sounds. On the flight in, I'd prepared quite the diatribe about the emergency cell phone, but decide on a hug. He almost drops the cup. I let go and smile at his bemused expression.

Colin gestures at a screen on which soldiers and tanks are traveling across barren countryside. "The Russians have mobilized?" he asks as I sip my coffee. Definitely needs vodka.

"The Germans and the French, too." Keith removes his rifle and places it on the gun rack. "They've given us a deadline of three weeks to abandon our bases in Europe. Full U.N. backing."

"Three weeks? That's not enough time," Colin says.

"It's that or war. Things are already getting pretty hostile. Another embassy got torched last night. It's not a good time to be an American." Keith sighs. "Makes you miss the good ol' days when everyone was united against the dragons."

"At least we weren't killing each other." Colin grabs a cup and leans against the console. "It was a mistake to release the battle-room footage."

"Oh, you mean footage that showed humans using dragons to kill humans?" Preston says, livening. "The world has a right to know."

Colin waves a hand at the screen. "Haven't enough people died already, Jedi?"

"I guess we should just let the government do whatever they want, right, Sarge?"

I slump into the chair beside the portable heater as their discussion intensifies. They both seem so damn certain. A year ago, I had the world figured out, too. The government was good. Dragons were evil. I miss those days.

"What do you think?" Preston asks me at some point.

"Leave her out of this," Colin says.

I pinch the bridge of my nose. "I don't care. I want to rescue Allie. Does anybody know where Oren's headquarters are?"

Keith massages my shoulders. "I'm sorry, Mel."

"You have to know something."

"We're working on it, but nothing useful right now. Our capabilities have been severely hamstrung." Keith takes the seat beside me, runs a hand over his naked scalp. "A couple weeks ago, the Dios ambushed us when we were transferring hideouts. We've disbanded for the most part." He indicates the touchboards. "We're running skeleton surveillance, and that's about—"

"I don't understand what this has to do with Allie," I say.

"We thought they were after Baby. James thought it could be Allie," Preston says.

Keith frowns at him, then gives a brief shake of his head before he can say anything else.

"That ship's sailed, Keith. I know," I say.

Preston furrows his brow. "You know?"

"Yeah, Evelyn was in Dillingham to rub it in." I try to get the timeline straight in my head. A month ago, James contacted me to say good-bye. Right before he defected? A couple weeks later, the Diocletians waylaid Keith and the Grunts. Shortly after, the Greens began their mental assault in search of Allie. "Was James with you when they attacked you?"

Neither of them can meet my gaze.

"He was on the other side? Why? He knew Allie and Baby were on the island."

Keith stares into his coffee. "No, he didn't. We never told him where you were."

My breath knots in my chest.

"After Georgetown, we were worried he'd go rogue," Preston says, "so we kept him out of the loop. He was so angry. At the military. At the dragons. At us for not rescuing you guys sooner. I'm sorry."

"He never asked me where we were," I mumble. In all our conversations about being fine, he never asked. "Wouldn't he have asked? If he was after Allie, wouldn't he have asked me where we were?"

"He knew you had strict orders to stay silent. Maybe he didn't want to make you suspicious," Colin says.

I shake my head. "Why come after you? He knew you didn't have Allie."

"We've been running interference against them for the past several months," Keith says.

"They came after all our groups," Preston adds. "James probably didn't even realize it was us."

"Dragon exposure," Colin says. "It screws your head up."

"That's government bullshit," I say. Keith lays a hand on my arm, but I shake him off. "In Dillingham, Oren mentioned something to me about multichannel telepathy and Allie. Do you know what he's up to?"

"We've been trying to figure that out," Keith says. He nods at a screen tape labeled *Drone Network*. Little black dots crawl across a white map of North America, with the heaviest concentration in the pair of drone zones, fifty-mile-wide swaths of land that enclose the evacuated territories. He points out a green blip in the evacuated territories, about a hundred miles north of Denver. "This is the first positive signature we've seen in weeks."

Colin examines the screen. "That one's us," he says, then explains our ruse with the drone.

"Didn't make sense," Preston says. "Not enough bang."

"Bang?" I ask.

"We thought maybe Oren was setting a trap. He's done it before," Preston says. "But except for blitzing us, he's been pretty quiet for the past month. A few of his standard propaganda vids threatening retribution and mayhem, but nothing major. There couldn't be a better time, either. The military's focused on Europe, and the new conscripts aren't battle-tested. Only one reason he's gone to ground. He must be constructing his death star."

I barely hear that last part. "They reinstituted the draft? What's the entrance age?"

Keith rises. "You guys need sleep."

Last time, the government lowered it to fifteen. Sam's birthday was in November. He wouldn't have waited for conscription notification, either. Could already be in boot camp. Could already be at war. "Where's my brother, Keith?"

"You need sleep. We can discuss this later."

"I'll sleep when you tell me where Sam is."

Colin nods to Preston. "Show her."

I gape at him. He gives me an apologetic smile, then drops his gaze.

Preston pulls a computer tablet from a cabinet.

"Put that away," Keith says. "She doesn't need to see this."

This? Show her? "I know you think you're all protecting

me." I push myself out of the chair and set my mug on the table so I don't hurl it at somebody. "I've seen the way you look at me. I get it, I really do, but I will not be a victim of your sympathy. And if you stand in the way of me and my family, I'm done with you."

Keith takes the tablet from Preston. "A couple of weeks ago, the government launched another *Kissing Dragons* spinoff called *The Frontlines*." He angles the tablet so I can see the screen and taps the play button on a video titled "KDF—Welcome to the Suck."

The screen remains black as a dragon roars and the crackle of fire escalates from the tablet speakers. Transitory silence is followed by breathing—quiet, quick—and the nearby clamor of tumbling rocks. The camera cap is removed to reveal a town in ruins. The view zooms in on a Green as it paws its way through a heap of rubble. A dusted sign at the heap's bottom identifies the wreckage as Kiddy Kare Preschool. The view pans up. In the distance, seen through a fissure in a building, Greens and their insurgent riders lay waste to the rest of the town.

There's a triumphant yowl, and the view returns to the heap of rubble. Risen to full extent atop the fallen preschool, gold eyes gleaming, the dragon clutches a child's lifeless body in its claw. It raises the corpse to its mouth.

"Now!" someone shouts. A half-dozen All-Blacks burst

into view. They dash forward, blasting away with their machine guns. The Green recoils under the barrage and unleashes a ball of flame that fills the screen.

When the orange haze of fire fades, the dragon lies limp and glowless atop the rubble. A soldier sits beside the Green's head, the dead child clutched in his arms. A flash of silver catches my attention. Before I can identify the source, the video shifts to dragon jets that just appeared from offscreen. They engage the remaining Greens in a dizzying firefight.

The view pans left to show the close-up of a smiling teenager wearing body armor over dragon camos. The green-and-red scales that adorn his helmet glitter in the sun. He scuttles toward the dead dragon. Three other men—no, boys—converge around him.

"You all right, newb?" the teenager calls.

The video zooms in on the soldier atop the rubble. He looks up, and it's Sam. I knew it would be, but I can't check my gasp. The Sam I left in Mason-Kline was full of mischief and laughter.

That Sam is gone.

He climbs down the rubble, kicks away some debris, and sets the body on a patch of asphalt. I think it's a girl, no older than five, but it's hard to tell because smoke obscures her face. Sam unclasps his bloodstained silver necklace and puts it around her neck.

He glances down the road, where an injured dragon has fallen. He readies his weapon, then looks back, his grimy face tight with anger. "Let's kill 'em all."

He looses a primal scream and leads the charge forward.

As the racket of footsteps and gunfire recedes, the video hones in on the silver pendant of Saint George that dangles from the necklace Sam laid on the child's body. The screen darkens around the famed slayer until nothing remains but his silver spear and the crimson-touched dragon pinned beneath it.

"Join us for the premiere of *The Frontlines*," says Simon Montpellier, the narrator for all the military's propaganda shows. "Watch boys become men, and men become heroes."

The video ends.

"Rewind it," I say, glad my voice comes out strong.

"Melissa, I don't think . . ."

I snatch the tablet from Keith and return to the portion of the clip where I'd seen that flash of silver. I pause and zoom in. I'd hoped it was the Saint George pendant reflecting the sunlight, prayed Sam didn't share our family curse, but the starburst of light appears at the corner between his helmet and his close-cropped red hair, where there should be nothing but receding darkness.

The tablet winces in my grip. I set it down. "How long have you known?"

"They aired the first episode a few weeks ago. Storm-trooper boot camp," Preston says. "Sam and Alpha Squad just went on their first salvo. Don't worry, Cosgrove, it's mostly fake."

Mostly fake, but not that glint of silver.

"If Oren's been off the radar, it must be. Your brother's safe, Melissa," Colin says.

"Safe?" I trace the CENSIR line along my head. Colin reaches for me, but I shrug away. I look at Keith. "Do you have a way to contact my uncle?"

"He's an FBI analyst, Melissa. He won't have access to military or BoDA databases."

"I remember him telling Sam that he knew some D-men." Back when Sam wanted to interview a BoDA agent for a "dream job" class project. "He can point me in the right direction."

Preston shakes his head. "They'll be monitoring his phone lines."

Plan B. "You got a car?"

"Your uncle's actions are already under intense scrutiny." Keith doesn't say it, but I know he means because of me. "It's too dangerous, Mel. You need to lay low until we figure things out."

"I've figured things out, Keith. Allie's gone silent. My brother's trapped in some military prison camp being tortured and exploited just like I was. I can't sit here and lay low. Help me, or get out of my way."

"There is one thing you could do that could help them both," Preston says.

"We discussed this," Keith says. "Absolutely not. I don't want her involved."

"I'm already involved."

Colin claps Keith on the back. "Why don't you wait outside, Major?"

"He blames himself for what happened to you," Preston says when he's gone. "He blames himself for Sam, too. Try to be easier on him."

"I'll be easier on him when he stops treating me like a child. What's going on, Preston? No more secrets."

He drops into a chair. "Everything's completely hosed. The Reds who weren't killed have gone into hiding, and those of us who didn't join Oren—"

"There were others?" I say.

"The pull of the dark side is strong. News reports suggest that Greens across the globe are flocking to Oren's call. Unimpeded, of course."

"No doubt," Colin says. "I bet the rest of the world's thrilled."

"Yep. Not their problem anymore. We think he's got at least three hundred now."

"Holy hell," Colin says. He sips from his coffee as he examines the touchboard map.

"Yeah. The apocalypse is coming if we don't do something." Preston looks at me. "That's where you come in."

"If it helps my brother or Allie, I'll do whatever I can, but I don't see what good I can do."

"You don't realize how popular you were, do you?"

I catch his meaning. "You can't be serious."

"Showing the world the cruelty of men does us no good if everyone believes dragons are monsters. We need to show them the truth."

"The Greens are monsters, Preston," I say.

"We have to try something. War's coming."

"And I better choose on which side of the fence I'll stand, huh?" I say, earning me a couple of confused expressions. "Never mind. I don't see how I can help, but I'll do it, Preston. I'll do anything I can. We can discuss details tomorrow. I'm tired."

"Jedi. I'll have to get supplies anyway."

He leads us to an adjoining room occupied by several cots, a folding table, a couple of kerosene lamps, and a heater. Based on the Monopoly money and playing cards on the table, it appears our arrival interrupted their entertainment for the morning.

Preston departs with a bounce in his step that awakens

a pang of guilt. I push it away and make for the bed in the darkest corner.

Colin grabs my hand and brings me to a standstill. "I'm not going to let you sneak off."

I fixate on the wrinkled leather of my hiking boots. "What are you talking about?"

"What was your plan? Were you going to fly Grackel out in the middle of the night? Walk to your uncle's?"

I glare at him. "Don't try to stop me."

"You don't get it," he says, cupping my face in his hands and pulling my gaze to him. "I'm with you, Melissa Callahan. I'm always with you."

14

11:05 p.m. Preston's snoring on his cot, and Keith drove off thirty minutes ago in his truck to run some errands. I slip a letter beneath his pillow and tiptoe from the room.

After kissing Baby good-bye, with a reminder to obey Grackel, I hurry down the escalator. Colin greets me at the baggage claim, a pair of machine guns slung over one shoulder, our go bags over the other.

I push open the sliding doors that lead outside. Gusts of wind kick at us. Heads down, we make our way to the Prius parked in the loading zone. It used to be Dad's. The license plates have been changed, but the scratches along the driver's side are unmistakable. The thumbprint scanner on the handle accepts my fingerprint, and the doors unlock.

"You know Keith could have changed ID allowances anytime?" Colin says.

"What's your point?" I climb into the driver's seat and shut the door.

Colin gets in, screwdriver in hand. "Ten to one I won't have to reprogram it, either."

I place my thumb on the scanner beside the driving column, and the car starts. He sticks the screwdriver in the glove compartment, gives me a tight smile.

"Preston said it's a three-hour drive to the nearest store. You actually think he's gonna hit up a 7-Eleven at ten thirty at night?"

"Yes, I do. He's less likely to be spotted now," Colin says, which is the same reason we're leaving late. The drone zone's more active at night, but the patrolling UAVs become much more focused on the skyways than the highways.

"It's easier this way," I say as I maneuver out of the parking lot.

"He's gonna be real upset to find you gone, Melissa."

"He'll understand," I say. "I thought you said you were with me. So stop trying to talk me out of it."

Colin nods, locks his jaw, and stares out his window.

I drive us to the economy lot. Squatting on his haunches between stripped cars, Randon gnaws on the remnants of a deer. He spits out antlers and lumbers over.

"Any word from Allie?" I ask. The dragon springs off his feet, latches his talons around the car chassis, and picks us up.

She still sleeps.

Skimming over fields and deserted highways, Randon carries us to Rapid City, South Dakota, near the edge of the drone zone. We take shifts driving. Except when there's no other route, we stick to the back roads on our way to Ann Arbor.

I'm not even sure if Uncle Travis and Aunt Susan live there anymore. Five months ago they did. Along with Sam. I know that much from the drone surveillance my captors showed me in Georgetown. However, with all the paparazzi and journalists swarming them because of their relationship to me, my aunt and uncle might have gone into hiding.

If they're not there, Dad's at the Detroit VA, getting treatment for his paralysis. He'll know something. I reach into my jacket pocket for his letter, worrying over a pair of sentences written near the end. *Your brother loves you, Melissa. One day, he will forgive you.*

Or will he turn out like Claire? A reconditioned monster? That look in his eyes from the promo video, those angry words—they haunt my quiet moments. Perhaps the dragon was fake, perhaps the dead girl, too, but that hatred was real.

When they threw me into the reconditioning chamber, I came a cycle away from hating not just dragons, but also Mom, who they portrayed as a murderous insurgent. Sam already blames me for Dad. It wouldn't take much to push him over the edge.

But I will bring him back. As I stare down the highway, I repeat this to myself. Because I can't bear the alternative—that Sam's lost, too.

Colin obeys the rules of the road to the letter. When on empty streets or traveling through abandoned towns, I drive well above the speed limit, ignoring traffic lights and stop signs because it keeps the adrenaline going and me from fixating on how fast the clock changes while the scenery doesn't. I slow when Colin reminds me about the drones, but my foot's back to the floor within a few miles.

We meet our first counterterrorism patrol at the South Dakota-Minnesota border. In the faded light of the rising dawn, Colin pulls up to the control gate. A soldier steps from the guard post and orders us out of the car. He's dressed in a parka and dragon camos. It's the first time I've seen the standard-issue black fatigues in person since Georgetown. I shut my eyes, repeating my mantras, but can't stop trembling.

Colin squeezes my leg. "It's going to be okay. Let me handle this."

We get out, and he hands the soldier our phony IDs.

"How's the grind treating you, Corporal?" he says, affecting a slight Southern accent that reminds me of someone I once knew.

"Cold. Slow."

Colin laughs and claps him on the back. "Better than hot and fast."

"Amen." The corporal examines our IDs. He scrutinizes Colin, then me. I stare over his head at the field of dirt and speckled snow behind him and focus on identifying Colin's vocal doppelgänger. Someone from Mason-Kline? No matter how hard I concentrate, I can't remember a name, much less the twang of a single Kansas farmboy.

"So what brings you two this way before hours?" the corporal says.

"Didn't know they reinstituted the curfew. We don't get much news out on the frontier. Keep your head down and stay out of trouble, right?" Colin says with a smooth smile.

"Frontier, huh? Ex special forces?"

"The few, the proud, the crazy."

"Don't know if you heard, but they closed the frontier down about a month ago. No civilians allowed."

Colin winks. "It used to be you just had to avoid the dragons. Now it's the drones, too. Still, it's a pretty good life if you work it right. Lets you forget about the world for a little bit."

"There's a dream. Don't know what you've heard, but we got another war on the way."

"I miss chasing scales." Colin taps his left temple. "Can't see a lick out this side anymore, though, and the army's got no use for one-eyed snipers."

The corporal gives Colin our IDs. "Where you headed?"

"Ann Arbor, to visit my girlfriend's father. He was injured in a car accident."

"My apologies, but I'm going to have to check your car before I send you on your way," the soldier says. "Please open the trunk."

Colin unlatches the rear hatch. "New protocol?"

The machine guns are stowed in a hidden storage compartment beneath the trunk floor. I wanted to bring them in case our cover got blown and we needed to fight our way out of a situation.

Seemed like a good idea at the time.

I reach a quivering hand under my jacket for the Beretta I took from Keith's weapon rack, but hesitate when Colin gives me a slight shake of his head.

He follows the soldier to the back of the car, staying no more than a step behind him. Neck snapping distance.

"It's complete horseshit," the corporal says. "They stick us out here in God's crack, looking for ghosts. Yeah, the surgers are out there somewhere, waiting to cut our throats and steal our children."

"And eat your pets," Colin says.

The soldier chuckles, gives a cursory glance into the trunk, and closes the hatch. "Don't get me wrong, the surgers need to be put down quick, particularly those Dios, but we'll see a tidal wave out here before we find one of them coming at us, rolling in a Prius. And God only knows I'm not gonna be checking a Greenie for its credentials, 'cause my ass'll be hauling."

They come back around the front, and the corporal opens the passenger-side door for me. "Sorry to have wasted your time. Hope your father's all right, ma'am."

"I didn't know you were such an actor," I say once we've put some distance between us and the border.

"I did a few plays in high school."

"You don't strike me as a drama geek."

He grins. "I was a drama stud, thank you very much."

"You're proud of yourself, aren't you?"

"A little bit."

"Would you have killed him?"

His features harden. He turns on the sat radio, cranks up the volume on the metal station, and accelerates until we're twenty mph over the speed limit. Thirty-two mile markers later, he pulls over to the side of the road, shuts off the radio, and looks at me. "Were you afraid or hopeful?"

It takes me a few seconds to figure out his words, a good deal more to figure out my answer. "Both."

He flinches, doesn't speak for a minute. "What about me?"

"Hopeful," I say without hesitation.

He leans over and kisses me on the cheek, then eases the car back onto the road. He switches the radio back on and sets it on a station I prefer. I rest my head against the window and watch him through half-closed eyes.

Hopeful. Yes, so very hopeful.

As we head farther east, the counterterrorism checkpoints increase, as do the number of drones in the sky. Fallow fields and abandoned farms give way to the near-ubiquitous blackness of civilization.

Electronic billboards crop up along the highway. They intersperse PSAs reminding people to report suspicious activity to the Bureau of Dragon Affairs with promotions for *Kissing Dragons, Kissing Dragons: The Other Side*. . . .

And then I see my brother's face. He's the forty-foot-tall centerpiece of a six-soldier team of hard-eyed teenagers. *Kissing Dragons: The Frontlines* flashes beneath their angry visages.

Colin squeezes my knee. "It'll be okay."

I try to believe that.

In Chicago, tanks and armored personnel carriers

intermingle with the ant parade of black cars that marches into the maw of the downtown abyss. In the shadows between buildings, in parks, in plazas, artillery and missile launchers gaze at the cloudless sky. These are the decorations that comforted me in Arlington until Mom died, and now they remind me of Sam.

We stop at an underground fuel station. Colin returns from the mart with my requested bag of Cheetos and a Mountain Dew, then heads back inside because they have a landline. While he calls his parents to let them know he's still alive, I devour my food and contact Randon.

Allie still sleeps.

The blackness of city fades back to farmland. The billboards here, nonelectronic, encourage young men and women to enlist in the various military branches, warn of the approaching apocalypse, implore you to store your precious keepsakes in underground banks.

We reach my aunt and uncle's house more than an hour after curfew, according to the loudspeakers that blare across the city. No cars in the driveway; none on the adjoining curb. No lights in the windows, but that's a curfew mandate.

I ring the doorbell. It doesn't work.

Colin knocks on the door. Nobody answers. He knocks louder.

"Go away!"

"Uncle T, it's me," I say.

The door cracks open. A flashlight's shined on my face. "Melissa?" He glances skyward, then pulls me into a dark hallway. Colin squeezes in behind us and shuts the door.

"Sorry about that," Uncle Travis says, leading us down the basement stairwell. "Thought you were reporters."

"Who was it?" Aunt Susan calls from the lit room at the bottom of the stairs. I stumble at her voice. So familiar. Painfully familiar.

She sits on a couch, a tablet on her lap, a textbook beside her. Put her hair in a bun, take off ten pounds, and darken the gray hairs, and she wouldn't look a wrinkle different from the Mom I see every day in my head. She glances up, puts her hand to her mouth, then stands and opens her arms. "Well, come on now, get on over here and give me a hug."

We embrace. "You're not mad at me?" I ask.

"Travis, go get us something to drink. You want some—" She notices Colin. "Who's this fine young man?"

I introduce them.

Uncle Travis studies Colin. "Former All-Black? Nice as it is to see you both, I'm not sure why you—"

"Travis, where are your manners?" Aunt Susan says. "Be a host and get us some drinks."

He gives a short bow impeded by a belly that's grown substantially since I last saw him. "Brewski?"

Colin waves him off. "I'm fine, sir."

"What about you, Mel? Got some Shirley Temple mix."

"Not a word," I say to a grinning Colin. "Actually, Uncle T, if you have some brandy . . ."

"That would be swell," Colin whispers in my ear, and I have to bite my lip to keep from laughing.

"How 'bout a Coke?"

"Travis, get her a drink. Get me one, too," Aunt Susan says. "Why don't you go help him, young man?"

"Yes, ma'am."

"So polite. And quite handsome," she says once they're gone. "What's this nonsense about me being mad?"

"After Mom . . . ," I say, but can't finish the thought aloud. After Mom died, I stopped visiting during summer vacations. "I'm sorry, Aunt Sue."

She hugs me again. "You silly girl. You don't apologize for anything." She helps me out of my jacket and we sit on the couch. "So what's the story with Mr. Brown Eyes? Boyfriend?"

"I'm not sure."

"He is," she says. "Olivia would approve. I wouldn't tell your father, though."

"Have you seen him?"

"Two weeks ago. The stem-cell therapy is helping. He can form simple words now."

"He's gotten my letters?"

She nods. "You're all he wants to talk about. You and Sam."

"Does he know? About Sam and that show?"

She flattens the pleats on her skirt and frowns. "He wasn't thrilled. None of us were, but it's what Sam wanted."

"You know they're doing the same thing to him that they did to me."

"I don't think so, Mel."

I tell her about the CENSIR I saw.

"He calls every week," she says. "He seems happy. He feels like he's making a difference."

They let him call? "They must be manipulating him."

She takes my hand between hers. "He volunteered, dear. For that CENSIR thing, for the show, for all of it."

No, no, no. Not Sam. "Did he even read my letters?"

She doesn't answer.

For as long as I can remember, Sam played at hunting insurgents and dragons. Now he's doing it for real.

And I'm on the other side.

15

Aunt Sue says Sam calls every Tuesday around noon. I have one day to figure out what to say to him. Sitting at the desk in his room, surrounded by his *Kissing Dragons* posters, I run through draft after draft, then open the letters I'd sent him, looking for inspiration.

"He was a big fan?" Colin says, startling me.

I look over my shoulder. He's staring at the near life-size poster of L.T., the newest of the fab four. Colin sets a tray with a sandwich and bottled water on the side of the desk I've been stationed at since morning.

"I thought you weren't talking to me," I say.

He rubs my shoulders. I tense. He lets go. "I don't think this is a good idea, but I'm done trying to talk you out of it."

Everybody tried to talk me out of it. Aunt Susan thought

it would upset me; Uncle T believed it could endanger Sam; Colin, pulling me aside, warned that Sam could betray me to the authorities, hinted that I was jeopardizing the safety of my aunt and uncle.

They're all right, of course, but I have to do something. He's my little brother. I need him to be my little brother again.

Colin returns sometime later with a plate of spaghetti. "You need to eat."

"Later."

"Your aunt and uncle should be back soon," he says. "Any luck?"

"You're right, this is stupid." The sun's setting on another page of hollow words, paper-ripping strikethroughs, and rampant doodles. I add it to my collection of uselessness and stare out the window at the black-brick dormitories across the street.

"It's not stupid, Melissa. Caring is never stupid."

I wad up the first letter I sent Sam, in which I apologized for the mess I'd made.

"The last time we talked was during the interview." *Kissing Dragons: The Other Side.* The posters taunt me with their presence, but I've yet to tear them down because they remind me of him. "I remember his last words. 'You don't talk to me.' He was so angry. I didn't mean to ruin his life,

Colin. I just want to make things better, but I don't know how."

"I can talk to him. Soldier to soldier."

"That's nice, but he doesn't know you from Adam."

Colin inhales, blows out a long breath, then knocks on the poster of Frank behind him. The rugged *Kissing Dragons* leader stands in the foreground, arms akimbo, legs spread. A dragon-slaying superhero. A tied-up Red lies in the background. The three other A-Bs crouch around it. Colin's finger extends to the one wearing the cowboy hat.

"I should have told you this earlier. It's not something I'm proud of."

I brace. "What are you talking about?"

"There are many rules critical for a successful dragon hunt," Colin recites the show's famous tagline, dropping into that Southern accent. Thicker this time. I know that voice. I hate that voice.

I get up, leaving my hands on the desk because my legs feel weak, and work my way to the bed. Dad bought Sam the Frank poster for his eleventh birthday. Sam had wanted J.R., the young cowboy who dashed into dragon battle with more bravery than sense, but Mom hated him most, so she and Dad compromised.

J.R. I always assumed they were initials, but in Dillingham, in the delirium of waking from anesthesia,

Colin had mentioned something about "Junior."

In the picture, Junior's too small to make out his face, but I remember him well from my stay in the quarantine cell, where they tortured me with an endless loop of *Kissing Dragons* episodes.

I squint at Colin, wondering whether he hid behind CGI or makeup. J.R. had had a Wyatt Earp mustache, a scar on his chin, and a darker complexion. I don't remember the eyes because he wore his hat low—part wrangler, part rogue—but I do remember the accent, how much it grated on my nerves.

"You died," I mumble. "Season two. Episode thirty. The Scarlet Scourge killed you." Fake. Everything's fake. I almost let myself believe, too.

"I wanted to tell you—"

"Get out." I suck in a hitching breath. "Get out!"

After he leaves, I sit on the bed, arms around knees, rocking myself, closing my eyes tight to the tears.

"Melissa?"

I open my eyes, wipe away the wetness. Aunt Susan's lowering the blackout blinds. The clock on the wall reads 8:15, an hour since the light went away. "Your father's here," she says.

That's right. She and Uncle T went to get him. Life goes on. I get to my feet. Aunt Susan takes my hand. "You okay?"

"Fine," I mumble. "Do you have some makeup? I don't want Dad to see me like this."

She leads me into her bathroom and pulls out her box of supplies. I blow my nose with a tissue she offers. "Why do boys suck, Aunt Sue?"

"It's their nature. What happened?"

I tell her as she helps me fix my mess of a face.

"That must have been hard for him to admit," she says.

I give a bitter laugh. "That's something Mom would say. Or this grumpy dragon I know."

"He should have told you a long time ago, Melissa. Don't pucker." She glides a stick of Crimson Fire along my lips. "He does not strike me as a coward, though."

"No. I've never seen him scared of anything."

"So why not tell you about this?"

I blot my lips on a tissue. "Because he was embarrassed. Because he's been trained by the military to be secretive." She waits. "Maybe because he knew they tortured me with the show and he knew I'd hate him if I found out."

She touches the tip of my nose, the way she did when I played guessing games with her as a little girl. "And yet he still told you."

"Can we stop? I don't know what you're getting at."

"Yes you do. If you had a choice, would you rather admit a dark secret to a stranger or someone you love?"

I pull back. "Love?" The word hums in my brain, painful and persistent.

"You should see the way he looks at you."

"I have."

"Then you know I'm right."

"Did I mention that I killed his sister? That reconditioned girl in those vids. Have you seen them?"

"Horrible things we do to each other in the name of victory. History repeats itself not because we forget it, but because of who we are," she says.

"Is that what you teach your students?"

"I try not to be so bleak. It's bleak enough out there without the truth getting in the way." She applies concealer. "Does he know?"

"I told him." Only after several weeks, only when I wanted him to leave me alone. But he didn't. He never left me alone. I measure Aunt Susan's curious smile and struggle against the emotion. "You think I'm a silly girl, don't you?"

"That is our nature. Life would be so tedious if we weren't," she says with a gentle laugh. "Your uncle Travis is probably boring your father to death with stories about his writing, and it's about time we saved him."

If not for my hair, I'd look halfway pretty. "You have something to cover this monstrosity?"

She returns with a gray flat cap and tugs it down over my ears.

I smile at my reflection. "I look ridiculous. You think they'll like it?"

Grinning, she mouths "They" and hooks her arm through mine. "Always a stunner. I got a little secret for you. Your father's not going to care. And neither's that boy of yours."

I want to apologize to Colin, want him to see me in a somewhat presentable state, but the door to his room is closed, and I've kept Dad waiting too long. I spot Dad two steps from the bottom of the stairs. Goose bumps break out across my arms, and my throat tightens.

"Look who we've got here," Uncle Travis says, waving at us from his position on the living-room piano bench. "The two most beautiful women in the world."

Dad rotates around, using a mouth tube to control the chair. His arms hang limp in his lap; his legs dangle on the footboards, skinny and crooked. But his eyes, oh, God, his eyes, they find me and they widen, and his lips move too, ever so slightly, but up in a hint of a smile.

"Mel, Mel," he says, a croak, but his voice, his glorious voice.

Three quick strides, and I'm hugging him.

"Dad," I whisper, smearing makeup and tears on his U of M sweatshirt. "I've missed you so much."

"You look good," he says with some effort after I let go. I leave my palm on his cheek and sit at the edge of the recliner so that his face fills my vision.

"I feel good," I say, and laugh when I realize it's true.

"Trav says you have friend," he says. "I want to meet him."

I wipe at my eyes with the back of my hand and kiss him on the cheek. "Be right back. Don't go anywhere."

I race up to Uncle T's office. I knock, but nobody answers. "Colin, I'm sorry."

No response.

I turn the knob, expecting it to be locked, but when it gives, worry creeps over me. I push the door open to a depressing darkness. I flip on the light to a more depressing emptiness. Atop the folded blankets on the couch, beside the rolled-up sleeping bag and the pillow that looks unused, I discover a note, scrawled on an FBI-emblazoned notepad.

Melissa, you know how much I hate running away, and I apologize for that. There are things I want to tell you, but I'm not sure how without making you hate me. I wish I had the strength to walk tall and speak the hard words loudest, as my father taught me. I must figure out how to make things right, if such a thing is possible.

Please thank your aunt and uncle for me. When you talk to your brother, trust that beautiful heart of yours. You will always be in mine,

Colin

That night, after the curfew speakers quiet and the lights go off and I finish the bottle of Korbel's on the office couch, I unroll his sleeping bag. I curl around the pillow and wrap myself in the blankets.

Images of bodies falling into a ditch rage in my dreams. I am the gravedigger, forced to pull off hoods from the faces of the dead. Mom. James. Allie. And now Colin's gone to sleep, too.

I wake drenched in sweat. After toweling off with the blankets, I scavenge the house for more alcohol, find nothing but a case of beer by the sideboard. Warm and nasty. Fighting my gag reflex, I down two cans in quick succession.

I stumble back to the office. The room spins a moment, and I'm vomiting. While drinking another beer, rambling to a rudely unresponsive Grackel, I clean the mess. I roll up the blinds, unlatch the window, and toss the towels onto the roof to cool off. The sleeping bag reeks of barf and liquor. I attempt to push it out the window, too, but can't make it fit.

I drag it outside and hurl it onto the lawn. I sit on the porch and drink. I return inside for another beer and a sweatshirt. When I come back out, I kneel beside the sleeping bag and sniff at it, imagining myself a determined bloodhound.

Unable to locate a scent other than mine, I point myself in the direction of the highway and walk. The shadows of trees loom over me, the purr of distant wind and unseen drones accompanying my trek.

I run out of beer and toss the can into a gutter, then the sleeping bag. A minute or thirty later, the dragons come, breathing fire and vengeance.

The hallucination passes. I dig into my pants for Dad's letter, but find only Colin's note. Blubbering his name, I search for the sleeping bag without success.

Lost, I return home.

16

The trill of the phone sends my heartbeat into apoplectic overdrive. I fold Colin's note along the well-formed creases, jam it into my pocket, and head for the kitchen. Aunt Sue, phone pressed to her ear, waves me over to the table where Dad sits.

I didn't want him or anybody here for my conversation with Sam, but after Aunt Sue found me this morning passed out in the foyer, she insisted, and I was in no condition to argue.

I take the empty chair that faces the tablet screen.

"You linked in, Sam?" Aunt Sue says. My image pops up in the screen corner. I bite into my lower lip, furrow my eyebrows, loosely clench my jaw, trying to adopt an expression that conveys love, but I come off looking ill and constipated.

A bright light draws my attention to the larger box on

the tablet. It fades, and Sam's face appears. For a moment, he's my little brother again, but then his smile drops and the soldier from the video is staring at me, a statue carved of loathing. A statue with a CENSIR on his head.

An hour ago, I settled on a script for different scenarios, most revolving around this reaction, but I cannot remember a word of it.

"Hi, Sam. I've missed you," I whisper without breathing.

Silence. Infinite.

"Say hi, Sam," Dad says.

Sam's green eyes narrow a hair more, his thinned lips purse to near vanishing. "What do you want?" His voice is deeper than I remember. Harder, like the rest of him.

"Are you okay?"

Sam glances over his shoulder. "I need to go."

"Please, don't."

"You're putting everybody in danger," he says. "Nothing new for you."

"Sam," Dad says.

"And you dare use Dad as sympathy bait."

"Sam-uel All-en Call-a-han," Dad sputters, drawn and slow.

"Dad, please," I say. He grumbles something unintelligible and speeds from the room.

"What do you want, traitor?" Sam asks.

"Sam, don't—" Aunt Sue begins, but I wave her off.

I feel at the scar under my tufts of hair. "They're not hurting you, are they?"

He snorts. "You think talking to dragons makes us special?"

"No. I need to know you're okay, Sam. Please."

He continues, not hearing me, or not caring. "We're freaks of nature, Melissa." He taps his CENSIR twice, hard. "This is our protection against their infection, and I will wear it until every last one of them is dead."

"What about Mom?" I say. "Was she a freak?"

"Mom was misguided." His features soften for the briefest moment. Then back to stone. "Look what happened to her."

"The dragons didn't kill her, Sam. You know that."

"What I know," he says, glowering at something offscreen, "is that without dragons, Mom would be alive, Dad wouldn't be quaded in a chair, and you wouldn't be on our hit list."

I remove the tablet from its stand, jerk it close, and peer into the camera. "Would you do it? Line me up and pull the trigger? Look at me, Sam. You know who I am. Dammit, look at me! Would you do it?"

He glances up, eyes brimming with wet conviction. "In a heartbeat."

The screen goes black. I lay down the tablet and slump into the chair, hyperventilating.

Aunt Sue squeezes my shoulder. "You tried, Melissa."

"I told myself I wouldn't get upset. I meant to tell him I love him. No matter what happened, I promised myself I'd tell him that."

"He knows you do. Deep down, he knows the courage it took."

"Courage? I never feel brave," I say. "Scared and sad top my list." Courage isn't even in the small print.

"That's what courage is, dear. Acting in spite of your emotions, not because of them."

I laugh so I won't cry. "Philosophy 101?"

"No. Your mother taught me that."

I leave immediately. Aunt Sue and Dad plead with me to stay, but it's too dangerous now. Would Sam report them for harboring me? Would he give me up to the authorities? I'm not sure which hurts more, the fact that I don't know the answer to those questions, or the look on Dad's face as I pull out of the driveway.

Figuring my way out of Ann Arbor keeps me distracted, but once I reach the interstate, I can't hold back the tears. It wouldn't be so bad if I were driving a different car, but the Prius has too many memories.

We went on our family vacations to the Shenandoahs in this car. We drove to Arlington National Cemetery for Mom's service in this car. We moved from Virginia to Kansas to start over in this car.

We had more important conversations in this car, Dad and I, than anywhere else, because that's when he had time to talk. We discussed dragons and Mom and my sessions with the grief therapist.

I learned how to drive in the parking lot of Mason-Kline High in this car, Dad at my side, ever encouraging even as he held on to the now-faded door handle for all it was worth, even after I sideswiped a chain-link fence when I swerved to avoid a squirrel. I remember the excitement of getting my driver's license, and how it was quickly tempered by my new role as chauffeur.

Take Sam to his track meet. Take Sam to the movies. Take Sam to school. For a period of three months, I couldn't imagine anything worse than having a younger brother.

I look in the rearview mirror and see the empty backseat where I forced Sam to sit because I didn't want him up front with me. I recall his impish smile, his irksome questions about my nonexistent "love life." I couldn't get to our destinations, couldn't be rid of him fast enough.

How many times did I tell him "I hate you" growing up? Ten, a hundred, a thousand?

Did I ever once tell him "I love you"? I can't recall.

The longer I cry, the more I expect Grackel to chime in with her redundant advice, but she doesn't, so I contact her.

What do you want, human? she says, brusque even for her.

"Anything from Allie?" I ask aloud, trying to imagine I'm not alone in this car.

She hears, but she cannot hear.

"What does that mean?"

If I knew what it meant, I would have told you.

"Is something wrong?"

No. What do you want, human?

"I just need somebody to talk to."

I have big ears and you have big emotions. I can hear you wherever you are.

I consider disconnecting but decide a pissed-off Grackel's better than the silence. As I reach the southern outskirts of Chicago, I recount my recent interactions with Sam and Dad, share some of my car memories.

Then I tell her about Colin. She lets me ramble. I spend at least ten minutes discussing Aunt Sue's theory. Could he actually love me?

"Can you contact him for me, Grackel?" I ask. She doesn't respond. I'm not even sure she's listening. "Grackel? Please, if you—"

Kill emotion, human, she snarls, and disconnects. A

couple of miles later, I realize she must have learned of Colin's *Kissing Dragons* role before I told her. Maybe he confessed. Maybe my emotions gave it away.

I understand her anger at Colin. But why's she taking it out on me? I spend several more miles searching for an answer, keep returning to the only one that makes sense.

Because I don't hate him. I can't. We've all done bad shit. Learn from it, move on, forgive the best you can.

How can you forgive? Baby's voice is the tiniest whisper in my head.

She sends me a series of images from the Georgetown ER, focusing on the four stations where Mengeles tortured dragons to determine their weaknesses. At the nearest, the Red strapped to the slab still retains a healthy glow as flamethrowers douse her. Two more Reds, fading fast, undergo a variety of experiments at Chemics and Impactions. The Green at the final station, subjected to high-voltage electrocution, is nearly glowless. On the slaughter slab at the far end of the hangar, All-Blacks dismember a previous "test subject" with chain saws.

The images move from the dragons to the dragon talkers. There's Evelyn, smiling at the Thermals station, flames reflecting in her eyes. Two boys who I knew only by their assigned numbers interact with the Reds at the middle stations. They're dead now, like those dragons, like the willowy girl at Electrics. Lorena. Beautiful, alive Lorena.

Baby transmits one final picture, lets it linger. It's of me, staring at her, shock and horror and grief etched in my features. It's from the day the All-Blacks and Mengeles torture scientists dragged her into the ER, her wings broken, her glow dim.

How can you forgive?

"I can't, not them. Never them. But Colin—"

Is one of them. How do you know he wasn't there?

I pull over to the side of the highway. I struggle to breathe but can't seem to find any air. I'd never fathomed the possibility. But it's possible, so very possible. I reach into my pocket for his note, which I've already read too many times. *There are things I want to tell you, but I'm not sure how without making you hate me.*

Was Colin a soldier in one of the military's talker camps? Maybe even Georgetown? He didn't work in the ER, he wasn't a guard for the girls' barracks, nor was he one of those who visited late at night to swap favors. I remember those men. They frequent my nightmares.

But there were plenty of other roles. Maybe he tended the boys' barracks, maybe he was one of the soldiers in the battle room. Maybe he just did what he was told. If ordered, would he have put a CENSIR on my head, shocked me senseless, killed me? In that other life, would he have called me glowheart and despised me?

I don't know. Doesn't matter anymore anyway.

I read the note one last time, then rip it up. I'm lowering the window to toss the remnants when the dragon sirens atop Chicago's skyscrapers awaken. I scan the cloudless sky but don't see anything other than a few drones. I check my rearview mirror. The skyline looms large and ominous, several military helicopters buzz around, but that's it.

An automated voice booms from the sirens. "Report to your nearest shelter. Failure to comply will result in jail time or a heavy fine."

This must be a scheduled attack drill. Major cities perform them at least twice a year.

The billboard ahead indicates that I need to take exit 51E and proceed to the Fulton River Public Dragon Shelter. Armored personnel carriers and cop cruisers are already maneuvering through the city to establish choke points that funnel us there.

Two choices. Haul tail to the next exit ramp, turn around, and pray I make it out of Chicago before they barricade the roads, or continue on to the shelter, hope my fake ID holds up, that nobody recognizes me. . . .

I'm already flooring the accelerator by the time the last piece of Colin's note flutters from my hand.

17

The red cascade of taillights ahead of me signals the end of my getaway attempt. Two armored personnel carriers barricade the highway, forcing everybody to exit at Union Avenue.

I'm soon surrounded by hundreds of All-Blacks. The majority usher civilians from buildings. Dozens more direct traffic with machine guns or batons, turning us until we're headed north. I search for escape paths, but APCs and tanks block the major intersections, cop cruisers the smaller ones.

Though I'm but another black car in a black sea of activity, I feel like I'm the centerpiece in a giant funeral procession. And it's not just the soldiers peering through the windows of my Prius hearse. Other drivers, their passengers, the growing herd of pedestrians. All of them can see me; most of them probably know me. The knit cap tugged low over my ears and the sunglasses obscuring half my face are insufficient shields to the thousands of eyes out there.

Our funeral crawls past tightly packed buildings that crowd the road. I keep my chin tucked to my chest, partly to obscure my face, partly to examine the emap on my lap. I look for an alley or a covered parking lot to hide in.

"Remain on the path," a bullhorn-amplified voice yells.

"Failure to comply will result in a heavy fine."

"Follow directions. Move along. The faster you comply, the faster we finish this exercise."

I peek up and see several college kids in Urbana-Champaign sweatshirts sitting on a bus bench, arms linked. Three A-Bs gesture at them with batons. An argument ensues. It ends quickly, with the soldiers arresting them.

I look around, notice more people in handcuffs. I wipe the sweat from my palms, crack my window. Behind the sound of sirens and more bullhorn commands, I hear people chanting antimilitary riffs, which the A-Bs ignore as long as everybody follows their orders.

Those who don't follow orders are brought to heel with batons, pepper spray, and handcuffs. A few people have attempted to slip free during these dustups. So far, nobody's made it.

I need a bigger distraction. . . .

Waiting for my opportunity, I watch another scuffle break out on the sidewalk. An A-B clocks a sitting Mohawked man until he stumbles to his feet; a second cuffs him. The bullhorn bellows for order, warns people to behave. Half a block ahead, soldiers quarrel with a group that refuses to vacate a Starbucks.

Somebody shrieks behind me. In my rearview mirror, an old man dressed in a hideous pinstripe red suit swings his cane at A-Bs herding him and others from an Italian restaurant.

The nearest A-B kicks away the cane and puts Old Man in handcuffs. The two women accompanying him, his daughter and granddaughter, I'm guessing, attempt to backtrack to retrieve his cane. Soldiers intervene.

"Remain on the path!" the bullhorn orders.

Granddaughter argues with an A-B, Daughter smacks another one. They're handcuffed, too.

Without his cane, Old Man has trouble keeping up, and on the far side of the causeway that separates the restaurant from a clothing shop, he collapses onto a bench. When he ignores an A-B's order to rise, the soldier jerks Old Man to his feet, grabs hold of an arm, and drags him along at a hitching gait. Old Man grimaces and yelps, but the soldier doesn't care.

Others do. They shout curses at the A-Bs. Several form a

wall, blocking the way.

The bullhorn crackles. "Move along or you will be prosecuted!"

The protesters remain steadfast. A soldier draws his pistol and raises it overhead. When nobody budges, he fires a warning shot. A second soldier pepper sprays them. More A-Bs charge in with batons, but none of those from my vicinity.

Time's running out.

I look at Old Man, who's slipped free of his A-B escort during the commotion. He's leaning against the wall of a storefront, hands on his knees. He's flustered, short of breath, and not at all deserving of what I'm about to do to him.

I whisper an apology, then shout, "Watch out! Old Man's got a knife!"

The nearest A-B whacks Old Man with a baton, sending him to the ground. The surrounding protestors ignite and swarm the soldier. Several more attack his buddies. The A-Bs directing traffic race over to help.

I pull to the side of the road, snatch the map, and slip out the car door. In a low crouch, I scuttle between vehicles, working my way back toward the causeway that splits the restaurant and clothing shop. Behind me, gunshots erupt, these from machine guns. Someone cries out.

Everything escalates from there. I can't see anything

from my position between two SUVs, but I can hear it all. Car alarms and panicked honking and feral shouts intermingle with dragon sirens and bullhorn yells and trilling gunfire.

And above everything, the screams, though I'm not sure all of them are real.

I break cover and dash into the causeway. There's a micro park to my left, a few benches to my right, but nowhere to hide. Ahead of me, an access road separates the causeway from an empty parking lot.

I scurry forward, am almost to the road, when I hear voices coming from around the corner. I back into the shadows of the restaurant facade and press myself against the wall. Two A-Bs go running by, the sun reflecting off their scale-covered helmets.

Keeping a tight grip on my Beretta, I edge to the corner. I can see a building adjacent to the parking lot. It's either an apartment or a dorm complex. If it's the latter, it'll have a dragon shelter, which means the A-Bs won't search it. One gigantic, flashing problem. A cop cruiser blocks the end of the access road, no more than twenty feet away from the building.

I peek around the corner to check the other direction. The road curves out of sight, but that's where those two soldiers came from.

The riot's dwindling. A couple of stray gunshots still

echo, a few moans penetrate the whir of sirens, but that's it.

". . . are aware that several people responded to this drill inappropriately," the bullhorn speaker is saying. "Anybody found hiding will be prosecuted to the fullest extent of the law. Return of your own free will, and we will be forgiving. Remain on the path. Do not make us tell you again."

I'm about to freak out when I notice the five-foot-high brick wall ten or so feet to my right. It's behind that Italian restaurant. Dumpster!

I push myself over the wall on my second try, am thrilled to discover that the Dumpster's enclosed on all sides. I tuck the Beretta into my waistband, lift the Dumpster lid, and make myself cozy in days-old food discards.

Soon I hear a male voice and two sets of approaching footsteps. I sink lower, keeping one hand on my gun, the other over my mouth.

As they come closer, I discern words. "Yes, sir." Pause. "No, sir." Pause. They pass in front of the Dumpster. "Right away, sir."

"What's up?" another voice asks.

"Cap says we gotta hump uptown."

A groan. "More babysitting?"

"Ground support."

"Good. You see that damn trust-fund hippie who tried to get his swag on with me? Put his ass in place."

"Yeah."

"Little punk bastards."

"They do think it's a drill. . . ."

Their footfalls dwindle. They continue to talk, but I'm no longer paying attention.

"They do think it's a drill!"

If it is a real attack, where are the dragons? Where are the dragon jets? Where're the fire and the death? I don't know, but they must be coming this way. And if they're coming this way, to a city like Chicago, with its advanced dragon defense system, that can mean only one thing.

Oren and his Greens.

I want to flee, want to become light and speed far away from the scent of putrid tomatoes. But I can't. Not until the soldiers and cops have evacuated the area.

I prop open the Dumpster lid with a to-go box to let some light in. As I examine my map for the best route out of this nightmare, I listen to the thrum of cars and the echo of bullhorns, I listen to the dragon sirens, but mostly I listen for the dragons.

18

When Mom died, I figured that was the end of her life. But Keith, her army copilot for several years, visited often, providing Sam, Dad, and me with hundreds of new memories.

Like the time she briefed her flight crew an hour before they launched on their mission to Denver. The city was under siege by a fleet of Reds. Straight-faced, she handed out *Playboy*s and ordered everyone to "alleviate their nerves."

That was the first half of the story, one of Sam's favorites. One of Dad's, too. But right now it's the second half of the story that most resonates.

When they arrived in Denver, not much was left but ashes.

"Destruction and death everywhere you turned," Keith said. "But the worst things were the dragon sirens. Many of them still blared throughout the city. But they sounded different. . . . Humanity's got an echo. In Denver, that echo was gone."

It seemed profound to my fifteen-year-old mind, humanity echoing, though I never fully understood what he meant. And up until a couple minutes ago, a part of me wondered how that could be worse than thousands of scorched corpses.

Now, with the bullhorns and the vehicles gone, and nothing but the sirens blasting into forever, I hear the emptiness. And as I crawl from the Dumpster and climb over the wall, I understand.

Here, on the vacant streets of a massive metropolis, I'm the only person left on the earth.

I emerge from the causeway, expecting to find blood and bodies from the riot—the precursor to the apocalypse. I am relieved when I discover only rubber bullets and a few other silent hideaways scurrying for vehicles. Citations flutter beneath windshield wipers, but I don't see any boots on tires. Must not have had time.

I warn the people about the impending attack.

"They would have run something on the emergency alert system," a man says.

"The A-Bs would have told us," another says, though at least he glances skyward.

"If you thought so, why didn't you go to the shelter?" a

woman asks, then sucks hard on her cigarette.

"Shelters might not be safe," I say. "Get out of Chicago."

I sprint back down the street, find the Prius. I hop in and floor it. A few blocks down, as I'm about to make a left turn and head west until I can't anymore, I spot five people handcuffed to a long bike rack on the sidewalk. If not for the red suit among all the black, I probably wouldn't have noticed them.

Old Man's laid out, unmoving. Daughter and Granddaughter tend to him. The other two, wearing Urbana-Champaign sweatshirts and bruises on their faces, are rattling their handcuffs. When they see me stopped in the intersection, they wave for help.

Shit.

I park the car and hurry over.

The shorter boy gives me a tremulous smile. "Wouldn't happen to have a hacksaw with you?"

I ignore him and nod at Old Man. "Is he okay?"

"He's unconscious," Daughter says. "We tried to call 911, but our signal's down."

"Bastards went straight gangsta on his head with their bully sticks," says the other boy. "Thought he had a knife. Dude's rockin' a cane. He was in freakin' handcuffs."

"I'm not sure if this'll work, but I've got a gun," I say, which draws worried looks from the women and impressed ones from the guys.

"A lady packin'. I like that. What dorm you at?" Shorty says.

"Quiet. Hold still." I place the muzzle against the chain that connects his handcuffs to the bike rack.

Shorty's smile evaporates. "On second thought, maybe I'll wait for the scale chasers to come back."

"This isn't a drill," I say. "I overheard a couple soldiers talking. Dragons are coming."

Shorty nods several times, excited for some reason. "No wonder they were so amped. Never seen them like that about a drill. Freakin' scale chasers."

"K-Dawg was saying something about a cover-up," the other boy adds. "He heard some background chatter on the military channels. . . ."

"You're wrong," Daughter says. "They wouldn't leave us here."

"Classic scale-chaser misdirection," Shorty says. "Rumors were starting. They wanted to put a damper on it. Tied us up to prove it is a drill."

"So they'll come back for us, right?" Granddaughter asks, glancing at Old Man.

"For sure," Shorty says.

"Look around you. They're not coming back. Hold still now."

"No, no, they'll come back. They wouldn't ditch out on

us," Shorty says, pushing at my leg. The others agree with him.

There's no time to argue. I remove my cap and ruffle my hair until they can see the scar from the CENSIR.

"The military doesn't give a damn about you," I say, amazed my voice comes out strong.

I wait for Shorty to recognize me, but it's Granddaughter who speaks up. "You're that executioner girl from K.D."

Now they're all squinting at me. Realization dawns on Shorty's face. "What the hell are you doing in Chicago? You part of this attack?" Again, the idiot sounds more excited than worried.

The dragon sirens cut out for a message.

"Thirty Greens inbound from Milwaukee. Headed south at full flame. Seek shelter immediately."

The sirens pick back up again, halting every few seconds to repeat the warning.

"Thirty!" Granddaughter's face drains of what little color it had.

"Milwaukee's ninety miles north of here," Daughter says.

"How fast do dragons fly?" Shorty asks, all excitement gone.

"Lot faster than you," I say.

Shorty extends his cuffed arm as far from the bike rack as it'll reach. "What are you waiting for, dragon girl?"

I shoot. Shorty lurches to the ground with a cry. As the gunshot echoes through the emptiness, I examine the links. The bullet didn't leave a mark, except for the one on Shorty's face from shrapnel spray.

"Try again," he says, eyes on the sky, unaware of or unconcerned about the blood running down his cheek.

The others slide down the rack as far as they can. I back the gun away a foot. Shorty covers his face with his free arm.

Three empty clips later, the handcuff links are barely dented, dozens of gunships and drones are flying in to form a perimeter around downtown Chicago, and Granddaughter's crying. She goes hysterical when I tell them I'm going to get a bigger gun from the car. "You can't leave us. You can't leave us!"

"I'm not leaving you," I say.

I'm turning around when Shorty clutches at my ankle with his free hand. "Don't leave. Please."

"I'm not leaving. I promise." I pull free and scurry to the Prius.

I start the car. Their pleas turn to yells and their yells turn to shrieks as I roll away. I crank up the radio, which plays the emergency message on every station. A block away. Two blocks. Three. They're beyond sight now, but I can still see their eyes, still hear their voices. Louder than everything.

"You can't abandon us here!"

"Please!"

"Don't let us die!"

A block later, the emergency message updates. "Greens incoming. Seek shelter."

I keep the accelerator floored. Buildings and stoplights blur by. I'm nearing ninety when the opera of war ignites. Missiles scream toward the heavens; artillery and explosions provide the accompanying drumbeats.

I glance north, toward the cacophony. The military doesn't seem to be firing at dragons. They're creating a giant black cloud in, around, and over downtown Chicago. Gunships and drones circle the expanding nebula.

A honk pulls my attention back to the street. A car's speeding right for me. As I swerve out of the oncoming lane, the driver flashes his lights. There's a concrete barricade several blocks ahead. Soldiers patrol the other side. A few notice me and raise their machine guns. Doubt these contain rubber bullets.

I hit the brakes and cut the wheel a sharp left onto a street that stretches to the horizon, but it's also blocked by a barricade. No soldiers, though. There are a few cars in the area, parked haphazardly, doors flung wide. I screech to a halt and leap out of the Prius.

I glance back. The blackness has swallowed Chicago, extending inland from Lake Michigan and reaching high enough to block the afternoon sun. The artillery and missiles continue to fire into it. The drones have disappeared, and the gunships dive in and out at regular intervals.

On the other side of the barricade, I search for a car, find a Ford Explorer at the second intersection. The driver door's open, the thumbprint scanner that controls ignition has been smashed. Wires dangle from beneath the steering column. I click a couple of bare ends together, but I have no clue what I'm doing.

I'm sprinting toward the next abandoned car when I hear the roars. I look over my shoulder. A gout of blue fire erupts from the black haze, chasing a gunship. A Green the size of a semi bursts into the open and corkscrews left in hot pursuit. The helicopter banks up to avoid the flames, only to be incinerated by a second dragon exiting the cloud.

More gunships fall, more dragons emerge. Five, ten, fifteen . . .

They spread out, descend to rooftop level, their carpets of flame unrolling in parallel swaths, igniting everything they touch. At full speed, they will reach me in a matter of minutes.

I reach the car, an older model. Someone has already shattered the driver's-side window, ripped the visors loose, and trashed the storage compartments. I spend too many seconds looking for keys anyway.

I'm exiting the next useless car when I hear a rumble of rolling thunder. A flock of dragon jets blisters by overhead. A hundred, maybe more.

The Greens roar and move to engage. They send a tidal wave of fire hurtling across the sky. The jets counter with an armada of missiles. The sky splits apart in a thunderous explosion, forcing me to shield my eyes.

When the light settles, eight dragons remain, but they're retreating north. The jets pursue.

No, I am no dog to cower with tail between legs. The guttural voice is loud and angry inside my head. The largest Green does a sharp backflip, then incinerates two jets and rockets past the others.

You cannot leash Thog! he declares between torrents. He swerves up, down, sideways, crashing through buildings, slicing through trees, on a flaming roller coaster of destruction ever southward. Toward me. Toward Old Man and his family and those two college boys.

Jets chase Thog, but he's too erratic for their missiles.

Thirty dragons were too much.

But now there is only one.

I run. Back between the concrete slabs of the barricade and into the Prius. I'm making a three-point turn when Grackel enters my head.

Do not do this, Melissa.

"I have to," I say, gunning it.

You do not even know if they are in danger.

I honk the horn to the rhythm Mom used on her final ride. Thog doesn't notice. Grackel somehow does.

Do not discredit your mother's memory with this foolishness, human. She wanted to save you.

"Then she would understand. As should you," I say aloud, and send her my mental picture of her broken tail.

That was different. I knew I would escape, Grackel says. *I am old, you are not. Do not do this. Please.*

"Kill emotion, dragon," I say fondly. "Look after Baby for me."

Thog weaves in and out of view between two high-rises, then drills through a third, which collapses behind him. He must have lost his rider, which makes him blind in all this blackness.

I resume honking.

Where are you? Thog sweeps his head back and forth in wide arcs, his scythe of fire slicing across three city blocks. *Where are you? Talk to me, you treacherous human!*

I don't understand what he means by that second part, but I oblige and orient him to my location.

Thog tightens his wings and accelerates for an attack run. I take the nearest right, honking and providing directions the entire time. He appears in the rearview mirror, a flying freight train of annihilation. His gold-eyed headlights hone in on me; the flames come.

Fiery tongues lick at the car. Sweat soaks me. If I can keep Thog on the straight long enough, the jets can lock in and bring him down. Old Man, his family, those two college boys will be safe.

And I will die. For the first time in forever, I am at peace. I know what I'm doing is right.

Go left! Grackel screams.

Her voice so startles me that I obey on instinct and jerk the wheel that way. But I'm going too fast. As the car flips, I notice a couple of things.

Foremost, another Green in front of me.

Second, the banshee wail of a nearby missile.

The world becomes a tumbling mess of blacks and Greens as vicious roars thunder all about.

Then it ends.

19

The dream always starts the same way. Lorena and me sitting in the barracks bathroom, *Kissing Dragons* playing on the thinscreen. Claire's nearby, her face stuck somewhere between a snarl and a scream. Only her eyes move, from me to the show and back to me.

Gunshots erupt from outside. Dragons roar. I turn to ask Lorena what's happening, but she's transformed into a corpse with bullet holes for eyes. A rivulet of alcohol trickles from her lips.

The noise of the battle intensifies. I leave the bathroom to investigate. My feet stick in a layer of liquid, but I can't see what it is because the thinscreen's off. Calling out names and numbers that go unanswered, I feel my way to the door.

It opens on its own. Sunlight blinds me. I look back into the barracks.

Daggers of light illuminate a floor coated in a crimson film, broken only by the meandering path of my footprints. My eyes drift up. Every bed appears to be filled. The blankets that cover the bodies begin to creep down to reveal dead faces. They're all the same.

Allie.

I bolt out the door. The Antarctic snow is warm and soft, like bread a few minutes out of the oven. I look down. Not bread. Flesh. A human abdomen. I attempt to retreat into the barracks, but Georgetown's disappeared, replaced by an endless field of bodies. I know them all. The man I'm balancing on died in my battle-room attack on Montego Bay. As did the children pressed shoulder to shoulder on either side of him. I saw the adjacent woman in the reconditioning chamber. There's Sheriff and Old Man. Ahead, I spot Claire and Lorena.

I flee, keeping my eyes locked on the horizon. The sun drains from yellow to black and the sky shades a dark red. My foot lodges in an armpit or a groin and I trip forward. I reach out to break my fall and find myself inches from my mother's face.

Her eyes open. "Run!"

I do.

I stumble onward, slip again.

This time it's Dad, his eyes paralyzed, but not his mouth.

"Run!"

I fall again.

Sam. Glaring. "Run!"

Then Allie. Smiling. "Run!"

Colin. "Run!"

And as I push myself up, he turns into Claire.

I run.

I trip again, but this time my hands fall into emptiness. I'm spun around so that I'm facing the sky. The bodies on either side of me link their arms through mine, jam their legs against me. Feet above me curl into my hair and lock my head down. Fingers entwine my toes.

I'm sinking, sinking, sinking . . . becoming one with the dead.

Then I see the light above me, swelling larger and brighter.

Green, the entrance to hell. I blink and it's gone and there's only darkness. The smell of pine trees and earth reaches me.

Another blink and James is there, crouched beside me, close enough to touch, if only I could move my arms. But I cannot move, nor can I speak. I can only look at him. And

I do, for as long as my eyes will stay open. His black hair's cut too short and his blue eyes carry that ever-sadness, but it's him.

"You're not supposed to be here," he says, a world away. He digs me out from the wreckage, cradles me in his arms, looks at me in a way that makes me want to forget about the pain erupting through me. But it's too much.

The dream boy drifts from sight.

Awareness returns with a low buzz.

I push through the heaviness and force open my eyes.

Blackness.

That buzz intensifies until it strikes through the numbness and drills into my skull.

Someone's calling out something.

A number, maybe?

A jet of liquid hits my face. Salty, familiar, but I can't place it. I get another burst on the other cheek. The jets slap me back and forth. Sensation trickles into my body, and soon I feel it all.

The bandages compressing my ribs.

The cuts stinging my face.

The shackles digging into my wrists overhead, stretching my arms from their shoulders.

And that ringing, so sharply resonant, means a CENSIR,

means that hell will have to wait while crueler demons take their flesh.

"Twenty-Five?" The electronically deepened voice, so distant before, now booms from above.

I shudder. "No. No!"

The jets shut off, the ringing subsides.

"What were your plans, Twenty-Five?"

"What happened?" I groan. Even my toes hurt.

My CENSIR jolts me.

"What were your plans, Twenty-Five?"

"I don't understand."

The wall in front of me lights up with a panning image of downtown Chicago. What's left of it. Rescue crews are already picking through the rubble.

How long have I been out?

I search for memories of what happened after the car flipped.

Nothing.

"Why were you in Chicago?" Interrogator asks.

"Did the shelters hold up?" I ask. "Did that man in the red suit make it? He was on Halsted Street near the—"

Another jolt. "Answer the question, Twenty-Five."

If I lie, the CENSIR will detect it, so I stick to the generic truth. "I was headed back home."

"You're telling me your appearance during this attack was a coincidence?"

"Don't you think I would have been flying a dragon and not driving a car?" I say, which earns me another jolt. "Yes, it was a coincidence."

A couple more questions to verify my bad luck, then: "You went to see your family in Ann Arbor in search of your brother."

Not a question.

The throbbing in my ribs intensifies. "Sam tell you that?"

There's the briefest pause before he says "Yes," but it's enough. He's lying.

For a moment, the pain of everything dulls. Sam didn't report me.

"Where were you headed?"

"Home," I say.

I receive a sharper jolt. I bite hard into my lip, choke back a scream.

"Don't make me ask again. You know what we're capable of, Twenty-Five."

Far too well. But I won't betray my friends. Never again.

My CENSIR shocks me hard enough to rattle the chains overhead. I scream.

"Where is home?" Interrogator asks after I've quieted. "If you do not cooperate, we will recondition you."

I let my tears run.

"Saint Matthew Island," I mutter, which is as much a home as any.

Silence. Does he detect the half lie?

I'm starting to think he's no longer there when another picture flashes onto the wall, showing the inside of Kanakanak Hospital, cordoned off with crime-scene tape, the sheriff and his deputy laid out on the floor, necks twisted to dead.

"Was this you?" Interrogator asks.

"I was there. I didn't kill them." Another half lie. "Oren and his Greens were after Allie. Twenty-One."

"Why?"

"I'm not sure. Oren mentioned something about her being tangled. Something about multichannel telepathy."

"She can talk to multiple dragons at once?"

"Yes."

"You can't?"

"No."

"Do you know anybody else who can?"

"No. I don't understand. Why is she so important?"

Interrogator ignores my question, asks me dozens of his own about Oren and his Diocletians, often repeating them in different ways. I provide him Evelyn's name, a guesstimate of the number of dragons at Oren's disposal, and basic information that anybody could glean from news reports or

Oren's propaganda vids. Otherwise, my answers are a variation of "I have no idea."

"How did the insurgents find Georgetown?" Interrogator asks after finishing his Oren line of questioning.

"There was a tracker in my arm," I say.

"Was?"

"After we escaped Georgetown, it was removed."

"What about the others?" he asks.

"Others?"

My CENSIR jolts me. "Loki's Grunts? Where are they?"

"Most of them are dead," I say. After a sharper reprimand, I admit another generic truth. "Only Keith and Preston remain."

"Where are they?"

"I don't know," I say.

The jolts sharpen, my screams weaken, my thoughts crumble.

"If you do not tell us the truth, we will hurt someone you love. Think on that, Twenty-Five."

I'm lowered to a sitting position, shackled wrists laid in my lap. The thinscreen shuts off, and it starts to rain. It's that same concoction from the jets. Salty and metallic, and this time I recognize it. They used it during my reconditioning. I'm lucid enough now to know it's not blood—too watery. Not human, at least. Could be dragon.

I let my tongue pull in a few drops to wet my lips and lube my throat, then push away the thirst that twists my insides. I attempt to stand, wanting to get a better sense of my prison, but the chain connected to my shackles is locked rigid and I'm pushed back to the floor. There's enough play for me to sit or lie down, nothing more.

A minute or so later, the overhead sprinklers shut off. I expect another round of interrogation or the next phase in the torture progression—images of dead Chicago cycled rapid-fire on the thinscreen, or maybe episodes of *Kissing Dragons* played in an endless loop . . . just don't let it be that show with Sam.

I wait, but nothing happens. I listen. For footsteps somewhere outside my cell, for voices, for anything at all. Rain drips from my hair in fading intervals, and sometimes I rattle my bound hands just to hear the *clink* of the connecting chain. But that's it.

The world's gone eerily silent, and I am but a ghost in it.

20

The blood rain's at it again. It seems only minutes ago that the sprinklers shut off, but I've thought that before. I keep track anyway. That and my bladder are the only metrics by which I can measure time's ebb and flow.

Sprinklers: fourteen. Me: six. My best guess is that it's been four days.

I take my few sips, then start my silent count. One scale chaser, two scale chaser . . . In sixty scale chasers, the sprinklers shut off. My shivering lasts another several minutes. Afterward, I struggle to find the relative peace of nightmares.

"We will hurt someone you love," Interrogator said. They need time to collect collateral to ensure my cooperation. What's taking so long? Who will they torment me with?

Though sometimes it seems like they've left me here to

wither, I'm sure they're monitoring my emotions via the CENSIR, and I want them to know that fear does not top my list.

I glower at the invisible cameras that are surely watching me and think about Mom and how the Green that killed her was part of a secret army project to control dragons, a project they later forced me to partake in.

I think about Dad, once powerful, broken when the military came to Mason-Kline to kill Baby and the other dragon children.

I think about Sam, that wild-haired, wild-eyed kid in a Prius, the brother who loved me before the government convinced him I was a traitor.

I think about Allie and the video those guys showed me in that Dillingham diner.

I think about Baby, another child tortured and rolled out in front of the cameras, all in the name of ending this war.

And I think about James, the boy who loved dragons like my mother loved dragons, the boy I never really got to know. The military didn't kill him, not in a flesh-and-blood, Mom sort of way, but what's the difference?

I'm wondering what would have happened if we'd met in a better world . . . when the sprinklers start up again.

Already? It was only minutes ago that they turned off, no more than an hour, I'm sure of it.

One scale chaser, two scale chaser . . . but the rain doesn't stop when I reach sixty, nor a hundred, and soon I'm soaked and shivering.

And then it does stop, and a strange mechanical noise echoes from afar. The chain connected to my shackles retracts, pulls me into tiptoe standing position.

It's time. Now they're going to activate the thinscreen. "We will hurt someone you love." Dad. It's gotta be Dad. They used him against me before. They know how important he is to me. Confess, or he dies. Would they actually kill him?

I don't know, but if I see him, I will break, so I squeeze my eyes shut. A stalled breath later, a sharp brightness shines through my eyelids; an uncomfortable warmth envelops me. I squeeze tighter.

Minutes pass. My CENSIR remains dormant. Nobody comes on over the speaker system. All I can hear is the fast drip of liquid onto metal as I twist on my tiptoes, the chain above me spinning back and forth in calm gyrations. My shoulders burn.

I peek out between my eyelids, am blinded momentarily. When my eyes adjust, I see that the thinscreen's off, that the illumination stems from a row of floodlights along the ceiling. My scrubs aren't the black, prison-camp issue I envisioned. White once, they're now stained scarlet.

"What's going on?" I ask.

Nobody answers.

I look for the cameras, find them in the corners. Not invisible at all. You can find similar models in department stores, the ones you sometimes wave at and wonder if there's someone on the other side watching. . . .

With sudden horror, I notice how the lights, so bright, converge on me.

Spotlight me.

I'm the one on display.

Beneath my scrubs, now semitransparent and clinging to my skin, I'm naked save for the wrapped bandages around my stomach. Bedraggled, dripping blood, I'm in a macabre peep show.

I try to remember Keith and Baby and everything I need to protect, but they are the merest shadows to the horrid image fixed in my head: Dad, trapped in his wheelchair, made to watch me suffer.

"Keith and Preston are—"

My CENSIR delivers a sizzling shock. Four more, and I'm screaming and writhing. I've barely quieted to moans when nozzles emerge from the wall and pummel me with geysers of blood rain. Feels like someone's digging through my stomach to yank out my spine.

I close my eyes as the world spins, struggling to recall what my captors want. A location. A city. What city?

"Ann Arbor . . . Mason-Kline . . . ," I blurt between gurgled screams. "Chicago . . . Arlington . . . Charlottesville . . . Manassas . . . Topeka . . . Wichita . . . Kansas City . . . both of them. Saint Paul . . . Rapid City . . . Montego Bay, Montego Bay, Montego Bay! Georgetown . . . both of them. Dallas . . . D, D, D . . . Dillingham! Dillingham! D, D, D . . . Detroit . . . Michigan . . . Ann Arbor . . . Chicago . . . Dumpster . . . D, D, D . . ."

I black out.

I'm revived with low-voltage prods from my CENSIR. The geysers are off, but it hasn't been long, because I'm still drizzling everywhere.

"Are you okay?" Interrogator asks seconds later. Did I hear him right?

"Please let him go," I say.

"Answer the question, Twenty—" He stops. Several seconds later: "Answer the question."

"What question?"

"Are you okay?"

"I'm okay," I say. "I love you. I'm sorry."

Abruptly, the lights shut off. I'm lowered to the ground.

I curl into myself, tuck my tears into my elbow so Dad won't see, and eventually sleep.

I'm awakened by a raging fire in my shoulders. I'm upright, already in torture position, and back in the spotlights, but my clothes are stiff and dry. And opaque.

"Denver," I say before the nozzles change that. My voice comes out weak, so I repeat myself. "They're in Denver."

Interrogator ignores me.

"What do you want?" I shut my eyes. It's all I can do not to cry. "What do you want? I don't know anything else! Let Dad go."

The speakers crackle to life. "We do not have your father," Interrogator says.

"Who do you have?"

"Nobody of your concern."

Then why am I strung up like this? "Who do you have?"

"Quiet now, Melissa. Behave, and this will all be over soon."

Melissa? In Georgetown, they only called me Melissa when they wanted something from me, something they couldn't wring out with threats or torture. But I have nothing to offer anymore.

I gasp. Maybe it's the person on the other end of the camera feed who has what they need, a boy who knows what it's like to flinch when you hear anybody, anybody at all, mention the numbers twenty-five or twenty-six.

"James?"

I'm ignored.

"You can't trust them!" I shout. My CENSIR delivers a string of sharp electrical bursts that set my teeth chattering. And I know I'm right. James is here.

"We will not tolerate your disobedience," Interrogator says.

"I'll be okay," I say, lifting my head and giving my bravest smile for the cameras. "Don't tell them anything. Don't worry about me—"

These jolts come faster. Electric fire fills my lungs. My vision clouds, dark floaters hopping everywhere.

A bang echoes from the speakers.

The jolts cut out, and I'm dropped to the ground. I spasm. A warm sensation floods my head, and the *clang* of metal sounds nearby. Through the floaters and the haze, I notice a flash of silver on the ground. My CENSIR, I think.

"I'll be there in a second," someone says. Not Interrogator.

Gunfire erupts far away. Pistol shots respond, these closer, some just outside my cell. The battle grows louder, but more sporadic. And then the gunshots cease altogether.

Muffled footsteps click my way.

The door bursts open.

I can't see much, but I can see enough to know it's a soldier. Dragon camos, a rifle or machine gun slung over one shoulder. He's here to finish me off. That's what they did in Georgetown.

Another step and he's in the spotlight, almost close enough for me to touch. He crouches in front of me, comes into focus.

The soldier is Colin.

21

He removes my handcuffs, plunges a needle into my arm. "This is Dilaudid. It will help with the pain."

He gently probes my body, wincing when I wince, apologizing when I cry out. In between cataloging my injuries beneath his breath—abrasions, bruised or broken ribs, possible internal bleeding—he informs me that we're in a Bureau of Dragon Affairs office in Indianapolis, that it's been two weeks since Chicago, that he's sorry for leaving me.

There are things I need to tell him, but I can't remember what they are.

He prods at a grouping of welts along my forearm, asks if they injected anything into me. I give a weak shrug. "What about food? Did they give you anything? We have to make sure they can't track you."

I attempt to speak, manage a moan that only deepens the worry etched in his eyes. I jab a shaky finger at the nearest puddle of blood rain. He relaxes a hair.

After cocooning me in a jacket that smells of sweat and him, he scoops me up as if I'm nothing, pulls me to him as if I'm everything. He carries me into a hallway lined on either side with narrow steel doors. Black-suited BoDA agents lie slumped everywhere. For a second I'm back in Mason-Kline. Getting shot in that bivouac by the D-man. James carrying me from the wreckage into carnage.

James!

A couple of blinks later, we're at an elevator. Colin leans me against the wall and presses his hand to the imprint scanner. As the door slides open, I work through the ache strangling my throat and murmur, "James. I think he's here."

The concern in Colin's features vanishes. "No, Melissa. It's his fault."

Colin picks me up and moves into the elevator. He presses the up button on the control panel.

"Please," I croak. "Help him."

"He's the big fish they want," Colin says. "Anyway, he'd want you safe. That's why he came back, wasn't it?"

"Please."

He clenches his jaw, shakes his head. "There's a shift change soon. We don't have time."

"Allie," I say. "He knows—"

"He doesn't know," Colin says, softening a hair. "He doesn't know where she is, Melissa. They were asking him when I entered the control center. I'm sorry."

The elevator dings.

"Quiet now," Colin says, setting me in the front corner.

In one quick motion, he draws his sidearm, mounted with a silencer. The door slides open to a drab lobby. A man in a black suit's leaning over a curved desk to talk with the woman behind it.

The woman's eyes widen. She blanches as Colin lifts his gun and, with a whistled *whoosh*, nails the agent in that place where brain stem meets neck. Kill shot. He turns the gun on the secretary, and she swallows her scream.

"Don't even think about that panic button," Colin says. He presses the stop button on the elevator panel, then steps into the lobby. "What's your name?"

"Buh . . . Buh . . . Becca."

"You have kids, Becca?" Colin asks with another step.

"A son." She swallows. "Jeffrey."

"I had a friend named Jeffrey growing up," Colin says. "I liked him. He died in the war. He was only sixteen. Do you know who I am, Becca?"

Becca gives a furious shake of her head, smoky lines of makeup tears streaking down her cheeks.

"And you won't press that button when we walk out," Colin says with another step.

"I won't press it. I promise to God I won't. Please don't hurt me."

"I'm not going to hurt you. But you need to calm down."

If anything, her sobbing intensifies. The noise masks the sound of my clumsy crawling. Colin's another step away, coaxing her with words, his gun never straying from her head, when I struggle up to my knees and limply throw my palm against the stop button.

As the elevator doors slide shut, I see Colin spin toward me.

As I hit the down button, I hear Becca scream.

And then I hear a gunshot.

The elevator hits bottom; the doors slide open. Bio-print scanners control access to each cell. There are plenty of hands in the hallway. Will dead ones work? Even if they would, I'd have to lift somebody up to put their hand in position.

I'm not sure I can even lift myself.

In nae. I crawl for the smallest corpse—a blonde who'd be pretty if not for the penny-sized hole between her eyes. As I grab her collar, I think of Colin and his advice back on Saint Matthew Island.

"Always go for the kill shot." In our ice cave, whenever it was his turn to perforate the crate, he'd knock out one or two bull's-eyes, maybe come close to a few others. A survey of the seven or eight men and women scattered through the corridor tells me he was holding back.

So many secrets.

Scooting on my butt, I drag the woman inch by snail inch toward the first door. I'm not even close when Colin comes running out of the elevator. He stops short, wearing an expression that says he wants to rescue me from the unrescueable.

I bite into my lip. "Were you... were you in Georgetown?"

He crouches in front me, his face inches from mine. I look away. He unwraps my hands from the woman's collar and takes them between his. I pull them free.

"I'd heard of it, but I was never there," he says.

"James and I were," I mumble, staring at the dead woman's face. I feel nothing for her. She is but a broken doll. I force myself to look at Colin and decide that I will believe him. I must. "You were there, too."

His brow furrows. "I wasn't. I swear to you."

"We're fragments, Colin. All of us. James, too. Broken." My head hurts. I close my eyes for a moment. "Just trying to figure out... how to be unbroken." I clutch at him. "Please, Colin."

Colin tenses but nods. "Okay."

He starts to lift me, but I shake him off. "I want to walk."

With an arm about my waist, we trudge by door after steel door, our footsteps the only breaks in the silence. My breath remains thick in my lungs, my tongue thick in my mouth, but some coordination returns. I'm still rickety, but at least my legs don't feel like buckling every other second.

"How . . . how did you find me, Colin?"

"The tracer in your arm."

"Keith said . . . said he removed it," I say. I have a scar on my right bicep where they operated.

"He couldn't bring himself do it," Colin says, but I barely hear him.

Baby!

"I caved," I say. "I told them about Denver. . . ."

"They evacced right after Chicago," he says. "Standard protocol. They're safe."

"I can't reach her, Colin, I can't reach her," I mumble, hyperventilating. I lose my balance. He catches me.

"Signal's blocked down here," he says. "They're fine. Baby says hello and, I quote, 'If the scale chaser doesn't bring you back in riding condition, I am going to turn him into an ice sculpture and drop him off a mountain.'"

I cough out a laugh.

We pass an open door. I peek inside. Spotlights illuminate chains dangling from the ceiling, rivulets of blood rain seeping into a drain. I look at Colin. He nods.

Two cells beyond mine—two worlds apart—Colin stops walking.

"I have to warn you, he's not who you remember." He gives me a wan smile, then pushes on the door.

The prisoner, bathed in a yellow glow from the thin-screen video feed of an empty cell that I assume is mine, sits shackled at room center, rocking himself in slow arcs. His left arm appears dislocated or broken, his right's heavily wrapped beneath his own crimson-stained scrubs, and his face is so bloated by injury I'm not even sure it's him.

Not until he looks up and I see his eyes.

"What are you doing here, Sarge?" James whispers. "You're wasting your time."

Colin squeezes my shoulder. "You sure about this?"

"We can't leave him."

Colin kneels beside James to uncuff him.

"Get him out of the CENSIR first."

"It stays on," Colin says. "It's set to passive inhibit. Nobody can hurt him."

"Passive slave, huh?" James rubs at his wrists, his smirk contorting into a grimace.

Colin pulls a needle from his pocket. James's eyes go wide. "Stay away."

"It's a painkiller." He brushes James hands aside and injects him in the shoulder. He lifts him to his feet. "Move."

James limps forward. Colin wraps an arm around my waist, takes a long breath that does nothing to calm the tension that so palpably suffuses him, and guides me out of the cell.

"This all you, Sarge?" James says, surveying the carnage. He foot-nudges a gun from the hand of a dead agent slumped against the wall. He bends over to retrieve it.

"I wouldn't do that," Colin says, drawing his own gun.

James straightens, glances back with that smirked grimace. "Nice work."

Colin tenses further, waves James forward with his gun.

On the elevator ride up, Colin tells us his plan for escape. In the lobby, I don't see that secretary behind the desk, but there is another bloodstain on the wall behind where her head would have been.

We exit into a parking garage, where Colin directs us to the Humvee marked U.S. ARMY that's parked in a handicap spot. He loads us in the back, puts bags over our heads, handcuffs us to the doors.

We drive off.

"This the Krakus transfer?" someone asks a couple minutes later. The gate guard, I assume.

"King of hearts and queen of spades," Colin says. He sounds almost jovial.

"Treat them right," the guard says with a laugh, and we're on our way.

Colin removes my hood. I look back, half expecting to find a road of bodies leading to a torture fortress, but we're on an ordinary street surrounded by ordinary high-rises in an ordinary city.

Everything's so damn ordinary.

I take a deep breath, repeat my mantras, and contact Baby. She squeals and cries and laughs. I can almost see her, body wiggling back and forth with delight, stomping around, causing a minor earthquake, and it alleviates some of the hurt. I talk with her for a few minutes, assuring her I'm very okay (though a little too warm and in need of a good frosty kiss), then ask Grackel for an update on Allie.

She is sleeping again, human. . . . It is strange, human. When the Greens were attacking, she was awake, I am certain of that. It was as if she knew I was speaking, but she could not hear my words. I do not understand what is happening.

Grackel's confusion terrifies me, but it also provides me clarity.

I look at myself in the rearview mirror, my new ordinary. I hold on to the image of the hideous train wreck that is Melissa Callahan, Twenty-Five, the queen of fucking spades, and make a decision.

I'm done running.

I'm done hiding.

I'm going to save Allie.

I'm going to join the Diocletians.

PART II
KISSING DRAGONS

22

At a middle-of-nowhere motel that evening, while James is showering, Colin sits me down on the bed, where he re-dresses the bandage around my ribs and applies antiseptic to various abrasions across my body. Another dose of pain-killers helps keep the pain in the background.

"You want to talk about it?" he asks.

He means the torture. "I've been doing a lot of thinking." I chew at my lip, wishing the room's mini-fridge held something other than water bottles.

He takes my hand. "What is it?"

"Allie . . . Oren's done something to her." I recount my conversation with Grackel.

"It's probably a bad coincidence."

"You don't believe that."

"I don't know what to believe. At least we know she's alive."

"And nothing else." I shake my head. I'm only stalling. I have to tell him. I know what his response will be, but I have to tell him. I look at him, pull my hand free. "You have to let me go, Colin."

His eyes widen with comprehension. "Melissa, you're not thinking straight."

"I'm thinking straighter than I have in a long time," I say. "I can't sit around and hope that things work out okay, because they won't. If I infiltrate them—"

"Say you somehow do infiltrate them. They'll make you do things, horrible, horrible things."

"What was that secretary's name?" I ask. It's a cruel shot, but it doesn't faze him.

"You're only going to get yourself killed," he says, almost pleading. "Oren's not an idiot. He'll know what you're doing."

"Not if James vouches for me."

"The Diocletians work in isolated cells, Melissa. James wouldn't be able to get you—"

A clatter of metal sounds in the bathroom. Colin bursts through the door, reaching for his gun. I'm two steps behind.

James lies in the tub, shower curtain draped over him,

plastic rings strewn everywhere. The rod to which Colin cuffed him dangles over the edge.

Chin to his chest, he glares at us through matted black hair. "Get out!"

Colin holsters his gun. He grabs me by the elbow, but I shake him off. "He needs help."

"He didn't want my help earlier." He lowers his voice. "And I promise you that he doesn't want yours."

"Doesn't matter what he wants." I retreat from the bathroom, return a few seconds later with Colin's medical supply bag. "Give me the handcuff keys."

"No."

"He's not going anywhere," I say.

"No."

"Sit on the toilet and point that gun at us if you want, but take off those goddamn handcuffs."

He retrieves the keys from a pocket and presses them into my palm. "He's dangerous, Melissa," he whispers to me, then leaves.

"Get out," James says when I uncuff him. I reach over him and shut off the water. "Get out, Melissa."

I dig through the bag until I find a syringe of that Dilaudid stuff and an antiseptic towelette. I lower the curtain enough to expose his torso. Vicious scars, fresh and enflamed, undulate along his back and chest. He grunts a curse, flails limply, the shower rod clattering against the acrylic. I push him down. He's too weak to resist.

I use the towelette to clean an undamaged patch of skin along his left shoulder, just above the tattoo that encircles his bicep. *Drink the Wild Air.*

"What happened to our salubrity?" I jam the syringe into his shoulder.

"Get out. Please," he says through clenched teeth. A tear slips free from his right eye. "Please."

"Shhh. Save your breath, farmboy."

I pat him dry as gently as possible, though he grimaces with every touch. He passes out. I check his pulse. It beats strong, angry almost. Dragon exposure? I push the hair from his eyes. Even asleep, he appears tormented.

In our two-hour car ride, I spoke no more than a few words to him. But now . . . I cannot bring myself to update him on the awesomeness of my life since we went our separate ways, and it hurts too much to discuss Allie. I decide to tell him about Baby, hoping my voice filters into the darkness, provides him some flicker of light.

"She's one of the few good things in this entire mess," I whisper as I dab at his chest with antiseptic. "Don't get me wrong, she's turning into a real pain in the ass."

I move to his stomach, smearing ointment everywhere. "She's so incredibly stubborn. She's grown enormous.

Keeping her in line was difficult enough before, but now she's a damn flying brontosaurus. I don't think she realizes how strong she is. One time she got so mad. Nearly caused a cave-in. Grackel was livid. And a little bit terrified. And you know Grackel. That's saying something.

"She'd hate me for telling you this, but she misses you. Allie misses you. I—" My hands ball into fists. "They're just children!"

I bite hard into my lip until the desire to hit him passes. It takes a while. I wipe an arm across my eyes to clear them and continue treating him in silence.

After applying bandages, I call Colin, who helps me dress him in mismatched Walmart clothes. We carry him to the bed.

I'm checking his pulse again when, out of my peripheral vision, I see Colin coming around to my side, a pair of needles in his hand.

"What are those?" I ask.

"Sedatives. I'm sorry," Colin says, and drives one into my arm.

I slap him. "You asshole."

"I need to go grab some things to get us through the checkpoint. I can't risk you doing something stupid."

My eyelids grow heavy. He kisses my forehead, lays me down. His footsteps echo into emptiness. From across the universe, I hear a door open and shut, a car engine rumble to life.

I fight the urge to sleep. Opening my eyes requires effort. Sitting up proves a struggle. Unzipping his backpack is damn near impossible. I fumble through it with clumsy fingers, not sure what I'm looking for. Tablet, needles, underwear, gun clips. No gun.

In a pocket, I find a pair of metallic flash drives. There's something familiar about them. A couple of groggy blinks later, I remember where I've seen them before. Preston procured several drives like these from Georgetown; he used them to make his RedJediGrunt vids.

Repeating my mantras does nothing to quell the shaking in my hands as I struggle to stick the first drive into Colin's tablet. A file folder opens. It contains a dozen videos, ranging in date from a week ago to yesterday. My trembling subsides. This isn't Georgetown.

I load the first video. Via infrared cameras, it shows me hanging from a chain, jets of blood rain assaulting me until I wake. I tug out the drive, swap it for the other one, load the last file in the folder.

James dangles from a chain similar to mine. He's soaked in blood rain.

Blink.

He's screaming.

Blink.

"Where's the next attack, Twenty-Six?"

My eyes snap open at Interrogator's voice. A woman's in the room with James now, a whip coiled in her hand. She steps in front of him. It's the pretty lady from the hallway, the one Colin shot between the eyes.

"Oren doesn't operate like that," James says.

The woman strikes in a flash, the whip slicing into James's back. He cries out.

Blink.

". . . he gave us . . . orders . . ." James is saying between heavy breaths. "Two days before the attack . . . didn't know before."

The woman removes a bottle from her pocket, dips latex-gloved fingers into it, and rubs a substance into a fresh laceration. James writhes and wails.

"Twenty-Six, you expect me to believe that you're just a common soldier in the Diocletian army?"

Blink.

". . . telling the truth." James clenches his jaw. "Check my CENSIR."

"You've managed to fool us before, Twenty-Six."

"I don't know!"

The screen in front of James bursts to life. There I am, spotlighted in my cell, soaked with blood rain, screaming.

Blink.

"I don't know!"

On the screen, my CENSIR jolts me several times in rapid succession, and the geysers of blood rain open fire. They feed the audio from my cell into his.

"Stop lying," Interrogator says. "Where were the other riders?"

"Others?"

I get shocked again. James attempts to shut his eyes, but they shock them open via his CENSIR.

"In your trio, you were the only rider on your dragon," Interrogator says.

"Huh?" James says. Sounds drugged.

They shock me. They shock him. We scream.

Blink.

". . . this makes any sense. What's this have to do with the girl?" Interrogator asks.

"I don't know why Oren wants Allie," James says. "Please stop."

"Tell me something new, Twenty-Six, and I'll end Twenty-Five's suffering."

"Okay . . . okay . . . I've got a theory. . . ."

Blink.

23

The thrum of highway beneath tires lulls me awake. Something's itching at my eyes. The car's unfamiliar. And for a few seconds, so is its driver. A wig of shoulder-length black hair covers Colin's head; tinted glasses hide his eyes.

"How you feeling?" he asks.

Asshole. "Where are we?"

"Almost to Iowa. Your name's Jill," Colin says. "I'm Mike. He's Justin. We're on a weekend excursion to the Badlands."

I check my reflection in the rearview mirror. I've got blue eyes and a blond wig that's nothing like the one I wore for *Kissing Dragons* but reminds me of it nonetheless. I look more like that dragon queen than the girl I used to be. Will I ever get to be Melissa again?

I look away. A seat over, "Justin" wears an Ohio State University cap, tugged low to hide his CENSIR. No handcuffs anymore. Makeup conceals bruises on his face. Brown-colored contacts do not conceal the rage. He catches me watching him and shuts his eyes.

Rows of corn blur past my window; the memory of the torture video comes into focus. I want to ask James about his theory on Allie, but I don't know how to broach the subject without arousing his suspicion about my intentions. I don't know how to talk to him at all.

Colin turns on the radio. The silence intensifies.

I contact Grackel and Baby in spurts, but the distraction of their conversation only serves to remind me how empty it feels in the car. I do not know these people anymore. Colin with his secrets, James with his darkness.

We reach our first checkpoint a mile before the Illinois-Iowa border. No less than fifty All-Blacks monitor the highway control gates. Several patrol the queue of vehicles with bomb-sniffing dogs; the rest lurk in sandbag fortifications with enough weaponry to annihilate a mountain.

When it's our turn, an A-B sergeant orders us out. I cross my arms over my chest to control my trembles and lift my eyes skyward, praying he thinks me annoyed and not ready-to-pee-myself terrified.

While he scans our fake licenses into his tablet, another

soldier searches the car. Nothing in the glove compartment or center console except for some wadded-up receipts and loose change. From the trunk, he removes a pair of over-sized backpacks. He lets the dog sniff at them, opens them up, inspects the contents. Colin's tablet, some MREs, a couple of canteens, three blankets that appear to be made out of aluminum, a set of binoculars, a bundle of rope. No ammo, needles, or flash drives.

"What are your intentions?" the sergeant asks.

"Headed for the Badlands, man," Colin says. He's affected a dopey-eyed look. "Heard there are some killer dragon skeletons to check out."

The sergeant scowls. "That's near the drone zone. That's off-limits."

"No way, man. They're closing the frontier?"

"It is closed. You stay on this side of it. And no souvenir hunting."

"We look like we want to do any dragon dancing, man?"

The scowl intensifies. "You know what I mean. Don't bring back any . . . mementos."

"Only pictures and good times, man."

"Stay alert, obey curfew, follow signs, and keep out of trouble." He returns our IDs, we get back in the car, and I start to breathe again, though it's another ten minutes before my heart rate settles to anywhere close to normal.

On the outskirts of Des Moines, traffic slows to a crawl again. Signs along the highway indicate that all civilian traffic must take the next exit. Except for a herd of semis, most of the vehicles are already military. Drones crisscross the cloudless sky.

The semi in front of us switches lanes, giving me a view of the highway ahead. Hundreds of troop transports form a convoy that plods west, toward the evac territories. Beyond the trucks, I see tanks. Beyond that, I cannot distinguish, but the snake of vehicular blackness stretches to the horizon. I think of Sam, tell myself he's in some film studio somewhere.

"It'll be Armageddon," James says.

"Isn't that what you want?" Colin says.

"The dragons never had a choice in the matter."

"You did."

James doesn't answer, his gaze returning to his window.

We drive on. North and west, muddling our way through checkpoint after checkpoint. Traffic thins until only that strained silence accompanies us. We reach Badlands National Park around sunset and pull off to a scenic overlook. Prairie dogs bark at us from afar.

"Pretend like you're tourists," Colin says. He indicates the drone that circles overhead. It's the only one in our vicinity, but there's little else to observe other than us. "The frontier checkpoint's a ten-minute walk from here. We wait for nightfall, then we go."

"Won't it still be able to track us?" I say.

"The boy scout's got it all figured out," James says, flipping his fake driver's license around in one hand. "That's what the Mylar blankets are for, right?"

"It'll block the thermal imaging for a short while." Colin pops the trunk. "Long enough for us to put some distance between us and its cameras."

James rolls down his window, flicks the license away. "You know, for a fugitive, you sure seem well connected."

Similar thoughts have crossed my mind too many times.

I trudge to a railing that overlooks a canyon bulging with hills made of red-striped rock. I spot no dragon skeletons, though. On a nearby information placard decorated with a frontiersman (the nineteenth-century version) and a couple of prairie dogs, somebody's added a ravenous-looking Red to the mountainous backdrop.

James limps up beside me, sneers at the image. "They'll always be monsters. Better to play the part than to die a coward."

There's no courage in what the Diocletians have done, I want to say, but I need his alliance. Colin stands a dozen feet from us, binoculars raised to his eyes. I lean closer to James. "I don't trust him."

"Neither did Keith at first," James says after a long silence. He stares off toward the horizon. "Thought maybe he was working covert ops. But he told us the location of another talker facility. This place called Banks Island. Polar bear territory. There were only three talkers there, dead, of course, but we recovered design schematics on a new CENSIR.

"Thing was," he continues, "Oren already had those design schematics. Stole them two months before. Maybe the army already knew about the breach. Whatever. Keith believed him. Didn't hurt that Georgetown Claire was his sister."

"That not enough?" I ask.

"Maybe. Blood doesn't necessarily mean allegiance."

"Sam," I whisper, his name out of my mouth before I can stop it. I glance at James, hoping he didn't hear, but he's looking at me.

"I'm sorry."

"Doesn't matter. Just another thing they've taken from me."

He nods. "There was one thing about Sarge's story that never really worked for me. He was supposedly a grunt in the U.S. Army, so how'd he know about that facility? He claimed to have served there, one of the pro-military talkers, but they send the scale-chasing talkers to more hospitable locations."

I think of Colin's note. *There are things I want to tell you, but I'm not sure how without making you hate me.*

"There's been something bothering me," I say. "I can't stop thinking about it."

"What?"

"There was only one way in and out of that BoDA detention center."

James nods. "The elevator."

"Right. So he had to come in that way. But he didn't kill that secretary or that agent until we tried to leave."

"Huh?"

I explain Colin's and my first trip up the elevator. "And there's something else. Colin was in Interrogator's control room before he rescued me. But I don't remember hearing any gunshots before that."

James smirks. "They knew him. Or knew of him. They trusted him."

I trusted him. "He told me that Keith didn't remove the tracer from my arm. He told me that's how he found us."

"Of course he removed it," James says. "I was there. I watched." It was the day after we escaped Georgetown. The medics had performed the impromptu surgery in a cave somewhere in Argentina.

"You're sure?"

"Yes. Keith was worried they'd figure out the tracking frequency."

"He's working with the government," I speak the truth a part of me has known since Indianapolis. I warn Grackel about Colin's allegiance.

He is not our enemy anymore, human, she says. *Kill emotion, human, and see his heart.*

That doesn't make any fucking sense. I keep the thought to myself, but Grackel must pick up on it.

If he is our enemy, how come we are already not dead?

I ignore her, look at James. "We need to leave. Tell me the name of a Green. I'll call them—"

"You don't need to escape him, Melissa," James says. "He wants to protect you."

"Protect me?" I almost laugh.

"I don't know what he's about, but he came back for you, Melissa. He killed for you. That's who he is now," he says softly.

I don't want to think about who he is. It doesn't matter anyway. Not anymore. "You remember when we first met?"

"Dragon Hill."

"You told me there was another war coming. I think it's time I choose a side."

"This isn't your war, Melissa."

"Are you kidding? Look at me. Look at what they've done to me."

"Oren won't accept you," James says.

"Why don't we let him decide?"

"You know why I came back for you in Chicago?" he asks. "Because . . . never mind." He sighs. "Grackel contacted me and told me what you were doing. Who does that? What sort of person takes on a Green with a Prius?"

I shrug.

"A fool," he whispers, and I'm not sure whether he's talking to me or himself. "The Diocletians destroy fools."

24

We rappel into the Badlands swathed in aluminum foil. Well, Colin rappels. James and I struggle in our descent, groaning and grimacing the entire way, but finally make it into a canyon between the striated mounds of red rock.

We hobble west, Colin leading us with a flashlight and an old-school paper map. The expansive quiet, the Mylar blankets wrapped around our shoulders, and the ruddy landscape call to mind one of those cartoon shows Sam liked growing up. Something about explorers colonizing Mars, only to discover that the Red Planet was already populated by dragons.

An interplanetary war ensued.

Grackel, you guys come from Mars?

What is Mars?

A different planet.

She goes silent, and I know she's searching her memories, know that she'll find nothing. One of the few things that truly frustrates her. Fifteen years ago, over the span of several months, Reds, Greens, and Blues popped up across the globe. All in the same mysterious way—full-grown, lethal, and without any knowledge of the past.

Probably not, I say. *How would Blues have gotten here?*

She laughs, a guttural, awful sound. I like making her laugh.

Even if Blues could fly, it doesn't make sense. If dragons are from another world, why come to ours? Was their planet dying? That's the go-to explanation by the extraterrestrial theorists. Not the most harebrained theory, but close.

I don't know if that cartoon ever explained why the dragons decided to come to Earth. That wasn't the point. It was a boy show, full of bloodless battles that always ended in the death of dragons. Of course there were always more dragons for the next show.

The only dragons on this version of Mars are long dead. We came upon the first an hour in. Wingless. Definitely not suited for interplanetary travel.

Another dinosaurlike skeleton appeared, then another. Soon the foothills of red rock gave way to exploded prairie and foothills of dragon bone. They're everywhere, scattered among the detritus of savaged earth, though none are close to complete. Fractured by war or dismantled by scavengers. Not a skull or claw in sight, the favored showpieces in cabin lodges around the world.

We pass through a broken barbwire fence and soon arrive at the epicenter. At least two dozen incomplete skeletons ring the caved-in remnants of a stadium-sized hole.

"Blue Rez One," James mutters.

Colin walks the hole's perimeter, directing the flashlight beam into the dark spaces between the rubble.

"Is this field trip your idea of a lesson, Sarge?" James says.

Colin doesn't answer.

"Eye for an eye and the whole world goes blind, is that it?" James runs a hand along a stray rib bone wedged into the ground.

Is that why Colin's pit stopping at this erstwhile dragon "sanctuary"? For a visual comparison? Shrink down the bones, replace the broken rocks with broken buildings, and it's easy to see the similarity.

Colin drops to his knees, shines the flashlight into the abyss. Beneath those broken rocks lie the skeletons of dragon children.

"What the hell are we doing here?" I ask.

"We need to take cover." He removes several glow sticks from his backpack, then a bundle of rope. He secures it to a nearby skeleton and drops it into the crevice. "There's a cave down there. We'll be able to rest without worrying about the drones spotting us. Hurry now."

"Clever, isn't he?" James says on his way past. I don't understand the comment until I look into the hole. The rope barely reaches a partially obscured cave, which sits off the edge of a ramp blockaded on both sides by collapsed earth.

An easy way in, a not-so-easy way out.

I'd hoped to escape tonight. Slip out while Colin's sleeping. I bet I could make it back up that rope. But no way James could. Not without Colin, healthy and strong, pulling him from the depths.

James goes down the rope first, Colin goes last. And I'm stuck in the middle.

Colin preps a dinner of MREs. He offers us some pills that he says are painkillers. We both refuse. James takes his meal to the front of the cave. I take the front corner. Colin joins me.

"How are you doing?" he asks.

My ribs ache. My legs are sore. "Fine."

"I know you're angry. . . . I just can't have you doing something stubborn, Melissa."

I stop nibbling at my pork ribs to glance up at him. The glow stick protruding from his shirt highlights his concern in yellow. Asshole.

"I don't want you to get hurt," he says when I don't respond.

"You gonna drug me again? Put me in handcuffs? Lock me up? You gonna keep me safe?"

"You've been through a lot, Melissa. You need time to recover."

Recover? I snort.

"What about Baby?" he asks. "You're the only one she has left."

"She has Grackel. . . ." I look at him. Fuck, I hate him. Fuck, I love him. "She has you."

"You know that's not the same."

He's not gonna let it go. He's not gonna let me go. "You're right. Of course, you're right. It's just . . . I miss her so much, Colin. And I was supposed to protect her . . . and I didn't . . . I didn't protect her at all. . . ." I let myself go. I let him hug me, and I let myself cry into his shoulder.

I let him make a bed for me. I let him lie beside me, let him hold me. I pretend to drift off, and then I wait.

When I'm sure he's asleep, I tiptoe my way through the darkness toward the cave mouth. James is little more than an outline in the limited moonlight from above. Head dipped to his chest, he chews slowly on a granola bar.

"No," he says as I sit beside him.

"But—"

"You know the biggest difference between Greens and Reds?"

"Thirty thousand dollars," I say. A dragon-hunting joke that elicits a sarcastic snort.

"A Red will kill you because it has to. A Green because it can." He shifts position, stifles a groan. "What would it be like to feel no guilt?"

He envies them. A part of me does, too. I don't want to think about that. "You mentioned that Grackel contacted you," I say. "I didn't know you guys were still on speaking terms."

"It was a one-time thing," he says, which is similar to the answer Grackel gave me when I asked her about it.

"Good timing for me, then," I say. "Give me a name, James."

"No."

"We'll both die if you don't."

His jaw clenches. "The wrong memory, the wrong look, the wrong smell, the wrong direction of the wind . . . it doesn't take much for a Green to decide that you're better off in its belly than on its back."

"Give me a name."

He taps his CENSIR. "You're unprotected. They'll scour your soul—"

"Give me a name."

"You don't understand what they're like, Melissa. What they'll do to you."

"Dragon exposure, huh?"

"Yeah."

"I've been around plenty of dragons."

"You don't get it," he says.

"Are we going to have to do this all night?"

He scowls. "What about Colin? He won't make it."

I do not hesitate. "He made his choice. Give me a name."

And he does.

25

I tell Grackel my intentions. She thinks I should wait to make a decision until my head's clearer—telling me to kill emotion at least three times before she concedes that I can't—but she does agree that if I do this, I must cut all ties.

I should say good-bye to Baby, but I don't know how, so I just tell her I'll be gone for a while and to listen to Grackel.

Please don't leave me alone. You're the only human who talks to me anymore. Please don't leave me.

I'll be back. I promise.

I thought you loved me. I thought we were sisters.

Always. Forever, I say, and disconnect before my resolve fails me.

✳ ✳ ✳

Hello, Praxus, my name is Melissa Callahan. I'm a talker friend of James Everett, who is currently CENSIRed. We need your help.

Shutting out the sounds of James's haggard breaths, ignoring the percussive thrum of my heart, I listen.

My only previous experience talking with Greens was in Georgetown. I can't remember one that didn't threaten to kill me. I expect the same from Praxus, but when I hear the tiny ringing noise at the edge of perception that indicates he's picked up my call, there is only silence.

And the ghost eyes. Probing my mental blockade, searching for a way in.

A shiver runs through me. I clench my hands, but James intercepts me, slipping his fingers through mine. "If you fight it, Praxus will never accept you."

His touch calms, his words provide clarity. Horrible, horrible clarity. This dragon is not my enemy, but my friend.

A friend full of death and destruction.

I must give that to him, I must embrace the one emotion I've managed to suppress. I must give him my rage.

So I think of Georgetown. I think of Major Alderson and the All-Blacks. I think of how they abused me for just being me. I think of how they threatened my family, how they convinced my brother I was a traitor. I think of how they tortured Baby. I think of Lorena, executed in the barracks bathroom with all the other talkers.

Then the dragons came. Spouting hellfire and retribution. I didn't see my tormentors die, but I hope they did. Every last one of them. I imagine how they burned, how they screamed . . . imagine Lester and Patch drowning in flame . . . and it's not enough. They deserve more. They deserve to burn but never die . . . constantly burn and burn and burn!

Praxus begins to purr.

I think of Major Alderson, coming into the reconditioning chamber to kill me and Allie. I think of Allie, stabbing him to death with her dragon brooch, and I only wish I'd been the one able to do it.

My hands are clenched into fists, and I'm snarling and I can't stop it. I want to kill them all. Again and again. Kill them in brutal and beautiful ways—

A pressure ignites in my skull. I moan.

"Disconnect, Melissa," James whispers. "Disconnect!"

I shake my head, clench my jaw. I must be strong—

An explosion of memories swarms me.

Not mine. Praxus's.

Swooping down from the cloudless sky into a frenzied crowd.

Attacking a day-care center.

Fighting another Green. Ripping it apart, scale by scale.

A thousand more like this, in a jumbled blur.

The pressure abates, then is gone.

The body of a scorched boy materializes in front of me. To my left, a Red screeches its death knell. To my right, an old woman cleaved in half gurgles a plea for salvation.

With every heartbeat, new victims appear. Faster and faster they come, bodies piling up all around. The smells, the screams, the tastes . . .

Death, death, death. Everywhere.

It is glorious.

More! More!

At some point I start laughing. "What would it be like to feel no guilt?" Guilt! Hah! In this world, where the end can come from any direction, what's the point of it? Live in the sunshine, swim the sea, drink the wild air's salubrity, and kill anybody who gets in the way.

No, not killing. Controlling one's destiny. Own or be owned. Dominate or be dominated. Two choices. Perish with the weak or flourish with the strong.

I sweep a hand at the memories around me and laugh louder.

Forget the weak.

I am strong.

I am powerful.

I am . . . being kissed?

I blink, and a black-haired boy is there among the dead. His lips are on mine. I try to pull back, but he overpowers me. He cups my cheeks in his hands, presses harder, full of fire. He bites my lip with such force that I cry out. But it is a good pain. I feel alive and whole and unstoppable. I bite back, drawing blood.

Harder and harder we go at each other. Kissing and biting and kissing some more. I tear off his jacket and shirt, grapple at his jeans, but whenever I attempt to proceed past his buttons, he deflects, whispers "Not yet," then resumes kissing me.

His words incite me. A challenge. I bite harder to distract him, dig my nails into his scarred back. He groans in pain, in ecstasy, but still he keeps me at bay. I remove my jacket and shirt, press myself to him. I can feel his heart beneath mine, racing toward annihilation.

I want more. I want all of him. "I will win," I whisper, and chew violently at his ear. I will win. I will dominate and own and control.

Praxus continues his slideshow of carnage, but it fades to the background, as does the rest of the world. It is just the boy and me, bound in our battle of savage lust.

Only to be interrupted by a guttural voice.

I will find you. You are mine.

The boy bites me once more, and this time the pain shooting through me holds no pleasure.

He notices my grimace, releases me, and backs into the shadows.

Cool air pricks my skin. My jacket and sweatshirt are next to me, but I only have a vague memory of removing them. Of kissing that boy. Of biting and groping . . . I hurriedly cover up, looking away from the darkness where he sits.

It takes me minutes to remember his name. I can barely remember my own.

"Why didn't you tell me?"

"I tried."

I wipe a stray tear from my cheek. "You should have tried harder."

"Tell you that they corrupt your memories, that they make you forget who you are?" he says from the darkness. He sounds a mile away. "Would it have mattered?"

No.

When I'm sure my voice won't tremble, I ask, "Why'd you do that, James? Why'd you kiss me?"

He doesn't answer right away. "There are worse addictions than wanting to be happy."

He doesn't elaborate, but it doesn't take me long to figure it out. The memories of our kiss have already faded to wisps, but those of Praxus remain vibrant. The accompanying bloodlust, however, has diminished to a background itch. If not for James diverting my attention . . .

I close the gap between us. I can see little beyond his blue eyes and the stern outline of his jaw. I press my hands to his cheeks. He flinches, tries to pull back, but I don't let him.

You are mine.

But I'm not. Because of James.

"Thank you," I whisper, and he relaxes.

I kiss him for real this time. Bodies sore, lips bloodied, it's an awkward and at times painful thing. But we carry on, and I am filled with a joy that only minutes ago I would have killed for.

26

Praxus reintroduces himself bright and ugly in the morning with a flurry of images, the stench of burning skin, and the taste of charred flesh.

But he does not stay long. He lifts me up for a few glorious seconds, then lets me fall.

"Are you okay, Melissa?" the black-haired boy says. I have a strong urge to attack him, to drive my talons through his heart.

"Leave me alone," I say. Over his shoulder, I see the soldier boy watching us with an incomprehensible look. I clench my claws and retreat to the alcove, where I eat my bloodless meal in silence. I catch them both eyeing me from time to time, but they remain safely distant.

Minutes pass before I remember myself, remember them.

A part of me still wants to kill them.

"We should be going," Colin says from the cave mouth, binoculars pressed to his eyes. His manner is far too neutral for my comfort.

"How are you feeling?" James asks after Colin's disappeared up the rope.

Like when I need a kick of alcohol, but ten times worse. "Don't suppose you'd kiss me again."

"It won't matter," he says. "Praxus knows you're resisting. The challenge of breaking you excites him."

Before I can respond, he leans in with a gentle kiss.

"I thought it didn't matter," I say.

James gives me a humorless smile. "Doesn't."

"I'll be fine."

He doesn't say anything.

"Look, you've recovered from it, haven't you?"

He doesn't look at me. "Yeah."

"That's why the government developed the CENSIRs in the first place, isn't it?" I snort. "Not as punishment. But protection."

James shrugs.

Colin calls again.

"You better go first." I push out a laugh. "Otherwise he might leave you here."

"Yeah."

Ten minutes later, it's my turn. I secure myself, give the rope a yank, and up I go. I'm nearing the top when the wall in front of me disappears. The rope, too.

We're amid the clouds, hovering.

Hunting.

There. The faint odor of sweat, the low thrum of a pounding heart. Our heartbeat accelerates. We descend.

In the distance, a climber scales a cliff.

We glide in. A soft green glow appears on the sandstone. The climber looks over his shoulder. The scent of urine overpowers the sweat one.

He freefalls down his rope. Fire warms our throat, but we do not release it. We swoop in wide arcs, ever downward, as if out for a casual flight and not an afternoon snack.

The urine scent dissipates. The climber reaches a ledge, scurries toward a small cave. We can almost feel the hope swelling in him. He thinks if he plays it right, maybe he can escape. He is a fool, but his false belief excites us, so we let him have it awhile longer.

A while passes. We give him warning with a full-throated roar. We could roast him in a second, but we want him to hold on to that hope. They are sweeter that way.

He sprints into the cave, and he thinks he's made it, but we are a lightning bolt. We dive at a steep angle, our wings scraping sandstone. We zip past his hideout, hear him exhale in relief even as he continues to tremble.

Perfect.

We make a sharp U-turn, flipping upside down. Our eyes meet. His widen for the briefest moment before disappearing with the rest of him into our claw. He struggles in our grip, so we dig our talons into him. Blood flows; a divine aroma rises. We quiver as he cries out.

"Melissa, stop it!"

I blink and that soldier boy's there, teetering on the edge of the dragon hole. My fingers are embedded in his forearm. A black-haired boy stands behind him, arms wrapped around the soldier boy's waist, tugging him backward. They are strained with their efforts. Weakening.

"Fight it, Melissa," Soldier Boy says. I hear the fear in him. "Think of something that makes you happy."

"I make my own happiness," I say, digging deeper, feeling Soldier Boy's blood pump around my talons. He winces. His feet slide an inch, then another. I could kill them with one quick jerk, prove to them that I am alpha. I smile up at them. "Does it hurt?"

"Remember when you played fetch with Baby?" the black-haired boy says. "You remember that?"

His words give me pause. "Baby?" The name is foreign to me.

Melissa. Her voice crashes into my thoughts. An image

pops into my head of a young Silver chasing after a tennis ball.

I release my grip on Colin. He pulls me to the surface, dumps me there. He glares at James as he retrieves gauze from his backpack to dress his bloodied forearm.

"Sorry," I say, though I'm not. I know I should be, but I just don't care anymore.

He nods, never looking at me. He finishes, spools up the rope, grabs his pack. "It's a long day. No point in delaying."

What's wrong with you? Baby asks as James falls into step beside me.

I ignore her. "If I get like that, stay away from me," I say to James. "And never bring Baby up again."

"I'm sorry," he says, more in understanding than apology.

Baby continues to talk at me, grows more distraught by the second at my responding silence. The hollowness inside me swells in lockstep.

Why don't you talk to me anymore?

It's safer that way, I want to tell her, but I know she will never accept that. Unable to find a good answer, I finally say, *I love you and mind Grackel.*

Melissa, please don't go. Don't leave me. . . .

I listen a second longer, then block her out and push onward.

❋ ❋ ❋

Sometimes Praxus waits fifteen minutes, sometimes an hour, but he always returns. It's only noon, and the boy at my side already wears a dozen fresh scratches and bruises thanks to me. More and more I find myself looking at his wounds and smiling.

Yet he stays close.

Soldier Boy does not. Except for a few directional commands and reminders to remain alert, he pretends to ignore me. But sometimes I see him glancing back, the hardness in his features ruined by the sadness in his eyes.

"Where are we going?" I say to Black Hair as we hike across another stretch of long-abandoned farmland.

"Somewhere safe. You'll be safe, Melissa."

He uses that name whenever he addresses me. Melissa this. Melissa that. I hate that name. I leer at the gash in his shirt. "Safe? You can't even protect yourself."

"You need to block him, just for a little while, Melissa. Find something happy."

My gaze travels from the gash to his lips. Last night, this morning. I know the kisses happened, but I can hardly remember them. I remember the blood, though. The way I bit his lip.

"Kiss me, boy." He shakes his head.

"Kiss—"

The world shifts.

Jaw spreading wide, fire bursting forth, we chase a noisy yellow Volkswagen down a suburban street. Humans flee in their chaotic way. Black houses ignite left and right beneath our flame. Trees explode.

The car continues to honk. Not in the panicked way of the weak, but in rhythm.

A war cry.

The warrior looks over her shoulder at us. The urine scent is thick in the air, but not from this one. She stinks of something different, something we do not have a name for. It sickens and enrages and thrills.

Then we are atop her, bathing her in our flame. She screams, her stench gone in an instant, swallowed by ours.

We are invincible!

Another scream echoes from the depths, the world returns to its pathetic normal.

I'm on my knees, cradled in the arms of a boy who reeks of impotence. I thrash in his grip as he pulls me to my feet. I break free and snap a side kick at him. He jumps out of the way.

"It's going to be okay, Melissa."

I trace my tongue along my lower lip, gnash my teeth.

"It's going to be okay, Melissa."

I lunge at him, he evades. "Coward!"

"Think of your family, Melissa. Sam, your younger brother."

An image of a redheaded All-Black flashes through my thoughts. He sits on a pile of rubble beside a dead Green.

"Scale chaser," I hiss.

"What about your father? He wrote you a letter. Preston delivered it. Remember the words, Melissa."

Another image.

Cripple.

I feign contemplation, swipe at the boy. He is too slow this time, and I slash him across the face. He recoils. Desperation tinges his face, but he does not relent.

"Olivia Callahan. Army pilot. Looked just like you, Melissa. Bravest person I ever met. She loved you guys so—"

"Mom," I whimper, remembering. The yellow Bug. Washington, D.C. I was not in the sky chasing her, but in a dragon shelter listening to her play hero, listening to her die.

Praxus stole the memory from me, twisted it around, had me kill her. I enjoyed it. Her screams linger, pained and wonderful. I bite hard into my lip to distract myself.

Too hard. The skin breaks, and I taste blood. My blood. Her blood.

And just like that, my tears are joined by laughter. Great, sobbing laughter.

"Melissa?" James says.

I get it together. Barely. "Praxus is reconditioning me, isn't he?"

He embraces me. "We will get through this, Melissa."

I don't believe him, but I take small comfort in his "we."

Soon enough, the small comforts vanish.

There is only desire.

Praxus slakes my thirst more often now. In between flying high, I'm stuck trudging across barren fields with this coward boy who calls me a name I do not recognize and begs me to remember things that do not interest me. I am sick of his soft words and soft looks. I want to strangle him, hear those words suffocate in his throat, watch those pathetic eyes bulge from his head. Yet he always hovers just beyond the reach of my talons.

The soldier boy doesn't simper or cower like this one. He's all confidence and fire as he plows forward. I smell the delicious aroma of condescension on him, along with a delightful dash of sorrow.

Near dusk, Praxus and I attack a new city. Black buildings, black smoke everywhere. Through the darkness, we hear a car honk at us. There! It honks again, beckoning. Another war cry. The driver emits that same scent as the previous one.

Our skin warms, our hackles rise, our breath comes faster. We move to intercept.

"Fire! Fire! Fire!" We exalt in the heat that rises in our throat, but it sticks there, and the car disappears around the corner. We crash through a building in chase and come face-to-face with another Green. The rider atop it launches a missile at us. Pain explodes through my chest, I fall to my knees.

Explain, Praxus says, the first thing he's said to me all day.

I don't understand.

He zooms in on the flipped-over car, on the driver.

A girl. She looks familiar. She looks alive.

Explain, Praxus repeats.

I don't understand.

He provides more images. A man in a red suit cuffed to a bike rack, along with four other humans. That girl from the car trying to shoot off their handcuffs. The girl fleeing the city, only to turn back around.

Explain.

I don't understand.

Explain.

I growl, tired of this mystery and his demands. *Why are we not killing them?*

I feel him smile. *Soon.*

The girl disappears.

Farmland returns.

The sun sets.

A green star rises with the gloaming.

Black Hair yells a warning to Soldier Boy.

Death comes.

27

Ⱥ line of azure fire streaks through purple puffs of sunset clouds. A drone plummets, explodes. Soldier Boy orders us to a black barn two fields over. He looks at me as if he expects an argument. I give him a worthwhile scowl but a grudging nod.

Black Hair interprets the situation with more clarity. "Run, Colin. As fast and far as you can. Praxus will kill you."

"Praxus." Soldier Boy recites the name as if it's an epithet. He steps up to Black Hair, eyes ablaze. "I should put you down for this."

"Maybe later. Right now, you're the one who has to worry."

Soldier Boy shakes his head. "Drone goes down, dragon

jets scramble. In a few minutes, your friend will be dead and Melissa will be free."

"Will there be enough?" Black Hair says. "Given everything that's happened, how can you be sure the dragon jets will even show?"

They continue to argue. They make the mistake of forgetting about me.

I sift through dead weeds and find a suitable rock. I'm tiptoeing into position behind Soldier Boy when a raspy voice startles me.

You condemn cowardice, yet only cowards sneak up on their enemies.

True, but I don't care. I cock my improvised cudgel, focus on his brain stem. Kill shot. Always go for the kill shot, somebody once told me.

I swing. Somehow Soldier Boy ducks away, as if he has eyes in the back of his head. Or a raspy voice in it, I realize as he spins toward me. Before I can strike again, he grabs hold of me, whirls me around, and twists my arm behind me until I cry out and release the rock.

Two Reds emerge from the clouds overhead. The dim one with the mangled tail descends toward us as the other bellows and launches itself at Praxus. Brightening, Praxus tightens his wings to his body and accelerates with his own roar.

RPGs shriek back and forth; invisible bullets purr across the sky. The dragons evade and resume their collision course. The Red's quicker, darting around Praxus's bursts of fire, but it can never get close enough to do any real damage to the larger dragon. It's nothing more than a pesky gnat.

Soldier Boy's grip on me loosens a notch. I glance at him. He's fixated on the battle. I groan. "Colin, you're hurting me."

"Melissa?"

"Yes," I whisper. "What's happening to me, Colin? I'm scared."

He leans in. "It's going to be okay, Mel—"

I whip my head into his jaw. He staggers. I thrust my elbow into his gut, donkey kick a kneecap. He doubles over, letting go of me altogether.

I throw another elbow at his Adam's apple but am jerked away by Black Hair. He flings me to the ground, straddles me, pins my shoulders. I knee him in the groin, slip an arm free, and straight punch him in the nose, followed by a jab to the solar plexus.

Blood pouring from his nostrils onto my neck, he grabs my wrist, smashes it to the ground. He clamps his legs around mine, flips me over, puts me in a chokehold. I thrash, but he is stronger than he acts.

"I'm sorry," Black Hair says, and presses hard against my

throat. My breath weakens. The distant music of roars and gunfire fades, my resistance wanes, my vision tunnels on that dim dragon hovering above us.

A rider dismounts via the rope ladder hanging from its shoulder. He hurries over, grapples with Black Hair.

"Get off her, James." His voice, muffled by an oxygen mask, sounds a mile away.

Soldier Boy yanks the rider away. "She's not right, Preston. Dragon exposure."

"That's not real," the rider says.

"It's very real," Black Hair says. "She'll be fine. Go. Now, before it's too late."

"It already is," I want to tell them, but I can't speak.

They argue, but I can no longer make sense of their words. A dragon scream pierces the night. The rider blanches, and in the moment before everything goes dark, I think I hear him say, "Keith."

28

I wake with a headache. Not a normal one. CENSIRed.

A heaviness weighs on my wrists. Shackles.

I force my eyes open.

The edges of a steel ceiling come into view.

I struggle into a sitting position, clanking the entire way. I'm in the corner of a room of indeterminate size. The fading light from a pair of hand-crank lamps illuminates my cot, a nearby toilet, a shelving unit laden with water bottles and canned food. The steel walls around me disappear into shadow after a few feet.

Chains thicker than my thumb connect my shackles to bolts in the concrete floor. I give them a yank. The metal bites into my wrist. The limits of my leash allow me to reach the toilet and shelving unit. After relieving my bladder, I forage through the pop-top cans of ravioli.

"Sorry, Melissa, not the greatest selection." Black Hair steps from the shadows, a tablet clutched in his left hand, his right arm bound in a sling. He cranks the nearest lamp to full brightness to reveal a dozen more cots and shelving units scattered throughout a large room, though my sleeping cubicle is the only one outfitted with a toilet, provisions, and manacles.

"What happened? Where are we?" I ask as he sits in a chair beyond my reach.

"Somewhere safe, Melissa," he says. "Detox usually takes several days." He indicates my manacles. "Until then, we need to protect you from yourself."

I offer up an agreeable smile. "I am harmless."

"There's no point in lying, Melissa." He taps his own CENSIR, shows me his tablet. *CENSIR for Melissa Callahan* is written above a 3-D image of a brain. Flashing red text on the right side of the screen indicates my *Current synaptic state* as *Violent, dangerous to others.*

I lose the smile. "What do you want?"

He loads a picture on his tablet of a stern-faced man in army dress blues. The name tag on his uniform says CALLAHAN. "Do you recognize this person, Melissa?"

"The cripple." Before he was crippled. "And stop saying that name."

"Melissa, he is your father. Peter," Black Hair says.

"I don't see the relevance of who he was."

Black Hair pulls up another picture. A ginger in dragon camos. He sits atop a pile of rubble beside a dead Green. "Melissa, this is your brother, Sam."

"If you want me to play this game, stop calling me that."

He nods, loads another picture. The woman from the yellow Beetle, in dragon-riding attire.

I roll my eyes. "Has to be my mother. I suppose she's alive."

"No."

"Too bad. Means I can't kill her for real."

I grin at Black Hair. He moves on to the next image in his slideshow.

At first I don't recognize her. Not with the makeup, long hair, and full cheeks. She shares an obvious resemblance to her mother, though, which helps me remember. Cut away the brown locks and twenty pounds, and she's that girl in the black car in the black city.

I hone in on the wrinkle of expectation that creases Black Hair's forehead. "My sister?"

His tablet indicates my lie, but he doesn't call me on it. Instead he tosses me a compact. "You don't have a sister."

I check my reflection, gasp with feigned drama. Yes, we look alike, but that girl is not me. That girl was a fool. I toss the compact back. "You tried to save her, didn't you? But you couldn't. You couldn't save her, could you? Could you?"

He rises.

"Couldn't even save yourself," I call after him.

"Tomorrow will be better, Melissa," he says calmly, though he makes his escape from the room a hair too quickly.

Using my manacles as an improvised whetstone, I sharpen a half-dozen ravioli lids into jagged shivs. I slice up a bedsheet for handles. Then I practice, accustoming myself to the weight of the chains and the feel of my makeshift talons. They will no doubt fold against bone, but should make it through skin and sinew well enough.

I wake with tears on my cheeks. Black Hair sits nearby.

"A memory?" he asks.

"A nightmare." One of many. The girl was in all of them. Sometimes she was younger, and her mother was around and her father was healthy. Most were more recent: climbing a hill with her friends to take a picture around a dormant Blue; stargazing with Black Hair atop a stone tower; sitting in a room surrounded by people who stare at her with loathing, except for her father, who can express no emotion because of his crippled nature, but somehow the emotion—something far kinder than loathing; something I can't quite wrap my mind around—leaked out anyway.

All the emotions did, hers in particular. Too often it was a mixture of fear, anguish, or, worst of all, that one the cripple had, which popped up in all the scenes with her family, that Silver, or that annoying little talker girl.

Black Hair looks at me with clear expectation. He wants to talk about these nightmares of mine.

I head for the toilet. "Can you give me a sec?"

He spins around, retreats to the door. I recover my sharpened ravioli lids from beneath the mattress, wedging them between my fingers. I keep my hands relaxed so they remain concealed.

I flush. "Who is the black man with the scar on his face?"

Black Hair returns. "Oren. What did you think of him, Melissa?"

"He takes what he wants at any cost. He is not afraid."

"In a world of cowards, that must be nice."

"Yes."

"How do you feel?"

I chew at a blister on my lip. It's all I can do not to look at his throat. I must focus elsewhere. I settle on his shoes. "These nightmares, they are the girl's memories?"

"They are your memories, Melissa. They will grow stronger. The ones Praxus fed you will dissipate. You will return to normal."

"Whose normal? Yours? That's what you want, isn't it? Somebody you can protect, somebody who needs you. Somebody to make you feel important. Because you don't feel important, do you?"

He chuckles. "That Melissa never needed me." He loads a family portrait. "Tell me about your dreams."

I slump onto the bed. "There's no point fighting it, is there?"

"The faster you cooperate, the faster you'll be free."

I sigh. "The first one was a long time ago. Melissa was eight or nine. The principal stood in the door of her classroom. A visit from him only ever meant one of two things. Fortunately, somebody hadn't died. Melissa's mom was going to war."

"Olivia," Black Hair says.

"Yes, Olivia. Mom. Melissa stood on the curb and watched her go."

"How did she feel?"

An image pops into my head. The girl and her family in a field of black crosses, everybody dressed in bright colors. A knot forms in her throat. I cannot breathe. Her tears swell in my eyes. I force them back.

"Are you okay, Melissa?"

"Terrified," I say through gritted teeth. "She felt terrified."

"And you? How do you feel?"

"Strange, uncomfortable." Good, ambiguous terms.

He checks his tablet. "What happened next?"

I tell him everything. Black Hair interrupts to supply names of people and locations, which I subsequently use to show my progress toward reformation. New memories blindside me along the way. I cry her tears at the more painful recollections, laugh when appropriate. By the end, my eyes sting from her weakness.

Black Hair has edged closer to hear, the tablet set aside long ago.

I finish with the dream of him. "Melissa and you were on that stone tower—"

"Shadow Mountain Lookout," he says.

For a second I'm in a bivouac, and he's cuffed to a chair. A beautiful woman lies on a gurney nearby, pale and lifeless. Tears streak his face, and he is brittle with pain. A blink, and I'm back in chains and he's staring at me.

"Your mother had just died," I say, as if trying to get the facts straight.

He swallows. "Yes."

"I'm sorry."

"Doesn't matter. What were Melissa and I doing there?"

"You were showing her the stars. . . ."

"But she already knew them, didn't she?"

"She did. She liked the feel of your arms around her. She felt safe in your arms." I let her sorrow creep over me. "That's all we ever wanted. We just wanted to be safe, James. I just wanted to be safe, James. But there was nowhere safe."

He gets up. I clench my hands into fists, exposing the sharp edges of my talons. He crosses that invisible line that I marked in my head yesterday. "You will be safe, Melissa."

I spring from the bed, slash at his throat. Come up a foot short. He doesn't so much as flinch. He indicates my chains. "Adjusted them before you woke. It's okay. This is not unexpected. But I think we made good progress today, Melissa."

I glare at him. "You set me up."

"If you hadn't been so determined to conceal your intentions, you'd have been less cooperative. Tomorrow will be better."

I won round one, but round two I must grudgingly concede. Round three, however . . . "Yes, tomorrow will be."

But first I must get through today. We are at war, she and I. Her memories continue to attack in sharp bursts. I exercise at max intensity to combat the onslaught. Push-ups, sit-ups, jumping jacks with my shackles. When I'm desperate, I hit my healing rib, screaming at the fire that spiderwebs through my chest. Pain helps fight thought better than anything.

But I grow tired.

She does not.

✺ ✺ ✺

I wake with the name Baby on my lips, the smell of mountain air in my nostrils, and a lightness in my heart. The crank lamp is at full brightness. Morning, I suppose. Black Hair is nowhere in sight.

Between exercises, I look for him. The light dwindles, but he does not show. Perhaps he is out of tricks, perhaps he is afraid of me or, as I realize mid push-up, he knows his presence is no longer needed. . . .

The Silver appears in front of me, her glow dim. *He said you won't have to worry about things like Georgetown, stupid TV shows, or insurgents. He doesn't mean it, Melissa.*

My arms give out. I collapse to my stomach and cry. I'm not sure whether they are the girl's tears or mine.

"James!"

He does not answer.

I am repulsed by the desperation that infects me, but I cannot keep from calling again. "James!"

He does not answer.

The third time I break off before his name can escape my throat. I smash my fist into my rib. No! I will not let them defeat me. I roll onto my back and crunch the girl's frailty into oblivion, envisioning ways in which I will kill him, should he make the mistake of ever freeing me. Then the next memory hits, and I am empty again.

He lied to me.

Today is not better.

Nor tomorrow.

Days pass. Black Hair remains a ghost, though the lamp continues to taunt me brightly each morning. I tried to stay awake last night, but he must have waited till my body surrendered before entering the room. He must be monitoring my CENSIR on a regular basis, but if anything, this realization only makes me feel lonely, abandoned.

Makes me feel weak and insignificant.

Like the girl.

"No!"

I hurl ravioli cans, smearing walls with sauce that reminds me of blood. But blood no longer excites me. It only orders up memories of Georgetown and the slaughter slab and more tears. But I hurl them anyway.

Maybe my tantrums will force them to restock.

I perk to every creak, every groan that echoes from beyond the walls. I coil with anticipation, but the sounds fade into imagination too fast.

Sometimes between futile outbursts and futile exercises, I call for Black Hair. "James!" Other times I curse his existence. Sometimes I want him to sweep into the room and hold me to him and lie to me that everything will be all right. Other times I want him to hold me to him and lie with me so that I can catch him unaware and claim one final victory.

I imagine him there on my mattress and slice him apart with my talons, but I am interrupted by a vision of him with a sword jammed into his stomach. Me holding the hilt. Then I'm crying again. Slicing and crying, slicing and crying.

When Black Hair's not tormenting me, it's the girl's dysfunctional family or that needy silver dragon or that annoying little bitch with her yes, yesses and no, nos. Their names dance on my lips, but I'll be damned if I'll slip and give them sound, too. More push-ups, more sit-ups. More pain. Always more.

"I'll be damned." I laugh and cry and this time I'm sure they are my tears.

I am damned.

That night, I hear explosions. As I lurch up, that stupid yellow car flashes through my mind's eye. The car horn blares. Closer, in the infinite blackness around me, the red-haired boy whimpers and the cripple offers bullshit words of comfort. The girl stifles sobs.

"Go away!" I yell. "Go away!"

For once, the hallucinations listen. For the most part. The car horn dies. The boy and the father go silent.

The explosions, however, louden.

The earth trembles.

Shelves rattle, cans tumble to the floor.

A flashlight beam sweeps my way, and I flinch, expecting a gunshot and Major Alderson behind it. Except this time, I make no move to avoid it.

But there is no gunshot. The flashlight comes closer.

"Melissa, are you okay?"

I don't recognize this memory.

The crank lamp flares on. A boy around my age smiles at me. He wears a Confederate-flag bandanna. A rectangular piece of paper protrudes from it, taking up the space between his left eye and ear. Something's written on it, but he's too far away for me to read the words.

"I'm Darryl, though everybody calls me Double T. Talker Talker," the boy says, his words made of rapid-fire twangs. "James asked me to check on you, and I figured things got a little strange and you might be having some questions. If I do say so myself, given the circumstances, you are doin' mighty fine."

He gives me a slow once-over, and I wonder if this is the first time he's ogled me. Or just the first time while I've been halfway conscious.

"Where is James?"

"Old John didn't like the way you and him were treating. Thought you might be getting him soft, which is the last thing we need right now, ain't it?" He glances at his tablet, grins at the sight of my shredded mattress. "How 'bout you?

You still got the itch in ya?"

I shrug.

"Divine intervention, this thing." He flicks his bandanna, eliciting a dull, metallic echo. I squint, notice that it bulges in a circular pattern along his brow line. He smiles, a crooked thing. "We all wear them. Well, not the berserkers. Those are Oren's elite—"

Another explosion detonates. More cans fall. I cringe, pull my knees to my chest.

"Don't sweat it, we are straight impenetrable down here," Double T says. "Army's just blowing the sin outta the mountains. Idiots don't know nothing about nothing. Old John says even if they knew our position, they'd have to go bunker nuke on us to reach this far down. Could you imagine? Nukin' your own country?"

I wait for the next explosion, shudder. "I don't feel safe here. Is there somewhere else we can go? I bet you've got somewhere safe you could keep me. I'd be very appreciative."

"Rules are rules. A few more days before you're right, though James thinks it might be taking longer with you." He whistles. "Mind merging with a Green like Praxus without a CENSIR to slow the flow."

He pulls a strip of beef jerky from his jeans, offers it to me. "Old John says it's my nicotine patch. Gets me through the tough bits."

"No thanks."

"Suit yourself." He rips off an edge with his teeth, grins between bites. "Something about the texture. Nothing to compare with tripping the Green fantastic, mind you." He takes another bite of meat, speaks through it. "How're your memories? Any coming back? James told me to ask for your mother's name."

"Don't recall."

"You know your name?"

I don't answer.

"Can't say I'm surprised. It'll just be blankness for a while. That's the way it always goes. The dragons blare their music into you so you can't hear nothing else. Bam, bam, bam." He snaps his fingers in fast succession. He claps loudly, taps his CENSIR. "Then the music dies, just like that. All you wanna do is get it back. But they're not there to give it to ya, so you gotta get it yourself." He starts snapping again, though I don't think he's aware of it. "It's that itch. Oh, and you wanna scratch it so bad. Keeps us sharp, Old John says."

He notices his fingers, reddens as he clamps them into a fist. He stuffs the last of the jerky into his mouth. "Just got out of a second stint of detox myself." He beams. "Two weeks without an incident. Old John says it's best for us recent graduates to work the rooks because we're wearing the same shoes, only a little more worn in."

"It's nice that he trusts you with breaking me in, but . . ."

"But what?"

"Well, what if you get an itch?" I hold up my manacled hands. "I'm completely vulnerable."

He shakes his head, adamant. "You got nothing to sweat from me."

I sigh with exaggerated relief. "You know, I think we can be friends, Double T." I soften my voice and smile. "Very good friends."

Blushing, he pulls out another stick of jerky, thrusts it at me. "You best be having this. Old John says the lady drive goes through the roof during detox. The man drive, too, but that's always there, ain't it?"

He chuckles, blushes deeper.

"That so?" I say, grinning.

He rubs the back of his neck, lets out a whistled breath, glances toward the door. "Old John's right dubious about you. Says you caused problems in bear country. Says you're dangerous."

"Isn't that why you're here?" I ask. "For danger?"

He checks his tablet, and I see some of the blood drain from his face. "You got the itch."

"I got a lot of things." I recover several ravioli lids from beneath the mattress and fling them at his feet. He dances out of the way as if they're bullets. Laughing, I arch my back. "I am very dangerous. James couldn't handle me? Can you?"

He looks over his shoulder, back to me. Sweat beads his brow. "Goes against the rules."

"You're in charge, right?" I ask. Batting my eyelids, I gently rattle the manacles to remind him.

He hurries toward the door, trips on the leg of a cot. For a moment I fear he's going to chicken out, but instead he closes the door. He returns with a goofy grin. "You are trouble, aren't you?"

"With a capital T," I say, emulating his accent. "Double T."

He chews on some more jerky. "No, no, no. I can't. James would kill me. Told me he would if I tried anything."

I roll to the left half of the bed, pat the open area beside me. "I won't tell anybody if you don't." I lick my lips. "Come on, Double T, I can see that itch of yours growing."

He sets the tablet on a desk and crawls in beside me, his gaze locked on the foot of space between us as if it's a crocodile moat. I look at the square of paper that sticks out from his bandanna. The words written on it are upside down.

Me, Darryl Thompson, aka Double T.

I am a St. Louis Cardinals fan.

And something else I can't read.

He glances at me and I smile, which sends his focus back

to the shredded sheets. I reach for his face. He flinches as I grab the square of paper wedged in his bandanna and pull it free.

I am a vegetarian.

I flip the paper over. It's a close-up picture of him, complete with bandanna and goofy grin. There's a hand on his left shoulder, but whoever it belongs to has been cropped out.

He's looking at me all sheepishly. Coward.

"You should smile more," I say. I give him back the picture.

He tucks it back into his bandanna and grimaces. Or maybe it's a smile. Hard to tell.

I move closer. He tenses.

"I've never done this before," he whispers. His breaths come in short, pathetic bursts.

"Neither have I." I pry the jerky from his fingers and take a bite. Doesn't help the itch. "I'm a vegetarian, too."

He scooches over an inch, stops.

Another explosion.

The bed trembles. Not as much as him.

I grab his head between my hands and pull him to me. I press my body to his and kiss him with the full force of my desire.

His cowardice quickly gives way to lust. God, he has all

the skill of a blowfish. A blowfish with breath that stinks of cured meat.

I force him onto his back, throw one leg over his hips to straddle him. I rise up onto my knees, draping my chest over his. Calloused hands fumble beneath my shirt. I kiss him harder, reach beneath the bed for the ravioli lids I didn't discard. I grab two for each hand, slide them between my fingers. I poise my hands on either side of his neck, clench them into fists.

I clamp on to his tongue, twist hard, taste a rush of blood. He lurches forward with a scream stifled by my teeth, and I drive my talons deep into the soft spots of his neck. Scarlet life pumps over my knuckles, sprays my face. His fingernails dig into my skin for a second, and then it's over.

I rock back and tug out my talons. I shove him off the bed before he can further stain it. He flops about, gurgling and gasping, but soon enough Double T is done talking.

I search his pockets for a key to my manacles, discover only a handful of jerky strips, a Velcro wallet, and a miniature Swiss army knife with a dulled blade shorter than my pinkie.

Using a length of sheet and two unopened ravioli cans to weight each end, I fashion a crude grappling hook. Thirty or so tries later, I catch the leg of the desk and pull it toward me. I crank the lamp, then turn my attention to the tablet.

Password protected.

I check Double T's wallet for clues, find four more pictures inside, each encased in a plastic sleeve. Cropped to hone in on single faces, they display the rest of his family. On the back of the first three, he's written their names, their relationship to him, their birthdays, and the day they died.

Mom and sis long ago in a *Botched drone strike in Knoxville*, according to the note beneath their death date. His father three weeks back in *Chicago—the Blitz on the Bears*. *Sic semper tyrannis* is written beside his birthday, the letters thick and dark, as if retraced several times.

The final photo shows his older brother in an All-Black outfit. Besides resembling Double T, he looks vaguely familiar, though I can't say why. According to the back, he's apparently still alive. At the bottom is a phone number and more retraced words. *NEVER CALL.*

I try various name and birthday-death day combinations for the tablet password. I try simple variations—0000, 1234. Random ones. Alphanumeric words. Nothing works.

"You're starting to piss me off," I say, looking at him. Blood spatters his face and the square of paper is still lodged in his bandanna. I tug it free, check it over again to see if I missed anything.

Useless. But maybe the little squirrel's got something else in there.

I jerk the bandanna free.

Red hair.

I shudder.

I don't want to look, but I can't help it.

Beneath drooped lids, the green eyes are slack.

"You know who I am. Dammit, look at me! Would you do it?" I scream at him.

In a heartbeat. Is what he's supposed to say, but he doesn't say anything.

Because he's dead.

I crash to my knees.

He threatened to kill me, but I killed him.

I killed him.

I killed him.

I killed him.

I hug him and cry into his shoulder. "I'm sorry, Sam. I'm so sorry."

The explosions end, the walls stop rattling.

Real?

I approach the heap of crimson-soaked blankets in the corner, lift the edge of one enough to see the body. Still there. Still dead. I study the face a second longer, just to be sure. Not Sam.

A Diocletian. That's who I killed. An evil dragon rider. A bad guy.

Why couldn't you have been a bad guy?

Fuck.

At least he's not Sam.

Fuck.

I wait until the crank lamp fades, crank it back up, check again. Real. But not Sam.

Fuck.

Fade, crank, check.

There. Always there. Never Sam. But always there.

I should close his eyes. At least I should do that. Say a prayer for him. Something.

But I can't.

Why can't I?

Fuck.

I throw the sheet back over his face. "Why couldn't you have been—"

"Don't feel bad."

I spin around. A man watches me from the doorway. He looks one part king, one part gangster, one part psychiatric patient. Dressed in white scrubs, he's got a brownish-red beard that belongs on a lumberjack and a devilish grin that belongs on the Cheshire cat. He's wearing a CENSIR. A gold-plated Beretta protrudes from his shoulder holster.

I quickly wipe at my eyes.

"I'm O.J. Double T the first dandelion you . . ." He makes a *tsk*ing noise and slashes a finger across his throat.

"Maybe."

"Don't be shy. We were all quite impressed."

He walks over, still with that grin. From his pants, he pulls a key, which he uses to unlock my handcuffs. He taps my CENSIR. "This stays on. I'm sure you're fine with that."

I nod.

He heads for the exit. "You coming?"

I glance over my shoulder. "What about . . . ?"

"Double T? We'll get somebody in here to clean up that dandelion. Not your problem anymore."

"But . . ."

The grin falters. "You coming or not?"

Coming.

Beyond the thick steel door is an underground highway. Flickering lights run the length of the arched ceiling, illuminating four lanes that extend into darkness in both directions. Doors are recessed into the tunnel walls every couple hundred of feet. Stenciled letters indicate their purpose. Directly across from us is Prayer Center U5-372. The room in which I spent the last several days is Shelter U5-2153.

This is an understate. We took a field trip to a prototype my freshman year, built deep beneath the streets of D.C. A relic. Our guide told us it was the only one in existence, a quarter complete before construction got scrapped.

"Thought there was only U1," I say as O.J. directs me to an armored SUV—military, I think, but painted white and with #1 inscribed all over the hood and doors—idling in the access lane.

"Learn that in your history books?" His voice goes theatrically gruff, his face dramatically stern. "Last defense against the dragons? Worst-case scenario?"

"Something like that."

"Yep. And they wouldn't tell you differently." He pulls onto the road with a smirk. "A devil they don't want you to know."

I give him a questioning look.

He laughs. "It's like when we armed the Afghans against the Russians. That's what my G-Pop said. Yep." He adopts an old-man voice. "'A circle of screw-you gratitude.'"

I glance at him. He's back to the grin, his eyes fixed on the empty road ahead. Fixed, but half glazed, like he's reminiscing. Or batshit. Completely.

Wish I'd brought a ravioli lid with me. Or ten.

We speed past more blast doors with faded markings and numbers on the adjacent walls. *Dragon Shelter U5-2149. Supply Depot U5-371. Mess Hall U5-148* . . . there's nothing to indicate where we are, no signs of Allie anywhere. Or anybody, for that matter.

"Where exactly are we?" I ask.

"Down below."

Double T said something about bombing mountains. "The Rockies?"

"Could be."

A few minutes later, we pass a prayer center with the words *Klyv's Klan* written beside it in hand and a graffiti picture of a cartoonish Green hugging some smiling white-cloaked teenagers. The next prayer center belongs to Praxus's Posse. Praxus looks meaner than Klyv.

O.J. makes a left turn down an access road. The tunnel presses in around us. The flickering decreases, the lighting brightens. *Restricted Zone* is written in large red letters every hundred or so feet.

"You good at anything?" he asks.

"I can shoot."

"That's what all the dandelions say."

I force a smirk, mimic the throat-slashing gesture O.J. made. "I can kill."

He touches his nose, points at me. "Got me there." His grin widens. "We'll see how that works when you're not surfing scales."

We approach a guard station. A metal gate lies crumpled off to the side. White-cloaked soldiers lurk behind sandbags. Half have their machine guns and rocket launchers aimed in the direction we're headed, the rest have them trained on us.

O.J. slows, flashes his lights in a sporadic pattern. The soldiers lower their weapons. He flips them off as we pass.

The tunnel terminates at a pair of blast doors, each as big as a Blue. They appear to be jammed, open wide enough for a couple of people to fit through. A faint green glow comes from the other side. A dozen armored SUVs are haphazardly parked near the opening.

As we get out, a guard emerges from the shadows on our right. Young face. Sane eyes. "This her?"

O.J. nods.

"Thought she was taller."

"Thought she was cuter," another voice calls from the left.

"Where's Double T?" somebody else calls from the darkness.

O.J. inclines his head at me, makes that slashing gesture again. I feel sick. "Ravioli lids. Turned him into jerky."

They offer compliments.

I ignore them and follow O.J. through the blast doors into another tunnel that's clearly been widened by dragons. Broken concrete and shredded mannequins clutter the sides. On a fragment of wall still intact, I discern what appears to be a three-pronged propeller inside a yellow triangle. Up ahead, mixing with the sporadic growls of Greens, I hear something similar to gunfire, but it doesn't sound quite right. More of a soft hiss than a metallic purr.

Around a bend, the tunnel splits in two. A pair of Diocletians guard the one to the left. Behind them, the tunnel narrows to its original size, unrenovated by dragons. I spot more of those yellow signs. These have words beneath. DANGER: RADIOACTIVE MATERIALS.

We go right, toward the Green glow, the growls, and that strange gunfire. The broken walls and broken floor shift to solid stone. I smell something unpleasant, but it's too faint to place. A breeze swirls. Cold, but I refrain from hugging myself, because O.J. keeps glancing at me with that stupid grin.

The tunnel opens into a cavern stockpiled with weaponry and split in two by a gargantuan wall. White and lumpy, as if made of giant interconnected seashells, it's covered in graffiti. The wall stops a few feet short of the ceiling. The green glow emanating from the other side illuminates overhead sprinklers that cast a mist of fine spray in the dragons' direction.

On this side, beyond pallets of machine guns and rocket launchers, two dozen or so teens in white scrubs and bandannas are shooting up mannequins. A spindly man paces back and forth behind them, shouting instructions about breath control and muscle relaxation.

"Welcome to the arena, dandelion." O.J. says, ushering me toward the shooting range.

Their guns resembles pistols, but blockier. With one shot, heads explode, limbs sever. With two, torsos crumble. A conveyor system brings up the next mannequin while the shooter reloads. A digital scoreboard that hangs from the ceiling tallies each kill.

I do a quick survey of faces, but don't recognize anybody

except James. He's near the far end, no longer in his sling. He fires with rhythmic precision, every shot a head shot. His name's at the top of the kill list.

He is a killer, I remind myself.

Just like me.

A couple of people notice our arrival. James glances my way. It's the briefest thing.

But his next shot doesn't hit the head. It doesn't hit the mannequin at all. It pulverizes a chunk of the cave wall behind the conveyor system.

"Cock bait crawls in here, and you skipped right over the rusted rails, pretty boy," the instructor says. "Get your mind right!"

James nods once and resumes decapitating dummies.

"Ready for some fun?" O.J. grabs one of the blocky guns from a pallet and tosses it to me.

It's got two switches. I recognize the safety, but not the bottom one. I eject the clip. The bullets resemble sharpened rectangles. Thin. The clip probably holds forty rounds.

"New scale-chaser joy toy we ransacked in a raid a couple weeks back," O.J. says. "They call it a railshot. Meant to penetrate dragon hide. They come with toxins and stuff you dandelions played with in Georgietown. Our engineers modified it for our purposes." He indicates the switch beneath the safety. "Adds a plasma burst. A miniature chain reaction that liquefies your target from the inside. Only thing it won't melt is the sun."

I start for the nearest open mannequin. O.J. grabs me. "Where you going?"

"To have some fun."

"Shooting stuffed dolls doesn't mean anything. You said you can kill. We'll see." He points toward that seashell wall that separates us from the dragons.

"Are you taking her riding, O.J.?" James asks.

"Back in line, pretty boy," the instructor says.

O.J. holds up a hand, spins around.

Everybody stops shooting, and I'd swear the dragon growls quiet a notch, that the glow in the cavern brightens a couple of notches.

I look over my shoulder. This time James's eyes do linger before shifting to O.J. "You can't do this. She's not ready."

O.J. smiles at him. "You said something, dandelion?"

"She just got out of detox. You can't send her out."

I switch off the safety, wheel around, and blow the head off the mannequin behind him. A couple of people whistle. Others laugh. I grin at James. "I'll do just fine, thank you very much."

He ignores me. "You know I'm right, O.J. Praxus could berserk her if you restore any part of the connection this soon."

JOSHUA McCUNE

"I don't plan on restoring it. I need to know how well she flies."

"You can't be serious. The sky's crawling with DJs."

"Good talk. Get back in the line before I berserk you. Vincent, I expect this from the dragons, but not these little dandelions."

The instructor's features tauten as he gives a curt nod.

He looks at me. "Come on, let's see if you can shoot anything besides dolls."

We head for the seashell wall. Closer, I see it's made of armor plating—a mishmash of destroyed vehicle hulls fused together.

That unpleasant smell intensifies. My nose wrinkles. "Roses?"

O.J. indicates the misters above the wall. "Helps mask our odor. You allergic or something?"

"No. Just don't like them."

"That's unfortunate," he says, like it's not unfortunate at all. "Why do you think we wear white?"

I'd never thought about it before. "Because they wear black."

"Yin and yang, huh? That's how your government sells it."

"Not my government."

He shrugs. "Greens are a feisty bunch. White soothes them."

I imagine a Green basking lazily in a field of white roses and can't help laughing. O.J. looks at me like I'm the crazy one, which gets me laughing more.

We pass a stairwell that drops into a causeway beneath the wall and come to a U-shaped bank of lockers. Each has initials taped to it.

I follow O.J. to a locker marked D.T. It contains a white cloak, body armor, a helmet, some goggles, an oxygen mask attached to a breath pack, several Confederate-flag bandannas, and a perfume bottle.

Affixed to the inside of the door is a palm-sized mirror with the word *You* written in black marker. Pictures cover the rest of the space. They show Double T and his family, their names written on each one. He's the only one smiling in any of them.

O.J. uses a black magic marker to cross out D.T. Beside it he writes *25*.

I grit my teeth and pull out the body armor.

"Not your size," he says as I screw with the buckles, "but we'll get that worked out . . . if necessary."

Too big, the heavy vest digs into my shoulders. "It's fine." The helmet's got a couple of dragon-jet stickers affixed to it. They're scored down the middle. Kill tokens, I assume. I put it on, tighten the straps. Smells like Double T. I think of Allie. *In nae.*

I slide the goggles over my eyes, tug on the white cloak and breath pack, then head for the stairwell. I glance over my shoulder at O.J., who seems slightly bemused. I push out a grin. "You coming?"

"You forgot this," he says, tossing me the perfume bottle.

I sniff it and blanch. But it's better than Double T's scent.

"Don't be shy now," he says.

I douse myself in the rose stench.

We pass under the wall and ascend the stairs at the opposite end of the causeway. "Getting scared, dandelion?"

I ignore him.

This part of the arena is larger. Can't see the ceiling, not even with the glow of four Greens providing generous amounts of light. Each dragon is contained in a cage of forearm-thick steel grating that disappears into the darkness overhead. They prowl close to the bars, snarling and smoking and growling at each other nonstop.

A dragon zoo. Or rodeo, given the harness and saddles mounted on each one. And I'm the cowgirl up next. I take small comfort in the bulky collars that encircle their necks. Similar to the ones the military used on the dragons in the battle room to control their fire and punish them when they got out of line.

"They're your prisoners?" I ask, unable to keep the surprise from my voice.

"God, no. They're ascetics. This is but a means to an end."

A Green in the right front cage spins around and locks in on me. They are indistinguishable save for slight variations in size, but I know this one's Praxus. He opens his mouth wide to roar, but it's choked off almost immediately as veins of lightning erupt from the collar and ripple through his body. Baring his teeth, he half stumbles, half charges us. Out of the corner of my vision, I see O.J. smiling at me. I hold my ground, though I can't help tensing.

Praxus plows into the grating. It bows with his weight. Electricity explodes from his collar, races through him. His glow flickers, and he crashes to the ground.

"I think he likes you," O.J. says. "You didn't answer me. Scared?"

"No."

"What would your CENSIR say?"

"We gonna sit here all day chatting?"

A bioprint scanner controls access to each cage. Digital placards along the top identify the occupants. Praxus appears knocked out. On the other side of the cave, Klyv puffs smoke at me between ululating growls. The two in the back cages stalk back and forth, convicts sizing up their next victim. Or meal.

So much for roses and white—

Somebody touches my shoulder, and I flinch.

"You know what smells worse than anything, dandelion?" O.J. asks, and presses his hand to Praxus's scanner. The cage door swings open. "Fear."

I roll my eyes, squirm free of his touch, and step inside.

He closes the door. The deep echo of metal shoots a shiver through me.

"Alone?" The question's out before I can stop it.

"This is your party. I've decided I halfway like you," he says. "Try not to wilt out there."

"You gonna at least open up communication?"

"We never shut it down," O.J. says. "He just can't shade your brain with dragon love."

"He's not talking to me."

"Greens aren't known for . . . chatting. You should appreciate that."

The insurgents of Loki's Grunts used ladders to mount their dragons. There are no ladders here. Which means I'm gonna have to climb up Praxus. Even lying down, his knees tower over me. Scrabble up his tail? Not sure if dragons are like horses, but coming up on a Green from behind seems ludicrous at best, even if he is comatose. But it's the only option.

I take a deep breath, pictures O.J.'s asshole smirk in my mind, and push forward with zeal.

Then Praxus decides to wake up, and my zeal vanishes.

He lumbers to his feet. The chill in the air is long gone, and the oven's ramping up faster than the Green's glow.

He cranes his head forward until it hovers a foot over mine, growls in a way that evokes memories that made me quiver with ecstasy a few days ago and now remind me how easily he can rip me in half.

Two choices. Give into my fear and hope he doesn't eat me . . . fuck that.

I stand straighter, clench my fists, and glare right back at him. He snorts a cloud of black smoke into my face. My eyes mist. I choke back the coughs, blink the sweat from my eyes, and smile. He bares teeth that make a shark's look playful.

Baekjul boolgool. I open my mouth and roar. It's a mouse squeaking at a lion, but as I'd hoped, this lion tries to roar back. He gets electrocuted into a drunken stumble. I laugh. He ejects more smoke in my face, thicker this time, warmer. Adds in a growl and some teeth gnashing.

I suppress my coughs, chomp back at him. "You gotta do better than that, Praxi."

He flicks me with a talon, and I'm suddenly flying. I smash into the cage wall. The air rushes from my lungs. Black spots swarm my vision. O.J.'s laughter fills my ears, along with dragon trilling.

Once I'm sure I have my balance and breath, I push

myself to my feet and stand tall. Praxus raises a claw so that his scimitarlike talons dangle around my head.

I cross my arms. "All talk, no fire."

More trilling. But it's not from Praxus. He swivels about, glow throbbing, and glares at Klyv. Klyv bobs his head in a wobbly pattern as he stumbles back and forth with pronounced exaggeration. He's mocking him. He stops every few seconds to make that strange trilling noise.

Praxus looses a stream of black smoke at the other dragon, but it comes up a few feet short. Klyv trills louder. Praxus growls a low rumble, spreads his jaws. I see a mass of fire forming in the back of his throat. The moment it reaches his tongue, lightning courses through him. He slumps to the ground but is back on his feet in a blink. This time he pushes the fire out faster, the flames licking out from his lips, before the collar delivers another blast of electricity.

Praxus collapses once more, eyes fluttering shut.

Klyv's trills end. He flaps his wings once, twice, and takes off at a steep angle. Embedded in the stone above each cage is a hatch. Klyv scratches at his, talons shrieking against the metal. The dragons in the rear cages launch themselves at their hatches. Klyv growls at them. They growl back, add in snarls and snaps. The heat in the cavern reaches a full swelter, the light a terrifying shine.

"He wants to play," O.J. says. I peek over my shoulder.

He's got a phone out, which he uses to open the hatch over Klyv's cell. I see the beginnings of an expansive stone chute.

Klyv narrows his wings and zips into it. The other two Greens scream at O.J., who shakes his head. The one on the left attacks its hatch, using its head as a battering ram; the right attempts to unleash its fire on O.J. Both get electrocuted and plummet.

I brace for impact but am still knocked off my feet by the resulting tremor. The gunfire from the other side of the wall quiets as aftershocks ripple through the cavern.

"What in the living name of . . . ," that instructor guy says, bounding up the stairwell. James and the others are a step behind.

"Dragon games," O.J. says, gesturing at Praxus and me as if he's an entertainer introducing the next performance.

James looks from me to Klyv's empty cage. His features slacken. "Get her out of there. Get her out of there!"

"He's been surfing again," the diminutive girl beside James says. She's vampire pale and got a dozen piercings strewn across her face.

"Incorrect. You are all ignorant dandelions." O.J. waves a dismissive hand at me, then glowers at James. "You bring this girl to us, this known friend of the Grunts—"

"So was I," James says. "Her heart glows just like ours."

"Her heart glows Red and Silver. She killed one of our

own," O.J. snarls, and I realize he never intended for me to survive past today.

"You set him up," James says. "You knew Double T was weak."

"And so is she," O.J. says. "Good riddance to both of them!"

James lifts his gun at him. "Let her——"

He spasms, his knees buckle, and he falls to the ground.

"Much appreciated, Vincent," O.J. says to the instructor, who's pulled out his own phone.

"You wanna play cowboy, do it somewhere else," Vincent says, helping James to his feet. He turns to O.J. "I do not approve of this, John. We don't need to lose any more dragons, and we have orders about the girl."

Orders?

"I'm in charge of this operation, Vinnie boy, not you," O.J. snaps, jabbing his phone at the instructor. "They're getting antsy-pantsy in there. Doesn't hurt to let them blow off some steam, so it's not one of us getting their wrath——"

There's a screech overhead from the other side of the hatch that opens into Praxus's cage. My cage.

I backpedal to the corner farthest from Praxus.

"Don't do it, John," Vincent says. "This is——"

O.J. taps his phone. The hatch opens. Klyv plunges through.

Praxus startles to life with surprising speed, jumps out of the way of Klyv's talons, and whips his tail around in a vicious blur. It smashes into the larger Green's chest. Snarl-screaming, Klyv responds with his own tail strike. It misses Praxus, comes my way.

I drop to my stomach. A blast of warm wind tugs at my clothes; a pulse of intense adrenaline focuses me. As the dragons clash midair, all talons and teeth and rage, I low-scuttle it to the opposite side of the cage.

I draw the railshot, flip on the plasma effect, take aim—

A short jolt from my CENSIR staggers me. My hand spasms. The gun clatters to the stone. I start toward it, get another jolt that drops me hard to my knees.

"Desist!" O.J. says.

I crawl for the gun.

Another shock.

I keep crawling.

"Dammit, Vincent, stay out of it," O.J. says. "I will berserk you, you damn dandeli—" He grunts in pain.

I glance back.

O.J.'s doubled over. Vincent's ripped the phone away.

"Stop her!" O.J. bellows. "She could kill your dragon."

As I grab the railshot, half the people watching draw their weapons. Some are pointed at me, but most at each other. Praxus's Posse vs. Klyv's Klan, I assume.

"Stand down," Vincent shouts, but only a couple listen. A dragon screech draws my attention toward the ceiling. Praxus and Klyv are chasing circles, a viridescent whirl of claws and fangs and smoke.

I get to my feet.

"I don't want to kill you, girl!" someone says. I look away from the dragons. A guy with a shaved head has his gun trained on my forehead.

"Stay out of it, Joto," says that pierced vampire girl, her railshot pointed at him.

Joto flicks his gun toward the corner of the cage. "Let them fight it out."

I sneer. "Do whatever you gotta—"

The brightness and heat surge. I jump away from the steel mesh as a dragon crashes into it fifty feet overhead. The sizzle of electricity pulls at my hair.

The dragon falls head over tail. The other one pounces from above, talons and teeth extended. I'm about to become a pancake stain. . . . I grab the railshot and leap into a dive, somersault, roll, roll, roll—

The world thunders behind me; the floor quakes. I lift into the air, fall hard on my side. Pain erupts through my half-healed ribs. My vision tunnels on one Green straddling the other, wings spread, head lifted toward the ceiling, mouth open in a silent roar of victory.

Klyv.

He's forgotten about me.

Perhaps he never knew I was here.

"Stay out of it," James says, from what sounds like a mile away. I hear other voices, arguing, yelling, but it's all a blur of useless noise. Everything's on the periphery except Klyv.

I lift the railshot and roar at him. He cocks his head around halfway. I just get one eye, but that's all I need. For a moment, I am a speck of annoyance to him. In the next, his eye widens with comprehension. And in the next, it implodes in a mess of gore.

With a weak puff of smoke, Klyv tumbles off Praxus and slumps to the ground, his glow fading out.

The cavern goes graveyard silent momentarily, then I hear a couple of seething whispers and somebody's muffled cries.

Praxus stirs with a low grumble. His eyes push open, pass over Klyv, and find me.

That was my fight, human—

A retching noise interrupts him. Praxus jumps into the air as Klyv's body expands . . . and expands . . . as if a bomb went off inside him. With an eruption of bloody vomit, the dead dragon deflates into something withered and mushy.

And the stench. Makes me long for roses.

O.J. rushes into the cage, tears streaming down his

cheeks. He hugs Klyv's nearly unrecognizable head.

I can't help myself. "Told you I could kill."

O.J. wheels on me, his smirk somehow back, though twitchy. "Think you've made yourself a friend, do you? How about we leave you in here all night with your friend?"

I look at Praxus, who's still watching me. No, not my friend. Not sure what we are, but I don't think he knows either, and I consider that a victory. I look back to O.J. "There's worse company to have."

"Think you're a clever dandelion, do you? I'll show you clever, I'll—"

"I don't think so," Vincent says. He and the pale girl grab O.J. from behind. That guy with the shaved head darts me a super-pissed expression as he applies handcuffs.

"What are you doing, Joto?" O.J. says to him. "Klyv was our dragon."

Joto gives me another glare, then looks away. The girl winks at me as she grabs Joto's hand to console him, like she wasn't pointing a gun at him ten seconds ago.

"We checked your CENSIR," Vincent says. "You've been surfing the scales again."

"I'm doing fine. I'm in charge!"

Vincent waves at Klyv's carcass. "That is not fine."

"I wasn't going to let anything happen. It was just a test," he sputters.

"Like you didn't let anything happen to Double T." Vincent grabs O.J. by the scruff of his shirt, jerks him close. "Be lucky I don't report you."

O.J.'s eyes bulge. "No, don't. I'll get right—"

"Get him out of here," Vincent says. "Lock him in with Double T. Should help with his detox."

"What do you want us to tell HQ about Klyv?" she asks Vincent.

"We were running a check on the collar's telemetry control. That's what you'll tell them. But only if they ask. Got it?"

"Oren won't be happy."

"Dammit, T-Clef, just do it. I'll deal with Oren."

As she and that Joto guy drag O.J. from the cage, Vincent looks to me. "You ready?"

"Ready?"

He nods. "We still need to see how you fly."

"What about Praxus?"

With a snort, the dragon gets to his feet. He lowers his wings so that they scrape the ground.

Come, human, you have already wasted enough of my time. Death beckons.

30

Oxygen mask and goggles in place, I scrabble up his wing, hop over a saddlebag, and reach the saddle, a two-rider version. The gunner's seat has a rear-facing tripod mounted with a large-bore machine gun. I climb in the front seat, grab hold of the reins, and thrust my feet into the stirrups, which are farther apart than on a Red. I'm adjusting them back so I've got a better lean into Praxus's neck when he launches.

I buck hard into the cantle; a jolt shoots up my back. His laughter rings through my head. I triple wrap the reins around my hands and tug myself close. As we approach the open hatch, he pulls in his wings and pumps them in rapid bursts. We accelerate into the chimney. Wind blasts my face, stone rushes by; adrenaline shivers through me.

I focus on the green-tinted darkness overhead, take long, controlled breaths. My body stops trembling. I settle into his flap rhythm, learn his tail-swish frequency. I'm just growing comfortable when a ledge appears ahead of us. He doesn't seem to notice it. It's coming fast, will decapitate him. Us.

"Praxus?" I say, my voice muffled by the oxygen mask.

No response.

"Praxus!"

No response.

"Prax—"

He ducks right before impact, laughs as my heart remembers to work.

He jets sideways into a secondary chute, twists into a tight spiral, spins faster and faster. I close my eyes, but too late, the nausea's got me. I bite hard into my lip, clench down hard, but no, no, no . . . I vomit and vomit until I'm empty, and he laughs and laughs and never stops.

More twists and turns and spirals. I keep expecting to erupt into the sky, but there's only stone and darkness. We are a green comet shooting through an asteroid that seems without end.

He corkscrews left, makes a sharp upturn into another tunnel. The stone presses in all around. He dives up and down, barely avoiding outcroppings and jagged edges. He hits a stalactite with his tail. It explodes; a cascade of thunder escorts us forward. The only thing louder is his laughter.

I duck and swerve with him, huddle close. But I do not call his name again, I do not close my eyes, though my stomach begs me to. And I do not scream, because I know that's what he wants most. My body may fail me, but I will not give him my terror.

To distract myself, I start humming. The only thing I can think of . . . something I know far too well. I don't know if Praxus knows it, but it seems to annoy him, because his laughter ends.

Stop it.

I ignore him.

He barrel rolls three times. Once I finish retching, I resume humming.

"Are you delusional?" The voice in my head startles me into silence.

"James? How? How are you . . . can you . . ."

"If you want to talk to me, you have to say 'Radio on,'" he says over me. "These CENSIRs have built-in transceivers."

I resume humming.

"The *KD* theme song? Seriously?"

"Radio on. Is there a way to turn you off?" I ask.

Praxus enters a cavern littered with stalagmite and stalactite remnants. He changes course, sweeps along the perimeter toward a pair of intact stalactites that hang like vampire's teeth. He smashes through them. Pebbles bounce off my goggles, pelt my oxygen mask. One slashes my forehead. Stings like hell.

I bite hard into my lip, start humming again.

"Know the difference between bravery and stupidity?" James asks.

I keep humming.

"You don't need to impress anybody, Melissa. You just need to survive."

Yeah. "Well, you're distracting me. So get off my line so I can concentrate. Radio off."

Praxus shoots into another tunnel that banks into an angled ascent. I hum louder, so loud I can hear my echo through the rush of wind and the rumble of clattering stone.

Ahead, the tunnel becomes a wall. Praxus accelerates. Ramming speed.

He opens his mouth and roars. Flames burst forth. Not red, but that strange azure color. The fire blasts the rock, turning it bright orange.

We plow into the melting stone. Plow through it. Rock churns around us. Debris bombards me, warm and angry. Pain slices my arms, my face.

And then we are out, into a world so open and wide. I push the goggles onto my head for a better view. Stars glimmer, the moon shines. The shadows of frosted mountains surround us. Everything seems so pristine. Except for us. I stop humming. Praxus roars once more, plaintive almost, then goes quiet and damps his glow.

I do not like you, he says as he maneuvers into a calm glide. *But at least now your scent is manageable.*

I pull off my oxygen mask. The roses are gone, replaced by the odor of earth and char. I agree. A marked improvement.

My face and arms bristle with each gust of wintry wind, but there doesn't seem to be much blood. My jacket's torn in several places, my cloak's perforated and singed, but besides an array of scrapes and bruises, I'm all right.

We drop to the valley floor. Praxus's glow reveals a wasteland of craters, broken evergreens, and exploded stone. We skim low toward a wooded area untouched by war. He opens fire.

The flames dwindle. Deer are bolting in every direction. Praxus smashes through trees in chase. I get a few more scratches from stray twigs, a mouthful of pine needles. In a matter of seconds, he's got four bucks gathered up, one cradled in each claw. He dumps his kills on the ground, lands beside them.

Off.

I unloop the rope twined about the saddle horn and use it to rappel down his body. I want to stay close for the warmth of his scales, but the sounds of his feasting call up a jumble of memories. I plod through ankle-high snow into a copse, lean against a tree, and close my eyes. The sounds of sinew rending and bones crunching come and go. So do the dragon sirens and car horns and screams.

Not real. Too real.

"Radio on. James?" I say.

"Yeah," he responds right away.

I smile before catching myself. I don't know if he's looking at my CENSIR feedback, but I can't let him see that he affects me. "Just checking to see if you were still there."

"You okay?"

"Fine."

"They're okay," he says.

"Huh?"

"Colin and Preston."

Keith? "Oh."

"Thought you'd like to know."

"Sure."

"I'm not monitoring you," he says.

I want to believe him. "Did I pass the flying test?"

"You survived," he says. Sounds like he's smiling. "Still have to make it back, of course, but now that Praxus has some food in his—"

"How do you know that? Thought you said you weren't monitoring . . ."

"There's a camera in his collar." He pauses. "You know, I don't remember you being this crazy."

"Yeah, people—"

I gasp as snow splatters me. A hunk of deer leg is wedged in the ground a few feet away. Through the trees, I see Praxus watching me.

"Is that what I think it is?" James laughs. "Must like you."

"Yeah. Tons." I blanch at the raw meat. An olive branch? A test?

"You don't have to . . ."

"You can go now, James."

I grab the hoof and rotate the leg. Blood stains the snow. Praxus continues to stare at me. I spin it three more times before settling on a section with minimal gristle and fur. I lay it down, circle it again and again, act like I'm examining it for the choicest cut.

Praxus blows smoke at me.

I glare at him. "I am not a heathen."

But I can't delay any longer. I get on my knees, place my hands on the leg as if it's a giant piece of corn. Blood and grime slick my fingers. I bend over, press my face close.

I glance up at Praxus and smile in contempt.

I open as wide as I can and bite in. A rush of liquid fills my mouth. I swallow it, force my gag into a snarl. I throw my head back violently, rip a hunk loose.

"Melissa, dragon jets incoming," James says. "Get the hell out of there."

I figure he's trying to save me some grief, but then Praxus unleashes a tremendous roar. A full-throated "I ain't getting the hell out of anywhere" sort of thing. By the time I remember I've got raw deer in my mouth, he's scooped me up and dumped me on his back. I spit it out as we blast off.

I thought he was a streak of speed before. It's nothing compared to this. Up and up and up we go.

"There's a squadron on your six, still several miles out, but closing fast. You need to get out of there!"

I look around. Can't see much of anything. The higher and higher we go, the darker and darker it becomes. I strain to listen but only hear the howl of wind and the roar of a dragon. It's all getting farther away.

"What . . . what . . . are . . . we doing?" I ask.

Where are the invisible monsters, human? Praxus demands as James says, "You're taking the high ground."

"High ground? Monsters?" Doesn't make sense. "They . . . they can see . . ."

Where are they, human?

"Who?" I mumble.

"Melissa, do you have . . ."

If he says something else, I don't hear it. The moon's

disappeared. The moon's disappeared!

"It's gone! It's gone!" I try to scream, but my throat's blocked and the words can't escape. The stars are winking out, too. The whistling wind and roaring dragon go silent. My grip on the reins loosens. I slump backward, my feet catching in the stirrups. My head lolls back, and I stare into blackness.

No moon, no stars. Only blackness. Everywhere.

"Put on your oxygen mask!" somebody whispers in my brain.

Oxygen! I need oxygen. I take a deep breath. Pain stabs my lungs. The next breath is worse.

"Put on your oxygen mask!"

I fumble at my neck, find the mask, but can't seem to get ahold of it. My eyelids grow heavy. Everything's heavy. But still. Feels like I'm floating. Pinpricks of light dance through my vision. So pretty. I smile. This will be a good sleep. No nightmares . . .

A city on fire. Scorched bodies everywhere. We descend between buildings after a herd of fleeing cowards. We ignite them. Excitement tingles through us.

Then it's gone. The world's black again, turbulent.

You are better now. Tell me where they are, human, or I will dump you off my back.

"Put on your oxygen mask!"

The voices don't sound so far away, my fingers aren't so clumsy. I slip the mask into place.

"Slow breaths," James says as Praxus continues to threaten me.

The moon returns, followed by the stars. I lean into Praxus, grasp the reins, and get my bearings. We're in hover mode, perched above a cloud bank. I peer through the gaps, see only the jagged outlines of mountain peaks.

I remember my goggles, push them down over my eyes, switch them to infrared. Everything tints greener than it already is. Dragon jets are flying at us from the horizon.

I tense. Every instinct tells me to flee. But I can't. I can't be afraid. For the Diocletians to ever accept me, for any hope of rescuing Allie, I must be Green. I bite hard into my lip, tighten my grip on the reins, imagine these pilots were in Georgetown. The rage swells, the fear fades.

"Eighteen, coming in hard from your left, right above that three-pronged mountain," I tell Praxus. He whirls toward our enemy.

Tell James Everett to unleash my collar. My fire burns hot in my throat, and he is not listening to me.

"You turned off his fire?" I say.

"You need to get out of there." He pauses. "We can't afford to lose another dragon."

"Open his fire, and open our connection."

"No. You don't have the weaponry. He could berserk you."

"You opened it a second ago, didn't you?"

"You were dying!"

"I'm gonna die real soon if you don't open it again."

"That was a quick hit. I won't . . . we can't . . . dammit, Melissa, we can't afford to lose another dragon."

A dozen missiles launch, screech toward us. Heat seekers.

Death comes, Praxus says, and looses another sky-trembling roar. I sit up straight, draw my railshot, and join in.

"Dammit, Melissa. . . ."

Everything slows, everything brightens. The missiles, the jets, even the bullets. We can see them. Individual pellets of rain that somehow shine against the black backdrop of night. Our heart thumps a slow rhythm as we plunge through the clouds to intercept, to attack, to kill.

I destroy the missiles with the railshot. He takes out the jets with fire that starts off orange in the back of his throat and turns azure as a spray of liquid from his collar joins the flame just beyond his lips. Explosions warm the sky, their incessant vibrations pushing us into new attack trajectories.

There is no communication between us. He sees what I see and I see what he sees and we are one. We twirl and loop and roll, and they die and die and die.

Bullets slice through our wings, lodge in our scales. Pain

slashes through us, but if anything, it excites us. We roar and scream and take vengeance on the nearest target.

And soon enough, the roaring invisible monsters and their roaring invisible missiles are gone, and the only roars belong to us.

We are invincible. We are alive.

In a blink, the world darkens, my heartbeat accelerates, the cold returns.

"Are you okay, Melissa?" James sounds hesitant.

"Fine."

"What's my name, Melissa?"

"What?"

"What's my name, Melissa?"

"Why?"

"I need to know you're with me, Melissa."

Columns of fire plume from the darkness below, funeral pyres for our enemies. I shudder. I remember killing them, I remember reveling in our victories, in their deaths, but it seems an eternity ago.

"James. Your name is James. Are you satisfied, *James*?"

"Yes," he says, and I don't need access to his CENSIR to know he's lying. "You're sure you're okay?"

"A little cold," I say. Praxus burns hot beneath me, but there doesn't seem to be enough warmth in the world to overcome the chill that's settled in me.

31

When we return to the cage, Praxus gets shouts of adulation as a team of medics sets to work on his injuries with bullet forceps, morphine sprayers, and bandage rolls the size of hay bales. When I dismount, I get a CENSIR shock that drives me to my knees. Vincent applies a pair of handcuffs.

James lifts me to my feet, gently pulls down my oxygen mask. "What's my name, Melissa?"

"Again?"

Vincent strips me of my railshot. "Answer the question."

"James," I say as if it's an epithet. "And you're Vincent."

The towering instructor shows me his phone, which has a picture of my father in his army dress blues. It's the publicity photo from when he led the research team that discovered dragons can't see black.

"Who is this?"

"My father, before he was paralyzed in Mason-Kline."

Vincent scrolls back to his gallery—a folder labeled *Melissa Callahan*—and loads that picture of Mom, Keith, James and his parents, and Oren at Shadow Mountain Lookout. I identify everybody I know before he can ask. I point at James's parents. "I don't know their names."

"Michael and Dianne." James shakes his head at Vincent. "She didn't know."

We go through a few more pictures. Sam, Uncle T, Aunt Susan. "Are we done? I'm not . . ." What was the term? "Surfing the scales."

"How are you feeling?" James asks.

"Brilliant."

James flinches. "Brilliant, huh? Was that intentional?"

"Yes."

"Who said it?"

I can't help rolling my eyes. "Hector the director." Brilliant. Everything was goddamn brilliant, particularly if it involved slaying a dragon.

James's look of concern turns to one of puzzlement. "She might be okay."

"Maybe. T-Clef, Grizzly B." Vincent waves over that pale girl with all those piercings and a skinny guy whose arms are cloaked in tribal dragon tattoos. Vincent looks to

James. "You're dismissed."

"I'm sorry. *In nae*," James whispers, and steps away to join the other bystanders.

Vincent says something I don't hear because I'm looking at James, wondering what he meant by that. But his expression's back to guarded. Then I hear Vincent say something about sending me back to detox, and my attention snaps to him.

"I'm okay. I don't have the itch."

"Everybody says that."

"Look at my CENSIR. I'm fine."

"We keep her in cuffs, and we can handle this chica blindfolded," the girl says. "Come on, Vince. Pretty sad state of affairs if we can't." She hooks her arm through mine, gives this exaggerated smile, like we're besties about to go on a merry stroll. The skinny boy takes my other arm, though his smile's not quite so big.

Vincent grumbles something beneath his breath, checks his phone. "All right. Get her fed and cleaned up. Any misstep . . ."

"I got it," the girl says. She looks at me, winks. "I can tell she and me are gonna be one good we. Ain't that right, Missy C?" She seems very pleased with her rhyme.

I nod.

"I'm T-Clef," she says. "That's Grizzly B. Try to

remember our names. You'll probably be quizzed later." She laughs, but I know she's not kidding.

She introduces the rest of the Diocletians in the cage, Praxus's other riders. I hear a couple of murmured congratulations, get a couple of nods of respect, but most everybody keeps their distance.

"I'm really okay," I say as she and Grizzly B escort me into the causeway that runs beneath the wall. "You can let go."

T-Clef grins. "We could."

"But we won't," Grizzly B says. His voice is surprisingly gruff.

"You just got out of detox," she says. "Reconnecting you to Praxus so soon should have thrown you back down the rabbit hole. Yeah, you seem fine, but . . ."

"Unless . . . ," he says. He and the girl exchange a look.

"Prax? You think?"

He shakes his head. "You're right. Not Praxus."

"Unless what?" I demand.

"It's a possible explanation," T-Clef says to him.

"Maybe Everett didn't throttle the connection very much. Maybe Praxus didn't have enough time."

"Maybe. But they took out an entire squadron of DJs. And you know Prax doesn't need but a split second. You've been there. . . . Probably temporary lucidity."

"Or she's playing us. Didn't Everett say he figured out how to beat the CENSIR in Georgetown?"

Beat the CENSIR? "What are you talking about?"

T-Clef and Grizzly B keep talking over me.

"Yeah. Perhaps Prax connects with her differently," T-Clef says.

"Which makes her unpredictable," he says, and tightens his grip on me.

I stop walking. "What do you mean James beat the CENSIR in Georgetown?"

"Don't worry about it," Grizzly B says.

I glare at him. "I'm not worried."

"Too many variables, Missy C," T-Clef says. "Ride the wave until things calm down."

I want to scream. "There is no wave."

"Yeah, but seeing is believing, and we need to see a little more, you know what I mean? Don't worry, this is standard operating procedure." She drops to a whisper, as if we're not the only people on this side of the wall. "In fact, you're getting it special 'cause we like you. So come on now, let's play nice."

They tug me forward, keep talking as if I'm not there, conjecturing how I may or may not be under Praxus's spell, while I keep thinking about what they said about James and beating the CENSIR.

He was so cruel to me in Georgetown, but only when the CENSIR was on. When they allowed him to take it off for our *Kissing Dragons* scenes, he acted like he cared about me, acted really well. Said things and did things that weren't in the script that made me think he actually did care. Then they put the CENSIR back on him, and I was a glowheart dirt stain again.

After we escaped, he didn't talk to me in any substantial way except once, to apologize for the way he treated me. Head down, unable to look at me. Sincere and remorseful, or at least he acted it.

But why? Why would he have faked all that cruelty?

The only answer I can think of is—to earn our captors' trust. By proving that he hated me, he proved his loyalty to them, and thus earned time off from his CENSIR, which would have allowed him to communicate with other dragons.

Maybe Keith and Loki's Grunts didn't find Georgetown because of the tracker in my arm. Maybe James told them where it was. Maybe *Kissing Dragons* was reality, and everything else he did while we were there was the lie.

Maybe, maybe, maybe.

And what about now? Who is he now? I shake my head. Doesn't matter. He doesn't matter. I repeat this to myself as we wend our way back through the tunnels to the parking lot of SUVs.

The same guard from before greets us at the blast doors. "She already fritz out?"

"We'll see," T-Clef says. "But she's a pretty sick flier. She and Prax took out an entire squadron."

"I'd keep that on the down low. Joto's major pissed."

T-Clef laughs. "Doesn't take much. I'm surprised he's not here looking to get his ass kicked."

"HQ sent their team down south on a supply run."

As they continue chatting, I envision myself stealing an SUV and some of those railshots. Sneak into Oren's headquarters, rescue Allie, and make it home before dinner. Piece of pie. I snort.

The guard tenses, T-Clef gives me a worried glance. Grizzly B tightens his grip on me.

"I'm fine," I say, but nobody believes me.

We move on. I want to ask them about HQ, but don't want to draw suspicion, so I go with something innocuous. "The guards, they're not talkers?"

"No." T-Clef taps her CENSIR. "The Tatankaville talkers all have to wear tiaras."

Grizzly B notices my confusion, grins. "T and her nicknames. My real name's Bryan. Guess how many people know that?" He makes a zero with his hand. "Lucky I've got it printed on my locker. Otherwise I might not know it."

She waves her free hand toward the ceiling. "Sure, let's

call our cell G4N6C4. Rolls right off the tongue."

"It's G4N8C4," Grizzly says.

"Whatever. Tatankaville sounds much better."

"Because of the Colorado Buffaloes," Grizzly explains. I shrug. He shrugs back. "Yeah, I hadn't heard of them either. Used to be a college or something."

"And tatanka is the Sioux word for buffalo," T-Clef says with a proud smile. The smile vanishes faster than it came. "The people before us. You think the dragons'll remember us when we're gone?"

"Nobody'll forget you, my dear," Grizzly says.

They load me into an SUV. T-Clef drives. Grizzly sits in back with me.

"Windows down, volume up," she says, back to perky. She opens the windows, turns on the radio. She shuffles through her MP3 player, loads up a bass-pounding rock anthem that sounds like something Colin would like. I want to ask her to change it to something else but refrain.

She peels out and floors it. Shaking her head from side to side, wind whipping her hair across her face, T-Clef sings along. Grizzly B air drums it every which way and accompanies the deep-throated baseline. "Pow, pow, pow, pow, pow."

The walls zoom past, the vehicle trembles beneath us. One slight twitch of the wheel, and the bass line will end with a tremendous crash. I welcome the adrenaline that surges through me, distracts me from thought.

We pass the guard post and soon arrive at the main tunnel. After a stop at an infirmary so I can get my scrapes treated and an injection of morphine, we drive to the prayer center for Praxus's Posse.

"That's not cool," Grizzly B says as we exit the SUV.

The graffiti picture beside the prayer center's entrance shows a hulking Green, smoke rising from its nostrils, wings spread around a cluster of cartoon teenagers brandishing weapons and sneers. The guy with the Confederate-flag bandanna has a streak of red along his neck to mimic a throat slash. Closer, I see it's ravioli sauce.

"I bet it was Joto," T-Clef hisses, rubbing away the sauce with her hand. She looks at me. "It's really gonna steam his vegetables when we put you up there."

"Isn't he your friend?" I ask.

Grizzly B chuckles. "They're practically married."

"He's your boyfriend?" I look at her askance. "I thought you were ready to shoot him."

"Gotta keep his macho ass in check," she says. "We need more strong chicas in this joint. After Evie—"

"Evelyn?"

"Ah, that's right. Georgetown," T-Clef says. "Don't get me wrong, the girl's a real two-faced bitch, but she knew how to turn the screws."

"Did she ever," Grizzly B says.

"She dead?" I ask, trying my best to keep the hope from my voice.

T-Clef's smile says my best wasn't enough. "Nah. She got reassigned a few weeks back. Technically, it was a promotion. She's good with the Greenies. Crazy good. Has that rage." She looks at me, laughs. "You Georgetownians."

"Of course, the real reason is there was a little too much drama in Tatankaville," Grizzly B says, pointing at the caricature of James on the other side of the graffiti picture.

T-Clef winks at me. "He's all yours."

I want to tell her it's not like that—because it can't be like that—but it helps my cover, so I play coy. "We'll see."

We enter the prayer center. A couple of crank lamps illuminate a room intended to accommodate maybe two dozen worshippers. On the stage, beyond the pulpit, there's an upright piano.

"You play, right?" T-Clef asks as we skirt the stage.

"Played," I say. James must have told her that.

"Why'd you stop?"

"Lost interest." Mom died. How much had she told James about me in all those years she spent as the clandestine leader of Loki's Grunts? What else does he know?

"Shame. She's got the fingers for it," Grizzly B says.

Not quite as long as Mom's. Not when I quit.

They take me through a door in the back into a narrow hallway. Hung among the crosses, portraits of Bible characters, and scripture quotes are various score sheets. Stationary Marksmanship, Airborne Marksmanship, Speed and Agility . . . according to the date on the header of each, I've been here almost three weeks. I was in detox longer than I realized.

"We update them weekly," Grizzly B says, "except for this one." He jabs a finger at the last sheet. Kills. "This one's cumulative."

T-Clef writes *Missy C* at the bottom, right beneath *Double T.* "How many jets you take out?"

"Eighteen," I say as I scan the names on the list. *Jimmy E* is at the top of the list, with two hundred eighty-three kills. How many of those were from Loki's Grunts?

She puts *19* by my name. "Klyv counts, I'd say."

At the end of the hall is a conference room or something that's been converted into a barracks with a dozen cots, three folding tables, and four industrial shelves—one with games, one with books, and the last two stockpiled with ravioli.

T-Clef retrieves a roll of paper towels and three cans. She uncaps one, tosses the lid into a trash can, and gives it to me. "Not that we don't trust you."

"But we don't trust you," Grizzly B says with a grin.

"Never heard of anybody going dragon on somebody with ravioli lids before."

"Yeah." I set the can on the table. "I'm not hungry."

T-Clef scoops out a clump of sauce-encrusted ravioli and shoves it in her mouth. "Don't sweat it, Missy C, we've all been there. I tried to take out Joto's eyes with my fingers. Bastard was laughing at me the entire time. Like he wanted me to do it."

Grizzly B bows his head. "I attacked the walls. I was not very focused."

"Still aren't," T-Clef says.

They laugh.

I decide I like them, and I think they really do like me, so I take a chance. "Why do you think they sent Klyv's team down south?" Grizzly B stops midbite, his eyes narrowing with suspicion. I quickly add, "Because of me?"

T-Clef shrugs.

"It's not actually down south, like in Texas or something," Grizzly B says. "It could be east or west. Sometimes they go up north, might end up in the same place."

"It's not meant to be a mystery," T-Clef says, shooting him a look. "You know how we work, right?"

I shake my head.

"On a need-to-know basis," Grizzly B says.

T-Clef nods. "And the only things we need to know

are how to shoot and ride. We don't have thinscreens or sat radios or cell phones, we don't get updates about what's going on topside. We don't know what we're supposed to do next until HQ tells us."

Which means they don't know where HQ is, where Allie is. "Doesn't that frustrate you?"

"You get used to it. It's better that way. No point in worrying about things you can't change. Only clouds your brain," Grizzly B says.

"And we get enough clouding as it is," T-Clef says, tapping her CENSIR.

They laugh again.

T-Clef's face hardens. "Seriously, though, Missy C, questions are dangerous things." Back to perky and singing. "Ours is not to reason why . . ."

Grizzly B joins her for the last part. "Ours is just to fly and die."

32

Someone's playing the piano. I know the song. "Over the Rainbow." At first I thought it was a nightmare.

The piano stops momentarily, starts again. The same song.

I get up from my cot, wrap the blanket around my shoulders. Most everybody else appears asleep, though a quartet of boys is playing cards at the table near the entrance. In the crank lamp's light, I see Grizzly B bobbing his head.

I skulk forward, hear him humming along to the music.

"Yeah, yeah, yeah." The fat one rolls his eyes. "Wake up from your clouds and play your cards, G."

Grizzly B stops humming and shows his hand. "How 'bout them lemon drops?" He scoops the pile of tokens scattered at the table center into his stash.

Fattie notices me. He stands and blocks my escape. "Where you sneaking off to, Missy C?"

"Just need some fresh air."

"Fresh air. Good one." Cowboy and Skinny laugh; Grizzly B resumes humming and bobbing.

I shrug. "What's with the midnight music?"

Fattie hooks a thumb at Grizzly. "That's a generous way to put it."

"The piano," I clarify.

"Piano? Do you hear a piano, guys?"

Cowboy and Skinny stare blankly at me.

Fattie cocks his head. "You feeling that itch, Missy C?"

"Over the Rainbow" starts over.

"Stop messing with her," Grizzly B says. He looks at me. "It's a nightly ritual."

I frown. "They ever play anything else?"

Fattie snorts. "Feel free to put in a request if you don't like it."

"For all the good it'll do," Skinny says.

They laugh.

I start for the door, but Fattie sidesteps with me. "You want in, Missy C?" He indicates the table.

"I'm good, thanks. Now, if you'll excuse me . . ."

He doesn't budge. "You in Praxus land?"

I don't answer.

He grabs my wrist. "What's my name, Missy C?"

"I can't remember." It's true, but not for the reason he wants it to be.

"I don't think she is," Grizzly B says, eyebrows pinched together.

I prefer Fattie's leers over his scrutiny. I drop my voice low so only Fattie hears. "If you don't want me to hurt you in front of your friends, I'd sit back down."

"Brave words for somebody in cuffs," he whispers, but releases me. "Better sleep with one eye open tonight, boys," he says with a chuckle, and turns his shoulder for me to pass. "Wouldn't venture too far, Missy C. Not everybody's as understanding as we are."

He slaps my ass. It takes all my control not to whirl and knee him in the groin, but I can't afford any more enemies at the moment. I look at my feet and head for the chapel, the only way out of here.

The piano player starts over.

Rainbows and magic, dreams and lies.

As I round the corner, the piano goes silent. As I open the door that leads into the chapel, it awakens again. The same damn song, sad, happy, and beautiful all at once. And horrible. Above all, horrible.

James sits in the second of three rows, head bowed onto the back of the front pew. T-Clef's on the piano. Eyes closed, fingers caressing the keys, head swaying with the music, a small smile on her lips.

Neither of them seems to have noticed me. I skirt the edge, tiptoeing along the carpet. Come to a sudden stop when I hear James. He's singing. Not very loud. And not very well. But earnest. It almost sounds like he's crying.

I listen to him for an entire verse before it's too much. I take a step. The floorboard betrays me with a sharp creak. His head jerks up, and he's staring at me. For a second there is a rainbow in his eyes, and then the clouds return.

He rises, raises his hands in a defensive position.

"I wasn't sneaking up on you," I say.

He advances on me slowly. "What's my name, Melissa?"

I give it to him.

He looks at me, into me. "I'm sorry."

I shrug, my heartbeat accelerates. "About what?"

He nods toward the piano. "It helps calm the dragons."

"Oh."

"They'd never admit it, but they're scared."

"Why this song?" I ask.

"Because it has hope, because it promises a better tomorrow."

"You only believe that if you're a foolish bluebird." Or a foolish girl. My vision starts to blur. I look away from him. "Other songs are better for . . . hope."

"Maybe, but I know this song."

"Did my mother sing it to you?" I ask, unable to keep the bitterness from my voice.

He nods. "When I was younger. When my parents were away on missions and I was scared."

When she should have been home with me, when *I* was scared.

"It's my song. Not yours," I mutter. It was the first thing she taught me. I'd play it and she'd sing it. And even when she wasn't there, I could play. And the world was right.

And then the world wasn't. And there's no goddamn song in the universe to unbreak the broken.

"I gotta go."

He reaches for me. "I'll come with you."

I pull free. "Alone. I'm fine. Please, James."

I leave. He doesn't follow. The music does. There are three SUVs parked outside the prayer center. Each has a thumbprint scanner on the driver's door. Each rejects me. I bang hard on the window of the last one, but it's bulletproof or something, and now my hand hurts. And I'm crying and the goddamn music won't stop.

I run. Straight down the middle of the highway, as fast as I can. The music is faster. I lose my strength. I look around. I don't know where I am. Everything looks the same. Faded signs indicate a dragon shelter on my left, a supply depot on my right, another prayer center up ahead. The understate continues both ways into dark loneliness.

The supply depot's unlocked. Handcuffed, it takes me a good minute to crank up the lamp on the entryway table. Through a film of dust particles, I see row upon row of mostly empty shelves. Nothing useful. I slide over the pharmacy counter.

In the back I find some long-expired NyQuil. I down it in several gulps. I slump down, open a second bottle, close my eyes. I drink. And I sing. And I drink. And I sing.

And that's how James finds me. Slouched against the wall, caroling about bluebirds on rainbow dragon highways. T-Clef's with him.

"You're James, and you're T-Clef." I grin. "See, I know your names, but can you answer me this? Why aren't there any yellow dragons? Why didn't Blues fly?"

"It's going to be okay," James says as he scoops me up.

I laugh. "Liar."

He carries me to an SUV. T-Clef climbs in back with me, hums a lullaby as I lie on her lap. She cleans the tears from my face, then sits me up.

"Hold still now, and I'm sorry in advance." She grabs my hands, pulls them to her cheeks so that my fingernails dig into her skin. Before I can stop her, she drags them down her face, leaving bloody scratch marks. Then she slaps me hard.

I fall back against the door, feel a wave of nausea. She steadies me. "You okay?"

"What the hell?"

"We needed to make this presentable," she says. "I'm sorry."

James looks over his shoulder at me, grimaces. "It's best that the others think you had a detox relapse."

I get it. They'll leave me alone if they think I'm a ravioli-lid, might-go-dragon-on-you psycho, and not some weak girl who breaks down when she hears somebody playing a piano. I look at T-Clef, who's smiling at me even as blood trickles down her cheeks. "Thank you."

She winks. "Just don't make it a habit."

We drive back to the prayer center. James picks me up, then sets me on my feet outside the door. He and T-Clef grab me by the elbows. She presses a railshot to my ribs.

"If you could snarl a bit, that would help," T-Clef says.

"Think about what they did to your mother," James whispers in my ear.

It's the best thing to say, and the worst. Inside, the piano sits empty, but the song plays on.

33

An alarm clock's chirping at me. For a moment, I think I've suffered the most horrific nightmare, but then I hear the grumbling and groans. I open my eyes. Insurgents are crawling out of their cots.

T-Clef stumbles past me and smacks the alarm.

"What's my name, bitch?" she says, loud enough for everybody to hear. I hiss it at her. She jerks me up, jams the railshot into my ribs. I grimace out a growl. She keeps me at arm's length, marches me to a table. I get some mumbled catcalls and sidelong leers, but everybody keeps a safe distance.

She feeds me by tossing ravioli at my face, saying things like "This is how you feed crazy bitches" and "Does bitch want more?" She scowls at me throughout, and I try to focus on the scratches on her cheeks, but by the fifth time she's smacked me in the face with cold noodles, I'm half ready to really kill her.

When the can's empty, she gives me a slight nod, then hurls it at my face. I duck just in time.

"Come on, we're already running late, guys," Grizzly B says from the doorway. The few bystanders who stuck around to witness my humiliation and offer up their own taunts funnel out of the room.

"I'll be there in a little bit," T-Clef calls after them. "Gotta give her dessert."

Grizzly B gives me a thumbs-up and sprints off.

T-Clef cleans my face with a wet rag. "How you doing?"

"Where's James?"

"Said he had to do something. Think he didn't want to be here for this."

"How much longer we have to do this?"

"Usually it's a couple of days."

I glance at her. "You've done this before?"

"Lots. Though never pretend before. It's kind of fun, isn't it?" She retrieves a makeup bag from under her bed.

"What's that for?"

"I'm gonna rough you up some." She clenches a fist, fakes punching me, grins. "I've got a reputation to uphold."

I spend the rest of the morning handcuffed to a chair in the arena, watching everybody else blow up mannequins.

Mostly watching James. He leads the scoreboard. Others joke and laugh and kill efficiently, but he's stoic and focused and kills ruthlessly.

He's always seemed so confident, so sure of right and wrong. Real or not real? Maybe he's wearing a mask, too.

Wear it long enough, and is that who you become?

Who have I become?

It's been almost six weeks since I lost Allie, and I'm no closer to finding her. In the meantime, I've managed to make life worse for everybody I know. I can only imagine what the mask I wear resembles. Bloodied and battered and scarred with savagery. I don't know if I'll ever be able to take it off.

I break my promise and try contacting Grackel to see if she's heard anything from Allie, if she knows anything about Colin, but I don't get a response. The CENSIRs can be set to limit communication to specific dragons, so maybe I can only talk with Praxus.

I'm trying to reach her again when Vincent comes over for his periodic checkup on me. "What's my name?"

I give it to him. He scrolls through pictures on his phone. I give him those names. He checks my CENSIR readout, pats me on the shoulder, and resumes instructing the others on proper killing technique. In a few more minutes, he'll return to my chair and ask me the same questions.

What is my name? Who am I? Melissa Callahan,

Twenty-Five, Diocletian, Murderer?

At the end of the dummy decapitation session, Vincent orders everybody to gear up for dragon dashes. Cheers echo through the cavern as they hurry toward the lockers to change. Even James smiles. It fades when he glances at me. I give him my best fake smile, fine as fuck, but he's already moved on.

"You can hide who you are from them," Vincent says, pulling my attention from James.

The bald instructor towers over me, his eyes dark and unreadable. "But you can't hide the truth from the CENSIR."

I laugh at the irony. I wish the CENSIR would tell me my truth.

He frowns. "It's normal to come off the high and experience emotional reflux. It's not easy, what we do."

I look at him. He was playing along with my detox story for everybody else. He knows I'm not under Praxus's influence.

"I'm fine," I say, because that's the only choice.

"'Black care rarely sits behind a rider whose pace is fast enough,'" he says, removing my cuffs. "Luckily, we've got dragons."

The other riders are finishing gearing up when Vincent and I reach the lockers. He instructs me to wait with him until they've vacated the area. "You're dangerous," he says.

"At least for a few more days."

After everybody's disappeared into the stairwell beneath the wall, I'm allowed to change. The label on my locker now says *Melissa* in somewhat ugly handwriting. Inside, the pictures of Double T and his family have been removed. So have the Confederate-flag bandannas. The body armor's smaller; so is the helmet. The scored dragon-jet stickers on it look new. I don't count, but I suspect there are eighteen.

Inside the helmet, I find a package of earplugs with a sticky note taped to them in that same ugly handwriting as my name. *To help with the outside noise.*

"Go!" Vincent shouts.

Praxus launches toward his hatch with an earsplitting roar. In the other cages, Bakul and Erlik roar toward their hatches. Soon we're in our chute, swerving around, ducking under, and smashing through outcroppings. We zig and zag through tunnel after tunnel, sometimes shooting up, sometimes jetting down. Half the time my stomach's in my throat or feet, and the other half I'm too busy holding on to make sense of up or down at all.

Yet when we exit from our tunnel into the mammoth cavern that signals the halfway point of the racecourse, we're in last place. The other two dragons and their riders are already looping back toward their respective tunnels. Praxus banks hard right on an intercept path with Erlik. The smaller Green turns its head to growl at us, but stays on its line.

I yank on the reins, yell at Praxus to get back on course, but he doesn't listen. I use the command Vincent taught me before I boarded Praxus for my dragon dash. "Shock, pulse level one!"

Tendrils of lightning shoot from the collar around his neck. Praxus spasms, his glow flickers, but he's a stubborn bastard.

"Shock, pulse level two!"

He spasms harder, his wings hiccup, and we crash to the cavern floor.

You are craven, human. I should eat your bones.

"Bring it, Praxi, or stop wasting my time. We're losing."

Death is the only competition.

No wonder he's come in last in the five races before mine, by a good margin.

He sprinted all the way here just in hopes of fighting Erlik. Now that that's no longer a possibility, he's gonna lie here as long as he damn well pleases. Which would be fine by me, but I'm already persona non grata and I can't afford any more blemishes to my ravioli-stained reputation.

"The faster you are, the faster you get to kill things."

What do I get to kill at the end of this game of yours?

"The next time you want to go actually kill something,

they might send Erlik or Bakul."

I cannot help it if your kind makes foolish decisions.

I'm so frustrated I almost shock him again but stop myself. I know what it's like to be controlled, to be forced. I am not that person. I cannot be that person.

I go the taunting route, knowing that gets him hot under the saddle. "It's because you're injured, isn't it? That's the real reason. You couldn't even keep up if you wanted to. It's okay to admit weakness, Praxi—"

He rockets off the ground, hissing something guttural at me that's definitely not English. Might just be a growl. We zip toward the end of the cavern, where a mattresslike pad is pinned to the wall. It's got a red X on it. Makes me think of Colin and our crate training, but this time I'm the bullet.

Praxus whips his tail into the mattress. I hear an alarm bell in my CENSIR, followed by an announcement of our halfway time (six minutes and twenty-two seconds) and our time behind second place (one minute and thirty-seven seconds).

No way we're catching up, but it's not the other dragons I'm competing against. It's Praxus's other riders. I've gotta make up ten seconds if I don't want to end up in last place.

"So I can hum to you. . . ." I sample the *Kissing Dragons* theme song. "Or you can be a brave little Green and—"

I jerk backward as he accelerates to lightning-bolt speed.

I press against him, hold on tight, and enjoy the ride the best I can.

By the time we reach our cage, new riders are already mounting Erlik and Bakul. T-Clef, James, and the others from Praxus's Posse clap as we touch down. It's the standard response for a completed run. I'll call that a win.

Get off.

"Good job," I say.

Get off. With him growling and stomping about like a giant elephant throwing a temper tantrum, it takes some effort to descend the rope down his shoulder. I bang against his leg a couple of times and almost slip a couple more.

Once my feet are firmly on the ground, I look up at him. "That was fun. Thank you."

He snorts smoke in my face, slams his foot to the ground, knocking me off my feet.

I do not like you.

I smile at him. "I do not like you either."

I'd swear he smiles back. Or he could just be showing me how sharp his teeth are.

"Round two. T-Clef, you're up!" Vincent calls from the middle of the walkway that separates the four dragon cages.

T-Clef saunters into the cage, gives me a curt nod, then a wink when she's closer. "You got some heat in his beat, Missy C."

I exit the cage. People still keep their distance, but I do get a couple tips of the chin. James ignores me, his gaze focused through the bars on Praxus, but as I pass behind him, I hear him say, "You agitated him pretty good." Sounds like he's grinning.

"Riders ready?" Vincent bellows as I retake my probationary position beside him.

"Ready!"

"Go!"

The dragons disappear into the chutes. The cavern darkens. Still enough light from the crank lamps around the perimeter to show Vincent's scowl. "Next time, do better."

My heart sinks.

Then he shows me his phone.

Second place.

34

Two mornings later, T-Clef wakes me up by yanking out my earplugs and yelling, "Vincent says you're better!" She jerks me up and lets me out of my handcuffs. "We'll see!"

She punches me hard in the face. She'd warned me about it the night before—said it would have to be real, enough to draw blood—but it's still an effort to apologize as she stands there over me, celebrating her performance for everybody in the barracks.

"What was that? I didn't hear you!"

I lick blood from my lips like I'm supposed to. "I'm sorry."

She helps me to my feet and gives me a hug. "We're on the level now, Missy C."

I get some nods and handshakes from the others. James,

sitting cross-legged on his cot, reading *The Art of War* by Sun Tzu, seems oblivious. Except for a few cursory hellos and a not-a-big-deal shrug when I thanked him for the earplugs, he's acted like I don't exist.

I don't understand him.

In the arena, I'm given a railshot and allowed to shred mannequins with the others. It's soothing, except when Vincent's giving me tips. He doesn't sound or look a thing like Colin, but it doesn't matter. . . . It takes a little longer each time to look at the mannequin at the end of my gun and not see him.

I try to contact Grackel, but she remains unresponsive. "Kill emotion," I remind myself, and fire off my next shot.

Kill shot.

Today, we pair up on our dragons for what Vincent calls blitz runs, where the gunner shoots at targets affixed to stalactites and outcroppings with a machine gun armed with digital tracers. Scores are based on accuracy and flight time.

Since there's a new element in Praxus's Posse—me— Vincent mixes us in and out to find the best combination.

I'm hoping for T-Clef, but we both are good fliers and not so good at shooting shit on the fly. I do better with Grizzly B, though he shouts percussion beats between gunfire riffs that annoy both Praxus and me.

On my fifth round, I'm paired with our fastest flier and

most accurate shooter.

James gives me the token high-five he gives everybody. "Let's do this, Callahan."

Callahan? That's a new twist. "Fast," I say, striding into the cage.

I fly. He shoots. For once, I refrain from taunting Praxus, from encouraging him at all to make haste. Vincent insists that we do all our training unlinked—practicing blind-folded, he calls it—but even though Praxus can't read my thoughts, he must somehow sense them, because that venge-ful fucker goes warp speed the entire way.

Good job, Praxus says to me, glowing with delight as James and I swap seats. For our second run, I shoot at every-thing but the targets. Worst score of the day. Doesn't matter. Our previous one set an arena record.

That night, my earplugs in but unable to sleep, some-thing occurs to me. In our first run, knowing that we'd be paired if things went well, James didn't miss a single target.

We more or less repeat the same routine every day. Breakfast, shoot, fly, lunch, tactical training, workout, dinner. The tac-tical stuff involves games of laser tag in the arena or skulk-ing through darkened prayer centers to take out lurking dummies. The workouts—running down the understate or carrying/dragging mannequins around the arena between sets of push-ups and lunges and bear crawls—suck in the best possible way.

It's all an addictive roller coaster of adrenaline and exhaustion that kills emotion better than alcohol ever did. Except when I get off and look around, I'm in the same goddamn place I've always been.

Lost.

Fucked.

After dinner, we return to our respective barracks. Most play games, a few read. I stick to the card group, because they're the most talkative. Even though it's mostly banter, bragging, and flirtation, I have picked up some information along the way: it's been more than two months since they've gone on an op, Klyv's riders are still down south because they're "bonding" with a new dragon, O.J.'s struggling with detox. . . .

Nothing about Allie, but I keep playing because it's better than the quiet.

Tonight Fattie's in a foul mood, in part because I just put him in the basement in our hearts game by shooting the moon. Also shot him dead a couple of times in our laser-tag elimination match this afternoon.

Doesn't help that T-Clef keeps reminding him. "How's it feel to be in last, Burly B . . . again? Better pick up the pace, or you gonna be running janitor on the halls while the rest of us are lighting the fires."

"Imaginary fires," Grizzly B says, thrumming his cards against the table.

"Waiting for the storm to die down," Skinny says. He looks over his shoulder. "Appear weak when you're strong, right, bro?"

James doesn't look up from his book, but gives a thumbs-up. I focus on my cards.

"Come over here so I can whoop your ass," T-Clef says.

"Maybe next time," James says, which is what he says every time.

"He wants you to ask," she says to me.

I kick her under the table. "Maybe next time."

Skinny passes me three cards, gives me a wink. Even before I look at them, I know one is the queen of spades. It used to be a barb, but now we're an alliance against T-Clef and Grizzly B. Tonight, however, I'm playing for me.

"I miss the sky flies," Fattie says, playing the two of clubs.

"The acoustics in the tunnels are kickin'," Grizzly B says.

Fattie flips him off. "Don't give me your silver-lining horseshit."

"Missy C ruined it for the rest of us." T-Clef stands up, hips on her fists, head turned sideways in a superhero pose. "I'm Missy C. My first flight out, I'm going to attack an entire squadron of dragon jets. Because I am awesome."

I laugh. "It wasn't my idea."

Skinny rolls his eyes. "That's right. Blame Praxus."

Fattie frowns. "Praxus just wanted to get his shine up for a pretty girl."

T-Clef mimes sweeping the floor. "Can't blame a brother for good taste."

"O.J. would let us out there," Fattie says.

"O.J. gets things got," T-Clef says.

"Technically, it was Dragon Slayer over here who got Klyv," Grizzly B says. I flip him off.

Fattie leads with the ace of diamonds. "I'm not here to play laser tag."

T-Clef dumps a king of hearts on Fattie's ace. "You're here to pick up the cards, Burly B."

"If Vincent thinks he can distract us with some stupid games—dammit, Missy C!" he says as I throw my queen of spades on the pile.

"That's gonna put you out." I grin at his scowl. "You owe me a picture."

"Right now," T-Clef says. She stands on her chair. "Hey, posse, we're gonna add a plus one."

Most everybody bounds from their beds or leaps up from their chairs and files out the door.

"You coming, flyboy?" T-Clef says.

James gives a slight shake of his head to her, then a slight nod to me. "Good job, Callahan."

"Thanks, Everett," I say.

"When you guys gonna stop being awkward?" T-Clef says, pulling me out the door.

"When you gonna stop asking?"

"You like him, right?"

I shrug.

"What would your CENSIR say?" she asks.

It doesn't matter. We fly well together, we make a good team whenever we're in the same tactical group, but the rare pleasantries we exchange come at a distance.

I need to keep my distance.

We join the others outside the prayer center, where Fattie's already at work. He sucks at cards, he's a middling flier on his best days, but he's a wizard with the spray cans. People shout out suggestions for poses and expressions.

My graffiti self ends up crouching besides Graffiti Fattie, my head right at his waist level in a somewhat provocative manner; otherwise, Graffiti Melissa is rather badass. Arms folded across my chest, a stylized oxygen mask covering the lower half of my face, a miniature dragon jet cradled in one hand, a railshot with *Klyv* inscribed on the barrel (T-Clef's suggestion) in the other.

Fattie is adding in shading around my face to make me look extra menacing when the dragon sirens mounted to the understate ceiling blare to life.

The only thing louder is the cheers erupting all around me. A quarter mile down, Erlik's Eviscerists are pouring out of their prayer center. SUVs come blazing by from the other direction—Bakul's Banshees—honking and flashing their lights.

We're going to war.

T-Clef drives us to Dragon Shelter U5-2127, where dozens of SUVs are already parked. Several have logos painted on them. Inside, dozens of Diocletians are gathering at tables. Place cards tell everybody where to sit. Signs in the middle of the tables match some of the logos on the SUVs. At the front of the room, Vincent preps a projection screen.

I'm looking for my name when T-Clef lets out a loud squeal beside me.

"Joto!" She pushes her way forward. The crowd parts enough for me to see him. He's at a table for six near the back of the room. The sign in the middle has a black-and-white silhouette of a dragon and a soldier kissing. Behind it, surveying the room with a slight smirk, sits Evelyn.

I don't think she sees me. I start to turn around.

"Twenty-Five, you're with us." Her voice is saccharine and evil.

Of course I am. I turn back around. We exchange frozen smiles. The fates must hate me.

Which is why James is in our group, too. He shows up after almost everybody else has found their places, taking a seat between Grizzly B and T-Clef. He says a few perfunctorily pleasant things to them and Joto, then exchanges a curt "hey" with Evelyn that makes his nod of acknowledgment for me seem jubilant.

Vincent activates the projector. The room goes silent. Oren appears on the screen. He's in some cave that shines a bright green from all the dragons behind him.

"Hello, brothers and sisters," he says. "The time has come."

A boisterous cry goes up.

". . . sacrificed a lot to get here," he's saying when the shouts die down enough for me to hear him again. "I appreciate all that you've given. . . ."

The screen shifts to a news clip labeled "Victory in Tahoe" that shows snippets of a massive battle, ending with the aftermath of a broken and burned forest littered with dead Greens. All-Blacks escort a handful of smoke-stained Diocletians into prison trucks.

"They kicked our ass," Joto says as calls for retribution ring out.

The screen returns to Oren. "We lost many of our bravest brothers and sisters in this attack, soldiers and dragons who understood that their sacrifice will ensure our victory."

Vincent and several other Diocletians pass out tablets to each table as Oren continues to speak. "The government believes this last attack has crippled us." He waves at the dragons behind him and grins. "It is time for us to rise from the shadows and unleash hell. Sic semper tyrannis!"

The video cuts to black.

Everybody in the room rises to their feet with shouts of "Sic semper tyrannis!"

Mine's a half beat late, but except for a sidelong glance from Evelyn, I don't think anybody noticed.

"Your instructions are on your tablets," Vincent says. "You will find—"

"These are just coordinates with a time stamp!" somebody yells.

"Enter them into your GPS," Vincent says. "You will be given further instructions once you're under way. Make sure you arrive within the allotted time. All the gear you need should be in your vehicles. Be swift."

Once we've all packed into the SUV with the logo of the soldier and the dragon kissing, Evelyn fires up the nav system. I take a peek as she punches in the coordinates from the tablet. I was right. We're somewhere beneath the Rockies.

"Saint Louis," she says.

"How much time we got?" Grizzly B asks.

"Ten hours."

"Are we flying?" Joto says, incredulous.

Evelyn starts the car. The tablet screen goes white. She sets it on the dash so everybody can see, then hits the play button. A slideshow starts.

It's titled *Kissing Humans*.

35

T-Clef's singing again.

I peek through my eyelids. It's 3:17, according to the clock in the SUV dash. The understate shifted from paved highway several hours ago. The headlights show the edges of a smooth rock tunnel and an infinite stretch of blackness ahead of us. We're headed straight to hell. No signs, no markers. But that's where we're headed. As fast as we can get there.

We speed by another offshoot.

I'm reminded of ants. How far does the Diocletian colony extend?

"Come on, slackers, I'm tired of going solo," T-Clef says. "We're a team."

She sings louder.

Evelyn grunts something unintelligible from the driver's seat. Joto, riding in the back with our gear, joins in but doesn't know the words. James is immersed in a military history book, which he's reading by penlight. Grizzly B, little more than a shadow next to me, air-drums halfheartedly for a couple of lines, then fades away.

The song ends.

T-Clef sighs and leans her head against the window. It'll be a couple of hours at least before she tries again.

I shut my eyes. I'm exhausted, but sleep won't come. I can't stop thinking about what I'm supposed to do in a few hours. What I'm going to do.

Prove myself valuable, prove myself ruthless, and maybe it gets back to Oren, maybe I work my way into his trusted circle. Plan B is to get Evelyn alone and torture her for information. She was with Oren in Dillingham. Maybe she knows where he is now, where Allie is.

Way too many maybes, but I don't know what else to do. I feel like I'm running through a maze, blind and breathless and out of control, looking for a way out. Is there a way out?

The others seem to find sleep here and there, but it looks too peaceful to be real. How can this be real?

At 9:45 a.m., the GPS indicates we've reached our destination. In an alcove off the side of the tunnel, lights illuminate a narrow, open-air elevator with a waist-high railing around its perimeter.

Grizzly B and Evelyn go up first.

Thirty minutes later, it's Joto and T-Clef's turn. She wraps an arm through his backpack and around his waist, grabs a railing with the other. It wobbles. Joto looks ready to be sick. She presses the up button and kisses him on the cheek. "Wanna get frisky?"

He gives a tense shake of his head, his gaze fixed forward.

"He afraid of heights?" I ask once they're out of sight.

"Claustrophobic, too," James says.

"Chose the wrong occupation."

James smiles ruefully. "Side effect."

"Huh?"

"From his reconditioning."

I frown. "He was in Georgetown?"

"No. They escaped Krakus."

Him and T-Clef? I become intensely aware that James is looking at me in a way he hasn't looked at me in weeks. A pang stabs my chest. I look away.

"Krakus . . . um . . . that's where . . ." I try to compose myself. "When we were leaving Indianapolis, he . . . Colin . . . he said that we were the Krakus transfer. Where is it?"

"It's a mobile intercept base. The location changes all the time."

"Oh." I glance back at him. He's still looking at me like

he gives a damn. Who are you? I take a deep breath, ask the question I can't seem to shove away. "Did you beat the CENSIR in Georgetown?"

"Sometimes."

My next question's out of my mouth before I can stop it. "What about when we were shooting the show?" When his CENSIR was off? When he was nice to me.

He laughs. "How hard would it have been to get a kiss?"

"A simple peck?" I say, which is what Hector the director told me to give James after I'd failed to fake anything better.

The elevator arrives. We board. He's shaking. I don't know why. He swallows hard a couple of times as the platform lurches up.

"Nothing's simple anymore, is it?" James says, then kisses me fiercely. My knees buckle and tears well, but I pull away before they slip free.

"I'm sorry. I can't." I wipe my eyes and focus upward. We don't talk after that.

The elevator ends on a ledge twenty feet beneath a hatch. We take a ladder the rest of the way up, exit into a forest of towering pine trees. Our topside vehicle, a black Escalade, is parked nearby. Evelyn closes the hatch. Joto and Grizzly B use a pair of shovels to cover it with dirt.

Midday, we reach the outskirts of Saint Louis. As we funnel to a checkpoint, we put on our wigs, Rice University hats and T-shirts, then pop in our vid lenses.

"Roll time, people," Evelyn says. "Stick to the script."

"What script?" Joto says.

T-Clef smacks his shoulder. "This is gonna be on TV in a couple days, jackass. So don't act like a jackass."

"Mean like this?" He flicks his tongue in a suggestive manner at her.

"That's the special-edition cut," Grizzly B says. He and Joto laugh.

Newly instituted retinal scans identify us as a group of college students from Houston, here for the football game. After searching our SUV, the A-Bs wave us forward.

Beyond the checkpoint, an electronic billboard on the side of the highway broadcasts a news clip of the battle in Tahoe. VICTORY! flashes at the bottom.

Joto snarls at the next billboard, which advertises *Kissing Dragons* with a montage of Frank, Kevin, Mac, and L.T. on various dragon hunts. Frank, the fab four leader, drives a sword through a Green.

The billboard switches to a promo for *Kissing Dragons: The Other Side*. The left half shows a trio of Greens igniting Chicago. An insurgent with a monocle over his left eye fires his machine gun over the side of his dragon at the streets below. On the right side of the board, the same insurgent stalks a padded cell with a maddened grin.

"They caught Red Eye?" Grizzly B says. Red Eye's the focal point of the advertisement, but my attention's on the other two dragons. Both are riderless. Both are wearing collars. Neither seems to have trouble navigating the black maze of buildings. That dragon that chased me in Chicago—Thog—was riderless, too.

Where are you? Talk to me, you treacherous human!

In the Georgetown battle room, the military had us communicating with collared dragons from afar in various covert missions. Oren must have implemented a similar strategy.

We pass billboards with PSAs about the blackout policy (BLACK IS STYLISH, BLACK IS SEXY, BLACK IS SAFE) and dragon exposure (IF YOU SEE ANYBODY TALKING TO THEMSELVES, REPORT IT IMMEDIATELY TO THE BUREAU OF DRAGON AFFAIRS).

And then my brother's glaring down at me, along with the five other members of *Kissing Dragons: The Frontlines*. A portion of the billboard runs a clip of Sam leading a charge through the woods toward a Green that's laying waste to a squadron of All-Blacks.

Real?

"Fucking family," Joto says, and I almost lash out at him, but stop when I realize he's looking at the only girl in the group. I check the other TV soldiers, recognize the boy at the end. Double T's brother.

Following the map we retrieved from the SUV's glove compartment, we exit the highway in the industrial district and wend our way to an abandoned tract of warehouses. We reach the third one on the end. The bay door retracts.

An All-Black standing beside a Humvee waves us in. A balaclava covers his face.

"Locked and loaded," he says as we exit the Escalade. He nods to Evelyn, hops in the SUV, and drives away.

In the back of the Humvee, we find five sets of All-Black uniforms, railshots, and several backpacks.

"How much you think Oren paid him?" Joto asks as we change out of our fake student clothes into our fake soldier clothes.

"He didn't," James says. "His brother was in Georgetown. Fourteen." He shakes his head, his gaze unfocused. "He sounded just like him."

Joto whistles, laughs. "Fucking family."

We have to pass through another checkpoint to get into downtown Saint Louis. We swap out our vid lenses. We're now new recruits, here for Dragon Defense System Training. The checkpoint guards don't give us a second glance.

Loudspeakers command people to remain vigilant, report anything out of the ordinary. The instructions echo everywhere, without much interference. It's late afternoon, but except for A-B patrols, the streets are practically empty.

We park in front of a missile launcher squeezed between

two hulking skyscrapers. An electrified fence surrounds it. I watch Evelyn enter a passcode. The gate opens. A stairwell between the legs of the launcher leads down to a fortified control station.

"Turn your plasma shots on," Evelyn says.

"Maybe we shouldn't," Grizzly B says.

"Those are our orders."

"It won't look good if we're all getting sick on camera."

"You didn't get sick when Klyv got mushified by the queen of spades over here," Joto says.

"Joto," T-Clef snaps.

"I'm just saying. Dead is dead. What's it matter?"

He's right. What does it matter? I draw my railshot and switch on the plasma effect.

"Trouble understanding instructions, Twenty-Five?" Evelyn says. "You stay back. Look pretty. Or try."

That's my role. Wait for others to do the blood work, then come in and be recognizable. I have no delusions that Oren is concerned about my welfare. He just doesn't trust me. Which is maybe why he put Evelyn in charge of our little propaganda team.

Playing tame won't get me anywhere, though.

"Shoot me," I say, and shoulder past her.

"She mean that in the video way or the bullet way?" I hear Joto say behind me.

At the bottom of the stairs is another door. I enter the passcode.

Inside, three soldiers are monitoring touch consoles. I nail two of them in the back of the head. The third makes it around halfway in his chair before somebody else drills him in the neck.

Their bodies shrivel. The reek of overcooked meat floods my nostrils. Grizzly B runs out of the bunker. T-Clef retches but keeps it in. Joto doesn't.

My stomach twists, my heart, too, but then I think of Georgetown and how these bastards could have been in a control bunker there, monitoring my or Allie's reconditioning. How they could have been the ones responsible for executing Lorena and the other talkers when rescue came.

I grab the explosives pack from James, who regards the corpses with cold indifference, and set it the middle of the room.

"Pretty enough?" I ask Evelyn on my way out.

We keep the plasma off for our other four targets. Then we head a few blocks over to the riverfront, take some touristy videos, and drop off our remaining backpacks.

We're on our way out of Saint Louis when the loudspeaker message breaks from its automated loop for an "important announcement from the Black House." The billboards shift to live video of the president's press secretary.

We lower our windows.

"Good afternoon. The Bureau of Dragon Affairs has captured the Los Angeles terrorists, and we are hours away from catching the New Orleans bombers. If you think to help them, if you think to ignore them, you will be considered one of them.

"As always, we ask for your prayers for the victims, and we demand your vigilance to help us prevent further atrocities. United we are strong. God bless America."

"God bless her," Evelyn says. "Get me the tablet."

"Blew up New Orleans?" Joto says, opening the glove compartment. He hands her the tablet. "Damn. Never got to go to Mardi Gras."

"We're supposed to wait," Grizzly B says as Evelyn powers up the tablet.

"Oren would appreciate this. Better theatrics," she says, and taps the screen.

Four fireballs rise from downtown Saint Louis. We pull off to the side of the road and get out. Evelyn sets off the final explosives. They detonate in rapid succession near the bank of the Mississippi. It takes a couple of seconds before the Gateway Arch breaks from the earth and crashes into the river.

36

For episode two of *Kissing Humans*, we return to Tatankaville for a flight to roast a supply convoy.

Two of Bakul's riders are already suiting up when we arrive at the arena. Hawk's got a Mohawk, and Hook's got a hook where his left hand used to be. They're running scout duty for the mission. They don't look happy about it, but in the time I've been here, I've never seen them look happy about anything.

I don my body armor, helmet, goggles—

"Keep your goggles and mask off until you need them, Twenty-Five," Evelyn huffs. "They need to know who they're seeing."

Who are they seeing? "I liked her more when she was Talker One," I whisper.

"Yeah," James mumbles. I glance over. He's staring into his locker. I lean back, see that he's looking at the mirror affixed to the back wall. Like mine, it has *You* written in black marker across its top. A family portrait that must be several years old is taped to the bottom of the mirror.

"You all right?"

"Always." He closes his locker, puts on his helmet, decorated to the brim with dragon-jet stickers.

"Let's fly!" Evelyn says.

T-Clef kisses Joto on the cheek. "Don't do anything stupid."

"Stupid is in the brain of the stupid."

She laughs. "You're so stupid."

"Yeah, but I'm your stupid," he says, kisses her, then dashes off.

"Kick some ass out there," T-Clef says, way too excited, and gives me a hug. "And please watch him. Evie's a great rider, but she can be a bit crazy, and since he's supposed to be videoing you, he won't be as focused as he should be, and—"

I squeeze her tighter. "We'll make sure he's okay."

"If Evie happens to"—Grizzly B makes a slashing gesture across his throat—"in the process . . . well, accidents do happen."

"The thought hadn't crossed my mind."

"What would your CENSIR say?"

We laugh.

On the other side of the wall, we split into our flight teams. The dragons are glowing an eager shade of deadly today. Praxus still greets James and me with a grudging growl, though he does allow us to mount him with far less petulance than normal.

"How you feeling, Callahan?" James asks from the gunner's seat.

"Fine, Everett. You?"

"Fine." The built-in pivot mechanism that links the gun to his seat allows him to swivel around a hundred-eighty degrees. He turns all the way to his right, looks sideways at me. "Don't do anything crazy, okay?"

I'm not sure what he means by that, what he ever means anymore, so I ignore him.

"Let's roar and roll," Evelyn says via the CENSIR radio.

The hatch in the ceiling opens, and we launch. Minutes later, we're out of the mountain. Clouds line the sky like feathered speed bumps. The midday sun shines a dark shade of orange through my goggles. In the distance overhead, I spot the green glow of Bakul.

Praxus snarls, and his heat picks up. Erlik's flying right at us in a vertical ascent. Evelyn's at the helm, head pressed to Erlik's neck, blond hair streaming out from her helmet, machine gun strapped to her back. She's a goddamn modern-day Valkyrie.

Praxus whirls toward them, belching smoke from his nostrils. Erlik doesn't slow.

"Hold him still, Twenty-Five," Evelyn says. "And take off those goggles. How many times do I have to tell you?"

Praxus brightens. I can almost feel the fire filling his throat. Sweat trickles into my eyes.

"He's not the enemy."

They are all enemies, human.

"Get him under control, Twenty-Five."

Erlik's almost on us. His lips pull back, his eyes narrow. He tucks his legs beneath him and accelerates.

"He's not the enemy today."

You are wrong. Praxus opens his mouth, but no fire comes out. He roars. *Turn it on!*

Erlik swoops around us in a tight spiral. Praxus lashes out with a tail strike that jolts me hard in the saddle, but Erlik's swerved out of range, snarling or laughing at us, or maybe both.

"Get him under control, Twenty-Five. And take off those goggles!"

"Any suggestions back there?" I ask.

"I've been talking to him. He's not talking back," James says. "Praxus is not a pack dragon."

I snort. "Are any of them?"

Erlik wheels around for another pass.

"Get Praxus on the level, Twenty-Five. We need a good clean shot of you and James flying smooth. Like you actually know what you're doing."

"If she's so damn gifted with Greens, why doesn't she tell him?" I mutter.

"Because Praxus wouldn't connect with her," James says. His words give me a camera-worthy smile and an idea.

Praxus, Erlik is a slave. Look at him take orders from those humans. He must fly close so that they can film our magnificence. He is not a worthy enemy. He is not worthy of our attention.

Praxus doesn't answer, but his glow dims and his body cools to something south of sauna. He levels out and soars into an assured glide. Erlik makes two passes around us, comes in close a few times, Joto staring at us through it all. Praxus ignores them.

I pat him on the neck. *Good job.* He tosses his head back and smashes it into my nose. Blood pours out. As his laughter echoes through my head, I think of Baby. How she did the same thing. How she was so mad at me. How she felt so alone.

I shove her from my thoughts, wipe the blood from my nose with my cape.

"Are you okay?" James asks.

"Fine."

We continue on in silence at a steady glide interrupted by an occasional wing flap. It's horribly peaceful.

A minute later, maybe ten, Hook comes on over the CENSIR radio. "We got twenty birds coming in at three o'clock. Flying low. Intercept on our position in under a minute. Orders?"

"Engage. Fire's active," Evelyn says. "Twenty-Five, stay back this time."

Erlik bolts forward.

I put on my goggles and activate binocular mode. Even at ten times magnification, the dragon jets aren't much more than black blips against the blue sky. For a few seconds, I hear nothing but the rush of wind. Then I hear nothing but the wrath of dragons.

Wings pumping, Praxus accelerates to full speed. His fuming bellows are echoed twice over by Erlik and Bakul. *Death comes.*

"Twenty-Five, stay back," Evelyn says.

I consider her order for about half a second. To gain Oren's trust, I must erase the doubts in his mind he surely has about me.

I must be Green. I must always be Green.

Praxus, the slave's rider wants us to remain here.

They want the glory of flame for themselves.

"Back off, Twenty-Five."

"Radio on. Feel free to tell Praxus that yourself, Number One. Radio off."

"James, please get your dragon under control since Twenty-Five is unable." Evelyn sounds positively frosty.

"He's not listening to me," James says as Praxus overtakes Erlik.

"I'm gonna berserk you, you stupid whore," Evelyn mutters. I'm not sure she meant for me to hear that, but either way, she doesn't open my link to Praxus.

"When you're talking to Praxus, call out your instructions aloud so I can hear," James says. "Keep your head low. Keep your body tight. The DJ pilots are trained to aim for the riders. Don't be a hero, okay?"

I glance over my shoulder. He's got both hands around the machine gun, attention focused on the enemy. A fusillade of missiles races toward Bakul as half the planes veer out of formation and come at us.

Within seconds, we're in the middle of a firefight. We swoop and swerve and twirl through flak clouds, sometimes chasing, sometimes being chased. Missiles shriek, bullets purr, dragons roar. Cerulean flames roll across the sky. Explosions detonate everywhere.

I point out targets and pursuers to Praxus. James does,

too. His shouted instructions sound miles away. Everything does.

I manage to squeeze off a few rounds with my railshot while James blasts away on the machine gun. I imagine it makes for good video, but Praxus is the only one with any accuracy.

And then it's over. Couldn't have lasted more than five minutes. Twenty columns of smoke rise from the earth, distant funeral pyres that are already dwindling. Bakul has a few holes in his wings and Erlik's got a couple of broken talons, but that's it.

The dragons drop to the earth to feast on charred pilots. Knowing that they'll check the feed from my vid lens later, perhaps want to use some of it, I make myself watch. Thankfully it's quick work and we're back in the air in a matter of minutes.

We fly north. The clouds swell, the sky closes. Snow starts to fall. We put on our oxygen masks and rise above the storm. We turn west, deeper into the evac territories. Hook, Hawk, and Bakul patrol our perimeter in wide circles, eliminating a couple of drones along the way.

The sun's dipping into the clouds when the gray fluff beneath Bakul mushrooms with colors. Orange, yellow, red. Muted, but distinct. The reverberant bass of rapid-fire explosions follows close behind. The sky blackens with smoke.

I switch on my infrared, look down, and increase magnification. Artillery dots the mountains on either side of a twisty road. A convoy of a dozen or so transport trucks wends its way west. All-Blacks are jumping out of the back of a few, taking up defensive positions.

"Move in for the attack run," Evelyn says. "Take out the dragon defense systems first, then—"

"Hawk's been hit! Shit! Shit, shit—" Hook's words turn to a choked gurgle. Bakul swings his head around wildly. Panicking. Without his riders, he can't see the A-Bs or their weaponry.

Bullet tracers slice the sky around him. He wobbles into the clouds, blood streaming from his flank. A missile slams into him. When the explosion clears, he's gone.

"They've got more firepower than we anticipated," James says. "We should fall back."

"Only cowards retreat," Evelyn says. "We are dominant. Or did you forget that?"

"I didn't—" James begins, then stops. A moment later, he's firing his machine gun and shouting epithets at the artillery.

The thunder of war intensifies. Praxus tightens his wings and flips onto his side to make himself as small a target as possible. Which isn't small at all. And his constant loud-ass roaring might as well be a sign that says SHOOT ME!

When I explain this to him, he roars louder. James joins in.

The artillery fire comes our way. Praxus attacks at full flame.

"Radio on. Open my link with Praxus, Evelyn," I say.

"James is enough."

I'm half certain she wants to get us killed. "But—"

"Stop arguing. Follow orders. Take out the west ridge. Think you can handle that?"

"Radio off. Bitch!"

Evelyn, Joto, and Erlik dive down and make a strafing run on the near side of the pass. We sweep across the road on our edge. As explosions rock us from side to side, I shout out targets. Praxus's fire melts artillery into useless goo in a matter of seconds.

James blasts away nonstop, at soldiers, vehicles, anything in his line of sight. Linked to Praxus, his accuracy is near impeccable. He laughs and curses with every takedown. "Drink that wild air, motherfu—"

The world detonates. A hellish heat swarms us from behind. We somersault forward. Praxus's roars become screams. Then we're twirling sideways, downward. We tumble out of the flak. I lose breakfast into the blur.

Praxus rights himself. His left wing's got a massive hole in it. He flaps it at full speed but struggles to maintain altitude.

Glow dimming, growls mixing with groans, he veers into a gap between the mountains and settles on an outcropping that affords us a concealed view of the pass. Scorched trucks, artillery fragments, and charred bodies are strewn everywhere. I hear artillery and gunfire in the distance, but I think we're safe.

I remember to breathe. "Okay back there?"

"Outstanding. Let's take it to these bastards," James says. He grabs a missile from the quiver attached to the saddle and slips it into a rocket launcher mounted on the other side. He lifts it and aims down the road, at a truck swerving its way through the carnage.

"James, no!"

He fires. The truck explodes into the air, crashes down, and tips over onto its side. A couple of All-Blacks crawl out the back.

"For Mark and Steven and Grynax . . ." James grabs the machine gun and doesn't stop firing until he's out of bullets, shouting names the entire time, some dragon, some human.

The artillery explosions dwindle to silence over the next few minutes; the gunfire ceases. I hear a couple of screams here and there, some women crying, but I'm pretty sure that's my imagination.

"Where are you, Twenty-Five?" Evelyn asks.

"Radio on. Praxus is injured. Got shot in the wing."

"Can he fly?"

I ask him.

He looks over his shoulder and snorts smoke at me.

"Yes, he can fly. Probably not too far . . ."

"He doesn't need to fly you too far. It's showtime."

"Payback," James says, singsongy.

We glide from our hiding spot. Evelyn, Joto, and Erlik hover a few dozen feet above the carnage that litters the road. The Green's got a couple of bodies clutched in his talons. I notice one of them squirming.

His screams are real. And then they're crushed.

As the dragon shoves the soldier into his mouth, Evelyn points down the road. "We let a couple of the trucks make it through. The next artillery entrenchment isn't for a few miles. Stay low. And don't open fire until I tell you. Understand, Twenty-Five?"

I grit my teeth. "Yes, ma'am. But you might want to take James off the hook. He's a bit rabid."

"He's been disconnected for a while. He's got attachment issues," Evelyn says, clearly annoyed. "Follow on our left flank."

Erlik eats the other soldier, spins around, and flies off.

I will not follow that slave, Praxus says when I relay the plans.

There is a feast on the other end.

There is a feast here.

He drops to the ground, sniffs the air, swipes wildly in front of him. His talons slice open the canopy of a crashed transport truck. Two All-Blacks lie slumped against the sidewall. I don't look away, but can't help flinching at the crunch of teeth through bone.

"You wanted this, Melissa," James says, almost spitting my name. "You can't be weak. You'll get us all killed."

I flip him off over my shoulder. *We don't have time for this, Praxus. There is a better feast ahead.*

Then go get it yourself, human.

"Where are you, Twenty-Five?"

Praxus, the slave's rider thinks you can't keep up with the slave. I'm inclined to agree.

That does it. He launches himself, bellowing away. His balance is off, so we wobble some, but he makes sure we don't fall behind. Via the magnification of my goggles, I see Joto give me a thumbs-up. He turns over his shoulder and leans toward Evelyn.

"Get Praxus quiet, Twenty-Five. We want this to look good."

Praxus balks at my request until I remind him that the fear scent on the humans will be much greater if we surprise them.

We swerve around a bend, and the two transport trucks

come into view. The pass narrows. Praxus pulls in his wings a few feet so they don't scrape the sides. The trucks putter up a switchback and disappear from sight.

"Approach from behind on their level," Evelyn says. "Get up close. Keep it quiet. And quiet your glow."

Erlik banks up.

We continue to fly low. Snow melts in our wake. Praxus heeds my reminders for silence and dimness, though as we round the switchback, his glow starts pulsing. Like a heartbeat. It accelerates, brightens. Evelyn chides me. I tell Praxus to calm down. He listens for about a second, then he's pulsing again.

Their flesh is ripe. He quivers, does that purring thing Greens do.

The trucks struggle up the incline. Erlik hovers fifty or so feet above them. Chest angled up, wings flapping a slow beat, he flies backward at their lethargic pace.

Tell the slave's rider to turn on my fire, human, Praxus says as we close within flaming distance.

Evelyn wants us closer. "Gotta to see the flames in their eyes," she says. Those are our orders. Close enough for video from James's and my vid lenses to capture the terror on the faces of the soldiers before we kill them.

Murder them.

I must be Green. For Allie.

I remind Praxus that their flesh will be riper the more afraid they are. He happily glides into position over the rear truck.

"Now!" Evelyn says.

Praxus drops from the sky with a furious roar, talons extended. He digs into the canvas ceiling and peels it off. Two dozen soldiers sit packed together on benches that line either side. Out of the corner of my vision, I see James aim his machine gun at them, his body coiled with rage. The soldiers raise their hands in surrender.

They're all young, their faces more suited for prom tuxedos than dragon camos. I close my eyes and try very hard not to think of Sam.

Their flesh is ripe!

Praxus's glow goes blinding behind my eyelids.

"Open your eyes, Twenty-Five. Your fire's active. Kill them!"

"They'd do the same to us, Melissa," James growls behind me, again spewing my name as if it's a curse.

I open my eyes. And all I can see is Sam.

No! These are not warriors, Praxus.

They are all warriors. The heat swells in his throat.

These are children!

They are all warriors.

They are not even fighting back!

"Hurry up, Twenty-Five."

They are not worthy of your fire!

No, but they shall taste it anyway. He opens his mouth. Flames curl forth.

This is slave's work!

Praxus roars at me, then at Erlik, and veers off, his azure fire blasting into the mountainside.

"What are you doing?!" Evelyn says. Then: "You deserve this, Twenty-Five."

She says something else, but it is irrelevant. The sweet stench of terror fills us. The sounds of it, too. The coward warriors weep and whisper pleas for their pitiful lives to their pitiful God.

We whirl back around. The urine scent intensifies. Pathetic. They are not worthy. But their flesh is ripe. We land in front of them. One stands on trembling feet and raises a trembling gun at us.

We purse our lips together and shoot a dagger of hell into his chest. He ignites. The others scream. We press a finger to our lips. They hush. We snatch the melting one and eat him in front of his craven brethren.

A couple jump out and run for the embankment. We crush one in our claw, send the other one flying with our tail. The rest sit there, quivering or paralyzed. They are fully ripe now. We brighten.

"How many must die before you leave us alone?" James shouts behind us.

"Finish them, Twenty-Five," Evelyn says.

Twenty-Five? No, we are Praxus. We are alpha. We will enjoy our meal without the words of slaves infesting us. We shout our annoyance at them. "We will do this our way!"

As the slaves roar back at us, we grab the nearest coward warrior and pull him close so that we can see him. He wets himself. His brimming eyes go wide, his body slack. The last vestiges of adolescence slip from his face and he is naked in front of us, a baby.

Powerless, defenseless.

He is not worthy.

No, he does not deserve this.

This is wrong.

This is wrong!

Praxus drops the All-Black and recoils with a doleful wail.

As he lifts off, a flash of movement catches my eye. On the ridge above, a soldier aims his rocket launcher at Erlik. I squeeze off two quick bursts from my railshot. The second catches the A-B in the shoulder, knocks him backward. The rocket launcher fires its missile skyward; the soldier liquefies.

I vomit, Praxus dims.

What did you do, human? What did you do to me?

It's the first time I've ever heard a Green unsure of itself.

No, not unsure.

Scared.

The crackle of dragon fire echoes through my CENSIR radio. I glance back. Both the trucks are in flames. Too far away to see the faces of the dying, but I always see the faces.

37

Reds celebrate their dead with stories of the departed's feats, followed by a ritual burning.

Greens eat theirs.

Well, Erlik does.

Praxus is too depressed to eat, I think. After dumping James and me, he wobbled his way up to the peak that overlooks the valley where we found Bakul's remains. He hunkers there, his glow a low smolder. Sometimes he lifts his head to the heavens and opens his mouth, but nothing comes out, and I imagine him a wolf who's lost his howl.

"You're jacking us up good, sister," Joto says, his words barely audible over the sounds of rending flesh and crunching bone. He sits on a nearby boulder, machine gun laid on his lap, jaw clenched, Erlik's green glow cast across half his face. He glances at me and shakes his head.

A couple minutes later, he's looking at me again. Staring. Harder. Angrier. I pretend not to notice, wonder if he'll snap before James and Evelyn return from their search for Hawk. He grunts and turns away.

He does this a few more times, and then I guess he can't hold it in anymore. "T-Clef told me if I put a bullet in your head, she'd never forgive me, but sister, you are a disease that needs curing."

I look back to Praxus, suspect he's thinking the same thing.

"Aren't you gonna say something?" Joto says.

"What do you want me to say?" I squint at him. His grip has tightened on the gun. "You want me to apologize?"

"You killed Klyv. Bakul's dead because of you. And what about . . . ?" He points the machine gun at Hook's broken body, which lies beside me.

"If it's easier to blame me—"

He aims the gun at me. "It's your fault."

"If you say so."

He hops off his boulder and presses the barrel to my temple, jams my head sideways. "How many dragons have you killed?"

"Dozens at least. One of every color."

"You think this is funny?" He jams harder. With my

hands bound behind me with tie wraps, I can't keep my balance. I tip over onto Hook. His body's still warm. The faint aroma of roses still clings to him.

"Will killing me make you feel better?"

"Maybe."

I close my eyes. "Then what's stopping you?"

"We got orders." He pokes me with the gun barrel. "But what if I was to say you tried to run? Can't let danger bait like you get away."

"You'd only be doing your job." I roll onto my stomach. "You'll want to make sure to hit me in the back so your story holds up."

I hear him retreat a couple steps. "Why are you so damn calm?"

"How many dragons have you killed, Joto?"

"What? None. Why would I do that?"

I open my eyes. "How many humans?"

He taps the stickers on his helmet. "Jets count?"

They all count. "How many have you looked in the eye, right in the moment before they die?"

"What do you mean?"

"You've killed people, but have you seen anybody die? Because those are the things that stick with you. You don't need any memories of me haunting you, so if you're going to put me down, I'll try to make it easy for you."

"Fuck you. You're not better than me. Who the—"

"Marion, we need your help!" Evelyn calls from somewhere beyond Erlik.

He pokes me with his gun. "Don't move, or I will kill you. Close up, too."

I've managed to right myself by the time James, Evelyn, and Joto return with Hawk's mangled body. They dump him beside Hook. Evelyn retrieves binoculars from her pack and climbs the boulder. James slumps against it, legs pulled into his chest, head resting on one shoulder. Looks like he's mumbling to himself . . .

No. Singing. To Praxus, I assume.

Joto nudges me with his machine gun. "You moved."

"Shoot me."

He laughs. "Nah. Too easy." He pulls a strip of beef jerky from his bandanna, chews on it. He offers me half.

I ignore him.

"Anything?" James asks Evelyn.

She shakes her head.

"What's taking them so long?" Joto says. He checks his watch. "The extraction team was supposed to be here an hour ago."

"Maybe they ran into trouble," Evelyn says. She doesn't sound worried.

"You tried contacting them?" James says.

"We're out of radio range."

"You know what I mean."

"Our orders are for a communication blackout."

"That'll do us a whole lot of good if we get a squadron of DJs on us." Joto sneers at me. "We only got one good dragon left."

"We already let them know our status," Evelyn says. "I'm not risking a talker intercept because you're getting brittle. Take Erlik and head for checkpoint alpha. You, too, James."

James looks up. "Erlik and I aren't linked."

"Since when's that stopped you? We can merge you now, if you want."

He shakes his head. "You're not thinking straight, Evelyn."

"You don't trust me, bro?" Joto says.

"It has nothing to do with that."

Joto laughs. "What would your CENSIR say?"

James clamps his jaw.

Evelyn smirks. "Don't worry, James. I won't hurt her."

"I don't give a damn what you do to her, Evelyn. Praxus needs me," he says. I bite the inside of my lip. How can his words still hurt?

"Sing to them both, for all I care," Evelyn says. "Get going."

Erlik, glow soft, belly bloated, lifts lazily into the air, Joto at the helm, James in the gunner's seat. Evelyn cranks a lamp and places it on the boulder.

"You have to leave, Twenty-Five," she says.

I snort. "It's kind out of my hands at the moment."

"Haven't you already caused enough damage?" Did her voice crack?

"Klyv wasn't my fault. Neither was Praxus. You did this, Evelyn."

"Them?" She lifts her head, shuts her eyes. She doesn't talk for a while. Her words come out soft, pained. "You know, he was doing okay until . . ." She exhales. "He was finally getting over what he thought he'd done to you." She hardens, glares at me. "What did he ever see in you?"

Now I get it. Why she was in Dillingham and James wasn't. Oren must have decided James's feelings for me might interfere with the operation. Feelings for me? Real?

It doesn't matter. Nothing matters anymore. I look at Praxus, broken up there on the mountain. I blew my chance. I've lost Allie. I've lost myself. But at least I can make Evelyn suffer some for it.

"James is very important to me, Evelyn."

"But you're not like him. You're not like us!"

"You know what they say about opposites," I say. I adopt my most sisterly expression. "You need to let go, Evelyn. Georgetown, that was just an act. Surely you've realized that by—"

She draws a knife from her belt.

"Evelyn, wait . . ." I expect somebody to shock her into submission, but whoever's monitoring our CENSIRs doesn't stop her. Maybe nobody is. Maybe we're out of range.

She stalks toward me. "You're gonna get him killed."

I scooch backward. "Evelyn . . ."

"It's not fair, Twenty-Five. Three years . . ."

"What are you talking about?" I run into rock. The knife trembles in her hands as her eyes glaze over. Is this some side effect of withdrawal from her link to her dragon? T-Clef told me everybody reacts differently.

"Three years." She stares off into space. I press my back into the mountain, push my hands against the ground, and struggle into a standing position. She looks back at me, unfocused, right hand tightening around her knife. "I was there three years."

Georgetown. "It's gonna be okay," I say, because I don't know what else to say. She's off her chain and about to strangle me with it.

"It's not okay. I did everything they wanted! Everything."

She's almost within kicking distance.

"You can't have him, Twenty-Five."

I plant with my left leg and throw an unbalanced roundhouse at her. But she's quicker than I remember from Georgetown. She blocks it, sidekicks me in the gut. The air rushes from me. She whirls me around and shoves me against the mountain. I donkey kick at her. She slams her heel into my Achilles, and I buckle.

She twines her legs between mine, jams her forearm into my neck. I hear the rustle of her jacket as she lifts the knife.

"Evelyn, wait—"

The tie wrap breaks, and suddenly I'm free. I spin around. She's standing there, glaring at me. She has her cell phone out. She taps it. My CENSIR loosens. "Hit me."

I gape at her.

"You're gonna hit me, then you're gonna escape. Come on now, give me your best shot. You know you want to."

I want to dance on her grave, but not like this. "You're crazy."

"Get out of here. Call one of your Red friends."

I consider it. Run, hide, wait, and hope? No. But there is another option. "I'll go, but first I need you to tell me where Allie is."

She taps her phone. My CENSIR tightens. She grins, and evil Evelyn, Talker One from Georgetown, is back. "Radio on. We are a go for beta protocol, sir."

Praxus looses a mournful wail. Three green stars emerge from behind the shadow of a distant mountain. The extraction team. They were waiting for her signal. She set me up.

I charge her. She shocks me. I stumble, grab a rock. I lift it to throw at her and get a sharper shock. I let the rock fall from my hand, let myself fall hard onto my knees. I crawl toward her with exaggerated ricketyness.

"Pathetic," she says.

I spring into her midsection. The phone flies from her hand. I drive her into the boulder. Her head smashes against it. I punch her in the stomach. She doubles over. I uppercut her. She staggers. I throw her to the ground, get on top of her, wrap my hands around her throat.

She chokes and coughs and gasps. I think she's trying to say something. I squeeze harder. Her eyes go big and desperate; her irises shade a bright green. The heat swells behind me; dragon wind buffets me. I glance back in time to see a massive black claw coming toward me. It yanks me off Evelyn, swallows me in darkness.

38

My legs tingle, my breathing hurts, and the darkness enclosing me feels like it's spinning in chaotic gyrations, even when I'm pretty sure it isn't. I can't see anything, and the only thing I hear is the muted *whoosh* of racing wind. It's an eerie sound that echoes all around me.

I count time to stay oriented the best I can, to distract myself from worrying about what awaits me on the other end of this black journey.

Somewhere around hour three, we dive. My stomach jumps into my throat; the wind noise escalates, shifts to something with a more hollow resonance. We've gone underground.

After a couple of minutes of dipping and swerving on what seems like a downward trajectory, we slow to a glide and settle to horizontal. The spinning fades, and the wind softens enough for me to hear distant roars. Until my captor starts roaring, which drowns out everything. The heat picks up, and I'm soon drenched in sweat.

We land. The claw opens, and I drop onto concrete, hard on my back. A strident symphony of roars and growls surrounds me. A fog of bright green-tinted smoke swirls everywhere. It takes my eyes several seconds to adjust. Staggering to my feet, my legs half numb, I look around.

Through the bars of a dragon cage, I see that I'm in a massive terminal split down the middle by two sets of train tracks. Dragon cages line the walls in every direction. Collared dragons fill those cages.

Hundreds of them. Maybe thousands.

"Pretty," somebody says. I look over my shoulder. A woman with spiked pink hair is leaning against the dragon's leg. White cloak, no CENSIR, gun pointed at me. She's chewing on a straw.

"Where are we?" I ask over the roars. I can't stop sweating.

She tosses her gun high in the air, her eyes never leaving me, then catches it and thrusts it at me. "Bang, bang!" She spits out the straw, laughs. "What's the fuss with you, girl? Tide in the sky says you're washing out dragons with your reflux."

"I don't know what that means."

"What's any of it mean, girl?" She looks up at the dragon. "Shush now, we're trying to have a conversation."

The dragon stops growling at the Green in the adjacent cage to look at her. He bares his teeth and snorts smoke in her face, then resumes his growls, though at a quieter volume. The pink-haired woman laughs but cuts off abruptly to glare at me. "What did you say?"

"Nothing."

"You hold your horses, girl. Please and thank you. We'll fix you up with a fiddle and jump you over the moon lickety-split."

"Thank you," I say, because she's crazy and that seems like the best thing to say. She resumes spinning her gun. She stops every once in a while to "Bang, bang!" at me and laugh. I'm half tempted to tell her to shoot me and get it over with.

That's what they're gonna do. Execute me. First they're gonna interrogate me. On the flight in, that was the only reason I could think of for why they didn't kill me on the spot. I refuse to die a prisoner.

As I rub feeling into my legs, I watch her flip her gun, trying to get the timing of it down. But she's got no rhythm to it. I take a deep breath, call on the rage for everything that I've lost, and launch myself at her.

"Bang, bang!" she says with finger guns, then side-steps, grabs me by the collar, spins me, and drives me to the ground. Even in her body armor, she's not much bigger than a pixie, but she holds me down, not even breathing hard. "Hold your horses, girl!"

She laughs, lifts me up, shoves me backward. "You can try again, if you want."

I retreat to the corner. She picks up her gun from the ground and tosses it to me. She raises her hands. "Think you can do it, girl? Kill an unarmed—"

I pull the trigger. Nothing happens.

She pouts. "Had to empty it beforehand. I get a little itchy scritchy." She flicks her trigger finger. "Maybe next time. Give it back now. Please and thank you."

I throw it back. "What do you want?"

"World peace." She laughs. "Or a world on a fire. Pick your passion. Make it so it doesn't pick—" The roars and growls of dragons quiet; the glow in the terminal brightens. "Oooh, you're special. Getting to ride on the O-train."

I look down the terminal in the direction she's staring. The dragons are all looking that way too. I've never seen Greens do anything in unison. Or quietly.

A train glides toward us. The dragons track it. It stops outside my cage, and through the train's window, I see a girl in white scrubs, a CENSIR on her head.

Allie!

Something's wrong with her. Her lips are moving rapidly, like she's talking to herself. Her hands are pressed against the window, bandages wound about both wrists. Her gaze sweeps over me without recognition.

Oren and two hulking brutes exit the train.

"What did you do to her?" I ask.

He pushes a button on his tablet. The door to the cage opens. "You're too much like your mother, you know that?"

"What did you do?" I ask as his two guards grab me.

"I made a promise to her, you know. A long time ago, back when we were friends. We made promises to each other." He gives me a rueful smile. "I didn't want you to be part of this, Melissa."

"Then you shouldn't have taken Allie."

"I know what you think of me. I know what the world thinks." This smile is sadder. "War is hell, and it requires demons. Compassion only prolongs the suffering."

"What about her suffering?" I say through clenched teeth.

"I hope you can help her, but I need you to be calm. Can you be calm?"

I give a terse nod.

He waves to the guards. The moment they release me, I bolt onto the train, calling Allie's name. She doesn't respond, doesn't turn away from staring out the window. She reeks of urine and roses. The woman sitting beside her introduces herself as Elise, Allie's nurse. She's forty maybe, with ruffled brown hair and beady eyes that belong on a bird. Handcuffs hang from her belt loop.

"Talk softly," Oren says. "No fast movements."

Fast movements, slow movements, quiet, loud, Allie doesn't seem to notice anything other than the dragons.

She mumbles to herself as she scans the line of cages. "Strachen, Strubak, Sudanki . . ."

"Allie?" I say as the train takes off.

The dragons track her. She tracks them. "Talix, Tamrik, Tebum . . ."

I reach for her hand.

"Careful," Elise says. She unhooks her handcuffs, offers them to me.

I ignore her, remove Allie's hand from the window, lay it in mine. Her small fingers stay limp against my palm. "Allie?"

". . . Tesiv, Thaxx, Theule, Thog. Thog, Thog, Thog, Thog . . ." She keeps muttering the name. She cranes her neck to focus on an empty cage receding from view. She stands up, puts her free hand on my head for balance. Her fingers dig into my hair for purchase, but I don't think she realizes it.

"Allie?"

"Let her work it out," Elise says.

"Thog, Thog, Thog . . ."

Ahead of us, the tracks diverge toward two tunnels. We zoom into the right one. The cages disappear, and soon so does the green glow. Allie squeaks out a mewl, then goes silent, sits back down, and drops her chin to her chest. She crosses her wrists and starts scratching furiously at the bandages that cover them.

I intervene. It takes most of my strength to hold her still. "Allie?"

Nothing.

I look at Oren. "What did you do to her?"

"It's the CENSIR," he says.

"Take it off."

"It protects her," he says as the train slows.

"She can still hear them, you know?" She just can't talk to them. "The CENSIR doesn't work like it's supposed to on her."

"I know." He sounds sad.

The train dead-ends at a pair of elevators. Allie doesn't budge.

"You should put her in these," Elise says, once more offering me the cuffs. "It's for her own safety."

"She'll be fine," I say, more for myself than anybody.

I shift my grip from her forearms to her armpits and hoist her up. She crosses her wrists and resumes scratching, then leans backward. I almost drop her. I set her on the bench and wrest her arms apart. I wrap her hands around my neck.

"You don't want to do that," Elise says.

I scowl at her and hug Allie to me. She leans back again, but her hands catch on my neck. Her gaze tightens, her lips curl into an angry O. A moment later, her fingernails are digging in. Trimmed and dull, but intent. She breaks skin. I yelp. She digs harder. Elise pries her off me. Allie sits back down and goes back to clawing at her wrists.

Elise makes to handcuff her.

"Don't," I say. "Don't. Please."

Elise looks to Oren.

He nods. As I dab the blood away, he reaches into his pocket and pulls out the silver dragon brooch I gave Allie in Georgetown. He holds it out to her. "Come on, Allison, it's time to go home."

She shakes her head.

"Come on, Baby's waiting," he says, as if speaking to a toddler.

She looks up, holds out her hand. "Arabelle?"

"I'll give it to you when we're in the apartment," he says.

Stiff-legged, she follows him and Elise to the elevator.

Oren presses his palm to the adjacent bioscanner.

"U211," he says once we're all inside. We go up.

The floor indicator above the door starts at U600 and changes numbers (U599 . . . U598 . . . U597) about every second. Allie remains frozen at his side, arm still extended in a begging gesture. I crouch in front of her. She blinks periodically, but I might as well be invisible.

"Grackel's alive," I say.

Her eyes wrinkle, but that's it.

"Arabelle misses you," I say.

Nothing.

I push her arm down. She attacks her wrists again. I force them loose and hold her in an awkward embrace that pins her arms at her sides. "I miss you," I whisper in her ear.

She doesn't move, except to scratch at her thighs.

"It won't do her any good," Elise says.

I keep talking to her, holding her, but Elise is right. And after about a hundred floors, I figure out why. Allie's tangled, so when she's off her CENSIR, she's getting hundreds of murderous dragons sharing their thoughts with her, all at once. An endless flood of desire for death and destruction. And now that the CENSIR's protecting her from that . . .

I recall the euphoria of Praxus's presence, the abyss inside me created by his absence. Magnify that a hundred times over, and that explains Allie's current state.

Angry tears roll down my cheeks as I pry her hands apart

once more. She's already managed to shred through two layers of bandage. "You broke her. Why? For what? *Why?*"

"I'm protecting her," Oren says. "Protecting all of you."

"Protecting her?"

"As long as there are dragons in this world, Melissa, people like us will be a threat to them. We will be slaves at best in their eyes, like your brother, or we will be monsters."

The elevator stops. The doors open into a motel-style hallway, replete with white walls, cheap carpeting, and dismal lighting. "With your help, Melissa, she will recover, I'm sure of it. Come on, Allison."

He waggles the brooch at her. She trails after him.

We stop at the fourth door on the right, the only one in the vicinity with a scanner on it. Oren leads us into a studio apartment that stinks of ammonia and urine. The bed's got pairs of padded handcuffs at the top and bottom. Spots of blood sprinkle the daisy-print comforter. A cot has been set up at the foot of the bed.

"Elise will be by every few hours to check on her," Oren says.

"I'd keep Allie locked up in the interim," Elise says. "Plug her ears, blindfold her—"

My CENSIR shocks me into a stumble. "I need you to stay calm, Melissa. You are a guest here," Oren says. "You treat us well, we will treat you well."

A guest under constant surveillance, it appears. I was merely *thinking* about hitting her.

Elise gives me a sympathetic look. "It's really the best thing for Allie."

I think she believes that's the truth, and I don't know whether to hate her or feel sorry for her.

"I know it's not ideal," Oren says. "It's only a few more days. Keep her safe for a few more days, Melissa, and then you can have her back. Deal?"

Safe? I look from the bed's shackles to her, and my chest hitches. I swallow and nod.

"Arabelle?" Allie says, tugging at Oren's cloak.

Oren tosses me the silver dragon brooch. "The key to the manacles is on the nightstand. Get her to walk around every once in a while." He and Elise leave.

Allie stares at me. "Arabelle?"

I want nothing more than to give her the silver dragon, hoping it might somehow fix a small part of her, but she used the brooch to kill Major Alderson in Georgetown. I shove it in my pocket. "Not today."

She slumps against the wall and tears at her bandages.

I intervene.

I talk to her about Arabelle and Grackel, recount our experiences on Saint Matthew Island. Laugh and cry as I relive her feigned suicide attempt.

Nothing.

I talk to her about the make-believe island we had in Georgetown, remind her about the jazz monkeys and the Kremlin circus and the graffiti waterfall.

Nothing.

My arms weary from fighting her constant efforts to slash her wrists. As I shift my grip, I talk to her about our cheesecake escapade in Dillingham.

Nothing.

I hum "Over the Rainbow."

Her blink pattern slows, but I think it's just because she's getting tired. I wait for her to fall asleep, then put her in chains.

I test the door, am surprised to find that it's unlocked. I wedge it open with a bottle of cleaner I find in the closet. I investigate the hallway. At one end is the elevator. The bioprint scanner doesn't recognize my hand. Two hundred and twenty-three steps later, passing twenty-five doors on either side, I reach the other end. An exit sign points at a door that's also protected by a scanner. I test it with my shoulder. It's made of metal and doesn't budge.

I check the other doors in the hallway. They're unlocked. Beyond each, I find replicas of the room in which Allie and I are imprisoned, except unlived in. I don't think anybody's ever lived in them.

Every floor is spotless, every bed is made. Every closet and dresser is empty. Every nightstand drawer contains a neatly positioned brochure titled "Rationing Protocols," with water and MRE allowances dependent on some color-code system. At the bottom, there's a four-digit emergency contact number.

Every nightstand has a phone. None of them work. I try them all again.

"Where am I?" I ask near the end of my second go-around. I wait for an answer, but none comes.

The only thing worse than the silence is the hollow echo of my footsteps as I return to my room. I've never felt so alone.

I check on Allie—still asleep—then head to the adjacent room, where I try out the thinscreen. It works. I find a news station, flinch when I see video of James's and my attack on the convoy. They loop through it as pundits analyze our monstrosity. The part where I diverted Praxus from eating that All-Black has been edited out (I assume by Oren); the faces of the soldiers have been blurred (I assume by the news).

Not real. I'm not a monster.

Am I?

39

James and Colin fish on a flooded street from atop a missile launcher. James reels in a Green talon. Colin hooks a shrunken Red head. Praxus alights atop a hotel, a necklace of blurred All-Black heads draped around his neck. He opens his mouth and unleashes a hurricane of fire.

I lurch awake in a sweat. The stench of feces hits me. I stumble from my cot, feel my way to the nightstand, and crank the lamp.

Allie's a mess. Her arms strain against her chains, but otherwise she appears asleep.

I remove her soiled sheets and her soiled scrubs and throw them down the room's laundry chute. I uncuff her, carry her to the bathroom, clean her off in the shower. I talk as I apply rose-scented shampoo. I glide my finger along her nose to her chin. She opens her eyes, stares ahead blankly.

We return to the bedroom. The dresser contains several pairs of white scrubs and spare sheets. After changing her, I reshackle her to the bed. I work my way around her and fit the sheets into place.

I retrieve a pair of MREs from the closet and prep breakfast. I feed her pastries and wheat bread and applesauce. She chews and swallows everything without issue, as efficient and mechanical as a trash compactor. I talk and hum nursery rhymes and it doesn't matter.

Elise visits that afternoon to check on Allie. I ask if there are any drugs that might help her.

"He needs her lucid," she says.

"Extremely lucid," I say. "Where are we?"

"I don't know."

"What do you know?"

Her bird eyes narrow on me. "That you're lucky he didn't kill you."

After she leaves, I head next door. I watch the news for a bit. It's not me on there anymore, so it's manageable. They've captured other insurgents here and there. Not James, fortunately. Not Evelyn, unfortunately. The generals and politicians they interview seem to think things are dying down, that the recent attacks were last-ditch efforts. I don't think they believe that, but I don't think they know how bad it is.

* * *

By the third day, I'm desperate. Allie isn't any better. Nothing I do gets through to her. She reminds me of Claire.

The only thing that ever broke Colin's sister from her robotic stupor in any good way was watching *Kissing Dragons*. Probably because he was on the show, but I can't think of anything else. I unshackle her, hug her close, and turn on the thinscreen.

It's on an entertainment station.

"Is Hollywood their next target?" A glitzed-up reporter is interviewing an even glitzier guy as celebrities stroll in for some black-tie affair. A-Bs line the black carpet on either side.

"Man, B and C, they got themselves a vendetta, wouldn't be no surprise to me."

"B and C?" the reporter asks.

"Bonnie and Clyde. They straight aiming, and I wouldn't wanna be in their hairs."

"You never know when the great mother's going to call your name," the next interviewee says when questioned. "When it's time, it's time."

The reporter beelines it toward the outskirts of the carpet. She plants herself in front of Cosmo Kim, the fashion stylist who transformed me from a raggedy prisoner into a glamorous traitor for my interview on *Kissing Dragons: The*

Other Side. If not for her skills, I probably wouldn't be so famous. Notorious. Kim's pink suit belongs to a flamingo, her hair and glaring face to an ostrich.

"You worked with her, C.K. What was Melissa Callahan like?"

"You want to know what she was like, do you?" Sounds like she's been drinking. She rolls her eyes. "She wasn't half as pretty as I made her, and she wasn't half as crazy as they say."

"You afraid of what she's going to do?"

"That's what they want," she says gruffly. "*Bleep* them."

"Anything else you can tell us?"

"You need a new stylist," she says, and stomps on.

I laugh. Allie remains limp in my arms.

I flip through channels—a soap opera, a talk show with doctors discussing the effects of dragon exposure on adolescents (James and I are exhibits one and one-A), a news station discussing the recent arrest of three Diocletian terrorists in Los Alamos—until I find the *Kissing Dragons* network.

The fab four are hog-tying a Red in an enormous arena surrounded by walls of rubble—

Allie goes from catatonic to psychotic in an instant. She lurches free. "Malovo, Malovo, Malovo . . ."

She jumps to her feet. I dive for her, but she's too fast.

She hurls herself at the thinscreen. I pull her away, spin her around, hug her to me. She knees me in the groin, slashes me across the face. I stagger, lose my hold on her.

She presses her face to the thinscreen so that her eyes are lined up with the dragon's. "Malovo, Malovo, Malovo . . ."

Frank drives the sword through the Red's skull. Its eyes shut, its glow vanishes.

Allie screams. She falls to her knees and digs into her wrists. "Malovo, Malovo, Malovo . . ."

I get kicked and punched a few times but manage to put her back in shackles. I turn off the thinscreen. I pin her down until she stops writhing. It takes a while.

I look back to the thinscreen. Malovo? On the show, they called him Big Nero. The Destroyer of Rome. How did Allie know his real name? Was he one of her call-center captures?

A terrible thought occurs to me.

"Vestia," I say loudly. She was James's former dragon mount, a Red I helped kill in the Georgetown ER. Allie remains motionless. I lower my voice. "Malovo."

She goes into crazy tornado mode again. Shackled and undoubtedly tired from her previous episode, it doesn't take as long for me to subdue her. She will, however, need another change of sheets and scrubs.

I think of the way she reacted to the dragons when we were on the train, shouting out their names as we sped by . . .

think of Thog, that dragon that chased me in Chicago, how upset she got when she saw that empty cage . . . his empty cage . . .

Where are you? Talk to me, you treacherous human!

Was he talking to her?

Now he's gone and she can't talk to him anymore, and she blames herself. Just like she blames herself for Malovo. She feels responsible for them, responsible for all those dragons down in the terminal. Still alive.

That's why she's trying to kill herself. I thought it was because she couldn't talk to them or feel them with the CENSIR on, but it's not that at all. It's guilt. She's trying to kill herself so she doesn't kill more of them.

The tears come too fast for me to stop. I wipe them away, kiss her on the forehead. "*In nae*, right?"

It takes me some time, and a few more breakdowns, but I finally think of an idea that might help her.

"I need to take her outside," I say to Elise when she visits for Allie's afternoon health check.

"That's not allowed."

"I need to show her the stars." I grab her wrist. "Please. I know you want to help her, too."

She pulls free. "I'll do what I can."

That evening, there's a knock at the door. I bound from the bed, as if it's Santa Claus come to visit. Instead, I get

Satan's concubine and a squadron of armed white cloaks.

Evelyn. Prettier and faker than normal. She's covered in stage makeup and is dressed in a blue, green, and red sequined dress. The only real thing about her is the victorious grin.

"Hey, Twenty-Five. Didn't think to see you again, but very happy that you're okay."

I clench my fists. My CENSIR shocks me. Her grin widens. "Actions have consequences, Twenty-Five."

"Yes they do," I say. "What are you doing here?"

"I brought somebody to see you. Heard you two were friends. John!"

"Step aside, step aside," O.J. says, squirming his way forward. He's unCENSIRed, but his entire body twitches as if he's experiencing constant shocks. "You and me, Ms. Dandelion, we're right like rain. I made a mistake, and I apologize." He nods rapidly at me. "Now it's your turn."

"What are you doing here?"

He scowls and goes extra twitchy, then laughs and puckers his lips at me. "Kissing humans." He draws his gold-plated Beretta from his holster and conducts to some unheard song for a few beats. "I'm the director! Congratulate me."

"Congratulations," I say, just to shut him up. "Why are you here, Evelyn?"

"Special rehearsal for the special finale!" O.J. says.

She glances at him, annoyance flickering in her eyes, before she looks back at me. "We gotta borrow zombie girl for a little bit."

Two soldiers enter the room for Allie.

"Don't worry, we'll bring her back, Twenty-Five," Evelyn says. "No worse for wear. I promise."

"Hate me all you want, Evelyn, but she's just a child."

Her grin fades to something a little less spiteful. "Weren't we all?"

40

I turn on the thinscreen once they're gone, brace myself. Chicago was thirty dragons. Oren has enough firepower down in those cages to wipe out a continent. Any continent.

An hour passes. Two. Stories about the continued success of war efforts in the evacuated territories and terrorist readiness protocols that have been instituted across the country cycle constantly, but that's it.

Either the government's imposed a media blackout, or Oren's special rehearsal is somehow flying under the radar.

Not just under the radar.

Underground. All those tunnels. He could attack anywhere he wants.

Everywhere.

Sam, Dad, Colin, Uncle T, Aunt Sue . . . they could all be

in danger. And there's nothing I can do about it except watch and hope. . . .

Breaking news.

Does the world end at 8:14 EST?

But the world's not on fire yet.

It's a Diocletian propaganda video. Oren's in a cave, wearing his white cloak and his typical draconian expression. He's lit by a string of flickering incandescents that dangles from a stalactite.

"You think you know the truth about dragons, the truth that's been fed you by a government that imprisons children and forces them to participate in its attempted genocide of an entire species. . . ."

Silent clips of insurgents wreaking havoc—including a couple of me—intersperse his homily, though I'm not sure whether he added them in or if the media did.

". . . We will show you once and for all that everything you've been led to believe is a lie," he finishes. The screen fades. An image pixellates against the blackness. James and Evelyn. He's in a black jumpsuit; she's in a sequined dress. Outfits that mirror the ones he and I wore for our stint on *Kissing Dragons.*

Here they're not holding swords over dragons, but over shadowed outlines of strapped-down humans. The sword tips end in digital question marks.

In the space between James and Evelyn, glowing letters sharpen into focus.

Kissing Humans

The Finale

8/7 Central, Tuesday

Live

Within seconds, talking heads are analyzing the "dilapidated" setting, the lack of dragons in the video, Oren's "weathered" features, even the frayed threads in his cloak. They unanimously deem him a desperate and disturbed man stuck in the "abyss of insanity created by dragon exposure."

I'm sure that's what Oren wants them to believe. Over the past couple of days, I think I've figured out what he's doing. All the various terrorist missions he sent us on were diversions. Few that I've seen covered on the news involved dragons, and those that did were small operations in the evacuated territories, like our attack on that supply convoy.

Spread them thin.

Then strike en masse.

"Live," I whisper.

One day until the finale.

One day until Armageddon.

Maybe I can stop it.

I've thought about it before, hoped for a miracle, but there are no miracles.

There's only me.

If I'm brave enough, if I'm strong enough, maybe I can do what needs to be done.

I have to kill Allie.

I shut off the thinscreen, lie back on the bed, shut my eyes, and tell myself that is what I'm going to do. That is what I must do. For the greater good. She's not getting better. She won't suffer anymore. It's for her good.

It's the right thing to do.

It's the right thing to do!

It's the right thing to do?

I pull a pillow to my face and scream into it.

"Hello?"

I peek out from the pillow. James is looking at me, smiling that sad smile. "I heard you wanted to go outside."

41

"What are you doing here, James?" I ask as I follow him to the elevator.

"I wanted to apologize."

That's not what I meant by my question, and I think he knows that, but maybe he doesn't know the answer. You just end up in the middle of the suck and you don't know quite how you got there, or quite how to get out.

Allie and a couple of white cloaks are waiting for us in the elevator. They're each holding a hand, like they're parents taking a kid out for a stroll. A giant rag-doll, dead-eyed kid. My heart hurts.

"You think showing her some stars'll actually work?" a white cloak asks me on the ride up.

"Hopefully," I say, though a part of me hopes not. The

other part hopes to give her one last smile. "You a talker?"

"Nah. No offense, but y'all are nuts."

"A little," I say. "When the dragon's in your head, reality's amped up several clicks. When you lose the connection, you crash hard."

"Yeah, we heard. Herb, may his deranged soul rest in peace, said it's like cocaine."

"Sure."

"So you think showing her some stars will remind her that reality's not so bad?"

"No, reality sucks," I say, which gets the two white cloaks laughing. "You don't look at the stars to think about reality."

And their laughter ceases.

The elevator stops at the fourth floor. James guides us with a flashlight down a dark hallway into a darker tunnel. The faint aroma of salt mixes with stuffy air. The air thins, the smell intensifies.

Numerous twists and turns later, the tunnel ends in an enormous explosion crater. The steep slopes sparkle white in the moonlight. Almost like sand, but more granular.

Salt.

The stars twinkle overhead. I tip Allie's chin upward and point out constellations, sweeping from west to east like Mom taught me, and recount the limited mythology I recall, most of which involves Zeus putting creatures and people in the sky to prevent patricide, escape an angry lover, or honor a fallen hero.

"There's Orion. He was a great hunter. He's got a team of hunters with him," I say. I force her gaze in the direction of Rigel, the brightest star in the constellation. She blinks without seeing. "That star there, that's the great hunter Thog."

Allie awakens with a lurch, wrenching her head free of my grip. She writhes in the guards' grasp, kicks at them. She looks around frantically. "Thog? Thog? Thog?"

I grab hold of her chin. She fights me, but I finally tilt her gaze skyward. "He's up there."

"Dead, dead, dead!"

"Look. Look!" I nod at Betelgeuse, the second-brightest star in Orion. "That one there, that's Almac. And there's Curik. And there's Thog . . ."

I repeat every name I can remember, assigning them to different stars in the various constellations. After what feels like hours but can't be more than a few minutes, she stops fighting me. Tears stream down her face.

"It's okay," I say to the white cloaks. "Please."

They release her.

She points at a star in Cygnus. "Who's that?"

"Bornak," I say.

"That?"

"That's Korm," James says.

"I bet that one's Bryzmon. They were brothers," Allie says.

I nod. "It is."

She points. "Is that Helk? He was a feisty trickster."

"No, Helk's over there. That one's Ulg."

"That one, that bright one there," she says, indicating Venus. "Who's that?"

"That's Vestia."

James smiles a good smile at me, then looks back to the sky and closes his eyes.

"Vestia?" Allie's brows are furrowed. She shakes her head. "She never talked to me. I never made her go away."

"I did," I say. "I made her go away. But she's not really away. She's waiting up there for us in the next tomorrow. It's a lot safer and happier. They've got all that space to themselves. And nobody chases them."

"I want to visit them, yes, yes."

My throat tightens and I look away.

"They want that desperately," James says, "but not yet. They want you to be a bright star like Vestia, but to be a bright star, you have to live a bright life down here. It's the only way."

"They never visit me anymore. Every day somebody disappears. They don't say good-bye. I never get to say good-bye either." She sniffles. "I never get to tell them anything.

I never get to tell them that it's okay to be scared. And that they don't need to be angry and that they're not alone. The only time I talk to them, all they do is die. All I do is make them die. And I never got to tell them good-bye."

I pull her to me. She sobs into my chest.

"You know what that means when you don't say good-bye?" I say, thinking of Mom. "It means they're not gone. They're never gone."

"Those there," she says, pointing at the Pleiades, "can those be Mom and Pappy?"

"What do you mean, 'Can they?'" James says. "They are."

"See those two next to them?" James says. "You've got to turn your head sideways a little bit and squint."

She does, then nods fervently.

"Those are my parents," James says. He cups his hands around his mouth. "Hi, Mom and Dad!"

"Where's your mom, Melissa?" Allie asks. It's the first time she's said my name. Tears slip from the corners of my eyes. She notices. "Don't be sad."

"I'm not," I say, and it's only a half lie. I find Sirius and smile. "There she is."

"She's bright," Allie says, and waves. I join her.

We continue to say hi to those we've lost, and for a little while at least, the world down here feels a little less dark.

42

James gives her a piggyback ride back to our apartment. Allie draws constellations on his back with her finger, repeating the names of the dragons in them. Back in the apartment, she asks James and me to sleep with her. "I never had a sleepover growing up."

She talks about her dragon buddies and how they don't like being locked up ("even though they understand that it's because they can't mind their manners") and that they miss her voice ("though when I could talk to them, they told me I talked way too much and growled at me to shut up, but they were nice growls"). She drifts to sleep as she's telling us about a dragon named Vanorak. ("He has a very high opinion of himself . . . but he's got honor . . . most Greenies . . . tricksters . . . troll monkeys . . . bananas.")

James gets up. "You know the others figured there was no way for you to get through to her."

Others? I push out a smile. "Remember Myra's funeral?"

"I remember roaring with you."

Roar away the pain. What a quaint, futile idea. "I remember how when the other dragons incinerated her body, how her embers glided into the sky. That's what made me think of it."

"She'd be happy to know that some good came of that," James says.

"Yeah."

"Hey," he says. "It's going to be all right, Melissa."

I'm tired of lies, no matter how nicely they're spoken. "I saw your TV promo."

He grimaces. "Don't watch it, okay?"

"Wasn't planning on it." I swallow, look at Allie, but not for long, because it hurts too much. "Take her, James. Take her away from this."

"I can't, Melissa." He taps his CENSIR. "Even if I wanted to."

But he doesn't want to. "Why'd you join them? Why, James?"

"I wanted to be the hunter for once."

"My brother's out there, my father. . . ."

"They'll be safe," he says. Another nice lie.

"Just like Allie, huh?"

"We need to end this war, Melissa. We need to be free."

I pick up one of the shackles. "Free, huh? She's just a fucking child, James."

He hardens, his jaw clenching and unclenching. A few deep breaths later, he's calmed. "In a couple of days, you won't have to worry about any of this ever again. You take Allie, you return to Baby, and you live in peace."

I give him a tight smile. "Thanks for taking us outside."

"Yeah," he says, and leaves.

I check the hallway to make sure he and the guards are gone, then return to my room. I watch Allie sleep, which is a mistake. I turn on the thinscreen, mute it, and find the *Kissing Dragons* channel.

It's on episode twenty-eight, the hunt for Betelgeuse. J.R.'s still alive in this episode. I almost lose it when I see Colin smile beneath that cowboy hat. I shut off the thinscreen.

I do push-ups and sit-ups until I'm too tired. I take a shower. I check the thinscreen. Episode thirty-one. The fab four are out for revenge on the dragon that killed J.R. I switch the station and watch an infomercial until the Scarlet Scourge is dead.

In episode thirty-two, they're going after Big Blue, the Beast of Brazil, who led the attack on Rio a decade ago. In the prehunt segment, they show clips of Blue stampeding through rain forest and city, trampling everything in his path. They interview relatives of victims.

I know part of it's not real, but the destruction and the

death are real. I freeze the thinscreen on an image of a man kneeling in a graveyard. Black headstones extend out of sight in all directions.

I pick up a pillow.

Nothing happens.

This is the flaw in the CENSIR. It doesn't read your thoughts. Only your emotions.

If I were angry, it would tell whoever's monitoring my CENSIR that I'm "violent, dangerous to others." They'd shock me or incapacitate me, particularly if they knew what I was about to do, but I'm sure they don't see any emotion other than sadness.

I focus on the screen. I imagine Sam and Dad and Uncle T and Aunt Sue in that graveyard. I glance at Allie, and damn me to hell, she's got a small smile on her lips. And I hope she's dreaming a good dream.

I press the pillow to her face.

I can feel her breathing against me.

I push down.

"I'm saving you. I'm protecting you," I whisper, because maybe saying it aloud makes it true.

But I'm not strong enough.

I'm too weak to save her and too weak to kill her.

I throw the pillow aside, hug her to me, and tell myself nice lies that I will be stronger tomorrow.

43

Allie's arm dangles across my chest when I wake. I sniff. The faint scent of ammonia lingers, but that's it. I crawl out of bed, crank the lamp, and prepare breakfast.

The toilet flushes. I look over my shoulder. Allie trudges out of the bathroom, silent as a ghost.

"Hi," I say.

She doesn't respond. She's back to that monotonous blinking. She sits on the edge of the bed and eats breakfast. Beside me, but not with me. She stares at the wall, occasionally takes a bite. I ask her what's wrong, I talk to her about the stars and her Green buddies. She eats and blinks and never responds.

I think about suffocating her again. She wouldn't struggle, wouldn't make a noise. Would that be easier?

I'm throwing away the trash from our MREs when I hear her croak something unintelligible. I cup her face between my hands. "What is it?"

"Arabelle?" she says.

The brooch! I check the drawer where I'd put the silver dragon pin. Still there. I could give it to her, unwrap her wrists, let her kill herself. God, I am a monster. I close the drawer. "I think we lost her."

She shakes her head. "No, no. Arabelle and Grackel don't talk to me anymore. Neither does Randon. They must be in the stars."

And she'd blame herself for them, too. I gamble. "Did they say good-bye?"

She looks up, and her lips purse to the side. Finally she nods. "Yes. Arabelle said, 'See you later, gator baiter.' And I told her, 'After a while, cranky-dile,' because she doesn't like that because she thinks she's prettier than a crocodile, and I agree, but I like teasing, but then she didn't talk after that, no, no."

I smile. "Well, if they said good-bye, that means they're not in the stars."

"But why would they stop talking to me?"

"They don't want to distract you from helping your Green friends. Speaking of your friends, you remind them to be nice, okay?"

"I don't have any control over that."

"What do you mean?"

"Whenever I'm in the hive—"

"What's that?"

"It's what Mr. O calls the place with all the thinscreens."

"Does he have you talk to them?"

"I think so, but I don't know what I'm saying. I don't remember. It's a bad place." She shudders. "Kill the dragons, yes, yes, or the dragons kill them." She's silent for a while. "I don't want to go back there, but Mr. O says I have to. Just once more. To help the Greens so they can be free. They want to be free."

"You hold on to good thoughts, okay? You think of Arabelle and Grackel, and that'll help."

"And you too, right?"

I try to smile. "Yeah."

"That song you were singing to me the other day, I like it."

I sing her the chorus of "Over the Rainbow." "That one?"

She nods. "Can you teach it to me?"

By the time the white cloaks come for her, she's memorized the lyrics. She gives me a hug. "It seems like a happy song, but it's a sad one, isn't it?"

I compose myself. "It is if you don't have dragons."

"I think the Greens would like it." She hums it as they take her away.

A white cloak stays behind. He hands me a stiff manila envelope. My name's written on it in bubbly handwriting, a heart drawn over the I. "Evelyn wanted me to give this to you. She thought it might help with everything."

I can only imagine. After he's gone, I throw the envelope into the trash can, then turn on the thinscreen. It's 2:08 EST. The news is focused on the *Kissing Humans* finale, on figuring out who James and Evelyn are going to execute.

After a profiler dissects the trailer, they interview a bookmaker from New Vegas on the odds that it will be somebody famous (he doesn't think it will be), politicians who condemn the Diocletians, who condemn the media for stoking fear, condemn social networks for not blocking Oren's propaganda videos. . . .

Ticker tape scrawls at the bottom of a commercial for Dark Tide Detergent. *Dio Trio execution set for tomorrow morning. Opening Day finally commences at Fenway Underground. FCC ups fine to $10 million for broadcasting "indecent material." Physicists discover flaw in the Einstein-Rosen Bridge Theory. . . .*

It's all rather typical. Either the government doesn't know the attack's coming, or they're doing a good job of faking it.

It's gotta be the latter. They know Oren's coming. They

don't want to tip their hand. They don't want to spark panic. They're going to annihilate him.

I almost convince myself.

I try to take a nap, but that's not happening. I exercise, shower. I check the thinscreen again. Same ole, same ole. It's 5:11 EST. I want to freeze time or accelerate it, but I'm stuck in its slow progression forward.

I heat up an MRE. I nibble at parts of it, push it around some, nibble some more, but leave most of it uneaten. When I throw it away, I see Evelyn's envelope. I pull it out, wipe the MRE gravy from it. I run my hands along the edges. It feels like a photo, an 8 x 10. Evelyn no doubt meant to torment me with whatever's inside, but it actually does help distract me from thinking about the inevitable.

I come up with possibilities for what it could be. A photo of me on Praxus, killing those soldiers in that convoy; or maybe one of Double T's body. Probably with a written note of congratulations, just like she fake congratulated me for killing Claire when we were in Georgetown.

Or maybe it's something more trite. Her and James locked in passion. Wouldn't surprise me if she's the kind to video that shit. Prim and proper on the outside, all devil on the inside. The thought of her in a red latex outfit makes me both cringe and laugh.

Then I think of something far worse, something I would

not put past her. What if it's not a picture she took, but one pulled from the net? In Georgetown, they showed me drone surveillance vids of my brother to encourage my cooperation. Maybe inside that envelope is a still photo of Sam, looking up at the sky . . . a sky soon to be filled with dragons.

I know it could be a lie, something to flay my soul, but I have to know. I tear it open and pull out the picture.

It's not my brother.

It appears to be a video-captured image from the commercial she and James made for the *Kissing Humans* finale.

James is straddling an All-Black, a sword pressed to the soldier's neck. The A-B's gagged with rope, spread-eagled to a stone slab with shackles, and wearing a distinctive cowboy hat.

Colin.

44

Evelyn wanted to break me with this picture, but you can't break what's already broken. I've got nothing left to lose, and now she's given me purpose, which gives me clarity of thought for the first time in ages.

First, I need to get out of my CENSIR. In Dillingham, Colin used those heart defibrillators to shock the CENSIR loose. With a certain amount of pleasure, imagining myself snapping Evelyn's neck, I rip the thinscreen off the wall.

It crashes to the ground; the power cord shears off. Strands of exposed wire jut from the end. I grit my teeth and press the wire to my CENSIR. My knees buckle, and I black out.

Melissa.

My head pounds. It takes a couple of seconds for my

vision to clear, a couple more for me to orient myself to reality. I stagger to my feet.

Melissa.

Grackel!

You have been asleep for a long—

When did you last talk to Colin?

It has been a half turn of the moon.

Two weeks. *What happened?*

He said he was going to find you. He promised he would not come back until he did, silly human.

Silly, silly human. My throat constricts. *What time is it?*

The sun is close to the horizon.

But I don't know where she is, which time zone. It could already be too late.

I set the CENSIR on the bed, grab the dragon brooch, and hide in the closet. Whoever's monitoring me knows I'm no longer in it. They'll send somebody to check. If not . . . no. *In nae.*

I uncap a bottle of ammonia and press myself against the closet door, leaving the door cracked enough to give me a view of the bed.

Can you talk to Allie? I ask Grackel.

She hears but cannot hear.

Melissa! Baby says.

Hey, little one, I say, smiling my first real smile in forever.

I miss you. You keeping Grackel in check?

She's bossy. When are you coming back?

As soon as I have Allie. It won't be long.

You promise?

I promise. I need to talk with Grackel some more. Keep everything cold for us.

The coldest.

For how long, Grackel? I ask. *For how long has Allie been able to hear but not hear?*

An hour, maybe.

I'm warning her about the impending Green attack when I hear footsteps.

I gotta go, Grackel. Wish me luck.

What a silly concept, human. Be you, and you will do fine.

The door opens. A white cloak comes into view, a Beretta in one hand, a phone in the other. I spring, jabbing the ammonia bottle forward. Liquid flies into his face. He screams, staggers, trips backward onto the bed, losing the phone. I throw myself on top of him, knee him in the groin, and chop him hard in his gun hand. His fingers splay open, and the Beretta tumbles to the floor.

Flailing wildly and cursing, he catches me in the ribs with the side of his fist, gets in a glancing blow to my head. I stagger, knee him again. I duck and dodge a couple more blind strikes, spot my opening. I drive the silver dragon pin into his jugular and hold it there.

"Stop struggling, or you'll die," I say, blood sputtering from his wound. His breaths come sharp and heavy. His eyes are squeezed shut, his face contorted into a pained, angry grimace. He tries to throw me off. I shove in deeper. He cries out. "I pull this out and you bleed out, asshole."

He stops fighting. "What do you want?"

I take his hand and place it on the brooch. "Hold this tight."

I retrieve the gun from where it fell on the floor. I point it at his forehead. "Get up."

"I'm gonna die."

I pick up his phone. "Get up."

"Fuck you."

I take his hand that's holding the dragon brooch and jam it toward his neck. I wait for his screams to end. "Get up."

I keep the gun in his back and push him out of the room. I activate his phone. It's fingerprint protected. We reach the elevator. "Open it."

He presses his free hand to the scanner. The doors open.

"Where are they taping that *Kissing Humans* show?" I ask.

"The film studio," he murmurs.

"What floor?"

"U86," he says. The elevator ascends. "You gotta—"

I shoot him in the head. I lean down beside his body, grab his hand—damp with sweat— and press a finger to his phone's bioscanner. I search through it, but it seems that he only had access to my CENSIR. I dial 911, am not surprised that it doesn't work.

I search his body for anything useful, find an extra gun clip. I consider his body armor, decide against it. I'll need to be quick, and it'll slow me down. I position him in front of the doors, on his side so I can use him as barricade. I kneel behind him, propping my arm on his hip for stability.

I check in with Grackel. She hasn't been able to reach my brother or Allie.

The digital indicator is at U93 when I remember the brooch. I need to give it back to Allie. I tug it from his neck, wipe it on my scrubs, and pocket it.

The elevator stops; the doors slide open into a giant warehouse. The soundstage is on the far end, maybe two hundred feet away. It's outfitted with green screens and decorated to resemble a cave. James and Evelyn stand in front of sword racks on either side of the stage, proselytizing for the cameras directed at them. Their victims are shackled to adjacent slabs. It's too far for me to make out features, but James has the one with the cowboy hat. Evelyn's quarry is writhing against his bonds, moaning and squealing through his gag.

I count three white cloaks in the room, scattered around

the stage in an arc. Their backs are to me, but shelving and lighting block my line of aim on O.J. He's a few feet back from the middle of the stage, waving his gun around in the air, conducting to nonexistent music.

I have to get closer, get better angles. I scan for options, spot a perfect vantage point behind a row of equipment cases.

I climb over my dead-body barricade, get on my stomach, and army-crawl forward.

"Your government tells you that dragons are monsters," Evelyn's saying, her voice echoing from speakers on either side of the stage.

"Your government tells you that dragons cannot breed," James says. I lift up onto my knees, test my line of sight. No good.

"Your government tells you that dragon children do not exist," Evelyn says.

"Your government tells you that only monsters kill children," James says.

"Your government tells you, and you believe," Evelyn says.

I see them grab their swords from the racks.

Shit.

I rise up, quick swivel to my left, take a breath, and shoot. White Cloak One goes down.

"It's her!" Evelyn shrieks.

I spin right. White Cloak Two's swinging his machine toward me. I nail him in the chest—in his body armor. He staggers, sprays bullets toward me. One slices my calf. I buckle, squeeze off another round, miss.

I dash toward the wings. Gunfire chases me. I whirl around a lighting stand. It takes a couple of hits before toppling.

"Dandelion delight!" O.J. calls. A bullet whistles past my head. I zig, zag, dive behind a shelving rack laden with industrial boxes. Machine-gun fire rattles toward me from the other side of the shelving. Boxes tumble. One lands on my back; another slams onto my legs. I grimace, catch a glimpse of White Cloak Two's shins in the gap between the floor and the first shelf.

I shoot him in the left shin, then the right. He falls to his knees. I shoot him in the thigh. He falls to his stomach. I shoot him in the face.

I'm wriggling out from the boxes when somebody steps on my hand. A foot kicks my gun away. "You have a little more Green in you than I thought, dandelion."

I turn my head to see O.J. grinning all sorts of happy at me, his gold-plated Beretta aimed at my forehead. He crouches. The gun shakes in his grip, but even blind he wouldn't miss me.

"Was it the left eye you got my baby Klyv with?"

"I think it was the right," I say with a smirk.

"Yes, it was the right," James says behind him. There's a flash of metal.

O.J. turns his head a fraction. The sword connects with his neck, cleaves right through it. His body falls backward. His grinning face falls on top of me. I grab him by the ears and hurl him as far as I can.

"Sorry," James says. "I had to make sure it was a killing blow."

I wipe blood from my face. "Good job."

He pushes the box off my leg. "What are you doing here, Melissa?"

I jump up, grimace back the inferno that ignites in my calf, and grab my gun. "Did you kill him?"

"I didn't have a choice in this, Melissa," he says as I fish out a Mickey Mouse key chain attached to a pair of heavy-duty keys from O.J.'s pocket.

"Did. You. Kill. Him?"

"No."

My relief lasts until I skirt the shelving and get a view of the stage. Evelyn's got her sword perched on Colin's back, both hands on the pommel, ready to skewer him. A film of blood coats the blade, and for a moment I think it's his, but then he looks up, his eyes filled with sadness, and gives a slight shake of his head.

I train my gun on her.

"Put it down, Twenty-Five."

I stride toward her, my aim fixed in the spot between her eyes.

She raises the sword. "Don't test me, Twenty-Five. Look what I did to Hector . . . and I liked him."

Hector? I look toward the other slab. The *Kissing Dragons* director's Botoxed face hangs slack, one eye wide open, the other half shut. Blood drools from his mouth.

I keep walking.

She lifts the sword in a threatening-to-plunge motion. "You know me, Twenty-Five."

Too well. She'll do it regardless.

"You know who he is?" Evelyn says. Her superior expression shifts to something I've never seen from her before. Fury? Her voice and arms are shaking with it. "You know who he is?"

I stop walking. "Let him go, Evelyn."

Evelyn bristles. "He's the one who put us in Georgetown! He's the reason we're like this!"

"You have three seconds to drop the sword, Evelyn, or I'm going to kill you."

"He deserves it," Evelyn says, but releases her grip. The sword clatters to the stage. "They all deserve it! They all—"

She spasms, then collapses.

"You were going to kill her either way," James says, statement more than question. I glance back. He's got O.J.'s phone in his hand.

No, I was going to interrogate her, then I was going to kill her. I head for the stage. "Where's the hive, James? Where's Allie?"

"Melissa . . . I'm sorry . . . I can't . . . I just can't." He gets in front of me, and for a moment I think he means to obstruct me and that I might have to shoot him, but then he hands me the phone. It's on his CENSIR control screen. "You're going to have to incapacitate me."

"Don't make me do that. Oren's going to find out you helped me."

"Probably."

"Come with us."

"You and I both know that's not possible. Get out of here, Melissa. Head to the fourth floor and escape. I'll bring Allie back once this is all over. I promise."

I wish I could believe him, wish I could believe things will somehow turn out all right. "I can't do that."

"They're going to kill you."

"Probably. Good-bye, James."

He touches my cheek, pulls his hand back. "Good-bye, Melissa."

I look at him for a second longer, then turn away and hit the incapacitate button on the phone.

45

I hobble onto the stage, get on my knees, and remove Colin's gag.

"Hey, beaut—"

I kiss him.

"I don't like you as a cowboy," I say, tossing his hat aside. I use O.J.'s phone to remove his CENSIR.

"Your cowboy," he says with utmost earnestness.

I'm unshackling him when I catch sight of the cameras. Still filming? I stare into the lens of the one focused on Colin's execution slab. "Oren and the Diocletians will be attacking soon with hundreds of Greens! Get to your shelters! Get to your shelters!"

"Stay here," Colin says the moment he's free. Ignoring my questions, he jumps off the stage and jogs over to a row of equipment cases. He returns with a roll of duct tape and a microfiber cloth.

"Need to fix you up," he says.

I glance at my calf. Blood streams down the back of my leg from where the bullet sliced it. "I'm fine."

He crouches, places the cloth against the wound. As he duct tapes my calf, I search O.J.'s phone for information.

"What are you doing?" he asks.

"I'm looking for Allie. The hive," I mumble. Unable to find anything useful, I navigate to Eveyln's CENSIR controls. I shock her several times. Her body jerks and spasms, but she doesn't wake. I up the settings.

Colin takes the phone from me before I kill her. "I think I know where Allie is. There's a military com center for disaster protocol. Unfortunately, the only way to access it from here is via the hub."

I hop off the stage, swallow the grimace as pain shoots through my leg. I scavenge a machine gun from one of the dead white cloaks. "What's the hub?"

He loots the other body. "A massive underground train station, pretty much."

The dragon zoo. "How do you know that?"

He doesn't answer for several seconds. "There's a lot I need to tell you."

After I retrieve my Beretta, we head for the elevator.

"Start with where we are."

"Area 51."

"You shitting me? Is this where the dragons came from?"

"Oh, yeah, dragons, aliens . . . all part of the bigger government conspiracy." He sighs. "Rumors and smokescreens. Area 51 was designed as an underground community model for end-of-the-world scenarios. . . ." He trails off, gives me a quick glance. "Hey, about what Evelyn was saying—"

"Colin, I know who you are." I squeeze his hand. "Who you were, that doesn't matter to me."

"I don't want any secrets between us," he says. I can feel his heartbeat in his palm. He looks away, takes several deep breaths. "I helped design the original CENSIR. Evelyn was right. Everything that's happened to you—"

"I killed your sister. Let's focus on getting Allie back, then we can worry about who's the more horrible person, okay?"

"Sure."

"Look at me." I wait until he does, smile up at him. "Thank you."

"For what?"

For being foolish. For loving me. "For being you."

The elevator's closed. The indicator above says that it's at U599. Colin searches through O.J.'s phone for an override to the bioprint scanner. Unable to find anything, he drags

O.J.'s body over and places his palm to the scanner. The scanner flashes red. Rejection.

"He hasn't been dead long enough," Colin says. He looks over his shoulder toward the stage. "They know what's happened. Hold tight."

He sprints back toward the stage, returns a couple minutes later with a toolbox. He's trying to pry the scanner open with a screwdriver when the floor indicator starts counting down. U598, U597, U596 . . .

"You do that?" I ask.

"Nope. They're coming for us." He tosses the screwdriver aside, winks at me, very J.R. cowboylike. "You ready for some fun?"

"You and I have different versions of fun."

"Shock, awe, and confusion. Fish in a barrel." He sketches out a quick plan for us to ambush their ambush. They've got five hundred floors to go. We've got four or five minutes to prep.

While I set up a fortification of equipment boxes around a shelving rack that gives me clear aim on the elevator, he retrieves a pair of speakers and sets them up in the wings of the studio. When he's finished, he shoots out most of the lights in the room, except those in the vicinity of the elevator, which he calls the kill zone.

"When the doors open, they'll come at you with lots of

noise," he says, clipping a mic to my scrubs. I can barely see him in the darkness. "We come at them with more."

"Got it. Act hysterical." My voice blares from the two speakers.

"Pissed," he says, his voice also in surround sound. He dashes to the wall adjacent to the elevator, disappearing into the shadows beyond the kill zone.

I kneel behind the shelving rack, test my line of sight, and squeeze off a few rounds to get a feel of the machine gun's kick.

"Don't worry too much about accuracy," Colin says. "Just keep firing."

"Always go for the kill shot, right?"

"Thatagirl," he says. "And if—"

"Go time," I say.

The elevator arrives. My heartbeat accelerates; the doors start to open. I unload everything I've got, screaming and yelling at the top of my lungs. Colin's voice echoes beside mine, coming from everywhere at once, louder than the metallic growl of my machine gun.

White cloaks pour out of the elevator. A couple get razed by my bullets; the rest toss grenades in every direction. Colin emerges from the shadows behind them, opens fire—

The grenades detonate. I duck and cover as a hailstorm of floor and shrapnel pelts my bulwark of equipment boxes. By the time it ends, the battle's over. Colin's working his way through a field of debris and white-cloak carnage.

He's saying something.

It takes me a couple of second to hear over the ringing in my ears.

"Melissa?" My name echoes everywhere.

I stagger to my feet. "Here."

After a quick check on my calf, and a quicker debate of whether or not I'm up to this, we scavenge the white-cloak bodies for ammo, then get in the elevator. We tell it where we want to go, but it doesn't respond.

"Stand back," Colin says. Using the butt of his machine gun, he smashes the elevator's floor indicator. He hoists me up and has me pull out the indicator housing, a rectangular box that's connected to the elevator's internal framework by a braid of thick wires.

He examines them and jerks out a couple. The lights flicker. Emergency lighting turns on. He gives me a sheepish smile that's painfully adorable. He rips out a couple more, crosses them. They spark, and a moment later the doors close and the elevator lurches to life.

We descend.

46

We spend the ride down going over hand signals so we can communicate without talking. Doesn't do us much good once we hit bottom, though. It's pitch black in the train tunnel and uncomfortably silent. I press the machine gun close to keep it from rattling. We tiptoe forward, feeling our way to the edge of the platform.

I reach out with my machine gun, probing for a train, but there's nothing. Colin grabs me by the waist and lowers me onto the tracks. I hear him land next to me. The noise of him, his footsteps, his breathing, it's all too loud, but I'm not sure I could move forward without it.

With my free hand, I find his. He's sweating.

"Nervous?"

"Just hot," he says. "You?"

"Just hot," I respond, and take off before we get any hotter.

Fire shoots through my injured calf with every step, but I bite back the groans and force Colin to keep up with me.

Too many minutes later, I see the faint haze of the terminal's lights. No Green glow. The dragon cages are empty. Colin slows us, skulks ahead, machine gun poised. He motions for me to stop or follow every few steps. It takes all my effort to comply.

The terminal is empty. The expansive quiet reminds me of Chicago. No echo of humanity.

"You okay?" Colin asks.

"Fine." The path of dragon cages extends out of sight. To our right, there's another set of tracks leading into a different tunnel. "Which way?"

He checks my duct-tape bandage. It's stained crimson. "Melissa, you're not doing well—"

"Which way?"

He indicates the tunnel.

Before he can become too concerned, I pull him into the blackness of the other tunnel and set a brisk pace.

My lungs are burning almost as much as my calf when Grackel enters my head.

The attack has begun, she says, her voice resonating a little, which must mean she's in broadcast mode, telling Colin the same thing.

"How do you know?" I whisper aloud for Colin's benefit. Even that sounds like thunder in the dark quiet of the tunnel.

I can feel it. The air is alive with Green rage.

I drop into silent communication. *Do you know where?*

No, I do not know where. Feels like a lot.

What about my brother?

I have not been able to reach him, she says, for my ears only.

We reach the tunnel's terminus. Columns of light funnel down a bank of deactivated escalators, dimly illuminating the station's platform. Colin holds up his hand. *Halt.* He and the train he lurks behind are little more than gray shadows. He sneaks around it, climbs onto the platform, and scouts the escalators. He circles them twice before waving me forward.

I follow him up an escalator at a torpid creep. He pauses now and again, I assume to listen, though I'm not sure for what. That eerie silence from the terminal has followed us.

Can you tell Colin to hurry it up, Grackel?

Seconds later, Colin glances back at me and shakes his head.

He says that he is the trained soldier and rushing into the unknown is unwise, Grackel tells me.

Unwise, huh? I imagine he said something with a little more bite. He looks back again and holds up his hand, stiffer than normal, his eyes tight. Not just *Halt*, but *Halt!*

I push past with a glare and take the remaining steps two at a time.

The escalators funnel into a colossal concourse that reminds me of the one at FedEx Underground, where Dad treated Sam and me to soccer matches while Mom was on deployment. But there are no vendor stations or causeways onto a field here. It's all bland gray wall, demarcated in giant block letters with the inscription *A51-TAACOM.*

Colin looks both ways. "This is it. There will only be one entrance. Heavily guarded." He scans again, extra slow, even though there's not a ghost of a soul in sight. "Left or right?"

"I got right. You go left."

He grabs me before I've gone a step. "We're not splitting up."

"We're easier targets together."

"And you won't have anybody to guard your ass. I know this is hard, but we can't be rash, Melissa."

"Fine, but you've got to pick up the pace."

We scuttle across the concourse to the wall, stick close to its edge. Colin speeds up from snail to turtle. He scans ahead. I scan behind. Another escalator well appears on the opposite side. Then another.

I'm guessing we're about a quarter of the way around when Colin gives me the halt command, followed by a thumbs-down. He makes a circle around his eye with his fingers, then slinks forward at a low crouch.

I strain to listen, but beyond the whisper of my quick breaths, I don't hear anything but that vast silence.

He stops, holds up four fingers, then waves at me urgently. Retreat.

Grackel sends me an image as I'm backing up. Four white cloaks flank a set of wide double doors, the kind you see in a movie theater or high school hallway. Except these are metal and controlled by a bioscanner.

Colin scuttles toward me, a finger pressed to his lips. He takes me by the shoulders, looks at me, smiles. Somehow happy and sad all at once.

"What's wrong?" I whisper.

"I'm always with you," he mouths, kisses my forehead, and sprints back toward the doors.

Colin is going to draw them away from you, Grackel says as I start after him.

Tell him to go to hell.

But with my leg injured, I can't keep up. Just before he disappears around the curve, he looks back. His eyes wide and pleading, he motions for me to halt. And then he's gone.

Be still and listen, Grackel says with a telepathic growl. *You will hide in the black stairs. He is going to kill the four warriors in white. He believes this will bring reinforcements. He will lead them away. You will stay hidden until all is clear.*

We're not splitting up. We agreed.

Kill emotion, human. You are a warrior, Melissa Callahan. Warriors only bleed when the war is over. Go!

I send her my own telepathic growl as I scamper across the concourse to the escalators and take cover. I peek out, but can't see anything from my position.

Show me what he sees, Grackel.

No, human, you must concentrate on your task. Hold still. Be calm.

Dammit, Grackel, at least tell him to wait so I can give him—

Shots explode through the emptiness. Four seconds, maybe five, and it's over.

"Rule one of the hunt: never wake a sleeping dragon!" Colin bellows. He starts shooting again, bombarding the door and wall, by the sound of it. "I'm awake!"

He fires a few more rounds before fleeing. I hear his boots drumming the concrete. For one long held breath, he's alone. Then the avalanche comes, a fusillade of footfalls and gunfire in frenzied pursuit.

The pandemonium fades, the gunfire becomes more sporadic. I dread the inevitable silence that minutes ago was an ally but now will mean . . .

I push Colin from my thoughts and break cover. I dash across the concourse, staying light on the balls of my feet, machine gun gripped in both hands. I skirt the wall at a quick jog, freeze as I come around the bend and see Elise and two white cloaks treating the four guards laid out on the ground.

The white cloaks don't notice me. Elise does. She shakes her head, nods for me to retreat in the direction I came from. I shoot the two white cloaks in the back of their heads. She opens her mouth, I assume to scream. I drill her between the eyes.

The steel doors, now riddled with dents, are closed. Though Colin shot up about every inch of wall in the area, he left the bioscanner intact.

I check the bodies. One of the white cloaks Colin shot up still pulses blood from a bullet wound in his abdomen. With lots of grunting and cursing, I manage to prop him against the wall. I yank his arm up to the scanner and press his palm to it.

The door clicks. I open it. A tangle of voices swarms me.

"A-B squadron coming up E Street. I'm flanking around and coming in high."

"Take that, you scale sucking sons o' bitches!"

"Apaches spotted in the flak cloud. Disengage and regroup at beta mark."

"Don't wanna get burned, shouldn't have tickled my dragon!"

"Who's kissing who now?"

"Pentagon defense perimeter has been cleared. Let's move in for an attack run."

I steel myself and enter.

47

Allie's hive is a domed arena ringed from floor to ceiling with scaffolded cubicles, modular ramps, reinforced catwalks, and enormous thinscreens.

Hundreds and hundreds of thinscreens. From the causeway where I lurk, I spot a few that are blacked out. The rest bring back horrid memories of Georgetown in bright, vivid color. Aerial battles here, blazing skyscrapers there, death everywhere. . . .

On a cluster of screens to my left, through a thick haze of black smoke, I see the Washington Monument, the Capitol, the Black House, the Pentagon . . . all aflame. Farther down, I catch glimpses of the New Empire State Building, the Chrysler Building. . . .

Manhattan burns brighter than D.C., but I think that's

only because the buildings are taller.

White cloaks oversee the devastation. They wear head-sets and sit in high-tech armchairs that have joysticks built in on either side.

I watch one operator involved in a dogfight with a trio of DJs over the Potomac River for about three seconds before I realize what's happening.

In the battle room, talkers told the dragons what to do via verbal commands. Here, Oren's figured out a way to com-municate with them via joysticks.

More than communicate.

Control.

He's turned mass destruction into a veritable video game.

And the CPU, the queen bee, is Allie.

She's in the middle of the arena, strapped to a metal chair, a skullcap fixed to her head. Tubes protrude from its circum-ference and wrap around a center column, spiraling toward the ceiling. At the apex, they spread out and follow support beams to hubs that look like giant internet routers. Dozens of smaller tubes extend from the opposite sides and funnel into the thinscreens.

Even at this distance, a hundred feet, maybe, I can see that her jaw's locked open in rictus. Her eyes are rolled back in her head. On the rare occasion a screen blacks out—when a dragon dies—I hear her hoarse voice over the din, shouting the dead dragon's name for a few seconds before returning to her catatonic state.

White cloaks patrol the catwalks. White cloaks patrol the arena floor. I cannot rescue her.

Two choices.

Grackel?

What is it, human?

Did you ever hear my mother sing?

Once or twice. The old Red chuckles. *Her voice hurt my ears.*

Do you remember the words?

Of course. They were incredibly silly.

Could you sing it to Allie?

I expect her to go silent, but she must decide to include me, too. At first it hurts, and not just because her guttural voice screeches the lines, but soon . . . the emotions . . . I hear them in every word . . . feel them . . . they are not Grackel. They are Mom. And they are far more beautiful than any rainbow.

I swap my machine gun for the Beretta.

I steady my breath.

I raise the gun.

I listen to the song a couple more notes.

I blink away the tears.

I send Allie to the stars.